QUI TANGIT FRANGITUR

Also by Mark Hankin

(writing as T. J. Frost)

Final Passage

The Abigail Affair

The Shoot

Play the Piper

Fight for Life

MARK HANKIN

WHO
TOUCHES
ME
IS
BROKEN

This book is a work of fiction incorporating real persons, events and locations as detailed in the Notes and Acknowledgements. Any resemblance to other actual persons, places or events is purely coincidental.

Copyright © Mark Hankin 2019

The right of Mark Hankin to be identified as the author of this work has been asserted by him in accordance with the Copyright, Designs and Patents Act 1988. All rights reserved.

No part of this publication may be reproduced or transmitted in any form or by any means (electronic, mechanical or otherwise) without the prior written permission of the publisher.

ISBN 979-8839845930

Fast Editions
info@fasteditions.uk

Cover design by BespokeBookCovers.com

'Fiction has a role in recording history' – Jim Chestnut

Preface

My first contact with Ken Sinclair came on Thursday 14th March 2019 in a private message from a Facebook group called 'Writers Who Help Writers'.

> Dear Mark
>
> My name is Kenneth Sinclair (Ken). I have written my memoirs, focusing on events in October 1988 at which time I was a graduate trainee reporter aged 21 on the 'Today' newspaper.
>
> The editor sent me and my colleague Sarah Standen, another trainee who had become my girlfriend, to the Clyde Submarine Base, home of the British nuclear deterrent (then Polaris). The story of what happened there has never been told. I have records and documents that prove my account is true, including a handwritten letter given to me by Margaret Thatcher at 5.18am on Thursday 13th October 1988 in her suite at the Grand Hotel, Brighton.
>
> I am a journalist by trade, and I need help to finish my book and make it read more like a novel.
>
> I noticed from your posts that you offer ghostwriting services. I checked out your books written under your pen name Tim Frost and realised you could be the person

to help me. I have read all five of your novels.

I particularly enjoyed your comedy-thriller 'The Abigail Affair' and 'Play the Piper' with the unfortunate flautist.

With all your books, once I started I couldn't put them down, and read every spare minute, wearing out the page turn button on my Kindle halfway through 'Fight for Life'!

Forgive me, but it also helps that you, like me, are of an age and generation to remember the 1980s and the way things were then: technology, politics, cars, music, dress, girls, hairstyles.

If you are interested let's meet up soon to discuss my project. I cannot offer you a fee, but I have a royalty share proposition you may find attractive. As my health prevents me from travelling, will you come and visit me in Nottinghamshire?

I look forward to hearing from you.

Ken Sinclair

I reread the message several times, alarm bells jangling. I was editing the final draft of a book of my own for publication and could ill afford another call on my time.

Wary but intrigued, I Googled 'Ken Kenneth Sinclair reporter journalist Today newspaper 1980s'. No hits that included *Today*, but that was hardly surprising given the title folded in 1995. I did get results from magazines including *Shooting Times* and *Bike* but couldn't be sure if these were the same Ken Sinclair. If so, his areas of expertise were ... obviously ... guns and motorcycles. Another warning flag?

I dithered for twenty-four hours, then sent a polite message declining his invitation.

But that was not the end of the matter.

A few days later I received a second message from Ken. This one included a two-paragraph synopsis of his memoirs (what the publishing industry calls an 'elevator pitch'). He also offered to email a list of typographical errors in my own novels that he 'thought I'd want to fix'.

I didn't respond, but later that day he sent over his list of errors anyway: a Kindle clippings file of thirty-seven typos, spread across all my books. If nothing else, this proved he had read all my output, and with extraordinary attention to detail.

I emailed Ken's messages to my literary agent Sophie Silverman. She phoned me back fifteen minutes later in high excitement, saying it was the most intriguing pitch she'd seen for years, and whether true or not the story smelled like a bestseller.

So, despite my misgivings, I agreed to visit Ken.

He hadn't been exaggerating when he said his health was poor. The home address he gave for our meeting was a hospice.

I arrived shortly before midday on the following Tuesday at the modern low-rise complex. A care assistant took me to Ken's room. 'He's very weak,' she said before ringing his doorbell. 'No close contact, please.'

Ken Sinclair lay in bed, connected up to drips and drains and oxygen: a small man, doubtless further shrunken by his illness. Incongruously, his hair was thick, dark and long. Then I realised it must be a wig.

He greeted me with a wan smile and a wave of his free hand. Grey-skinned, gaunt and frail, he was not long for this world.

I took the visitor's chair.

'Welcome, Mark. Ken Sinclair. Sorry, I mustn't shake hands. I am living—correction, dying—proof that forty-plus a day is an unhealthy habit.' He spoke softly and with effort. 'The draft manuscript is on the table by the window. The brown suitcase contains my notes and documents. Have a read and a rummage and tell me if you can help. Take all the time you need. I'm not going anywhere. I may doze off.'

I crossed to the bay window which overlooked the gardens. The care assistant brought in my cup of coffee and I set to work.

I began with the manuscript and spent an hour and a half skim-reading and making notes. Then I explored the elderly leather suitcase on the floor. This contained reporters' notebooks; Boots wallets stuffed with six-by-four inch photo prints; a scrapbook of newspaper cuttings from *Today*, some with Ken's by-line, dated August to October 1988; cuttings from national newspapers, most dated 11th October 1988; a photocard Press pass to the 1988 Conservative Party Conference showing a very young Ken with big Eighties spectacles; more cuttings, loose, mostly from the 1990s, from assorted rifle, car and motorbike magazines; a box of Dictaphone tapes plus the original handheld dictating machine; two CVs, one typed on a manual typewriter and the other printed on a dot matrix printer (the type that screeched like a miniature circular saw); a tiny vintage Pentax camera; recent pdf printouts of 1980s Cabinet papers downloaded from the National Archives; more official papers and typewritten reports, many stamped 'TOP SECRET'; long curling faxes, faded to near-illegibility; a 1988 woman's pink Filofax; homespun Roneo-ed newsletters on coloured paper entitled *Faslane Focus*; a business card from Trade Wind Yacht Charters with an Indian name and an address in the Caribbean; the handwritten letter from Margaret Thatcher, prime minister in 1988, and another even more extraordinary document in her hand on three sheets of A4.

I examined the Thatcher papers closely, held them to my nostrils and inhaled.

Like everything in the suitcase, they were either the most elaborate, expensive, artful, accomplished, professional forgeries.

Or genuine.

I stood, stretched and returned to the bedside chair. Ken opened his eyes.

I said, 'May I record our discussion, please, to save taking notes?'

'Good plan. I used my Dictaphone all the time back in the day.'

'I'll take it on,' I said.

'Excellent. Can you make it read more like a novel?'

'Yes. It is already well written and could be published just as it is. But I think I understand what you are after. This is more than a memoir. It's really a love story, isn't it?'

He thought about this for a moment. 'Yes. I suppose it is.'

'We need more dialogue and more scenes. You have written mostly in narrative summary, with little direct speech. The facts and the events are all there, but without the emotional tug that a first-person account can give. And we must provide a physical setting for every chapter. At present there's too much soliloquy and exposition floating around in the narrative ether. I recommend we anchor everything to the time and place.'

'Yes again.'

'Also, you write from the viewpoint of an older man looking back. It would feel more immediate if the voice was yours as a young man. So, no retrospective self-judgement, no giving away what's coming up, and cut out phrases such as—' I consulted my notes—'"Thirty years of frustration with mobile communications began that morning when I saw a light labelled NSVC glowing". That takes us out of the moment. The young you didn't know that mobile signals would still be so crap today.'

'Yes, yes, of course. I get all that. Still, the older Ken is the one telling the story. Could we have a section from the present-day me, perhaps to introduce Chapter One? Like a voiceover at the beginning of a film? Then step back to 1988.'

'A framing of the narrative? That's a traditional device which would work well.'

'What about the footnotes? Do they add or distract?'

'I love them. They're a great way to explain stuff without holding up the story. Britain in the Eighties is a far-off land for anyone aged under fifty.'

A moment's silence followed. I lowered my voice and said, 'How much of it is true, Ken?'

'Every word. I'm a journalist. I report things. I don't make them up. Couldn't, anyway. I verified everything and cross-referenced it to the source material. Even the time checks and temperature readings are accurate, taken from my notebooks. I was a right nerd. Still am.'

I said, 'It would be good to reproduce some of your documents in the book. The two CVs, for example. They're so touching. And the official version of events, which seems to differ from your first-hand account.'

Ken grew more animated than I had seen him. 'Yes, yes! We'll do that. Put them in an Appendix. Give the reader both sides.'

'And a selection of your photos. The portrait of the two of you in your undercover disguises, for example.'

He chuckled. 'I believe I may have invented the "selfie stick". I constructed the gadget using an aluminium window stay, a tripod fitting and a remote shutter release. I tried to interest Jessops in manufacturing it, but they thought the market would be tiny for something so specialised.'

I said, 'Would you like me to rewrite a sample chapter, to show how I would tackle it?'

'Yes. Good idea. How about the one before the incursion, where ▮▮▮▮▮ comes for Sarah and catches the two of us *in flagrante delicto*?'

'I imagine that was very funny.'

'It was.' He chuckled again, and his laughter morphed into a rasping rattle of a cough. A full minute elapsed before he could catch his breath, reach out a shaky hand for a sip of water and continue. 'A USB thumb drive with the Word file is in my bedside drawer. Take it, and the suitcase.'

'There are many loose ends,' I said. 'Apart from the obvious unanswered question.'

'That's all for the Epilogue, which I have been unable to write. I can't manage my MacBook any more prone like this for long, and most of the time I'm too woozy from the morphine. Also I would find it too upsetting. May I brief you now, Mark? They say I have days or weeks rather than months.'

He spoke without fear or self-pity.

I realised I'd accepted the assignment without talking about money. I'd be in trouble with Sophie my agent. 'We need to discuss my remuneration. You mentioned royalty share.'

'A fifty-fifty split, with my half going to nominated charities and voluntary organisations. That should give you a good return. And the donations will serve as my atonement.'

'Very generous. I'll have to run it by my agent, but I can't see a problem.'

'I'll get my solicitor to draw up an agreement. She's coming in later with some changes to my will.'

I started on my list of questions. After thirty minutes I had most of the answers I needed, but Ken had tired. The arrival of the nurse to tend to his pain relief was my cue to depart.

I drove home in afternoon sunshine, Ken's suitcase in the boot and his USB drive in my pocket, wondering if my new client would survive even long enough to read my sample rewrite.

Mark Hankin
North Norfolk
England
November 2019

When I was one-and-twenty
    I heard a wise man say,
'Give crowns and pounds and guineas
    But not your heart away;
Give pearls away and rubies
    But keep your fancy free.'
But I was one-and-twenty
    No use to talk to me.

When I was one-and-twenty
    I heard him say again,
'The heart out of the bosom
    Was never given in vain;
'Tis paid with sighs a plenty
    And sold for endless rue.'
And I am two-and-twenty
    And oh, 'tis true, 'tis true.

From *A Shropshire Lad* by A. E. Housman (1859–1936)

Never Gonna Give You Up

MY NAME IS Ken Sinclair, and this is my true story.

I know where it ends, but it's a little harder deciding where to begin.

If I were a movie director, shooting the film of the book, I would open with a drone shot from on high. An elderly Volkswagen camper van winds along the side of a Scottish loch on a dreary autumn day, to the soundtrack of 'Never Gonna Give You Up' by Rick Astley. A caption appears on screen. 'Wednesday 5th October 1988, 1.35pm, 12°C, steady drizzle'.

Cut to exterior close-up through the windscreen. The wipers labour back and forth, clearing two interlocking semicircular areas of glass which frame the young occupants.

He is driving. His hair is longer than is fashionable for the era. Despite the weather, he wears sunglass clip-ons over his spectacles.

She also has big hair, a punkish candy floss mane with dark roots showing through, the whole effect that of a starburst on firework night.

Or a small, adorable nuclear explosion.

His plutonium blonde.

She wears heavy black eyeliner and mascara underneath chiselled Gothic eyebrows, like Siouxsie from the Banshees. Her irises are hazel but change colour depending on what she wears and the lighting.

He and she have been lovers for fifty-four days.

She will be missing, presumed dead, when the closing credits roll.

Neither of them can guess at this as they approach their destination, singing alternate lines of the cheesy Rick Astley song.

The camper van indicates, slows and draws up outside the gates of a ramshackle caravan site by the roadside. He turns off the cassette player. She reaches into the glovebox and takes out a pink felt drawstring bag.

Let's start my story here.

Peace

Wednesday 5th October 1988, 1.38pm, 12°C, rain

I PULLED the camper van off the road, through the gates and on to a bumpy forecourt of mud and sodden cinders.

All seemed quiet, with no peace protesters in evidence. The steady Scottish drizzle must have sent them to ground.

I applied the handbrake and cut the engine.

I recorded the time and temperature in my notebook, fresh from the stationery store and marked 'KS1' with a Dymo vinyl label maker.

I turned to Sarah and snorted with laughter.

'What's the joke, Maverick?'

'I still can't believe you did that to your hair. And now we have the earrings.'

'Just following instructions. Blend in.' She stuck out her tongue. 'You look equally ludicrous in those shades.'

'Definitely a Kodak moment.' I reached for my Pentax, screwed on the self-portrait device and we leaned together in our karaoke duet pose.

Only then did I unclip my *Top Gun* aviators, and the scene outside acquired some muted colour.

My first impression was of a South African township, with wooden shacks, caravans, tarpaulins stretched between trees, rusty oil cans serving as rubbish bins or braziers and massive cable reels on their sides as makeshift tables.

A sign on painted corrugated metal sheets announced 'FASLANE PEACE CAMP' against a rainbow adorned with multiple CND symbols.

Below this, a cartoon missile emerged from a submarine afloat in a loch. Hands of all colours reached out, and Munch-like faces screamed 'NO CRUISE! NO TRIDENT!'

A hand-painted sign on a shack read 'INFORMATION – LEGAL SUPPORT – VISITORS WELCOME'. The door stood open, and smoke puffed in a homely fashion from a flue jutting through the tin roof.

'Guess we check in there.'

We'd made it from London in two days, taking turns to drive, Sarah's Bon Jovi/Rick Astley compilation at full volume. We stopped for the night in a layby between Carlisle and Gretna Green, where we heated a can of baked beans with frankfurters, brewed tea and smoked a joint before retiring to give the VW's suspension a good workout.

We'd bought the camper from a Crocodile Dundee impersonator in the Caledonian Road for £350 in petty cash doled out by the editor himself. I was falling in love with the old van, its hooded chrome headlights so like the eyelids of a forlorn but faithful hound, and I was already in love with Sarah.

'Are you going to sit there daydreaming?' Sarah's voice cut through my reverie. I wound down the driver's window of the VW. This was necessary to get out, as the inside door handle was missing.

As I reached through the window, a tall guy around six foot with an aquiline nose and short hair ambled out of the reception shack. He wore a full-length transparent plastic mac.

He peered in through my window. 'Hey. Welcome to Faslane. Just visiting or do you plan to stay? I'm Jerry. Camp Commandant.' American accent, toothy grin.

'Ken,' I said, 'and this is my girlfriend Sarah. We'd like to stay a week or so. Keen to join the struggle.'

Jerry stared across me at Sarah. 'That's quite a hairdo. You two come far?'

'London.'

'You'll have visited Greenham Common on the way, then.'

Sarah said, 'No' at the exact instant I said, 'Yes.'

'Make your minds up, guys!'

I laughed. 'Yes, we passed it. No, we didn't stop there.'

'It's a women-only camp,' Sarah explained. 'No one with a penis allowed in. We couldn't both stay.'

'Okay. Rules for this camp. No alcohol, no drugs, no loud music after ten at night, no direct action without a resolution at Camp Fire, help with the chores, love everybody. There's no hierarchy and I'm not a commandant or leader or anything. You cool with that?'

We chorused, 'Yes,' and Sarah nodded, jangling her oversized earrings.

'Back up over by the gate. Tuck yourself in. You'll be fine there provided you can sleep through all-night construction traffic.'

'Will do. Thanks, man.'

Jerry leaned in further and dropped his voice. 'One more thing.'

'Yes?'

'Tone down the act a bit. You two are straight out of Central Casting.' He turned and sloped off back to his lair.

I wound up the window, started the engine and manoeuvred the van into the corner site.

'Looks like he rumbled us, Maverick.'

'Guess it's because we're clean and don't have BO.'

'We can soon put that right. I suppose we do look pink and scrubbed. We should have shopped at Oxfam. Our clothes are too new. Damn.'

'You were quick with that line about men not welcome at Greenham Common.'

'I'm Oscar material, you know that.'

'Almost like Jerry was expecting us,' I mused.

We got out. Opposite stood a lopsided psychedelic caravan with a sign saying 'MAKE BAIRNS NOT BOMBS. APPLY WITHIN FOR DETAILS'. Another van announced it was for 'WOMYN ONLY', with a frieze of alternating female gender signs and CND logos.[1]

Sarah said, 'At least it's stopped raining. Hello, who's this?'

'This' was a small boy running up, dressed in an orange one-piece nylon jumpsuit and pink wellies.

'I'm Archie. I'm four nearly five. You're pretty,' he informed Sarah.

A year older than my Susie.

'Well thank you, Archie, what a nice thing to say. I'm Sarah and this is Ken. What's that you've got?'

Archie held up a Fairy Liquid-bottle submarine with a cotton-reel conning tower and pencils for missiles. 'We're here because we don't want this to happen. Watch.' He crouched down, then jumped up and threw his model in the air. 'Psshwhoo!'

He retrieved his homemade Polaris and reinstalled the missiles with patient, chubby fingers.

'Did you make that all by yourself?'

'Yes. Joan helped. The toilet is there.' Archie pointed. 'The lock doesn't work so you close the door if you're a lady or you're doing a poo-poo, that means keep out.'

The door of the toilet caravan opened. A girl stepped down and approached. 'Hi guys. Welcome. I'm Debbie.' About our age, taller than both of us, blonde hair tied back.

'Ken and Sarah.' I extended my hand (hoping she had been able to wash hers) but Debbie marched straight up to Sarah and enveloped her in a hug. Then I received the same treatment. A tattoo of intertwined doves on her shoulder peeked out from under her home-knitted jumper.

'Peace, Ken.'

'Yeah, peace.'

---

[1] Feminists of the era using the spellings 'Womyn' and 'Wimmin' to avoid the subjugation implied in the syllables 'Man' and 'Men'.

'Come on, Archie, Joan and Colin will be back soon.' She took the boy's hand, turned to us. 'Archie's mum and dad. They've gone to town to sign on. You two on the dole or have you got dosh?'

Sarah said, 'We have some savings but we need to sign on too.'

'Helensburgh Job Centre. The bus stops right outside. I love your earrings, sister. You both members? Which branch?'

Again Sarah had the answer. 'I bought these at university last year. We haven't joined yet.'

'The peace camps are separate from the Campaign for Nuclear Disarmament. We believe in peace everywhere – Palestine, Burma, South Africa. We want Nelson Mandela released. CND is fine, lots of people belong, but they do try and dictate to us. They're not so keen on direct action—they only care about numbers at the big demos. You guys got any pot?'

At last, a question I could answer. 'Yes. But Jerry said no drugs or alcohol.'

'Not at Camp Fire, or when public are around, or outside where the police could see you. In your van is fine, same with booze. Sarah, I need more members for the Sisters' Swimming Club. You game, girl? Start the day right. Might muss your stellar hair and makeup though.'

'Sure,' Sarah said. 'How many go?'

Debbie stood for a moment admiring Sarah. She reached out and fondled one of my girl's jangly four-inch green and pewter enamelled CND earrings. 'Bev comes when she's around. Usually it's just me. I'll give you a knock at seven-thirty.'

Campers

Wednesday 5th October 1988, 6.35pm, 9°C, rain threatening

'IF NOT US, who?' Jerry called out.
 'Us!' we chorused.
 'If not here, where?'
 'Here!'
 'If not now, when?'
 'Now!'
It reminded me of the 'Dib Dib Dib, Dob Dob Dob' of my Wolf Cub pack, but the chanting seemed to energise the peace campaigners on this damp and gloomy Scottish evening.

We sat on logs, milk crates, salvaged car seats and camping chairs, hands linked as for 'Auld Lang Syne'. That was no problem with Sarah next to me on the right, but on my left sat Jerry, and holding hands with him spooked me out. How hard should you grip? Would we have to sit like this for the whole evening?

The fire in the centre of the group provided a flickering illumination, accented by the firefly glow of multiple cigarettes. Fearsome midges prompted frequent slapping and waving of hands.

We had agreed that I would observe the men, Sarah the women. Good practice for a reporter: remember names, faces and key facts without recourse to notebook and Sir Isaac Pitman's ingenious system.

One by one, the campers identified themselves and declared their dedication to the cause. Some stood, others leaned forward earnestly.

'Colin. Resident since 1982 with Joan and now our beautiful son Archie.' (Said son lay asleep in his mother's arms.) 'Five arrests, two nights in jail.'

'Joan. Mother and earth mother. Peace to all. One love, one life, one world.' She smiled from among her black ringlets, a placid woman with something of the Romany about her.

Both she and Colin were scarcely older than us, despite having a four-year-old child. Scottish accents, but not Glaswegian. Softer. Edinburgh?

Next up, a huge hairy Yeti with Elvis sideburns. 'Mitch. Fae Glesga, in case you didnae ken. Ah'm a sparkie, worked wae some of the lads on the Trident site. Hair-raisin' stories they tell. Here fur a wee spell tae install them solar panels Greenpeace gave us. Should have some leckie the morra.'

'Debbie. Six arrests, four nights in jail. Part-time hellraiser. Full-time gentle angry woman in a world of mad men. Making a difference, one day at a time.'

'Spike.' A skinny punk teen with a foot-high fluorescent orange Mohican, studs in his nose and rings in his ears. 'General troublemaker and pisstaker.'

Spike couldn't be older than seventeen.

My neighbour released my hand and stood.

'Jerry. A friend from over the water. Active in the US anti-nuclear movement for years. Got arrested at the Nevada test site along with Martin Sheen and Kris Kristofferson. Came over last fall for a conference, resident here since. I'm a lawyer, so bring me your questions about NVDA[2]. I'm not licensed to practise here, so don't ask me to represent you if you're arrested. And yes, I do have a valid visa.'

Jerry sat. To avoid holding his hand again, I got out my ciggies and lit two, passing one to Sarah.

The man on Jerry's left remained seated: a scrawny individual with tattoos on his neck and hands and probably many other parts of his anatomy.

---

[2] Non-Violent Direct Action.

'Norman. Ex-Royal Navy rating on the Polaris bombers. I drop in here every few weeks, tell a story. I'm a chef in civvy street now.'

'No jam tarts tonight, Norm?' Colin asked.

'Nah, sorry, mate. Can't sneak a tray out every time.'

Jerry said, 'Next please welcome and give a sign of peace or love to our brand-new arrivals, up from London in their smart VW camper van.'

I rose to my feet. Pins and needles shot through my calves from perching on the log. A heavy vehicle passed on the road and I waited until they could hear me, taking a drag of my ciggy.

'Thanks, Jerry and everyone, for such a warm welcome on a chilly evening.'

Spike said, 'Call this chilly? This is bloody tropical, mate. Wait till you're standing in a puddle outside the base for six hours holding a banner with rain running down your arms.'

'I'm Ken and this is my girlfriend Sarah—'

Now Debbie piped up. 'Ken, women aren't chattels. We don't own each other, and she will speak for herself. Tell us about *you*, man!'

I began to feel the panic of a wannabe stand-up taking flak on open mic night.

'Sorry, Debbie, I'm just so proud and humble to be in a relationship with this wonderful woman. I'm a photographer, at least I plan to be. Got this baby for my twenty-first birthday present.' I held up the miniature Pentax. 'Lots of my mates went into advertising or commercial graphics. I'm more into photography in the service of activism. Jeff Wall, the Düsseldorf school, if you're familiar with them.' I looked around the circle of faces in the flickering firelight and sensed that my fellow campers were in no way familiar with the Düsseldorf school or possibly any contemporary art movement. 'With your permission, I'd like to make a photographic record of the peace camp in action. Powerful images of resistance, like Leon and Jill Uris with their book about the Troubles.' That produced some nods of approval at last. 'Or

Don McCullin, with his pictures from the front line. Is everyone cool with me snapping them here day to day, and on the protests?'

I waited a beat. No one voiced an objection. Jerry said, 'We often have journalists turn up here, they're very welcome, but they have their own agenda, obviously not the same as ours. So yeah. Perfect, Ken. Just take care if you shoot near the base. The cops will try and confiscate your gear.'

I breathed out and sat. I'd got away with my tissue of lies.

'Everyone please greet Sarah.'

Sarah remained seated. In a clear, level voice she said, 'I'm scared.' After a pause, she continued, 'I'm scared witless and shitless by what's down there in the loch.' Murmurs of agreement at that. 'I'm scared for me, and I'm scared for all of us here, and I'm scared for the thousands of people who live in Faslane and Helensburgh and the millions who live in Scotland and the billions who live all over the world within range of weapons that can be unleashed at four minutes' notice and exterminate every living thing on this planet.

'I'm scared for Archie, and for children everywhere, and I'm scared for my own unborn babies.'

I raised a mental eyebrow at this, then remembered her line: *I'm Oscar material.* Still …

'I left university this summer and want to make a difference. I thought I'd need to get a job, but a few hours in this special place have shown me a different way. I feel at home. I sense a love as warm as that fire enveloping me. Thatcher claims, "There is no such thing as society". I'd like to invite that devil woman here, sit her down, give her a mug of tea and prove her wrong without saying a word or lifting a finger. We are society. Thank you for welcoming us. Just tell me what to do. I can cook, I can chop wood, I can clean the toilet, I can shout, I can sing, I can swim and I can climb. Maybe other stuff too like painting banners for barricades.'

Everyone sat still and quiet, transfixed by a performance so natural, eloquent and joyful that it didn't seem a performance at all (and perhaps wasn't?).

Debbie broke the silence. 'Girl, you got the spirit.'

I noticed that the youngster Spike had leaned forward, eyes wide, mouth hanging open. He'd fallen in love with Sarah too. Well, get to the back of the line, punk.

Only Colin shifted in his place and displayed signs of unease. 'Sarah, we all share your views. You and Ken seem a lovely couple. Your support and help are welcome. Just remember we're not firebrands here. Barricades yes, sometimes it's necessary, but no stone throwing or fires in the roadway. Just peaceful non-violent resistance. We've spent six years establishing this permanent presence. The local authority are on our side. We have planning permission for the caravans and sheds. We abide by the fire regulations. We don't litter or pollute. We work with the police for events like Hiroshima Day.'

'Good citizens. Sometimes too good,' Debbie muttered.

'God, you can be a boring jobsworth, Colin,' Spike the punk added.

Colin ploughed on undeterred. 'Go with the flow. Get to know us a bit. Just being here, all year, winter and summer, is so worthwhile. This camp will remain as long as Polaris and Trident are down there. But it's not the Cuban Revolution.'

Mitch, the hairy electrician, said, 'Ah've heard at Greenham Common women detectives are goin' in undercover, infiltrating the lassies. We worried aboot that here?' He looked directly at me and Sarah.

Colin said, 'There's nothing to infiltrate here. We are what we are. We have no secrets, no hidden agenda and the only crimes we commit are trespass and breach of the peace.'

Spike said, 'We should do more. Like, put a sub out of action. Wouldn't take much.'

Colin said, 'I'd love to get up close and personal with those bastard machines. But knock out a nuclear sub? How d'you plan to do that, Spike?'

'Dunno. Block a pipe or summat. While the girls go in topless on the canoes again as a diversion.' He leered at Debbie, then Sarah.

Jerry stood up. 'Let's talk more tomorrow. For tonight, we have our regular guest, Norman, waiting to share his experiences on those very subs. He's been up since three this morning, kneading and baking, and I think I felt a drop of rain, and Joan has her wonderful veggie stew bubbling away, so shall we move on? Norm?'

'Glad to. High time, I'm getting a well numb bum.'

Jerry left the semicircle and returned with an armful of logs which he threw on the fire. They hissed and sizzled. Norman rose from his place and unwound his lanky form. He appeared to have come down in the world since his naval career. His matted hair was greasy, and he stooped. He couldn't have been older than thirty. I hoped Norman's story would be succinct. I squeezed Sarah's hand and she squeezed back.

'The twenty-sixth of January. This year. Late at night. Down there—' he pointed through the trees towards the darkened loch beyond the glow of security and construction lights, '—we came this close to meltdown.'[3] He held his hands up, palms almost touching. 'I'm new on the Starboard crew of the *Resolution*. I'm on me first patrol, and the last, I'm pleased to say.

'The boat was alongside ready for sea. We were locked and loaded with all sixteen nuclear missiles, three Chevaline warheads on top of each, forty-eight big bangers altogether. That's more firepower on one submarine than all the explosives used in the Second World War ...' he paused for dramatic effect, '... *including* the two A-bombs dropped on Hiroshima and Nagasaki.'

The residents had clearly heard Norman's story before, but all remained rapt. The fire crackled and sparked as a new log settled in the pit. Rain fell in larger drops.

---

[3] The discourse of naval ratings consists of approximately 50% blasphemies. Some sailors can elevate the curse almost to an art form. As Norman was sadly not imaginative in this department, I have edited the profanities out of his account. I trust that what this Bowdlerised version loses in authenticity it gains in comprehensibility.

'Me and the other cooks, there's four per boat, we'd shifted and stowed a ton and a half of beef, fifteen hundred gallons of Younger's Tartan, five dozen cases of frozen fish and chips, enough bog rolls to go around the world twice, gammons, turkeys, a mile of sausages, sixty movies, you name it. Actually, Muggins here did most of the grunt work, being as I was the most junior and it was me first patrol. The Petty Officer did sod all except stride about with his clipboard.

'Anyways, we'd loaded it all and I was having a quick smoke in the junior rates' mess when the alarms sound off. Bells clang, hooters honk. Lads run up and down shouting. I poke me head out of the door. Ginger, he's the steward for the officers, tells me the reactor is overheating. Then Woodie the LMA[4], that's the Quack, bursts in and says, "Get ready to evacuate on the siren, lads. Put your smokes out. Leave everything. All got your dosimeters on? This is not a drill."

'The power to the main cooling system has only gone and failed. So the heat from the reactor has nowhere to go. The temperature on the dial shoots up like in a movie.

'Soon they are shitting themselves as the core temperature approaches one thousand degrees. Only a minute and a half before we have a meltdown and a big boom and our very own Chernobyl to keep Clydeside nice and warm and glowing with radiation for a hundred years.

'Two engineers race past the mess towards the reactor department. I catch a glimpse of Barney. Ever see a black fellow go white with fear? I saw terror in that man's eyes. He knows there's radiation escaping already where they're heading.

'Then the big siren goes off to evacuate. We're all pissing ourselves shitless. You can't hurry an evac. It's not like a plane with loads of doors and a nice bouncy slide down to safety. You have to go in file, take your time, climb up, keep your footing.

'Then we're all on the jetty. The commander—get this—is standing to attention in his underpants and a sweater with his cap

---

[4] Leading Medical Assistant (ship's doctor)

on. He takes the roll call, tells us to leave at the double, then Barney rushes down the gangplank and says he and his mate Little Bomber have started the diesel genny, and the core temperature is falling.

'We're told to stay off the boat with only the commander and a skeleton crew remaining aboard to run the reactor down. They take everyone's dosimeters and hare off to the lab. At midnight, a medic lumbers up in full hazard suit. He won't go aboard. He calls the commander out and tells him Barney's dosimeter is off the scale. He's taken two hundred and sixty times the safe daily amount of radiation. Barney comes down, more medics are standing on the jetty in their yellow spacesuits with a fire hose and a pail of detergent.

'They tell him to undress, chuck the bucket over him and hose the bugger down right there, stark bollock naked, this is January mind, from five yards away so they don't have to touch him.'

I turned to Sarah, my eyebrows raised. Could Norman's melodramatic account be accurate? Scary stuff, if so. Her lips were parted. I watched her moisten them with the tip of her tongue and a surge of desire flooded through me.

Norman continued, 'The ambulance rushes Barney to the Vale of Leven Hospital. That's the one at Alexandria they built special for us. Like a concrete shithouse. Designed to survive a direct nuke hit on the base. Lead-lined radiation isolation wards an' all. They keep Barney in a week, scrubbing him down in the showers every four hours day and night. The poor sod was lucky not to catch pneumonia. They told him he'd be fine, but he never went to sea again and left the service with—listen to this—a quarter of a million quid to keep his mouth shut for the rest of his natural. We doubt he'll get to spend too much of his payoff. He has to have cancer checks and X-Rays every three months. For life.

'Everyone else's doses are below danger level. Or so they say. But they record twelve times the background level of radiation at the Rhu monitoring station the next week. We stay ashore for fifteen days, with daily medical checks and Geiger counters clicking away everywhere, while a convoy of radiation clean-up vans work alongside *Resolution*. The bomber on patrol, *Revenge*, has to remain at sea and cover us.

'They decontaminate *Resolution*, fix the cooling system and—get this—discover hairline cracks in what they call the "trouser leg" joint of the reactor. Then the shit hits the steam turbine, because no other sub was ready to take over the deterrent. And it has to be continuous or we all lose our jobs.

'It went right up to Thatcher. She sent us out, knowing full well that there were cracks. That's why *Resolution* is in dry dock and *Renown* under refit now.'

'So they sent you out on patrol knowing about the cracks? That the sub was a death trap for you, never mind everyone else?'

'Right, Debbie. And guess what they said about the cooling incident to the Press? Sweet FA. Nothing. Denied any problem.' Norman dug in his pocket and produced a folded newspaper page.

The fire smoked and spluttered in the now-steady drizzle.

'Lend us your torch, Jerry. This is from the London *Observer* a fortnight later. I'm proud to say I was responsible.

'"N-sub minutes from disaster. The Ministry of Defence confirmed yesterday that a 'minor electrical malfunction' occurred on board the nuclear submarine *HMS Resolution* on 26th January. It insisted there had been no danger to the crew or general public. A spokesman—'[5]

Jerry said, 'Norm, let's move inside before we get soaked.'

In the communal caravan, Norman continued to hold forth over Joan's wholesome but virtuous vegetarian supper, which we ate from tin plates, washed down by mugs of tea. Our clothes steamed in the warmth of the stove and the smell of damp wool filled the foetid air.

Norman's scare stories included an account from a mate of his aboard the *Resolution* during the Falklands conflict. Norman claimed Thatcher ordered the submarine down to Ascension

---

[5] The article is reproduced in the Appendix.

Island and had the commander programme targets in Argentina for nuclear attack, mostly on islands but some on the mainland, including an army base not far outside Cordoba, a city of over a million. The crew weren't told, Norman said, as they were never given target details, but the ratings in the control room who entered the coordinates knew.[6]

After supper Spike produced a guitar and we sang 'Four Minutes to Midnight', a dirge which made me appreciate the artistry of Rick Astley and Bon Jovi.

Sarah and I pleaded tiredness and squelched back to the camper van in darkness.

We'd packed two hundred cigarettes, hash, whisky, notepads and ballpoint pens, twenty Kodak 110 film cartridges (a mix of colour slide and black-and-white in various speeds), a bag of 10p coins, spare batteries for the camera, porridge oats, tea and coffee, Marmite (for me only), UHT and dried milk and a selection of clothing already proving unequal to the challenges of a Scottish autumn.

No typewriter, though. That was deliberate. Even a small portable would make enough noise to betray us. And no torch. That was an oversight.

I slid open the side door and we climbed in. The pop-up roof provided ample headroom, but its thin fabric sides offered no insulation against the cold, damp night air.

'Put the roof down?' I asked.

'Yes, and start the engine, get the heater going. I'm taking off these jeans. My bum is soaked.'

---

[6] Whilst always officially denied and ridiculed, there is evidence that this story of Norman's might be true. Journalists Duncan Campbell and John Rentoul claimed to have seen copies of classified signals in their article 'All Out War' (*New Statesman*, 24 August 1984) and the allegation was vigorously pursued by anti-Thatcher campaigner MP Tom Dalyell, who cited first-hand confirmation from a retired Polaris submarine commander.

'Mine too.'

I spread our anoraks and jeans across the front seats. We sat side by side on the white vinyl sofa which converted (very soon, I hoped) into a reasonable double bed. I reached down two plastic glasses from the melamine cupboard above the tiny sink and poured us each a generous slug of Johnnie Walker.

'Peace.'

'Peace,' Sarah echoed.

'So how have we done?'

'Hard to say. I do feel guilty about the play-acting. They're such a nice bunch, so earnest, so naive. We could have owned up to being journalists and they wouldn't have cared. Why did Dennis want us undercover?'

'I don't know. But would they have spoken so freely if they'd seen this?' I rummaged under my rugby shirt and produced my second prized gadget, my Sanyo voice-activated Dictaphone. Still spooling away. I pressed Rewind.

'... about the play-acting. They're such a nice bunch ...'

'I'll be able to transcribe Norman's story word for word.'

'Is that legal? Can we tape people without their knowledge?'

'I guess so, in the overriding public interest. Don't fret, I won't get caught, and Dennis and the lawyers will decide.'

'I didn't buy everything Norm said. Like hosing down that fellow every four hours. Does that seem likely?'

'It's possible. Any radioactive contamination can be fatal.'

'What about the quarter of a million hush money? If we find the guy and it's true, that's dynamite. Norm might put us in touch.'

This was a great idea, but I didn't say so. My head spun from the neat Scotch. Instead I asked, 'What do you make of Jerry?'

'He marked us as fakes from the moment we arrived. But he said nothing around the fire when Mitch started on about spies. How will I manage this makeup with no bath or shower and no running water except from the standpipe? And my hair. I thought there would be electricity somewhere. How do they cope with that wee boy?'

I stretched over for notebook KS1. 'They're all grubby and pallid, as we will be soon enough. Let's have another look at what Dennis said.'

Sarah snuggled closer, peeped over my shoulder. 'With your outlines, it's more an impression than a transcript.'

I ignored this slur on my shorthand and recited. '"We received a tip-off from a reliable source in the anti-nuclear movement. I'm not telling you their name so you can't expose them accidentally or on purpose. This source said we should have eyes and ears in Faslane for the weekend of 8th/9th October, because something big is planned. The action or protest or statement or defection or whatever the hell it is will be timed to create maximum embarrassment for Thatcher on the first day of the Tory Party Conference in Brighton. It could even cause the Government to fall. I'm sending you two, and I want you undercover, and I want this story for us and us alone. The *Guardian* has had it too easy on nuclear defence. They have deep sources in CND and usually the first we know of something is when they print it. I've chosen you kids because I know you're bonking like bunnies and enjoy working closely together. Read the NUJ rules on undercover work before you leave."'

Sarah said, 'You're making most of this up. There's no squiggle that even remotely resembles "bonking like bunnies" and Dennis said he was sending us because no one knows our names or faces yet, and we need the experience.'

I said, 'May I continue? "Don't do anything illegal. Don't get found out. Protect the identity of any source. Check your facts. Phone in daily. Enjoy lots of regular sex."'

She didn't raise a chuckle. I closed the notebook. A fug had built up in the van. I reached over the back of the driver's seat and turned off the engine. 'Either Dennis's mystery source sold him a pup, or the campers have a dastardly plan which they're keeping to themselves.'

I slid a finger under the elastic of her knickers and gave them a twang.

She yawned. 'Not tonight, Napoleon. I'm bushed and I must get this makeup off. Say goodbye to Siouxsie.' She batted her long eyelashes. She did look tired. 'Will you go fetch me some hot water, lover? Our tiny kettle here is hopeless.' She fingered her earrings. 'I'll have earlobes stretched down to my boobs if I wear these again.'

'They made a point.' I drained my glass, slid the side door open. 'Oh no. Raining again.' I struggled back into my jeans and anorak and put the washing-up bowl on my head upside down. I slithered across wet leaves and mud towards the communal caravan from which hearty singing still wafted.

Coitus Interruptus

Thursday 6th October 1988, 7.10am, 10°C, rain

I AWOKE to a grey dawn and rain drumming on the roof.

I unzipped my sleeping bag, enough to raise myself on an elbow and check on Sarah.

Her breathing was gentle and even. Her nose twitched once like a cat's, but apart from that she didn't stir.

How beautiful she was! Cross as I had been at Debbie's starchy reprimand for calling her 'mine', I had to acknowledge her point. No one would ever own this woman, nor was she mine to parade as a trophy.

My mind turned back to the day we met, wide-eyed, nervous newbies in our first jobs. We'd greeted each other politely while waiting to meet the editor, Dennis Hackett. A whirlwind of introductions, demonstrations and showing-arounds followed. Heads swivelled everywhere. In the newsroom, the guys couldn't keep their eyes off my new colleague.

On the Tuesday, Dennis set Sarah and me to work on the obituary of dog trainer Barbara Woodhouse and we got to know each other.

We left the office for a drink in the nearest pub, just the two of us, on the Wednesday, and she accepted my invitation to the Odeon, Leicester Square on the Friday to see *The Unbearable Lightness of Being* with Juliette Binoche and Daniel Day-Lewis. The movie proved to be more erotic than I'd dared hope. Afterwards, we walked across to Chinatown and fed each other with chopsticks in a Gerrard Street noodle bar. Back on the street, she yawned, looked at her watch. 'Thank you for a lovely evening. This girl's ready for her bed.'

'See you Monday, then.'

She said, 'Oh. I was rather hoping you'd come home with me and we could sleep together at my place. Preferably having had sex first. But if you've other plans …'

Her face wore a wicked, teasing grin.

The date was 12th August 1988, and what a glorious Twelfth it ended up. The morning of the thirteenth started rather succulently too.

From that day on, our respective flatmates benefited less and less from our company.

I'm scared for my unborn babies, she'd said last night.

Was she already contemplating, as I was now daring to, a long-term future for us together? We'd known each other less than two months. Fifty-nine days, to be precise, which I like to be.

Another glance at Sarah. Still asleep.

The rattle of raindrops continued.

I considered my options.

Once assembled, the double bed occupied most of the floor area of the camper van, leaving only a handkerchief-sized space by the sliding door. I folded down the blanket which covered both of us and unzipped my sleeping bag with exaggerated care so the fastener wouldn't make a rasping sound. I brought my knees up to my chest, rolled to the edge of the cushions, drew aside the curtain and peeped out at a sodden vista of dripping trees, further blurred by my myopia. Looking down at the ground, I saw a huge puddle beside the van.

I eased open the door. The catch released with a snap.

I looked over my shoulder.

No sound or movement from my sleeping beauty.

I swung my legs down into the tiny footwell and slid the door open.

I poked my head out to confirm no one was around. Naked, knees bent, holding on to the doorframe with my right hand, I leaned out and peed on the leaf mould surrounding the puddle.

'Scooby-Doo, I want to be like you-hoo-hoo … so I can hang like you, piss like you, oo-oo-oo. Now wash your hands, ape man.'

'Sorry … tried not to wake you.' I twisted round, closed the door behind me and climbed back on the bed. I had to crawl over her to reach the sink and press the little plastic lever that produced a trickle of water from the tap. Straddled above her on all fours I was inviting her to grab me, which she did with glee.

'That's not fair!'

'It's not fair that you can pee anywhere, anytime, and you do, and I have to get dressed and trek over to the caravan.'

'No problem, I'll wait here in the dry for you.'

'I can hold on.'

'So I see. You'd better let go of me or face the consequences.'

She giggled. 'You need taking in hand. And your rear view on awakening is quite delightful.'

I dried my fingers on the blanket. She still had a firm hold of me, with predictable results. I unzipped her sleeping bag a little and slipped my hand inside.

She purred, catlike again, which reminded me. 'I've written a poem for you. Would you like me to read it?'[7]

'Yes. But not now.' Both her hands were at work. Well, two could play that game. Our lips met in a deep wet kiss. I unzipped the rest of her sleeping bag and shoved the quilting aside, then pulled the blanket over us.

'Just a little higher,' she whispered. 'Yes, yes. Oh, my word, yes … I do believe you're starting to get the hang of this.'

'Cheeky monkey yourself.'

---

[7] The poem, reproduced in the Appendix, is a parody of 'For I Will Consider My Cat Jeoffry' by Christopher Smart (1722-1771). Its combination of pretentiousness and puppy-dog devotion typifies the twenty-one-year-old me, in love and trying too hard to impress. I never did get to read it to her.

The rain renewed its pounding overhead and a gust of wind rocked the suspension.

'More.' She took my wrist and guided my hand. I kissed her ear, her neck. Her eyes closed and she arched her back to match the rhythm of my ministrations. A delicate flush spread downwards across her chest.

She began to moan, and her breathing became shallower. 'You bugger,' she gasped. 'Don't stop.' She stretched her arms out to either side and grabbed hold of the edges of the vinyl cushions.

The rain hammered down.

Slow hand ... who sang that?

Then an even louder sound.

A tremendous banging, a machine-gun rattle, this time on the sliding door.

What the hell?

'Sarah! Wake up, girl! The loch beckons. I have a costume for you if you want it. And a cap. Open up.'

Debbie!

More knocking and thumping. 'Can you hear me in there? Hurry up, it's pissing down and the sooner we're in the water the better.'

Sarah rolled her eyes, whether in ecstasy or exasperation with the interruption I could not judge. Either way she was too far gone to care. She managed to cry out, 'Debbie! Hold on. Just a moment. I'm ... I'm ... I'm just ... oh God, I'm just coming ...'

Scooped

Saturday 8th October, 8.50am, 10°C, rain

I PICTURED the editor leaning back in his ergonomic leather recliner, smoke spiralling upwards from his cigarette, feet on the desk, the Saturday first editions open in front of him.

Nice and warm.

I wedged the handset between my ear and my shoulder, took my own ciggy from the metal ledge of the phone box and sneaked a drag before replying to his question.

'There's something afoot for sure. We've gained the confidence of the peace campers. There are only six residents at the moment. Seven if you count Archie, but he's four years old.' The wind whistled around my feet. These flimsy new shelters offered neither the comfort nor the soundproofing of the classic red kiosks. There was a telephone at the camp, but Jerry had said it was out of order, which was lucky as I couldn't have used it for risk of giving us away.

Dennis said, 'Seven? Doesn't sound much of a story, Cocker. My source told me they were planning a spectacular. Do you think they've rumbled you? How's Sarah coping?'

I glanced outside. Sullen rain splattered the grey roadway. More of a Scotch downpour than a Scotch mist. My jeans clung to my legs, soaked yet again during the two-mile cycle from Faslane. En route, I'd spotted a pair of specks in the loch: Sarah and Debbie, both swimming strongly, raising no splashes. They were too far out for me to see if Sarah was wearing a costume.

'She's surviving. We have some promising ideas for features if nothing better comes up. The council is agitating to close the camp again. I've taken three hundred and forty moody photos. Ideal for a colour magazine feature. I even wondered if *The Times* …'

'You don't work for the bloody *Times*, you work for me.'

'We're all News International.'

'Watch it, Cocker. Remember where your loyalties lie.'

'Dennis, we can't report on a story that isn't here. Can you speak to your source again?'

'I already have. He repeated that everything will kick off tomorrow, Sunday. I'm disappointed you're not in the loop. Did they mark you as reporters, or did you upset them somehow with your smug metropolitan ways?'

'Neither, boss. There is one guy, Jerry, an American, who seemed to be expecting us, but he's said nothing since we arrived on Wednesday. The others have accepted us. Sarah has palled up with a girl called Debbie who—'

The editor harrumphed. The leather of his chair creaked as he swung his feet off the desk. 'I'm calling you back, Ken. I can't justify the two of you playing hippies on the banks of the Clyde any longer. The Tories are kicking off at Brighton on Tuesday, and I need—'

The throaty roar of a powerful engine drowned his words.

'Hold on, Dennis. Missed that. Some biker making a hell of a racket.' I wiped the condensation from the glass door with my sleeve and peered out.

The motorcycle braked and stopped at the kerb. A Triumph Bonneville T140, property of Mitch the electrician. The bike was a real hog which I'd drooled over since the first evening.

Even so, Mitch would have to wait in the rain while I finished my call.

'Ken? Are you there, mate?'

'Yeah … just a mo. while I find more 10p's, Dennis.' I delved into my sodden pocket, eyes on the motorbike. The rider gave a final thunderous blip to the throttle which vibrated the thin aluminium panels of the kiosk, then kicked down the stand, dismounted and took off his helmet, goggles and gloves.

I did a double take.

Her helmet, goggles and gloves.

The biker was not Mitch, but Sarah.

I fumbled coins into the slot. 'I'm listening, Dennis.'

Sarah marched up, flung open the door and squashed into the box with me. She pointed at the No Smoking sign, wagged a finger, lifted my cigarette between her thumb and pinky, made as if to drop it to the floor, then took a crafty drag from it instead.

I covered the phone with a wet woolly glove and hissed, 'What's up? I didn't know you could ride.'

'Quick, let me speak to Dennis. Developments.'

I lifted my glove from the mouthpiece. 'Dennis, Sarah is actually here now, and I believe she would like a word.'

'You didn't say she was with you. I wish you —'

She seized the handset. 'Dennis, sorry to barge in, but within the last hour I have discovered what they plan to do. It is big. You'll have copy for Tuesday's edition …'

A few minutes later, pedalling the communal push bike back to Faslane, drenched and cold, watching the Triumph shrink ahead of me into the distance, I reflected that had Sarah not arrived when she did, we would have been in the camper van heading south on the A1 that afternoon and in London on the Sunday night (when everything did indeed kick off). Even so, I felt upstaged when she finished the call with the editor, though we shared a brief kiss and a damp victory cuddle.

She'd made the breakthrough after swimming with Debbie three days running.

Now Sarah's name would go first in the by-line.

I had to push the wretched bike the final half-mile, the front tyre hanging off the rim following a ball-breaking encounter with a pothole full of rainwater.

Arriving at the camp, I wheeled the bike through the mud. I'd forgotten how wet you get on a bicycle in the rain. I shoved the crippled machine into its shelter and stepped up to the door of the communal caravan.

Sarah sat on the knackered sofa with the horsehair-sprouting arms, the only occupant, toasting her toes by the stove and rolling a cigarette. She'd changed into her dungarees and a thick woolly jumper and looked both snug and smug.

'What kept you?' she chirped. 'Make yourself a cup of tea, but don't settle in, we need more logs split.' She giggled. 'You're all steamed up about something.'

I had nothing to wipe my glasses with, so took them off. I stuck out my tongue, flicked her a V-sign, squelched to the stove and tipped the heavy kettle to fill a brown-stained mug promoting *Mick's Chicks – Free Range Layers*. 'So, how did that ambush happen? I had no idea you could ride a motorbike. Do you even have a licence?'

'Yes. There are benefits of having a family in the motor trade.'

I jiggled the teabag up and down with my fingernails. 'We all stood admiring that bike the first evening and you never said a dicky bird.'

'You never asked me. You and Mitch droned on about its cylinders and horsepower and electric start and the Les Harris mods and boy-racer crap. I could have been the invisible woman. Anyway, a girl must have a few secrets up her sleeve. No, don't come near me, you're soaking, and everything is dry in here.'

I scraped a folding chair across from under the grimy end window and perched as close to the stove as I could tolerate. I pulled out my pack of Benson & Hedges. Sodden, and squashed to buggery. I laid out the six fags on the stovetop, a row of bedraggled soldiers. 'So how did you wheedle the plans out of Debbie?'

'I've devoted quality time to Debbie apart from the swimming. I think she likes me.'

'That's good. I like her too.'

'No, you don't understand. I think she *really* likes me.'

'Oh. I did wonder.'

'She spilt the beans to me this morning out in the loch. Then we went to see Mitch. You'd already left to cycle to the phone. I knew I had to find you before you spoke to Dennis.'

'Just in time. Dennis was all set to despatch us to Thatcher's Nuremburg Rally in Brighton. How did you persuade Mitch to lend you his brand-new Bonnie? That's a grand's worth of heavy metal.'

'Easy. I told him you had cycled off to call your mother and beg her to send more money, but you'd forgotten your bag of 10p coins, and I didn't want you to reverse the charges to her yet again.'

'Journalism's wasted on you, you should be writing fantasy fiction. Ideally in a galaxy far, far away.' My icy hands, clamped to the mug, tingled as sensation returned.

She lit her roll-up. 'Also, I think Mitch fancies me too, and wanted to see me in leather. He takes a spare suit plus helmet and goggles everywhere in case he meets a nice girl like me, he said. He would have given me a ride to the phone box except he was up a ladder struggling with his wiring. Oh man, your face when I showed up!'

'Everyone fancies you, lover. You certainly look the business in leather. Talk about sex on two wheels. I could have taken you right there. Have you got a bike at home? Let's go touring together in the spring.'

'Ken.'

'Yes?'

'I told Debbie I want to take part in the raid. On Sunday night. When she confided in me I could hardly say otherwise.'

I put my glasses back on and her face sprang into focus. 'The editor said we mustn't break the law, lover. We'll be sacked.'

'I don't plan to break the law. Debbie will swim. All I have to do is wait by the outer fence with dry clothes, a towel and a blanket. I'll ask the cops on the gate to take them in for her. I'm just support. I won't go inside the base, I won't go in the water and so I won't break the law.'

'What about me?'

'What about you?'

'What will I do?'

'They need another fence cutter for the diversion.'

'Oh no. No, no. That means breaking into the base, or at least trying to. I can't afford to get arrested any more than you can.'

The door opened and Debbie entered. She took off her woollen bobble cap and shook her shoulder-length blonde hair free. 'Hey guys. Did your mum come good, Ken? What a bummer, running out of dosh.'

I stood up, because that's what well-bred young men do, then felt stupid and sat again. 'She'll put fifty quid in my account but says not a penny more.'

Debbie dumped herself on the sofa and put a muscled arm around Sarah. 'Hi, shore support team.' She turned to me. 'How about you, Ken? Guess you've heard the plan now? Are you in too? Or is your role to hang about the camp with your spy camera, ogling the talent?'

Sarah and Debbie erupted in childish snorts of laughter.

'You mean go in with Mitch and the boys? I don't know about that—'

Debbie leaned forward. 'They need four of you. One to work the bolt cutters, then he climbs through while the others hold the gap open. Then from the other side—'

'What about Jerry?' I said. 'Why isn't he going?'

Sarah said, 'Jerry stays on the outside so he can file the press release. This will get us into the nationals. If we're all arrested and in the cells, there's no one to handle the publicity.'

Without thinking, I said, 'I could do that.'

Sarah squeezed her eyes shut in disbelief.

Debbie said, 'What do you know about journalism and writing stuff, Ken? You're just a dilettante art-school dropout trying to be the new Ansel Adams. You should smuggle your dinky camera into the base and take action shots. We need Jerry on the outside like Sarah says. He knows about PR and all that shit.'

'Plus he has the mobile phone,' Sarah said.

I drained the dregs of my tea.

'Well?' Debbie arched an eyebrow. 'Are you with us, Ken? Are you a man or a wee, cowrin, tim'rous beastie?'

My heart thumped. 'Wee, *sleekit*, cowrin, tim'rous beastie, if anything,' I replied, to play for time. 'My mum will kill me if I'm arrested. With a criminal record I'll never get a job.'

'It won't come to that,' Debbie said. 'Mostly they just bang you up overnight, then the Procurator Fiscal writes you a stern letter saying you've been a naughty boy or girl and don't do it again. Check out the Legal Support hut, see the letters and advice there.'

'I already did. You're right, Debs, for a breach of the peace, lying in the road or handcuffing yourself to a gate. But what you're—we're—planning is far more serious than that.'

Sarah looked from Debbie to me and back like an umpire at Wimbledon but said nothing to help me out. If I hadn't been so cold and damp I would have been sweating.

The door swung open again and in ambled Mitch the Yeti. Only his lips, eyes and nose were visible among the abundant shoulder-length hair which framed his full set of sideburns, beard and moustache.

'Ah, here yeez all are. Ken, are ye with us, ya eejit?'

Incursion

Monday 10th October 1988, 12.25am, 3°C, dry, clear, frosty

'I STILL DON'T like it,' I said.

Sarah rolled up the bundle of dry clothing for Debbie in a red towel and crammed it into her own small rucksack. 'I'm not delirious about you joining the break-in crew.'

'As if I had a choice. My plan is to help with the cutting and scarper when the cops show up.'

'They'll clock you on the closed-circuit TV.'

There was barely room to stand in the camper. Outside the darkness was intense, with moonrise not due until 5.45am. A new moon, too, which would provide next to no illumination.

By then it would all be over.

With the pair of us in a police van heading for the cells, most likely.

I said, 'I play fly half, remember. I can hare it when I'm motivated. Promise you won't do anything rash yourself.'

'I promise. But I don't want poor Debbie setting off all alone. Once she's in the water and on her way, I'll climb back up and head for the North Gate with her stuff.'

'They patrol the main road all night, lover.'

'It's not illegal to walk with a rucksack even at one in the morning.'

'And when they spot *you* on the CCTV?'

'I'll tell the truth. There's no law against standing outside the base with a change of clothing either. They all know Debbie. I'll be fine.' She looked at her watch. 'Half past midnight.'

A tap at the sliding door.

'I expect we'll meet you coming back the other way,' I said.

'Yes.' She smiled, pale and tense in the dim glow of the battery lighting. Two inflamed midge bites on her neck suggested the handiwork of an apprentice vampire.

She slid open the door and climbed down.

The plan was for the girls to get a head start. They would use the culvert beneath the A814. This opened on to the old road that skirted Gareloch. Just before the base, the Timbacraft boatyard would afford Debbie cover and access to deep water.

Mitch, Colin, Spike and I would follow fifteen minutes later and create the diversion, drawing the MOD police and marines away from the waterside so Debbie could swim to the floating Admiralty Dock undetected, her waterproof bag of spray paints strapped to her waist.

We'd asked Debbie what she intended to paint on the side of *HMS Resolution*, the sub in the dock. She said she hadn't decided, but it wouldn't be polite.

It was a daring plan, almost military in its cunning.

My problem was that they'd designed the diversion to attract attention. Colin and the others were happy to be caught—wanted to be. A night in the cells was a badge of honour for them, whereas I'd blow my cover and get my name in the papers for all the wrong reasons. I would surely lose my job.

I searched for a ciggy and found a packet inside my sleeping bag with one remaining. We'd got through most of our supply already: smoke was the only defence against the clouds of evil biting midges which plagued the camp. In theory their season had ended the previous week, but no one had told the Faslane contingent.

As I lit up, I wondered how truthful Sarah had been about her intentions. My girl possessed a secretive streak, I was learning. She'd spent a lot of time alone with Debbie. All in the interests of the story, she'd assured me.

Smoke finished, I pulled on my ever-damp anorak and bobble cap and headed into the darkness.

Outside the communal caravan young Spike, an orange-crested cockatoo in a donkey jacket, banged his gloved hands together. Colin, chubby-faced and somehow middle-aged before his time despite his mullet haircut, fussed over his bootlaces and appeared nervous. Mitch the Yeti, wielding long metal shears, looked ready to take on all comers.

He leaned on his bolt croppers. 'Sure ye're up fur this, Ken ma man?'

'Can't wait.'

In a swift movement Mitch raised his meaty hands, extended the jaws of the huge cutters and lunged at my groin with a snarl. I leapt backwards, slipped on the leaf mould, banged my head on the window of the caravan and almost lost my balance.

The three of them laughed.

'Hey. Ease up. I'm on your side, remember?'

'We hope so,' Colin said. 'Mitch won't miss next time. Got your camera, Ken?'

'Yep.' I patted my pocket. I'd loaded 400ASA monochrome film and chosen the standard 24mm lens. I'd left the flash unit behind — it was as big as the camera itself, and its use would betray us.

'Everyone got torches?'

'No,' I said. 'We forgot to bring one.'

'Then you can't give us away, at least. Everyone got gloves?'

'No,' I said again.

'Not equipped fur this, are ye?' Mitch tossed me a pair of well-worn builders' gloves caked in dried mud.

'It's not that cold. Three degrees.'

Spike the punk said, 'The gloves aren't to keep your hands warm, you wally. They're to protect them when we cut the wire.'

Colin said, 'Let's move.'

We set off in single file, Colin leading and me bringing up the rear.

We descended a bank towards the stream which flowed down the hill behind the camp. As we neared the bottom I slipped on a patch of mud and slithered the final metre on my bum. The others didn't notice. My heart pounded as I recovered my footing.

They called it the underpass: a dank brick-lined culvert, mossy and slippery with weeds dangling from the roof. Mitch had to bend double and Spike walked bandy-legged to keep his spiky orange hair off the ceiling. Colin and I could stand. We sloshed along and the icy water soaked through my trainers in seconds.

The tunnel descended and I felt the faint tremor of traffic passing overhead. The splosh of our footsteps in the rank water echoed off the Victorian brickwork.

After fifty metres the culvert diverted left and a moment later we emerged on to the foreshore of the loch.

A broken-backed plastic kayak lay on the seaweed tethered to a rock by a weed-draped rope. The loom of the lights from the base glowed a sinister orange-yellow. The road now ran above us.

I turned, and my right trainer sank into the mud, held firm by suction. I tugged, my foot came out of my shoe, I lost my balance and plunged my sock into the oily water.

Spike grabbed my arm and I stayed upright. Once again my co-conspirators snorted with laughter.

We clambered up the bank, grabbing at bracken for handholds, slithering and sliding.

The old road to the base was in poor condition, potholed and crumbling at the verges. Below and to the left, the tide lapped on the shore and retreating wavelets sucked at the pebbles. We passed the sinister gatehouse of Shandon House on our right, the original entrance to the grounds of the mansion, now marooned on a strip of soggy woodland between the road we were on and the new A814 above.

Ahead I made out the base perimeter fence rising into the night sky. More fencing lined the opposite side of the road. I'd expected floodlights on every post, but the nearest were several hundred metres ahead. The posts also carried CCTV cameras with infrared night vision, so perhaps floodlights were unnecessary here.

They may have already spied us from their control room.

We didn't speak. Microphones on the fence would also betray our presence. Colin wanted them to catch us inside the base, not here on the public road where the cops would just admonish us and bundle us back to the camp in their van.

We trudged along, my feet chilled and numb in my soaked socks and trainers.

The Timbacraft buildings loomed out of the darkness, unlit but dimly silhouetted in the glow from ahead. We passed a series of workshops with galvanised roofing. The boatyard abutted the base and constituted a major security risk. If we were able to exploit it, so could really bad guys.

No sign of Sarah.

We crossed the forecourt of the boatyard. Hugging the ramshackle buildings, we arrived at the outer fence of Clyde Submarine Base, the most sensitive, secure and heavily guarded military installation in the UK.

From sangars inside, the Comacchio Group of Royal Marine Commandos would defend the base against attack, machine-gunning any mob or insurgent force threatening to overrun them, whether Russian, terrorist or civilian.

Despite the lateness of the hour, there was much activity within the facility. Vehicles moved along the internal roads, a giant crane swung, and orange-clad construction workers shuffled around. Clangs and bangs floated towards us on the frosty night air.

On the perimeter road beyond the tall fence, a group of pedestrians in plain clothes swayed down the pavement. One lurched into another and laughter echoed across the tarmac.

We waited, concealed by a Portakabin, and watched a stripy MOD police car cruise past the revellers.

'Good. It takes fifteen minutes for the patrol to do the circuit, so let's move,' Colin whispered.

We emerged from hiding and approached the fence. They'd upgraded this less than a year before, following many successful assaults on its predecessor by peace campers. Coiled razor wire lined the fence at ground level.

'Time, Ken?'

I pressed the backlight on my Casio.[8]

'One-twelve precisely.'

'Unclimbable. Uncuttable. The best wee fence that fifteen million pounds of taxpayers' lolly can buy. Let's see, shall we, laddies?'

Colin put his finger to his lips.

Mitch advanced on the roll of ground-level razor wire with his bolt cutters.

Colin hissed, 'Look!' and pointed. I wiped the condensation off my glasses and peered into the gloom. I saw it too: a gap in the razor wire fifty metres from where we stood.

'Aye,' Mitch muttered.

We sidled towards the gap. Amazingly, the razor wire inside the fence had also been removed.

The equivalent of a Welcome mat.

'Like takin' sweeties aff a wean.' Mitch squared up and hacked away at the fence at waist level, his arms two powerful pistons working to slice the weldmesh horizontally.

When he'd cut a slit about half a metre long, he paused and panted, 'Now pull.'

Our job was to separate the sections so he could continue shearing without tangling the jaws in the severed strands of metal.

Colin and Spike squatted down and tugged below, while I reached up and pushed the top section inwards.

Mitch powered on, keeping up a steady rhythm.

All four of us worked on like this, bunched up together.

At close quarters my co-protesters proved distinctly malodorous.

'Time check, Ken.'

'One twenty-three.'

---

[8] The TS-150, with analogue and digital temperature, world time map, five alarms, timer and stopwatch. 10 Bar water resistant, 10-year lithium battery. The watch stored the temperature readings, so I could recall and record them later, which I usually did at bedtime.

Mitch's breath whistled through his teeth. We struggled to force the fence apart, all panting now, arm muscles on fire from the effort of displacing the mesh.

When the slit had lengthened to about three metres, Colin said, 'Reckon that's enough. I'll go first.'

'Hold on.' Mitch closed his bolt croppers and sprinted back to Timbacraft. He hid the cutters underneath the Portakabin and returned in seconds. 'Thirty-five quids' worth. Dinna want them hauf-inched.'

'But you stole them in the first place, mate,' Spike said.

'Hurry, we don't have long,' Colin said.

I pushed the cut mesh while Mitch and Spike pulled. The slit parted. Colin climbed up and squirmed through. Mitch found it harder due to his height and bulk. His jacket snagged on a jagged cut end and he cursed in Glaswegian.

I tugged at his trapped sleeve and it came free, ripping the fabric. He landed inside with a heavy thump.

Spike followed, his head turned sideways so his impressive Mohican stayed parallel to the fencing.

That left me alone outside.

'Decision time, our Ken. Coming or nae?'

I climbed up and dropped through the slit which they held open for me. As the nimblest I had no problem.

The others let go of the fence and the two sections sprang back together. Even up close it was impossible to detect where we had effected our entry.

'Satisfied?' I murmured, looking from face to face in the gloom.

Three nods.

I'd passed the initiation.

'Now what?' I asked. They hadn't discussed (with me around, anyway) what we would do if we entered the base unobserved.

'See if we can get into the Red Area at least. The nearer the subs, the more fuss and noise when they catch us. Walk casual like we're sailors just back from clubbing. Mitch, lead on, you know the way.'

We crossed a scrubby patch of grass and set off towards the heart of Clyde Submarine Base. Street lamps cast pools of light, leaving dark areas of pavement in between. We passed the football pitch and crossed a rusty, redundant railway line.

Pallets of building materials, stacks of piping, oil drums, metal containers and skips seemed to occupy every spare piece of ground. Yellow-and-black tape dangled from temporary fencing. A small electric cement mixer lay on its side next to a pile of sand on a board.

The entire facility was a construction site, and a chaotic one at that. I took out my Pentax and started snapping, grateful for my little beauty's automatic aperture setting.

The patrol car didn't reappear, but ahead of us a guy came into view. He wore a white leather jacket with tassels and a wide-brimmed cowboy hat. He turned right, making unsteady progress. He stumbled off the pavement and swayed across the road, appeared to bounce off the opposite kerb and lurched back over the carriageway.

'Aff his heid,' Mitch chuckled. We quickened our step to catch up with the reveller. Soon we heard him singing 'Red, Red Wine' in a slurred Geordie accent.

To the north we glimpsed another foursome of partygoers, fresh home from Sunday night in the fleshpots of Helensburgh. Shouts and laughter drifted our way.

Despite our long hair, scruffy attire and unmilitary bearing, perhaps we weren't that conspicuous.

We caught up with Singing Cowboy and followed him a few paces behind.

'Heading for the subs,' Colin murmured. 'Hammered. And tomorrow he'll be on duty. Unbelievable.'

The drunken sailor stopped at a guard hut with a security turnstile. He hunted in his pocket and produced a pass. For a moment he got his tassels stuck in the turnstile. Then he was through.

We carried on past the sentry, who didn't even glance at us.

'Get tae! Thought we could tailgate Roy Rogers,' Mitch said. 'Nae ither way intae the Red Area.'

'We should have brought the cutters,' Colin said. 'May as well hand ourselves in now.'

'What's that building ahead?' Spike asked.

'Police station,' Colin said. 'Perfect. I'll go in, ask for directions to the Polaris jetty.'

'Aye, great.' Mitch grinned. 'Cannae wait tae see thae eejits' faces.'

So, this was it.

In moments I'd be arrested.

It all seemed so futile now: the planning, the bravado, the risks. All we'd achieved was a few minutes roaming around a low-security area of the base. And for that I had sacrificed my career.

I wondered how Debbie had fared and prayed that Sarah was safe and hadn't been arrested herself.

She at least deserved to keep her job.

For a crazy moment I considered staying on at the camp, becoming an activist. Whatever you thought about nuclear weapons, Clyde Submarine Base was a disgrace, a disaster just waiting to happen.

We gathered outside the police station and peeped in through the glass doors. Three officers were in residence. Two sat at a table, one with a copy of the *Sun* open at Page 3, the other reclining, feet up, phone to his ear, twisting the red cable around his fingers.

The third cop stood with his back to the others, spooning Nescafé into mugs.

My heart thumped. The moment he turned he'd see us.

The cop added water from the kettle followed by Marvel milk powder and prodigious amounts of sugar. He turned, took the mugs to the table and sat. I made eye contact with him, but he failed to register our presence, or didn't care—assumed we were ratings back from a fancy-dress party and would enter if we so chose.

He was more interested in Page 3 cop, who was talking and pointing at his topless totty.

Colin hesitated, his hand on the door handle. 'No. Those muppets don't deserve such an easy ride. Let's make their lives much more miserable. Come on, boys.'

We walked off unchallenged. Colin said, 'We'll rush the Maidstone Gate. When they see us, split up and run in different directions, find cover and hide. They'll set off the bandit alarm. Gives the girls every chance. Hope they haven't been waiting in the water all this time freezing their tits off.'

I said, 'Only Debbie is swimming. Sarah went along for moral support with a towel and stuff for when she's arrested.'

Colin said, 'Oh yeah, that's right.'

Spike chipped in with, 'Only Debs would swim without a wetsuit.'

Mitch added, 'She doesn't even bother with a swimsuit most days.'

We headed towards the loch, inky in the middle distance, the occasional ripple reflected in a floodlight beam. The astonishing amount of contractors' materials and rubbish aided our progress. We scooted across open ground to hide behind a pallet of tiles, dodged around yet another Portakabin and regrouped by a dump truck.

'Yon's the new trainin' school fur Trident.' Mitch pointed at recently poured foundations sprouting random lengths of rusty reinforcing bar. 'Or will be, if they ever sort their shit out. Already a year late.'

Stealthy now, destination in sight, we crept from hiding place to hiding place, one at a time, in a reasonable parody of a squad of paratroopers.

Then the Maidstone Gate towered in front of us, rolls of razor wire glittering in the glare of massed floodlights.

Time? 1.35am.

This fencing was higher than at the outer perimeter, with the barbed wire lining both sides at high and low levels.

But no sentries stood at the gate, which was closed.

Nothing moved.

No vehicle appeared.

And I felt no fear.

Instead I experienced an adrenaline surge of exhilaration. I had written off my job, and with it the anxieties of employment, and of deadlines, and of competing with Sarah for a by-line, and of scraping together enough each month from my salary to pay my exorbitant flat share.

Mitch whistled and said, 'Well would ye look at yon.'

Bandits

Monday 10th October 1988, 1.38am, 1°C

TO THE LEFT of the gate, almost concealed by yellowing bindweed and overgrown grass, lay two long extending ladders.

Heady with excitement, we extended one of the ladders and leaned it on the gate.

I clambered up. The others handed me the second ladder, which I hoisted over and lowered on the other side. The ladders were long enough to clear the rolls of razor wire on the top of the gate.

Mitch began his ascent. All arms and legs, he got himself caught up while transferring at the apex from one ladder to the other.

By now I was down inside the Red Area, while Colin and Spike remained outside.

Mitch couldn't extricate himself from the barbs and muttered more florid Glaswegian curses. Colin and I enjoyed his predicament for a while, taunting him from below, then we both climbed to the top of our respective ladders to help free him.

Headlights came into view.

The MOD patrol car approached at walking pace. I recognised the driver and his colleague, PCs Coffeemaker and Totty Ogler.

Spike, the only one still at ground level, leaned on his ladder and gave the cops a cheery wave and thumbs-up as they approached him.

Totty Ogler raised a hand in acknowledgement. Neither cop looked up, and so didn't spot the three of us perched in a huddle on top of the gate like a monkey family on a tree branch.

The car rolled past Spike without slackening pace. Its tail lights flashed a brighter red as the driver maintained his slow progress down the incline.

Colin said, 'The chippie has better security than this.'[9]

'Mind me best jacket,' Mitch grumbled as we tugged the clingy razor wire from his sleeve.

A minute later all four of us stood in the Red Area.

Mitch pointed. 'This way to the jetties.'

Construction supplies and equipment littered the ground. I took more photos.

A sign announced Berth No. 3, and beyond the sign a submarine conning tower jutted into the sky.

Another patrol car appeared from behind a shipping container.

Mitch left the carriageway and scurried over to a pallet dumped on the dirt, covered with plastic sheeting. He fished around and returned with a two-metre length of copper pipe, a polythene bag of plumbing parts and a mains extension reel. I took the reel, Colin took the bag and Mitch hoisted the pipe on his shoulder. 'Spike, just act like a plumber,' Mitch said.

'What does a plumber look like?'

'A lazy bastard teenager with a Mohawk, acne and a bad attitude, let's hope,' Colin said.

Spike raised his middle finger and gave Colin a hard shove into the roadway.

'At least we don't look furtive,' I said.

Mitch nodded. 'Yeah. Hide in plain sight.'

The police car's headlamps lurched upwards like searchlights as it negotiated a speed bump. Then the twin beams found us.

---

[9] The official account of our exploits, pulled together and rushed out by MOD staffer Brian Hawtin for a furious Margaret Thatcher, confirms all the shortcomings in the base security. You can read the full MOD report in the Appendix (minus the map showing our route, which remains redacted).

The car drew level. Spike banged on the driver's door and shouted, 'Dip your headlights, man! You tryin' to blind us or what? We got a job to do too.'

The driver wound down his window. 'You fellows on the *Trafalgar?*'

Spike said, 'Yeah, reactor emergency.'

'What's with all the radiation warnings? Never seen so much activity in the middle of the night.'

'Sorry mate, can't tell you any more. Classified.'

'Okay. You take care.' The window rolled shut and the car moved off.

Enjoying ourselves, we marched four abreast towards HMS *Trafalgar*. 'Hunter killer,' Mitch said, squinting up against the floodlights. 'Nuke powered but no nuke missiles.'

Colin said, 'Like *Conqueror* which sunk the *Belgrano*. Still an ugly bastard.'

We ducked behind a firefighting hose reel. At close quarters the submarine's size became apparent. The length of a football pitch, most of her mass below water, she exuded threatening power. The hull seemed to have a coating of black tiles like the scales of a fish.

High on the casing a sentry kept watch. At ground level, yellow tape with radiation warning signs surrounded the submarine. Pipes and cables led from the dockside to the vessel, supplying water and shore power, I guessed. Two mobile cranes reached high at what seemed impossible angles that must topple them.

Spike pointed at the nearest crane. 'How about climbing one of those?'

Colin followed his gaze upwards. 'Probably wouldn't notice us. Let's try for a bomber.'

We emerged from our concealment and walked on.

Because it had been troubling me since the police station, I said, 'You guys sure Sarah isn't swimming?'

'Your lassie'll be fine.'

'Don't you and your bird talk?' Spike said. 'Guess you're too busy shagging.' He opened his mouth and mimed panting. 'Can't blame you, mind, with her rack. How'd you pull that looker anyway?'

'When you grow up to be a big boy, I'll give you some tips about women, Spike.' I held up my cable reel. 'In the meantime, one more word like that and I'll tie you to a lamppost with this. Even better, I'll push you in the dock and get your fancy hairdo wet.'

Spike raised his hands. 'Hey, little man, can't you take a joke?'

Colin said, 'Spike, shut up, don't be such a twat.'

We passed two workers carrying a cylinder between them. It looked heavy. They paid us no attention.

'Liquid nitrogen,' Mitch murmured. 'For emergency reactor cooling.'

I tried again. 'Colin, tell me straight. Is Sarah swimming tonight with Debbie?'

Colin's expression told me the answer before he spoke.

'She didn't want you to know because you would have gone ape-shit. Sorry mate, you'd better take it up with her later.'

Reeling from the realisation that Sarah had deceived me, I plodded along with the others.

We approached another fence, another gate, with the heaviest fortifications yet.

Mitch said, 'Green Area. Polaris.'

Again, prodigious amounts of stores, equipment and building materials provided ample cover.

We hid and waited for ten minutes according to Casio. No sentries appeared. We crept forward.

The gate was locked, but unlike at the Maidstone Gate there were no floodlights. None working, anyway.

Several large waste containers stood lashed to the adjacent fence. We used these as ladders to effect a simple entry, in about one minute, over the gate and into the most sensitive high-security area of Clyde Submarine Base.

Why they called this the Green Area I could not imagine.

Inside, we proceeded unchallenged towards the waterside. We passed a yellow contractor's cabin, door open and lights ablaze.

The others strode on. I hung back and peeped inside.

No one at home.

Signs on the wall extolled the company's safety priorities and listed the nuclear accident emergency procedures. A row of hooks held the workers' civvy clothes, with their shoes lined up underneath. Two spare orange coveralls bearing the firm's logo hung like lurid animal pelts, with hard hats above.

The table held the essential equipment of the modern nuclear base worker: kettle, carton of milk, box of PG Tips, mugs, ashtray. The smell reminded me of a school changing room, even down to a distinct whiff of dope.

I exited and trotted to catch up with the gang. From behind, arranged in order of height with Mitch on the left, Spike in the middle and Colin on the right, they reminded me of John Cleese and the two Ronnies in that sketch about the class system.

I joined the group next to Colin. I knew my place.

'They're smoking weed on their break,' I said.

'Did you pinch any?' Spike asked.

We arrived at the Polaris jetty. A fin, even taller than the *Trafalgar's*, with a cluster of masts and antennae reaching higher yet, disappeared into the night sky.

There seemed to be no one about, and it was quieter away from the clangs and shouts of the night shift workers. With the darkened loch on our right we walked on, slowing our pace, still carrying our plumbers' props.

The jetty, about seven metres wide, ran parallel with the shoreline and must have been a quarter of a mile long. On its inner side, next to the shore, tugs stirred at their moorings. The submarine lay on the seaward side, in the loch.

As we approached the beast, I glanced up to the casing and spied a sentry patrolling towards the rear of the vessel. I put out my left arm to stop our party.

We backed up into the shadows and remained still and quiet for ten minutes this time, waiting for the sentry to reappear, a challenge to ring out or the alarm to go off.

Our breath condensed in the still night air. My feet were two blocks of ice.

No sound, no movement.

'What's he doing down the back end?' I whispered.

'They have to check the draught of the sub on the rudder once an hour. Make sure the bloody thing isn't sinking,' Colin said. 'Come on, I don't care if we get caught now.'

I *did* care.

We resumed our progress down the jetty. Loch water lapped at the scaly black hull of the submarine. A blue banner identified her as *HMS Repulse*, with the submarine's motto picked out in white letters underneath: *Who Touches Me Is Broken*.[10]

At the landward end of the gangway stood a wooden sentry box, homespun for such a high-tech vessel, reminiscent of a car park attendant's hut. Inside, two sailors sat side by side smoking.

I glanced at my watch. 2.06am. The tide was on the turn (I'd checked the tides, as well as the time of moonrise, in the almanac, telling the others it could be important. They had been blasé.)

'Gimme the cable,' Spike said, and snatched the reel from me. As if at a prearranged signal, which it obviously was, agreed upon while I was in the engineering contractor's cabin, Spike, Mitch and Colin strode out as one towards the gangway. A small gate barred their way but Colin, in the lead, pushed through it.

At the same instant, the wail of sirens rent the night air, coming from all directions, near and far, echoing off the buildings behind us and the submarine ahead.

Unseen loudspeakers crackled to life with a metallic, distorted voice:

'Bandit! Bandit! Bandit!'

A sailor emerged from the sentry box. He shouted, 'Hey! You three! Where d'you think you're going?'

---

[10] The Polaris submarine was the eleventh Royal Navy warship to bear the name, but the first to render the *Repulse* motto, 'Qui Tangit Frangitur', in English.

It was a dumb-ass question. My partners in crime were boarding *HMS Repulse*.

Colin shouted something over his shoulder about a reactor emergency. All three of them continued up the gangway at a trot, Mitch shouldering his length of pipe which flexed as he bounded after Colin.

The other sentry appeared alongside his colleague. The pair of them made no attempt to apprehend the intruders who by now had reached the casing of the submarine.

The Tannoy blared. *'Bandit! Bandit! Put on your hard hats. Lock all windows and doors. Guard all doors. Bandit! Bandit!'*

The last I saw of the trio was Colin descending through a hatch forward of the fin. He disappeared so fast I thought he might have fallen or slid down the handrail.

Vehicles converged on the scene and things got hectic. I turned and ran.

A searchlight beam snapped on, bounced around and tracked towards *Repulse*. I hared along the waterside the way we had come. In my peripheral vision I saw the silhouette of a commando, his SA80 raised in the firing position.[11]

From behind me came shouts, inaudible against the howling sirens, the distorted intruder warnings and the slamming of metal doors.

I was not the only one on the run. In fact, everyone was rushing about, like ants whose nest has been dug up by the gardener. Walking or standing still would have been far more suspicious.

Two MOD policemen raced past me. We crossed paths only a metre apart. They were talking on their radios, focused on reaching *Repulse*, and didn't register me.

Heart hammering, panting from my getaway, I passed between the metal-clad warehouses, hung a left and reached the yellow Portakabin, still open and unoccupied.

---

[11] I recognised the weapon because I'd held a prototype as a student when the Rifle Association visited the Royal Ordnance factory in Enfield.

I closed the door behind me, filled the kettle from a plastic jug and switched it on before turning to the coat rack.

I took down the smaller of the orange coveralls, climbed into them and zipped up, then crammed my damp bobble cap into a pocket and replaced it with a hard hat bearing the company logo.

I looked down. The legs were far too long. I spotted a pair of wellies in the corner and swapped them for my soaked trainers. The boots were predictably too large, so I rolled up the coverall legs, crammed them into the wellies and pulled more material down over the outside of the boots. This would prevent the wellingtons falling off, and I reckoned also increased my apparent height.

All this time, the noise, commotion and flashing of lights increased outside.

The kettle burbled and switched off with a click. I shivered—no, shook with tension. I had to use both hands to hold the heavy chrome kettle while I poured, and the teaspoon rattled against the mug as I added generous lashings of sugar.

The tea steamed up my glasses and soothed my parched throat. I returned to the clothes rack. With guilty, clumsy fingers I reached into jacket pockets. All empty. Hold on. Something in this one. A wallet, containing £25 in fivers, an Access card and a driving licence, all the property of a Peter Haywood of Greenock. In Peter's trouser pocket I found a pass holder on a lanyard. No pass inside, but I hung it round my neck anyway and replaced the wallet.

Footsteps! Someone outside the cabin. I turned to face the door as it crashed open.

A nuclear civvy worker dressed like me, except no hard hat. 'Hey, pal, seen any intruders?'

'No. Just me.'

'We have to secure everything and muster at the gate. Bogies in the water. I need to lock this door.'

I half-turned. 'How many intruders? Have they caught them?'

'No idea, the marines shooed us away when the bandit alarm sounded.' The guy put his head on one side. 'Have I seen you before?'

'Mark Bobbins. My first shift. Pete Haywood sent me for a torque wrench.'

'Well, forget about Pete's bloody torque wrench and get your arse down the gate, or it will be your last shift an' all, Lofty. Didn't you have the security briefing?'

I shook my head. 'The supervisor said they didn't do them at the weekend. Tomorrow instead.'

'And they call themselves managers. Unbelievable.' The worker donned the remaining hard hat. 'Put down the latch when you leave.' He spun on his heel and disappeared into the clamour of the base.

What next? If I joined the civilian contractors at the gate they would rumble me. There couldn't be that many of them on the night shift. Maybe only the dozen whose belongings hung in this cabin.

How long would the lockdown last?

Our gang of three inside *HMS Repulse* were already in custody, for sure. Had the Plods caught Sarah and Debbie too?

Thanks to my darling but devious girlfriend, neither would have a towel or dry clothing. After any length of time in the water, hypothermia was a serious risk. They were in swimming costumes, not wetsuits, and the air temperature hovered around freezing.

The brave, if reckless, swimmers needed my help, right now.

How could I get dry clothes to them?

I was staring at the solution.

From the hooks I selected two pairs of jeans, a short puffa jacket and a ski cap. I'd give my own anorak and bobble cap to Sarah. Shoes? Too hard to carry.

If challenged I would make up some bullshit story.

The siren and bandit alarm stopped.

I sneaked a look out of the window. The scurrying and shouting had abated. I reckoned they'd caught all the intruders (except me).

Time to go. But first, remembering I was a journalist, I dug out the Pentax and ran off a cartridge on the cannabis paraphernalia lying around the hut: the charred roach among the cigarette butts, the Rizla packets and the baggie in the bin containing a few shreds of leftover weed.

I considered taking the baggie as evidence, but realised this was a dreadful idea, certain to add a drugs charge to my own burgeoning rap sheet.

But I did return to the coat hooks and search in every single pocket, and that proved to be a shrewd decision.

As I rolled up the purloined clothes into an untidy bundle an explosion echoed from across the water.

Fugitive

Monday 10th October 1988, 2.20am, 1°C

MORE REPORTS rocked the base as I ran, not for the gate, but back towards the Polaris jetties. Every few seconds a dull *whoomph* generated a shock wave in the ground which I felt through the soles of my boots. A rushing noise followed, then a rattling or pattering sound.

A terrorist attack? What were the chances of them striking at the very time we were breaking in?

The action was out in the loch around the floating dock. This massive shed, located beyond the Polaris jetty, contained *HMS Resolution*, the target for Debbie's graffiti.

I passed *HMS Repulse*. At the sentry box, the two Naval orderlies we'd seen smoking earlier were arguing with two MOD policemen.

The four men paid me no attention.

Booom ...

A jolt like electricity ran through me as I realised what the explosions were.

Not bombs.

Not terrorists.

Depth charges.

The marines were trying to kill our girls by throwing grenades into the water.

A police boat came into view from behind the floating dock, its searchlight probing all round. Then I heard the throaty roar of a powerful outboard engine and saw the creamy wake of a rigid inflatable. No lights on the dinghy, but I made out a figure aboard raising an arm in a throwing motion.

Booom ...

The ground shuddered as the shockwave hit the underwater section of the dock. The sea glowed as if set alight. A plume of water some ten metres high erupted into the night sky and sparkled in the police searchlight's beam as it cascaded down, a few fat droplets of seawater wetting me like a sudden shower of rain.

I ran, shouting, 'Stop! They're only girls. Harmless peace campaigners! Don't kill them!'

The floating dock loomed massive ahead of me, filling my field of vision, a giant of a hangar.

HMS Resolution occupied the dock, raised up and suspended out of the water. She resembled a black jumbo jet with the wings removed. Below the waterline, marine fouling mottled and encrusted the hull.

Around the dock ran a perforated metal walkway, on which a Royal Marine sentry patrolled, weapon at the ready.

At the end of the Polaris jetty, a high fence halted my progress. I saw no way to proceed further except by jumping into the inky water and swimming.

This would defeat my aim of supplying the girls with dry clothes. Not that hypothermia was the main risk to them now. Still, I could use the jeans as tourniquets.

As I stood waving my arms to attract the sentry's attention, another explosion shook the concrete underfoot and more droplets of water pattered around me.

I yelled out in the gap between grenades, 'Stop! For the love of God, you idiots! They're girls—unarmed women protesters!'

The sentry turned and saw me this time. Had he heard me? He bent to talk into his radio.

Booom!

In the loch the RIB roared in tight circles as if driven by joyriding teenagers.

If either Sarah or Debbie remained in the water, they were likely to be dead by now. Explosives underwater cause more damage than in the air, because the water concentrates the shockwaves. Concussed, disorientated, drenched, gasping, gulping, the girls would find keeping their heads above water next to impossible even if they stayed conscious.

The police boat reappeared. It motored northwards, staying well clear of the grenade-happy joyriders in the RIB. I took off my glasses and wiped them. How many on the boat? Any girls visible? I squinted into the darkness, praying for a glimpse of Sarah's yellow loan costume.

Nothing.

I realised a minute had passed since the last grenade, and the note of the RIB's engine had reduced in both pitch and volume.

There was activity on the dinghy, which was now stationary, but of a different sort: shadowy silhouettes bending over.

They'd found someone in the water, alive or dead.

I decided to retrace my steps along the jetty to where the police boat would most likely dock.

I turned and collided with something solid and unyielding.

A marine, about my age but twice my size, stared down at me with a mixture of puzzlement and amusement.

'Place what you're carrying on the ground, nice and slow, then step back with your hands up, sir.'

I complied.

The commando's radio crackled. He inclined his head and pressed a button. 'I'm with him now.' He turned to me. 'What exactly are you doing here, sir?'

Lockdown

Monday 10th October 1988, 3.10am - 2.25pm, 23°C

DRUGS RIFE IN CHAOTIC NUCLEAR SUB BASE
**Trident construction workers have a high old time —
and not just the crane operators!**

Last night, with three campaigners from the Faslane Peace Camp, I entered the heavily fortified Clyde Submarine Base, home to the UK's Polaris nuclear deterrent.

These ageing submarines are soon to be superseded by the even more powerful Trident model, and in preparation for the transition Faslane has become the largest construction site in Europe after the Channel Tunnel.

What I discovered inside the base was a shocking catalogue of inadequate security bordering on negligence. Large numbers of civilian contractors are at work on the new Trident base by day and night. Their vehicles, cabins, equipment and stores have contributed to a chaotic security situation.

My photographs show numerous shortcomings in the defences, which allowed the three peace protesters to board the submarine **HMS Repulse**, *which was ready to leave on its top-secret twelve-week patrol and may have been already armed with its 16 Polaris nuclear missiles.*

I also discovered evidence that drugs are rife at the base.

It was feeble stuff, destined for the spike, and I knew it. Drugs were rife everywhere. This was 1988 — who cared? Half the population was stoned much of the time. The story lacked focus: was is about our incursion, with me undercover, or an exposé of security lapses, or drug-taking among contractors? Most pathetic of all was the admission that three of my co-protesters had boarded a nuclear sub but I hadn't.

My prose was turgid, with overlong sentences, two clauses beginning with 'which' in the same sentence and the use of generalities (*'chaotic security situation'*, *'numerous shortcomings in the defences'*) rather than specific details. *'May have been already armed'* was not only poor English but rotten journalism. It cried out that I did not know the answer.

At least writing gave me something to do, holed up in the corner of the canteen. I'd bought three postcards of Loch Lomond from the base shop and spread them out on the table around me as cover, and to deter anyone from joining me.

The pass I pocketed in the Portakabin had proved to be my lucky charm. The marine on the jetty, satisfied with my story and ID, took my arm, led me away and pointed out my exit route. He didn't even pat me down or he would have found both the reporter's notebook in which I was now writing and my Pentax.

More awkward to explain those.

At the gate I latched on to the worker who had interrupted me in the cabin earlier. He greeted me like a long-lost pal.

My nagging worry throughout the weary watches of the night that followed was that the rightful owner of my pass, one Roger McLelland, had alerted the Modplods, as the Ministry of Defence police were universally known, who would apprehend me at the main gate when it reopened.

Around me in the canteen, the excitement generated by the intrusion alert and the depth-charging of the loch had given way to resentful boredom among the night shift: several hundred staff and contractors, military and civilian, who found themselves confined to base hours beyond their clocking-off time.

By keeping my ears open and hanging around the coffee dispensers, I discovered that the marines had pulled one swimmer from the water alive and well and abandoned the search for a second.

I also learned that a 'member of the public' had triggered the bandit alarm by approaching guards on the South Gate with dry clothes for a swimmer.

That suggested Sarah had not gone in the water, but stuck to the plan she and I had agreed. One complication: the word was that a man showed up at the gate, not a woman. And Sarah's stated destination had been the North Gate, not the South.

Either the gossip was wrong. Or Sarah had changed her plan.

A little voice in my head kept telling me she was dead, and it was my fault, again, just like before with Susie.

You killed her. You killed her.

My pulse rate picked up. To arrest the impending panic attack, I forced my eyes to focus and reread my article.

A load of bollocks. The submarine buster boys would get the scoop. But my prose was so boring that at least I got my pulse and breathing under control.

Before long my eyelids drooped as a wave of fatigue engulfed me.

Stay awake, Ken, you dozy sod. Journalists have to stay up late. Do some bloody work!

Fired with fresh resolve, I started on a feature article. The peace camp and submarine base had much in common. Both were ostensibly dedicated to the same cause: peace. The nuclear deterrent was there to deter, never to be used. If you hitched a lift and asked for the peace camp, some wags would take you past and drop you at the North Gate, with the smug observation that this was the 'real' peace camp.

Both places had evolved from humble beginnings on long, thin, damp, cold, inhospitable and windy sites. Both were closed communities viewed with suspicion by large parts of the populace. Both were eyesores. Both were chaotic, with people milling around among piles of junk.

Comparing and contrasting the two places seemed a most promising tack, but needed a poetic or philosophical tone. The words wouldn't come, and my head kept falling forward. The pencil slipped from my fingers.

Twice during the night, I walked over to the bank of payphones and dialled the peace camp. Number unobtainable. After the second attempt I called the operator, who confirmed that the line was out of order. Curiously, though, she said no one had reported the fault.

At 6am the kitchen opened for cooked food. I took a tray, joined the queue at the servery and enjoyed an excellent full Scottish including porridge and black pudding all for £1.60, courtesy of a fiver of Roger's which I made a mental note to refund somehow.

A TV set hung on a wall bracket near the servery. *BBC Breakfast Time* came on air at 7am with Frank Bough and Jill Dando perched on the sofa. The news was of the upcoming Tory party conference in Brighton, and that the shadow Chancellor of the Exchequer, John Smith, had suffered a heart attack. It seemed like another world.

Nothing about the events at Clyde Submarine Base.

The sun rose and the hours limped by.

At 2.25pm I slapped down my pencil in frustration. Twelve hours now since the bandit alarm had gone off, and still no word when the lockdown would end.

I realised with a jolt that I could have phoned my story in to the paper from a payphone here. *Hours ago!*

The phones weren't in cubicles, but they had those hoods like in a hairdressers, and with minimal care I could have avoided the risk of eavesdroppers.

How stupid had I been! I could have been live on radio. *The World at One*, an hour and a half ago with James Naughtie interviewing me!

Dennis might have put the story on the wires as a teaser. My report could be on TV right now! '*Today* undercover correspondent reports from inside top-secret sub base'! Provided he didn't name me or show my picture, nobody would rumble me.

Kenneth Sinclair, the talk of the newsroom!

What a scoop I'd missed.

Idiot ...

Instead, your Faslane correspondent had moped around fretting about his girlfriend, then lined up to scarf down a plateload of bacon, eggs and fried bread.

I picked up my pencil and tapped it on the Formica tabletop.

Maybe just time to retrieve the situation.

I seized up my draft and scratched away in feverish haste to improve it. Out went *'numerous shortcomings in the defences'*, replaced by *'ladders left at security gates, bins lashed to fences, defective floodlights, missing barbed wire and Clouseau-like police patrols'*. I added details of our Ealing-Comedy encounters with the Modplods. I composed a short, grabby opener and removed the facetious subhead to the piece. The subeditors would rewrite the headlines anyway to fit the column space available.

Forty minutes later I had fifteen hundred words that resembled a functioning news article.

I pushed my chair back and headed for the phones clutching four 10p coins, change from my breakfast.

A group of guys had gathered around the coffee machines. Something about their huddled posture and murmuring voices made me pause. I walked across and earwigged. One of the group turned, saw my raised eyebrows.

People love sharing bad news.

'They've found a body. Half an hour ago. Washed up on the beach.'

Before I could open my mouth to frame a question the base sirens sounded. Not a long wail this time, just three short blips, followed by an announcement on the Tannoy: *'Lockdown ended. Resume normal operations and security.'*

Cheers erupted all around the canteen and everyone started getting their shit together and moving.

I prayed that Sarah was safely locked in the police cells and the body in the water was Debbie's.

My Lady's Chamber

Monday 10th October 1988, 2.55pm, 11°C

WE STREAMED through the North Gate like kids let out early on the last day of term. The Plods didn't even glance at our passes.

Wives had arrived in cars to collect husbands. Others headed for the bus stop. Nobody paid me any attention in the melee.

I set off down the main road towards the peace camp, a walk of around half an hour. When I was out of sight and the road was clear of traffic I nipped into the bushes. I climbed out of the orange jumpsuit and stuffed it behind a tree. I'd dropped the purloined jeans into a bin in the canteen toilets and abandoned the hard hat on a hook behind a cubicle door.

The moment I ditched the coveralls rain began to fall. At least my feet stayed dry this time in the stolen wellies.

As I walked, I tortured myself over Sarah's fate. Hope fought with despair. She was a powerful swimmer, but Debbie was in a different league, fighting fit, almost Olympic class. I'd back Debbie to escape the minefield over my girl.

But luck would have played a role. Maybe with Debbie in the lead, Sarah had time to retreat when the marines lobbed the grenades?

Torn between hurrying to get it over with and dawdling to put off the evil moment, I settled for a steady trudge in the strengthening rain.

All too soon, the peace camp hove into view ahead.

From afar the place resembled the *Marie Celeste*. No police vehicles parked up, no ambulance with flashing lights, no sign of life at all. Not even a plume of smoke from the big caravan.

I'd left the camp with Colin, Mitch and Spike less than fifteen hours earlier. It felt like weeks. And what a wretched homecoming.

I slowed my pace, clinging to hope for a few more seconds.

A wave of anguish and self-pity washed over me, compounded by thick, brain-cloying fatigue.

The drizzle had morphed into larger, scattered drops of rain, reminding me of the grenade explosions that had splattered me from way out in the loch.

I tried to imagine the horror of that deadly assault for a swimmer. The flash of the explosion underwater. The compression of the chest as the shockwave arrived. A gulp of seawater instead of air, followed by choking, sinking, a frenzied fight to reach the surface. Then another explosion, much nearer, and tumbling around, disorientated, a limb broken like a doll's, hanging by shreds of skin and sinew. An involuntary gasp, saltwater filling the airways, an out-of-body sense of peace as the brain capitulated and sensations faded along with consciousness. Then a lifeless, drifting descent to the cold, slimy rocks on the seabed.

I pushed open the gate and walked in, my heart pounding like a kettledrum.

Our trusty VW remained in its corner pitch, its hooded headlights a mournful reproach.

I stood still for a moment, my arms clasped around me, wet and cold, swaying with dizziness, overcome with guilt, remorse and self-recrimination.

Holding my breath, I opened the sliding door of the camper.

No Sarah inside.

She was dead. And I had allowed all this to happen. I'd volunteered for the decoy raid. Sarah's competitive nature had compelled her to take part too.

Sick at heart, I crossed to the communal caravan. No one at home there. No one in Jerry's caravan either, or in the wimmin's, or in Joan and Colin's old red bus, or in Mitch's frame tent, or Spike's bivouac.

I hadn't expected to find Mitch, Spike, Colin or Debbie, who would all be in custody. (Unless Debbie was dead.) But where were Joan, Archie, Jerry? Perhaps the police had rounded everyone up to 'help with their enquiries'. Or to identify the corpse ...

A voice cut through my reverie.

'At last! Clark Kent returns! Where have you been? Have you filed your story? I have!'

I whipped my head around. Sarah grinned at me from the doorway of the toilet caravan, tousle-haired and pink-cheeked in her Sloppy Joe sweatshirt, flip-flops and nothing else. She hurried across to join me and we hugged.

I found I could both breathe and speak. 'You're not dead.'

'What made you think I would be?'

Inside, we lay on the vinyl mattress and held each other in silence for at least a minute, until I became aware she was sobbing. I stroked her hair, stiff with salt. The last traces of her permed curls had washed out in the icy waters of the loch.

She said, 'You're all damp and smelly and lovely. I missed you. I thought you'd been arrested but you hadn't.'

'I was certain the marines had killed you. They found a body.'

She looked up at me through the tears. 'A body? Whose?'

'I feared it was you. Or Debbie.'

'Debbie's in the cells at Dumbarton nick with the others. And I'm here, alive, as you see.'

'How did you and Debbie survive the grenade attack? How did you get back here?'

'Oh, they were stun grenades, apparently. Flashbangs. To flush us out, not hurt us. They caught Debbie on the Admiralty Dock. There's a rubber apron all around it and she was sitting on that with me. We'd sprayed 'SCRAP TRIDENT' on the outside of the dock and we were getting cold. We discussed just swimming back, but she wanted to be arrested so she could appear in court and get more publicity. She said no need for me to get arrested too, and she would cover for me, so the moment the bandit alarm sounded she jumped and waved and whistled to attract the police boat. It took ages for the Plods to spot her even so. Meanwhile I slipped into the water and swam back to Timbacraft. I stayed under the surface as much as possible and no one saw me. The explosions were all behind me. I dressed and arrived here ten minutes later. What's the time? I've been asleep for hours.'

'Three forty-five. In the afternoon.'

'The court hearings were scheduled for three o'clock. Assuming they get bail they'll all be back by six. A body …' She pursed her lips.

'Who's at Dumbarton?'

'Mitch, Spike, Colin, Debbie and Beverley in the cells. Jerry, Joan and Archie to watch the hearing. Jerry will report the outcome to his pal at the *Scotsman.* He's already given him the intrusion bit. He also tipped off the *Glasgow Herald* to send their court reporter. Ken, my darling, you're shaking.'

A tear ran down my cheek. 'I thought you'd drowned. Who is Beverley?'

'She's a peace camper, been away in Edinburgh with the CND so we hadn't met her. She heard about our plan and conducted her own protest swim, off her own bat, at the other end of the base. She didn't tell anyone she would do it, but that's typical of her, Jerry said. Been arrested fourteen times. She got as far as the oil depot before they nabbed her. But we weren't the only ones in the water.'

'What—even more of you? Sounds like a right old swimming gala down there.'

'I'll come to that. First, how did you get away yourself? We were worried about you too. The men told Jerry you chickened out at the gangway. They got into the control room of *HMS Repulse*, poked around, took turns to sit in the helmsman's seat which is like an exercise bike with a steering wheel. Mitch inspected the secret charts and Colin tried to call the story in to the papers from the external telephone on the systems console. Only he didn't have the numbers. Spike wrote stuff on the nuclear missile launch panel with a marker pen. "Press to End World" and "Warning: don't touch me, I'm broken". Rather witty. When an officer finally burst into the control room Mitch said, "We're hijacking this submarine. Take us to Cuba." They had a hoot.'

'How did you learn all this?'

'The boys phoned Jerry's mobile from the cells. He gave them advice about a defence of challenging bye-laws.'

I sniffed and wiped my face. 'I spent half the night and all this morning in the base canteen undercover as a construction worker.'

'Wow. Great. You must have a scorcher of a story.'

'Not so. Most of the time I was working up a sulk because you deceived me about your swim. All the others knew. I felt a right prat. And I didn't chicken out. They rushed the gangplank and left me behind. Just then the alarm sounded so I took advantage of the confusion, disguised myself as a worker and stole a pass which got me out even though I didn't look anything like his photo.' I produced Roger's pass and showed her.

'Hmm, I agree he's not as good looking as you. So, you haven't filed anything?'

I shook my head. 'You say you have?'

She reached over for her notebook and flipped the pages. She'd scrawled hundreds of words of shorthand. 'I pleaded exhaustion this morning, wrote my copy, waited until everyone had left for Dumbarton then borrowed Mitch's bike and phoned it in from the call box. Like to hear it?'

'Yes. But what about the body? I think you know something too. Start at the beginning.'

She lay back on the bed and stared at the pop-up roof, its yellow fabric panels spotted with rain. 'I do feel bad about what I did. I put the swimming costume on under my clothes and convinced myself it was "just in case". At Timbacraft, Debbie went down the dock ladder. She said, "Come on in girl, the water's lovely," so I stripped down to my bathers and followed her.'

'What about the dry clobber? Did you swim back, collect that, then return on foot to the South Gate?'

She glanced towards the window. 'No. Jerry volunteered for that role yesterday. When he showed up at the South Gate, he tried to give the clothes and towel to the guards, but they hadn't realised there were intruders inside, either ashore or in the water. They sounded the alarm. Jerry gave the game away, he thinks.'

'I wish you'd trusted me with this. I was the proverbial mushroom, kept in the dark and fed a load of shit. Look at me, Sarah.'

She turned her head to meet my gaze. 'Yeah. I fouled up. Sorry. But you did the same, remember. You said you would only help with the fence cutting, then scarper when the cops showed up. Sauce for the goose and all that.'

'Touché. In my defence, I would have blown my cover by not following the guys. No cops showed up, so no excuse for me to split. It was crazy how easily we got in. We hacked away at that fence in direct sight of three CCTV cameras. Microphones listening everywhere too. Inside the base it was even easier to get about undetected.'

'You volunteered for the diversion party. We hadn't discussed that.'

'When we sat around in the communal caravan that morning you encouraged Debbie and Mitch, goaded me until I submitted.'

She said, 'Teased, not goaded.'

'No more deceptions. Complete trust. Always. Till death us do part. Agreed?'

'Agreed. Was that a proposal?'

We hugged. We kissed. I nuzzled her ear.

Sarah stroked my cheek. 'I thought you wanted to hear my theory about the body in the water.'

I positioned my palms flat on her chest and slid my hands from side to side, applying just enough pressure to locate her nipples through the thick cotton. 'Right now I'm more interested in this very live body, but go ahead.'

'You seem to have brightened up since you arrived looking like a damp dachshund. What you're doing is very nice but please take off your soggy anorak and jeans.'

'With great pleasure. Tell me all about the body.' I shrugged off the offending garments and hung them on the back of the driver's seat. We lay facing each other. A car drove by, tooting repeatedly, the tone of the horn dropping as it passed the camp. This was the signal of support. Vehicles that hated us sounded a long continuous blast.

'I didn't see a body, but as we sat on the apron of the floating dock, I spotted something moving … oh yes, carry on, just like that. The light wasn't great and it could have been a stick or a seabird. Then some bubbles came up. A snorkel! I pointed it out to Debbie. We watched and it moved northwards towards the Polaris jetty, staying close in to shore. Debbie thought it was a Navy diver. But they wouldn't have dropped the stun grenades if one of theirs was in the water, surely? How did you learn about the body? Any details? It could be important.'

I placed a gentle forefinger on her lips. 'Shhh. We can come back to this.'

She nibbled at my fingertip.

I said, 'Talking about sauce and geese, I've got a nursery rhyme for you. It comes with actions.'

'Like "The Wheels on the Bus"?'

'Yes, sort of. Ready? Here goes:

'Goosey, goosey gander …'

I touched her nose.

'Whither shall I wander …?'

My hands and lips began their exploration.

'Upstairs …'

She closed her eyes, relaxing under my touch with a long sigh of contentment.

'Downstairs …'

She got the idea. With a gleeful cackle she helped me out with the last line of the verse, guiding my fingers to their delightful, lubricious destination.

High Tea

Monday 10th October 1988, some minutes later

AS WE LAY enfolded, she murmured, 'Can I be cheeky and ask if I am your first?'

'First what?'

'Lover.'

I did my best Prince Charles impression, pulling the corners of my mouth apart with my fingers and keeping my teeth clenched. 'Whatever love means ...'

She giggled. 'Don't be silly. Am I the first woman you've had sex with?'

'Hmm. Depends what you mean by sex.'

'As a good Catholic girl I would use the Holy Father's definition from canon law. *Erectio, penetratio, ejaculatio.*'

'Do they have to be in that order?'

'Yes. Oh, you are hopeless!' She pulled the pillow from under my head and biffed me with it.

I said, 'Would it make you happier to believe you had deflowered a younger man?'

'No. Anyway you're not much younger. Two months or something. I'm just curious. If I am your first, you've learned fast. On the job, so to speak.'

I rubbed my nose against hers. 'I will not dignify your impertinent question with an answer. Would you like a cup of tea?'

'Yes please. And let's compare our pieces for tomorrow's edition, while there's no one around. And have a proper smoke.'

I pulled on my other pair of jeans and set the kettle on the tiny hob. Then I gathered the materials for a family-sized spliff. While I rolled and twirled and licked and glued and lit up, she read out her article.

Like me, she'd focused on the poor security at the base: the proximity of an independent business, Timbacraft, to the Polaris jetty; the absence of lighting along the foreshore, or any boom or barrier to deter insurgent boats or swimmers; the single dozy sentry inside the floating dock, with more poor lighting; and the lack of coordination between the marines, the Plods and the naval personnel.

Unlike me, she'd provided loads of context: the timetable for Trident, the local opposition to the construction, environmental and political issues.

I read her my piece.

As the atmosphere turned ever more herbal, we lavished praise on each other for our efforts. We agreed to wait for the return of the campers. The *HMS Repulse* Three could add colourful details about their stay in the sub. Then one of us would sneak off yet again to the public phone box to file more copy.

'Did you speak to Dennis when you called the office?' I asked.

'Yes. He seemed happy, but I sensed he had expected more.'

I opened the miniature wardrobe, found my other sweater and put it on. 'It all comes back to the body. Seems there was another protest or undercover op. last night. Which could tie in with Dennis's briefing. How can we investigate that?'

'Phone the base and ask them.'

'We'd get a "no comment". But we could call up the *Repulse*.'

She raised her eyebrows. 'Can you do that?'

'Yes, they put you straight through to the control room. They don't even ask who's calling, apparently, and if a rating answers they sometimes talk.'

'Amazing. Worth a try.'

The tip of the joint glowed as I inhaled. I held it a second, then blew the smoke out of the corner of my mouth. I passed over the spliff. 'Why didn't you go down the courthouse and report from there?'

'I'd have been with Joan and Jerry. No way to sneak off, like I could here all by my lonesome.'

'Didn't you want to see Debbie?'

'Well, yes. But she can wait. I'm not in love with Debbie, I'm in love with you, Dumbo. Did I tell you I listened to the whole *Today* programme on Radio 4 this morning? Nothing about our exploits.'

'Too soon.'

After several more minutes of popping and burbling, the kettle whistled. I reached over and made two mugs of tea. We didn't have any milk powder left, but I decided Johnnie Walker would serve just as well and sloshed it in, with her enthusiastic approval.

She said, 'Were you trying to propose to me back then?'

I said, 'Back when?'

'Then. Now. You know.'

'I think I was channelling my inner Freud.'

'A slip of a lad.' She giggled. 'We did it. We did it.'

'Had sex? We've done little else when left alone together for over ten minutes.'

'No, you dope-on-a-rope, I mean we got the story. Without blowing it. Our cover, I mean.'

We both dissolved into laughter. I declaimed, 'Hold the front page.'

She said, 'Watch out Bernward and Woodstein! Bernford and Woodwood. Redwood and Hoffstein. Holy crap, my brain is trashed. The two reporters. You know. Like you but even hunkier. In the film anyway.'

'Never mind them! We're gonna be ace hotshots! Shove over Peter Preston!'

'Yeah! Right! On yer pushbike, Dennis Hackett!'

'Gotcha, Kelvin MacKenzie!'

She shouted, 'And I'll eat your hamster any day, Clark Kent!'

'Shhh!' I stopped and stared at my anorak, hanging over the front seat. 'Shit. My pictures.' I reached into the pocket and took out the Pentax. 'They should be in London.'

'Well, get them there. You can borrow Mitch's Bonnie. He said to.'

'Ride down to Vauxhall Bridge Road? Six hours. Seven if I stay legal.'

She rolled her hazel eyes. 'No, put the films on the train by Red Star. Phone the picture desk to alert them, so they have the courier waiting at King's Cross. Call in your story to the copy desk on the way back here.'

'Red Star. Why didn't I think of that?' I flopped on the bed, laughing. 'The wheels on the train go round and round, round and round, round and round, whoo! whoo!—' I mimed pulling the whistle on a steam train.

She shook my shoulder. 'Ken. Do it. Take the bike. And while you're in Helensburgh, buy some fish and chips. I'm starving, and I can't take another of Joan's rehydrated veggie stews. Go on, go on. Get your pics to the paper and they'll be in tomorrow's edition.'

I sat up and tried to focus. 'I'm the worse for weed. And drink. But chips would be welcome. Hours since I had a decent fry-up.'

Sarah slid open the side window. 'More than I got. You'll be fine. Half a joint and a wee slug of Scotch, nothing. Way under the limit even if you get stopped. Clean your teeth though.'

'A hell of a big slug of Scotch. More like a cupful.' I rewound the film in my camera, opened the back and took out the cartridge. 'Sure Mitch is cool? Shouldn't you ride and take me pillion?'

'I've been out already. No need to both risk it. You go, Napoleon. Haddock if they have it, mushy peas, Irn-Bru. A shedload of chips. Get them well wrapped to keep them hot. And ride carefully, I need that food.'

'Right.' I collected my exposed film cartridges together, including the arty shots around the peace camp. The chances of them arriving in time for tomorrow's edition were slim, but just making the effort would score Brownie points.

I cleaned my teeth, dipping the brush into the remaining hot water at the bottom of the kettle.

'Hurry or the others will be here before you go. Helmet and goggles are in the top box. Keys are in the goggles. Good luck. Break a leg. Or rather, don't.' A pause. 'I love you.'

I found, put on and laced up my spare pair of trainers, my fingers tingling.

Ready, I stood in the tiny footwell and said, 'Will you marry me?'

'Yes, yes, of course, as long as you get back here pronto with fish and chips still hot. Go, go!'

My head as light as a helium balloon, I half-fell out of the van, clung to the door frame, pivoted on my heel and regained my footing.

I floated off in search of Mitch's Bonneville.

Bonnie

Monday 10th October 1988, 4.30pm, 13°C, sunny intervals

IN JEANS, ANORAK and old trainers I was ill equipped for biking, but I reasoned I'd be fine for the short ride into Helensburgh and back. Only ten minutes each way.

Aware I shouldn't be on the highway at all, I kept my speed down, rode by the book and arrived without incident at the Central Railway Station.

A wave of fatigue and dizziness crashed over me as I dismounted. I hadn't slept for going on thirty-six hours. I shook my head to clear it and trotted up to the entrance. What was a little tiredness? I had all I wanted in life now.

The owlish attendant in the Red Star office proved courteous and able to supply a suitable Jiffy bag, Sellotape and marker pen. He glanced at the address as I wrote. 'On account, sir?'

'Yes. When will it arrive at King's Cross?'

'Eleven o'clock, sir.'

I rejected the phone booth in the station as too noisy and insecure, and rode round to Colquhoun Square, the impressive central feature of the Victorian town. I'd seen a group of four old-style BT phone boxes there.

Pru the Prune, our harridan of a chief telephonist, put me through to Eileen on the copy desk. As I dictated, I could hear the click of the keys on her Hastech terminal over the evening buzz of the Vauxhall newsroom. I realised that if Dennis printed my or Sarah's piece that would be the end of our time undercover at Faslane.

A pang of regret accompanied this realisation. I was growing to respect and even admire my fellow peace campers, and I dreaded our denouncement as spies, our banishment from their simple, idealistic world, and the bursting of the love bubble that Sarah and I had spun about ourselves in that ancient VW on that clammy roadside.

I barged out of the kiosk. Next stop the Palace Restaurant.

A cold bottle of Irn-Bru and a well-wrapped haddock fish supper duly procured, I was back in the saddle homeward bound.

With the road to myself, I gunned the Bonneville and leaned into the curves. I had a serious case of the munchies myself now. Besides, the deal was to deliver the prize nice and hot.

Five minutes at this speed.

The sun, dipping in the sky, slanted its rays over the loch to my left, raising my spirits still further. On my second, or even third, wind I crouched low, working through the bike's five gears. I had the measure of this fine machine. To my surprise I sang aloud, channelling my inner Rick Astley.

'Never gonna give you up ...'

I clocked seventy through the village of Rhu. The Narrows flashed by on my left, a bottleneck in the loch formed by a long sand spit, on which you could walk out at low tide to get up close and personal with the submarines while keeping your feet dry.

Eyes on the road, Ken.

Mitch's goggles were a poor fit over my spectacles and restricted my field of vision.

'Never gonna —'

I glanced up and thought I saw light and movement ahead, around the next bend, behind a clump of scrawny saplings.

The trees whipped past on my left.

Yes, lights. Flashing lights!

I braked hard, changed down, tyres protesting as the heavy motorbike converted its momentum into heat in the discs and pads.

I rounded the bend. The verge between the road and the beach widened. My heart skipped as I saw a car parked up, flashing blue light on its roof.

Police in an unmarked, cunningly positioned out of sight to oncoming traffic, well before the end of the 30mph zone.

A yellow-jacketed officer appeared from behind a tree wielding a radar gun. He held the device steady in both hands.

His colleague emerged from the car, stepped into the road, held his hand up, palm towards me.

I glanced down at the speedo.

Even with heavy braking they'd clocked me at well over fifty.

I drew to a halt, engine burbling.

The one with the gun said, 'Switch off, sir.'

I killed the engine.

'Please dismount and remove your helmet.'

I kicked down the stand, got off and put the helmet on the saddle.

'You seem in a hurry.' He spoke in an accent I couldn't place. Not Glaswegian.

Short hair. Watchful eyes, darting everywhere.

'Was I over the limit, Officer?'

'The speed limit, the alcohol limit, or both, sir?'

I thought it best not to reply.

'Is this your motorcycle, sir?'

'Well, no, it's a friend's, to be fair.'

'Borrowed it, eh?'

The other cop, during this exchange, scanned the road in both directions. On the lookout for more victims, I suppose. He crossed to the car, turned off the portable flashing light and tossed it inside the vehicle.

My eyes flicked back to my interrogator. 'With permission.'

'Driving licence, please.'

I handed it over.

'So you've passed the test. Didn't your instructor tell you about speed limits and riding under the influence?'

'Yes. Sorry.' I hung my head, waiting for the invitation to breathe into the breathalyser.

The other cop returned, holding something glittery and jangly. *Oh shit ...*

He advanced and clicked on the handcuffs. 'In the car, please sir.'

'What about Mitch's bike?'

First cop said, 'You should have thought about that.'

Second cop took my arm, opened the rear door and did that thing where they push your head down to encourage you in. He scooted round the other side and climbed in beside me, bundling his yellow jacket under the seat in front of him.

The car was a Y-suffix Cortina, far from new, the grey vinyl of its seats scuffed and worn.

'Am I under arrest? What for?' I peered between the front seats at the dashboard.

No police radio.

My pulse raced.

The Bonnie started up. I twisted my head. The first cop sat astride the bike. He looked up and down the road, which remained clear. No other vehicles had passed since they stopped me. He bumped over the tussocky grass towards the water.

On the sand, the rider turned sharp right and sped towards the setting sun, the loch glinting behind him. He disappeared into the trees. A moment later he reappeared at a run, minus the bike but carrying our fish and chips, which he put in the boot. He jumped into the Cortina. The car rocked on its suspension as we dropped off the kerb and headed north.

I glanced at the passenger seat.

Not a radar gun, just a handheld searchlight with a trigger grip.

My fuddled brain fought to make sense of what was happening. I said, 'You can't leave Mitch's bike down there on the beach!'

Both cops laughed at this. But of course they weren't cops. Not Strathclyde civilian cops anyway. And not Modplods, who always wore uniform, and wouldn't be manning a speed trap down here.

I tried again. 'You haven't read me my rights.'

No response.

Who were these dudes?

Peace camp coming up on our right-hand side. There it was, smoke now rising from the communal caravan into the still, clear evening air. And our faithful camper behind the boundary fence, Sarah inside looking forward to her supper.

Nice and hot.

I glanced to the left. My backseat companion stared straight ahead.

I got the fingertips of both hands on my window winder, cranked, shoved my head out and yelled, 'Sarah! Sarah! Anyone! Help!' into the slipstream. The graffitied caravans and sheds flashed past. Then we were winding through the trees towards the North Gate roundabout and the village of Garelochhead.

The hand that grabbed my sleeve, followed by the jab of the needle, were the last things I remembered.

Mrs McCready's

Tuesday 11th October 1988, 8.30am, 19°C

MY HEAD POUNDED with a cataclysmic headache. My face and body dripped with sweat and my eyes stung when I opened them and blinked.

I lay in, or rather on, a single bed. On my back. Above me hung a chintzy lampshade.

I turned my head. Stripy curtains were drawn over a small dormer window. Sunlight filtered through and around them.

Not a police cell. But not a ditch or a cellar either.

I appeared to be dressed, apart from my anorak and trainers. I probed my left wrist. Good news: they hadn't taken my TS-150.

And I seemed to be uninjured.

My left arm, heavy as a sock filled with lead shot, wouldn't budge. I used my right hand to help it out until the watch came into my field of vision. I blinked and tried to focus, found the backlight and turned it on at the third fumbling attempt.

Having established the date, time and ambient temperature, I attempted to sit up, but my body was having none of it.

I leaned over the edge of the bed. A white chamber pot stood on the floor. A wave of nausea rose within me when I saw it contained puke. Mine, I guessed. Though there can't have been much to bring up.

I had no recollection of how I got to this place. I'd been unconscious or asleep for sixteen hours.

The fish and chips! They'd be stone cold. Ruined. Haddock, too. This seemed most important. Where had I left our supper?

I felt like someone had sawn open my skull and stirred up my brain with a wooden spoon until it was as mushy as Scotch porridge.

My stomach heaved at this thought of food. I retched, and my mouth filled with stringy saliva which I attempted to spit into the reeking potty.

The door to the bedroom creaked open. A woman's voice said, 'Ye'll be wanting a cup of tea, laddie, I'm thinking. And there's a piece of toast wi' Marmite to settle yer tummy.'

I wiped my mouth with my hand and twisted around.

A petite woman with a perm, in her sixties or even older, stood in the doorway bearing a tray with a steaming mug and a plate.

I heaved myself into a semi-sitting position. 'Where am I?' I croaked. 'Who are you? Why am I here?' I tried to swing my legs to the floor.

'Questions, questions.' She set her tray on a painted side table and replaced my legs on the bed with the skill and strength of a district nurse. 'If ye need the wee room, it's outside on the landing, but they've asked ye not to go doonstairs yet.'

She brought the table to my side, moved around the foot of the bed, collected the chamber pot and left the room. The door closed with the click of a latch.

Sensation had returned to my limbs and I found I could sit up. The scalding hot tea assisted with the revival process and I thought I could then manage the toast.

I took a cautious bite, then another. The buttery saltiness revived me further.

I got off the bed and bent down to lace on my trainers. The maniac in my head beat his bongos until stars danced before my eyes. I sagged down on the mattress.

Come on, Sinclair. You need answers. You must get back to the camp, and Sarah, and face Mitch and the others.

I stood, successfully this time, crossed to the window, pulled back the curtains and peered out. Below lay a small cottage garden, well tended, some annuals still in bloom, and beyond that a hedge and beyond that a hilly pasture on which a flock of sheep grazed in the morning sunshine. The light hurt my eyes. I drew the curtains again.

I exited the bedroom, stood still, listened. Male voices rumbled downstairs. I found the bathroom at the end of the landing. A new toothbrush and tube of toothpaste stood in a tumbler on a glass shelf under the mirror.

I looked like shit: furry tongue, pupils dilated, eyes red, black bags underneath them. A doped-up panda who'd been clubbing all night.

I unzipped and produced a thin trickle of dark gold pee. Very dehydrated. I cleaned my teeth, filled the toothmug with cold water and glugged it down, too fast, so I spluttered and choked.

I filled the hand basin with more water, ducked my face into it and dried myself with the hand towel presumably also provided by wee Janet, whose home I guessed this to be.

What the hell was going on? I took a few deep breaths, clenched and unclenched my fists. Time for some answers. I shuffled out of the bathroom and descended the narrow stairs, holding on to the bannisters on both sides as my knees buckled and my feet shot off in random directions like a Thunderbirds puppet.

My two abductors sat in the kitchen at a small round pine table, empty mugs in front of them. No sign of Janet.

'Feeling better?' the first cop impersonator said, the one with the fake speed gun. I wasn't good at accents. No way to place this guy's.

Let's call him Radar for now. My head pounded anew as I turned to look around, desperate for clues as to my whereabouts. As they'd brought me here unconscious, I had no means of knowing how far I was from Faslane. At least I was still in Scotland.

'Sorry about the amateur dramatics.' Radar twisted his thin face into an attempt at a smile. 'Sit down, Ken, and we'll bring you up to speed.' He turned to his partner in kidnap. 'Let's have another brew.' To me: 'More tea, Ken? Or we have coffee. Only instant, I'm afraid.'

'Coffee. Black. And answers. Like who are you two, where am I, and why, and give me a telephone to speak to my employer. This is outrageous.'

'Don't get all pompous on us, Ken. We've been generous to you so far. You'll get your phone calls. And I'll answer one of your questions straight away. You are in a safe house owned by nice Mrs McCready. Now we have some questions for you.'

Second 'cop', who'd handcuffed me and we'll call Trapper (and looked something like his *M.A.S.H.*[12] namesake, unlike his colleague) rose and switched on the kettle.

Radar continued, 'I need you to tell me everything you saw and heard inside the base.'

'What are you talking about? I'm a peace campaigner, but I've never been in the base.'

'The sooner you cooperate, the sooner you make your phone calls and get out of here. We have all day. You don't.'

'You'll let me go?'

'Yes. As soon as possible. It's up to you when.'

Trapper placed mugs of coffee in front of us, sat and spoke. 'You walked out of the North Gate yesterday afternoon dressed in contractors overalls. What were you doing in the base?'

'Are you recording this? Have you been spying on me?'

'No to the first, yes to the second. For your future reference, every phone box within ten miles of Clyde Submarine Base is monitored. Now answer.'

'I demand to speak to a solicitor.'

'No need. Nothing you say will go beyond the three of us. In return, we require that you do not make use of any information you receive except in the interests of national security. That is not the same as the public interest. Do I make myself clear?'

That was interesting.

---

[12] M.A.S.H. (an acronym for Mobile Army Surgical Hospital) is an American comedy-drama television series set during the Korean War. 'Trapper' was a thoracic surgeon and 'Radar' a corporal.

I said, 'No, you don't make anything clear. If you're CID, or MOD police, you're way outside your legal jurisdiction.'

'Do you deny breaking into the base?'

'Why should I tell you anything? You abducted me.'

Radar took over the baton of inquisitor. 'We invited you to help us with our enquiries. We offered to overlook your road traffic offences if you agreed. That remains the position.'

'I don't recall any of that, because you drugged me.'

'Lawful pacification. In your best interests.'

'If you are cops, show me your warrant cards.'

Radar sighed. 'Ken, you're a smart guy. Let me tell you what I can. We are plain clothes operatives with a great deal of discretion because of the national security aspect of our work.'

'Special Branch?'

No answer. I peered from face to face. Special Branch was the arm of the police force working for the security services. Their remit was murky, their powers wide-ranging, and they operated without obvious scrutiny except, one hoped, by the Government.

Trapper took over. 'You took part in the peace protest early Monday morning. You broke into the base, but you didn't board *HMS Repulse*. You disguised yourself and walked out when the lockdown ended. Later you rode into Helensburgh on your friend's motorbike, where you sent a parcel by Red Star to the *Today* newspaper and bought fish and chips for two. Can we at least agree on those facts?'

My turn to stay silent. Not much point denying what they knew to be true.

Trapper sipped his coffee. This was a civilised interrogation — so far. For now they both seemed to be acting 'good cop'.

An engine started up outside, followed by the crunch of tyres on gravel. Trapper turned his head. A red Nissan reversed across the kitchen window, Janet at the wheel, wearing a sensible hat. She engaged first gear and the car turned and moved away, its exhaust condensing in the morning air.

Things could get nastier now.

Radar's turn to speak. 'Did you know the women who swam into the base? The ones they arrested who appeared in court yesterday?'

They hadn't mentioned Sarah! I had to keep her out of this—whatever 'this' was. So I said, 'I know one of them, Debbie, but not the other, Beverley.'

'That's better. Well done, Ken. We're going to get on fine now. You're not a peace protester, are you?'

'Yes, I am. And a freelance art photographer.'

'Then who is the "employer" you referred to at the start of our chat? The one you wanted to telephone? Let's go into the hall, shall we, Ken, and you can use Mrs McCready's phone to ring your employer now. All right?'

I sighed. 'I'll answer your questions about my time inside the base.'

'Good call. Did you have any contact with the women swimmers while they were in the water or afterwards, during the period you were in the base?'

'No.'

Trapper leaned over the table. 'Think. Did you see, or hear of, anyone else in the water that night? Before you answer, Ken, we must counsel you to tell the truth. We can arrest and hold you on a charge of conspiracy to commit terrorism and will not hesitate to do so. Some have called our powers under the temporary legislation of 1974 draconian. But you'll know all this, as a diligent trainee journalist.'

'What makes you think I am a journalist, trainee or otherwise?'

'Wake up, Ken. You sent a package to the picture desk of the *Today* newspaper. In the pocket of your anorak you carried a reporter's notebook with the story of your midnight base tour. Some of it in shorthand. Before you bought the fish and chips you telephoned your editor, using the second box from the left in a group of four at Colquhoun Square.'

I put my elbows on the table and rested my pounding head in my hands. My memory and IQ had taken a hammering with the drugs they'd given me, on top of those of the recreational variety I'd taken myself. What was the point of trying to deceive these two?

They knew all about me, but perhaps not about Sarah's role. To protect her, I decided to offer up my information about the unknown swimmer, which seemed the focus of their investigation. And mine. A shared interest and concern.

I straightened my back. 'There was a rumour that a body washed up on the beach near the base. A diver or snorkeller.'

The men, side by side opposite me, glanced at each other. I tried to read their expressions.

Radar said, 'Did you hear where the body washed up? What was he wearing, did he have anything with him, who was he? Or she?'

'I eavesdropped on some maintenance workers. The Modplods will have the details. If you are who you claim to be, why are you asking me this—and not them?'

'Where was your girlfriend while all this was going on?'

'Tucked up in her sleeping bag at the peace camp.'

'Who was talking about this dead body? Could you identify them if you saw them again?'

'They were Cementation construction workers. One had a walkie-talkie. I might recognise him. Another was tall and blond, Scandinavian features. But I say again, why are you asking me?'

Trapper said, 'The jurisdictions within Clyde Submarine Base are complex. Each authority guards its turf. We have asked the MOD police for the information they possess. But we need other witnesses who aren't base employees facing the sack or a court martial and covering their arses. Ken, I'll tell you this much to show our good faith. The commandos injured the unknown swimmer with the propeller of their rigid inflatable. Those guys had a bad night. A seriously bad night. They failed to stop or catch you or the other protesters. While trying to flush you lot out, they killed this other swimmer. The Comacchio detachment commander is under arrest. We need a witness. You were there.

Did you hear or see what happened? Just answer these reasonable and vital questions and you will walk free.'

'Hold on. Let me try and remember.' I made a show of racking my brain, whereas I was playing time.

The marines *had* behaved with reckless abandon. And had Sarah been correct to say the grenades were harmless stun weapons? Who'd told her that? She and Debbie had parted company before the depth charging began and hadn't been in contact with each other since.

The sound of the explosions, the height of the water plumes and the seismic effect on the docks had led me to believe the marines were lobbing real hand grenades, and I didn't buy the alternative explanation.

Perhaps I was in a position here to serve the public interest, prevent a cover-up.

I took a deep breath. 'All right. The RIB was powering about at high speed and they chucked twenty or thirty grenades into the loch that produced a hell of a racket and water everywhere. They stopped suddenly. Then two marines leaned over the side to recover something, I assumed a swimmer, though I couldn't be certain, and whether he or she was alive or dead I also couldn't say. It was dark out in the loch and the RIB had no lights.'

Radar and Trapper exchanged glances again, and this time their emotion was in no doubt.

Triumphant vindication.

Trapper leaned forward, speaking in an urgent undertone. 'We think you saw the Royal Marines recover the swimmer or diver. When they realised they'd killed him, they panicked and threw the body overboard again, called off the search and skulked back to their barracks. They hoped the outgoing tide would deposit the victim miles from the base, wash him right out to sea even. Instead the poor bastard landed up on the Rhu Narrows, near where we stopped you. Now do you understand how important your testimony is?'

'Yes, I guess.' The commandos could just as easily have killed Sarah with their propeller or depth charges. Their violent, panicky response had been disgraceful and disproportionate.

'Ken, cast your mind back to that night. You're an observant guy. No wonder they chose you for a trainee post. Can you tell us: did the RIB's engine cut out abruptly?'

'Yes. It must have stalled when they ran over the diver.'

'They claimed they'd fouled the RIB's propeller on a fisherman's lobster pot marker. That's why the engine stopped and they leaned over. Plausible?'

'I guess … can't you identify the guy in the water?'

'His face is not around any more to help us. Sliced off by the propeller on the end of that hundred-and-ten horsepower outboard. Strathclyde CID are checking dental records and missing persons.'

'Can I go now please?'

'Yes, Ken. We'll put you back on your friend's motorbike. Make up some excuse to explain your absence. Don't be tempted to file a story with the paper about what you have learned, just yet. Keep your eyes and ears open. Tell Sarah where you've been, but make sure she promises to keep her pretty mouth shut. Any information, call us. In return, we promise to contact you if we ID the body first, and then you can publish an exclusive. We require that you run it past us and don't mention us. Now do we have a deal?'

'No charges for speeding or anything … else?'

'Nope. We don't deal in trifles, Ken.'

'How will we communicate? The phone at the peace camp is out of order. Anyway, they'll evict us as spies when they read today's newspapers.'

Trapper reached inside his leather bomber jacket and produced a mobile phone.

Not just any mobile phone. This was an Excell Pocketphone. The M2 model, no less.[13] You had to be a businessman or celebrity to

---

[13] On sale in late 1988 for £2,299 including VAT (equivalent to £6,322 in 2018).

afford one. British made, the first mobile in the world that you could ... well, carry in a pocket (as long as you didn't mind the antenna poking out). All the colour supplements carried the ad: a close-up of a business dude in immaculate button-down shirt and spotty tie, the phone peeking out of his shirt pocket.

'Yours,' Trapper said, and pushed it across the table. 'It's on Cellnet, which has the better coverage in Scotland.'

I picked up the handset. Two-tone black and grey. Soft touch keys, backlit. Lightweight, futuristic. Winner of the Queen's Award for Enterprise that year.

Portable, not just luggable at a pinch in a sturdy wheelbarrow like Jerry's Motorola.

Talk about a honey trap. I realised my face had split into a grin and my headache had faded to a background annoyance.

'Go on. Try it. Make a call,' Radar said.

I dialled the Speaking Clock.

'At the third stroke, the time sponsored by Accurist will be nine, seventeen, and thirty seconds ...'

'Clear as a bell,' I said.

'You can use it as a speakerphone, and there's a hands-free kit for your camper van.'

Embarrassed by how easily they'd bought me, I said, 'I still require you guys to identify yourselves. I need names, ranks, badges.'

'You'll find all that in your notebook, which is in your anorak pocket with your Red Star receipt,' Radar said. 'Now do you want to make those calls to your solicitor or editor or whoever, or get back to the peace camp where Sarah will be very concerned for your wellbeing? You rode off high as a kite and never returned. They'll think you ran off the road. They'll be searching the route for skid marks. Maybe Sarah will call the local police. That's a distraction none of us want.'

'God, yes. She'll be worried sick. I don't have Jerry's mobile number so I can't call him. I must get back.' I placed the M2 in my jeans pocket, taking care I didn't buckle the flexible antenna. 'What happens if our editor tells us to leave Faslane?'

'Use your initiative. Play for time. Find another place to camp if the Peace Corps evict you. Hang out in Helensburgh at the bars. Go drinking with Sarah. Perfect cover. The ratings frequent the Marlborough Head. We need to ID the dead man, Ken. And there may be other tasks for you. I hope we can build a working relationship of mutual benefit. Baby steps, no pressure, you can back off at any point. But I think you'll find that deep contacts within the security services are career-enhancing for an ambitious guy like you.'

Trapper looked at his watch. 'We collected the bike and it's safe in Mrs McCready's woodshed. I'll drive the Cortina and lead you to the main road. It's about twenty miles back to Faslane. That should give you ample time to come up with a convincing explanation for your overnight absence. In case you're wondering, the two of us ate your cod and chips when we arrived here last night. Mrs McCready reheated them and they were delicious. At least they didn't go to waste. No hard feelings, I hope?'

He grinned. We were all good mates now, or so he hoped.

'Haddock,' I said.

'Plenty more fish in the loch, Ken. Are we cool?' He extended his hand. I shook it.

'I guess.'

'Are you fit to ride back to Faslane?'

'Yes. I'll take it more carefully this time.'

'Good man.' He held eye contact for a beat.

His colleague shook hands with me too, saying, 'I put the accessories, the charger, car bracket, manual and leather case in the top box.'

Trapper said, 'We need a little tradecraft, starting with a parole.'

'Parole?'

'A challenge and response, so each party can identify the other on the phone, radio or whatever. Ours will be "raining" and yours is "weather". Never write these down. When you speak to us, include the word "weather" in the opening exchange. Whoever answers will work "raining" into their reply. If we call you, we say "raining" and you come back with a sentence including "weather". If you're with others, at risk of being overheard, or otherwise compromised, don't use the word. We will then have a meaningless dummy conversation. It all sounds rather Le Carré, but it provides essential safeguards. Shall we practise?'

'No need. I've got it. Weather, Raining. Let's move.'

Trapper said, 'One last thing. When you return to the peace camp, be wary of Jerry. We're not sure who he is, or what he is doing at Faslane. We've checked him through Interpol and his description doesn't match up with the activist the Yanks know by that name. Keep a close eye on him.'

Gone

Tuesday 10th October 1988, 10.26am, 9°C, overcast

THE EMBERS OF the camp fire smouldered in the pit. Jerry, outside the office with yard broom in hand, said, 'The prodigals return.' He shouted out, 'Ken's here.'

I turned off the Bonnie's engine, dismounted and kicked down the stand.

The campers emerged from their various sheds and caravans, gathered and stood around me in a circle.

Jerry, Debbie, Mitch, Colin, Joan and Spike all radiated contempt and distrust.

Only little Archie, holding Colin's hand, had a smile for me.

Mitch rushed to reclaim, and examine, his precious bike. 'Look, pal, ye wur tae borrow her fur errands. Not take aff like bloody Dennis Hopper and Jane Fonda. Fifty-eight miles ye've cloacked up.' He bent over to check the tyres, the suspension and the brakes, muttering.

'Sorry, Mitch. She's fine. I'll fill the tank today.'

Colin said, 'You missed all the action at the Sheriff's Court.'

I glanced at our camper van. Curtains drawn. Sarah catching up on her sleep. I had so much to tell her, so much to explain.

First, face the music here.

I asked, 'What happened?'

Debbie said, 'Reporters packed the public gallery. We're in the *Glasgow Herald,* the *Guardian* and big on the front page of the *Daily Express*. Might've been on breakfast TV but the reception was so shit we couldn't tell. All today's newspapers are in the communal.

Jerry had to hitch to Garelochhead and back for them, thanks to you two. We're out on bail in the sum of £50 each. Where's Sarah? She was a superstar in the loch. And what happened to you in the base? How'd you get out?'

My heart skipped a beat. 'What do you mean, where's Sarah?'

'As in, where is my swim buddy? Your girl. Remember her?'

Jerry said, 'Guess they took off for a celebration. Spent the night at Clatty Pat's'.[14]

Archie piped up. 'Sarah did a big brave swim with Debbie. I gave her my last Rolo like the girl in the cartoon, and the man said he loved her and quick draw me a bunch of flowers—'

Colin hoisted Archie in his arms. 'Hold on, big boy, we're talking grown-up stuff for a minute.'

'Aw Dad.'

Mitch said, 'Reckon the Loch Lomond Arms is mair their style for a randan, that explains the mileage.'

I put my hands over my ears. 'Stop. Stop talking all at once! Debbie, are you saying Sarah's not here? Not in the van?'

'Not when I last looked.'

'Shall we see if Sarah's in her van, Daddy?'

'Good idea.' Colin put Archie down and the pair of them set off to the VW.

My heart thumped at my breastbone. 'Not here? Where did she go?'

Debbie said, 'No idea. Thought she was with you.'

'When did you last see her, Debs?'

'On the Admiralty Dock, when she slipped into the water and swam back to Timbacraft. Not a ripple, sleek as a seal. I thought she'd come to the court hearing. Where have you left her?'

'I haven't left her anywhere. Christ. What's happened?'

Jerry said, 'She arrived back here around three am yesterday, shivering and shaking.'

I glanced across to the camper. Archie appeared in the doorway. 'Sarah's not here, Ken!' he called in a clear treble.

---

[14] Local nickname for Cleopatra's Nightclub in Glasgow's West End.

I said, 'Someone start from the beginning.'

Archie's mum Joan spoke for the first time. 'It was like Jerry said, she arrived back here on foot after the swim. I gave her a tug, tucked her up in your van. She started the engine for the heater. She was worried about you. I left her to sleep and checked on her at lunchtime. She wasn't hungry but she seemed fine, just tired. Not surprising, when she told me about the grenades, and how long she and Debs were out of the water waiting for the Plods to spot them. I looked in again when the bus was due as I promised, but she didn't want to come to the court hearing. Said she was exhausted, and thought she had a chill coming on from the swim, and should wait for you or news of you. We all got back to camp yesterday around five, no Sarah, you still weren't here, Mitch's bike was missing with both helmets and the spare leathers. Are you saying you didn't take off with her?'

I ran my hands through my hair, lank and in need of a wash in hot water. 'Jesus. No. I arrived back while you were all down in Dumbarton yesterday afternoon. I disguised myself as a worker on the nuclear reactors and hung about in the canteen and just walked out when the lockdown ended. Sarah seemed in good spirits, only hungry by then. I borrowed Mitch's bike to get fish and chips from Helensburgh while we waited for you to return. Sarah said that would be fine. To use the Bonnie. Mitch?'

Mitch scowled. 'I told your lassie she was welcome tae borrow ma hoag any time. I never told her to lend the Bonnie tae ye, or huv ye ride it an' give her a backie.'

Jerry said, 'I'm confused. Where have you two been since you ate the fish and chips?'

I felt the colour rising in my cheeks. 'I never made it back with the fish and chips. I've been ... sort of away by myself until now. All night.'

'So yeez hud a squerr go, eh?'

'Eh?'

Colin translated. 'Falling out. Ding dong. Argument. Lover's tiff.'

'No! Anything but. Listen to me, all of you. Where … is … my girlfriend?'

Mitch said, 'So ye sayin', you havnae seen the lassie since ye took ma bike tae Helensburgh, and ye've bin oot aw night by yerself, though you didnae argue wi her? Where ye bin, Fanny-bawz? Ye look like shit.'

This wasn't going well. Mitch appeared to be growing in stature by the second, working himself up. Shoulders thrust back, paw-like hands clenched, eyes blazing from among his shaggy facial hair, he scared me. 'It's nothing dreadful. I just needed some time by myself. Can we concentrate on Sarah and finding her?'

Jerry said, 'Ken, has something happened to Sarah? Did you have an accident on the road? You turn up claiming you haven't been with her, you didn't have a row, you rode into town for fish and chips but never brought them back and you've been out all night finding yourself or some crap. I think you know where she is. Should I call the police?'

'I swear I know nothing. All right, I'll tell you what happened. She and I drank some Scotch and smoked a little hash. I went for the fish and chips. I rode carefully, Mitch, believe me. Not a scratch on your hog as you see. On the way back I saw a police car on the verge just past Rhu. I thought they were after me. I'd been roaming the sub base for twelve hours and they must have seen me on CCTV. I didn't want to be arrested, so I went off road down to the beach and hid in the trees for a while. I lay down and the pine needles were soft and next thing it's morning and I've been out like a light all night. So here I am.'

'How d'ye explain the fifty-eight miles oan ma cloack? Awa an' bile yer heid, yer specky wee nyaff.'

'I can't explain. Perhaps Sarah took your bike after everyone left for Dumbarton and before I arrived yesterday. In fact, yes, that's it! I remember now, how did I forget, lack of sleep I guess, she said she had borrowed the Bonnie—to go to the phone box and call her mum to say she was fine. Because her folks know she is here, and they would see the news this morning and worry. After speaking to Mum, Sarah couldn't resist a spin. Perhaps she explored the glen road up over the hill. Why she didn't tell me I can't imagine. Felt guilty about the mileage. Yes, it's all falling into place.'

'Aye, right! Yer bum's oot the windae. Fust ye say ye've been oot like a light, then ye forgot for lack of sleep. Ma nan cood tell a better lie with her gob shut.'

Jerry's long face wore a worried frown. 'This is looking bad, Ken.' He addressed the others. 'Agreed I should call the cops? I don't understand what is going on, but Sarah is missing, and Ken is making no sense. I'm worried about Sarah's wellbeing and we are all responsible for each other in this camp. Anyone?'

Colin said, 'We want the civvies not the Plods. Make that clear.'

Joan said, 'Hold on, Jerry. If Sarah is missing, and God forbid some harm has come to her, we'll all be suspects.'

Spike jabbed a finger in my direction. 'I've never trusted you, Ken. Who are you? Why are you here?' He turned to the others. 'Reckon Ken and Sarah are MI5. She's split already, probably on the train to London as we speak. Meanwhile he tried to sneak the bike back and then he planned to hightail it in his van. Sarah's not missing at all and he knows it.'

'Spike, you're wrong. That's paranoid. MI5! Do I look like a spy?'

'Yes,' Spike said.

Jerry said, 'I'm making the call. Everyone stay on camp please. Mitch, make sure Ken doesn't do a runner in his van.'

'Aye. Wi pleasure.' He advanced on me and took a firm hold of my arm. 'Come wi me and we'll hae a nice sit an' a wee cosy chat i' the warm.' He led me towards the communal caravan. His lips almost brushed my ear as he whispered, 'If ye're Polis or MI5 I'll break yer airm, if ye've hurt the lassie I'll break yer neck.'

The campers dispersed. With a violent wrench I tore free from Mitch's grip and shouted, 'We must search now! She must have got worried about me when I failed to show with the supper. She could have taken the bus or hitched into Helensburgh. Or perhaps she got up early this morning, walked into Garelochhead to the shop, or maybe she's fallen ill. Let me check the van for a note. We're wasting time.'

Debbie said, 'When I looked in your camper this morning, I reckoned she hadn't spent the night there. The bedding was cold, and she hadn't had her early morning ciggy. Besides, Sarah would never go off by herself like that without saying.'

'You don't know that!'

The others regrouped, this time around me. I waved my arms, imploring. 'At least let's search the camp.' With a lurch in my bowels I realised what could have happened. 'She might have collapsed. Secondary drowning, have you heard about that? Water gets in the lungs, needn't be much, that inflames the lining and pulmonary oedema sets in. Can happen many hours after getting out of the water. You should have taken her to Casualty, Joan, when she arrived back here. Jerry said she was shivering. Christ, I'm sure that's it. Why didn't I think of it? I took the lifeguard's course. Idiot!' I struck my forehead with my palm. 'We need to search everywhere, right now. Fast. She might be in the underpass.'

Joan said, 'She could have gone into Helensburgh like you suggested, Ken, in search of you, and checked into a bed and breakfast when she didn't find you.'

'All these things are possible,' Jerry said. 'Let's not panic. But Ken is right about the drowning. So first we must be certain she's not around the camp. Then we call the cops. Or an ambulance if we find her injured. God help you, Ken, if you're winding us up, or you've hurt Sarah, or know more than you're letting on.'

'I'd never hurt Sarah! I love her. We got engaged yesterday afternoon. We're to be married.'

Debbie looked unimpressed. 'I don't think so, Ken. You're so smitten with her you're in a fantasy world. Sarah will never marry you.'

'What makes you say that? You barely know her.'

'Neither do you.'

Jerry raised his voice. 'Listen up, everyone! We will look for Sarah now and talk later. Mitch, you search the underpass and down to Timbacraft, on the route the girls took that night, in case Sarah retraced her steps—lost an earring or something. Joan, you take the office and the communal caravan and the unoccupied caravans between you. Spike: woodstore, tool shed, workshop, the derelict huts, the pallets and bins and the skip. Debbie, the women's caravan, Ken's camper, the bathroom and telephone caravans. Colin, hold the fort with Archie. I'll search with Ken up the bank through the woods to St Andrew's School.

'All of you, be on the lookout for any notes or evidence, but don't touch or disturb anything. The peace camp may soon be a crime scene. Be back here in twenty minutes, earlier if you find anything, in which case sound the airhorn and holler. Come on, Ken. You and I are going for a walk up the hill.'

Everyone departed on their assignment, moving faster than I had seen any of them move before. Mitch, Jerry and I passed between the office and the workshop and descended the grassy bank. Mitch ducked to enter the underpass which echoed with the gurgle of the stream, more water flowing than on the Sunday night. With reluctance, because I wanted to search the culvert too, I tore myself away and climbed up the opposite bank behind Jerry. An image of Sarah lying in the muddy water, face down, dead and dishevelled, made me shiver. I tensed as we climbed, blood roaring in my ears, waiting for a shout from Mitch of, 'Found her!'

Polaroids

Tuesday 10th October 1988, 10.49am, 9°C, rain threatening

THE DRIVEWAY to the school wound up from the main road via several hairpin bends. We emerged on to it from the vegetation about halfway up, both out of breath.

I'd learned from Colin that the special school for young male offenders had been closed two years earlier.

The main building was a former baronial mansion, a Gothic horror of towers, turrets and chimneys that they'd used as classrooms, offices and for dining. Nearby were the dormitories: three white-painted, single-storey wooden structures resembling military barracks.

The staff had lived at the bottom of the drive, just behind the peace camp, in prefab bungalows which the local authority had removed when the school closed.

It didn't seem likely that Sarah was up here, but we had to try.

'I'll check the house. You take the dorms,' Jerry said. 'Look for open doors, broken windows, anything.'

'Right-oh.' I jogged to the first dormitory and walked all around it, testing doors and windows, peering inside. The interior comprised one giant room with rows of iron bedsteads still in place. In the bathroom which occupied one end of the building, six cast iron baths stood side by side, behind them wash basins, urinals and a row of toilet cubicles without doors.

No wonder the boys placed here were disturbed.

Everything appeared sound and secure. Surprising, because unlike the mansion, they hadn't boarded up the dormitories. They would be ideal for squatting: more weatherproof and with better sanitary facilities than the peace camp.

I crossed to the second building, then the third.

Jerry emerged from the Dracula castle as I finished. He said, 'I got in round the back. Nothing. The roof is leaking and the place is rotten with damp and mould. Rat droppings, owl pellets. Furniture and junk lying around like they all just walked out. No one's been in there since it closed, I would say. Let's return to civilisation.'

Heavy rain fell as we slithered down the bank, grabbing at saplings to arrest our descent. The others had gathered in the communal caravan, all standing.

The day's newspapers littered the table, but no one cared about our incursion triumph any more.

Six hostile pairs of eyes fixed me with accusing stares. 'Anything?' I asked.

'She's nae here, pal.' Mitch's voice dripped menace.

Jerry said, 'Last chance, Ken. Do you know anything of Sarah's movements or intentions that you're keeping from us? If so, speak now.'

I shook my head.

'Could she have got herself arrested?' Colin suggested, hoisting Archie higher on his hip.

'Not here in the camp,' Jerry said. 'They would have told us. But they could have grabbed her on the road, say if she walked back towards the South Gate and they spotted her on the cameras.'

Debbie said, 'We can do no more ourselves. Time to call the police. Everyone agree?' Nods all round, including from me. 'Go get your portable, Jerry.'

Jerry said, 'Oh, I forgot to mention. No need. BT fixed the line. I tried it earlier and got the dial tone.'

I said, 'I'll come with you, Debs. When you've finished I'll call Sarah's mum and see if she's had word. Sarah would have phoned her if she got arrested. And if Sarah's in a hospital they would have called her mother too.'

In truth, the authorities were more likely to call *Today*, as Sarah's Press pass was in her purse.

I remembered with a jolt I had the Pocketphone in my anorak map pocket. If that rang I would be toast. Once I was alone, however, I could use the mobile to contact the editor and see if he had news of her.

The telephone caravan contained three folding chairs and a corkboard filled with scrawled scraps of paper and business cards. A modern green push-button telephone sat on a rusty picnic table, next to a well-thumbed plastic guard book containing typed sheets of telephone numbers.

Debbie opened the file and ran her finger down the list. I watched in silence as she dialled.

'Clyde Submarine Base? This is Deborah Barker from the peace camp. Please put me through to the police station.'

We waited. Debbie drummed her fingernails on the table, then leaned forward. 'Is that the MOD police? Do you have our campaigner Sarah Standen in custody, please? No, she wasn't planning a protest. No, you don't know her ... no, I've no reason to suspect that ... no to that either ... describe her? Attractive girl aged twenty-one, dark hair dyed blonde and curly, English and well educated, about five foot four, grey-green eyes.' She looked at me and mouthed, 'Tossers!', then into the mouthpiece, 'Well, why didn't you say that in the first place? Goodbye!'

She slammed down the phone. 'They're holding no one. On to the Helensburgh Constabulary.' She consulted her list and lifted the handset again. 'Yes, I'm from Faslane Peace Camp. Deborah Barker. Do you have my friend Sarah Standen in custody, please?'

They put her on hold, then transferred her. Debbie would have preferred me not to be there, but it was my fiancée missing. I wouldn't allow them to treat me like a criminal and I refused to play the role of suspect. As Debbie waited, then got through, explained who she was and repeated her message, I thought about Jerry.

He'd said the phone was working again, but I knew no one had reported any fault until I did so from the base canteen. Perhaps there had never been a fault, and Jerry had disconnected the wires himself, then reconnected them?

Trapper and Radar had warned me to be on my guard around him.

Was he a spy himself? American, a long-term resident with a history of activism, legal training … the perfect cover to win over the peace campaigners and elevate himself into a position of authority.

For all their protestations that the camp was anarchist, run by consensus without leadership or hierarchy, they all deferred to Jerry.

If he was (like us) an infiltrator, then for whom?

MI5?

Plausible. I guessed that MI5 and Special Branch fought over their turf.

We'd attended a seminar at the Wapping HQ about the roles of the various law enforcement authorities and the trainer had said as much.

'Not there? In that case I wish to report Sarah Standen as a missing person. No, don't transfer me again … God!' She looked at me in exasperation. 'She's not in their cells either.'

I sat on the rickety picnic chair, tense as a board, praying my new mobile phone wouldn't ring out. I remembered the accessories were on Mitch's bike, and needed retrieving.

Had Sarah done a bunk, caught the train home? Had she been abducted, as I had? A collapse from secondary drowning was the most alarming possibility. She'd made light of her swimming exploits, but as Archie said it was a 'big brave swim'. The loch would have been icy cold, despite the Clyde receiving the benefit of the Gulf Stream. And the air temperature had hovered near freezing (1°C was the lowest I'd seen recorded on my TS-150 during the incursion). They'd been out of the water, in swimming costumes, for an hour waiting for the Plods to spot and catch them.

'... I don't accept we have to wait that long. My friend would never ...'

The police were giving Debbie the standard spiel about missing persons. They wouldn't get involved in a hurry unless there was evidence of foul play or that the missing person was a danger to themselves or others.

'Are you saying you want us to come down the station, or not?' Debbie glanced at me, rolled her eyes, frustration and concern etched on her face. 'Why not today, then? The sooner you have a picture and description the better, surely? ...'

Debbie had the hots for Sarah, I was certain of it.

But it didn't matter to me. Nothing would matter if we couldn't find her. Alive and well.

Nothing would ever matter again if she was dead. A second girl's death on my conscience ... my life would be as good as over too.

'Yes, all right ... I guess ... thank you, Officer.' Debbie turned to me. 'Did you get that? At least forty-eight hours before they consider her missing. We're to call all her friends. The cops will need a recent photo of her. Ken, you snapped hundreds the other day when you had us all posing for your activism exhibition. Have you had those developed? Or do you have a picture of her in your wallet?'

The films were all in London. I didn't have another picture of her. What was the need, when I had the real live Sarah by my side every day and in my bed every night? The only picture in my wallet was of my Susie. All I could think of saying was, 'I took them in to Boots when I went for the fish and chips yesterday. They'll be ready tomorrow.'

'Phone the shop and see if they can do them today. First call Sarah's mum.' She held out the handset.

To play for time I unwound the curly cable which had tied itself into bunches and prevented you lifting the receiver very far. Debbie was tying me in knots too. I was tempted to confess all to her about us being reporters. Should I call the campers together and own up to the full story, including my abduction and recruitment by the two goons?

I had never met Sarah's mother. I'd met her father once, when he came up to London for a motor dealers awards event. We'd lunched at the cheerless Cranks health food restaurant in Covent Garden.

'Leave the bloody cord alone and make the call!' Debbie snapped.

I extracted the business card from my wallet and pressed the numbers on the phone.

'Standen Motors, Tracey speaking. How may I help you?' Tracey was loud and cheerful.

'Hello, it's Ken Sinclair, Sarah's ... boyfriend.' *I so nearly said colleague!* 'May I speak to Mr or Mrs Standen please?'

I pushed the receiver hard against my ear in case Tracey's voice, raised in pitch to cut through the din of the garage, was audible to Debbie by my side.

'Mr Standen has gone to recover an Austin 1100. Mrs Standen is off today. That's why you got me.'

'Is Mrs Standen at home?'

'No, she's driving to Coventry to see Sarah's elder brother. Can I help you, Ken?'

'Do you know if Sarah has been in touch with them recently?'

'No idea. Is there some problem? Isn't Sarah at work with you?'

'No. Please ask Mr Standen to call me when he returns, would you, Tracey?' I recited the phone number from the paper strip Sellotaped below the phone keypad and rang off. 'Both out.'

The door of the caravan opened. Jerry held a bundle of post, spotted with rain. 'Any luck? Ken, I need you a moment.'

Debbie said, 'Nothing yet. She's not in the CSB[15] or the town police cells. I'll try the hospitals next. Then Boots about your films. Give me the ticket, Ken. Jerry, if we can't track her down we need a full camp fire meet. I'm scared for Sarah.'

I said, 'Me too. The receipt's in my van. I'll be straight back.'

---

[15] Clyde Submarine Base.

My cover was wobbling, all set to collapse in a heap. There was no Boots receipt because I'd sent the films straight to the newspaper. The lies were piling up.

Outside in torrential rain I said to Jerry, 'What?'

'In your van, before we drown ourselves.'

We raced to the camper, piled in and sat side by side on the mattress where Sarah and I had made love the previous afternoon.

Jerry sniffed the foetid air. 'So much for camp rules.' From the clutch of letters, bills and a polythene-wrapped CND newssheet he extracted a medium-sized manila envelope. 'This was in the bottom of the mailbox. Hand-delivered before the mailman came, I guess.'

I seized the envelope, addressed 'K. Sinclair' in neat blue ball pen. Not Sarah's handwriting. I ripped it open. Several black-and-white photos tumbled on to the bed. They were from a Polaroid instant camera, with that distinctive wider border at the bottom. I picked them up and examined them one by one, passing them to Jerry.

The pictures were dark, grainy, flash-lit. Only one made sense: a close-up of the small brass nameplate on the fin of *HMS Repulse*.

The other shots were fuzzy, hard to interpret. Jerry and I pored over them, swapping them between us.

'Taken underwater,' I said. 'I assume they are the hull of *Repulse*. You can just see the outlines of the anechoic tiles.'

He held a photo up close to his beaky nose. 'I hope these aren't what I think they are.'

'The bulges? What could they be?'

'Possibly sonar sensors but I fear not …' He pointed out, in each photo, round protuberances like the nose cones of missiles. 'See here … and here.'

'What am I looking at?'

'Where the tiles are cut back. Those are limpet mines attached to the outer hull.'

'My God. Sarah thought there were snorkellers or divers in the water that night. And there was a rumour in the base that the marines had killed a frogman with the propeller of their RIB. Why have these pictures come to me?'

Jerry said, 'I have no idea, Ken. But I suspect you will find out soon.'

'What do we do?'

'Can we keep this between the two of us for now?' Jerry dropped his voice to a conspiratorial whisper. 'Debbie is such a loudmouth. She'll get us all arrested.'

Don't trust Jerry ... my abductors' words sounded in my head. Still, Jerry was right: Debbie was a loose cannon, impulsive and strong-willed. 'All right.'

'We need to raise the alarm. Debbie will be ages on the phone. Let's go to my caravan and use the portable.'

I put the photos back in their envelope and we scuttled down the gravel path to Jerry's caravan. He'd chosen one of the older vans as his home, and I saw why when we entered. A small wood burner glowed in the corner, making the interior warm and toasty.

Jerry heaved out his Motorola, a bulky handset connected by a curly cable to a box the size of a car battery. The cradle for the handset doubled as a carrying handle.

Primitive compared to my new Pocketphone: a latter-day field telephone.

I glanced around at home-made shelves crammed with legal textbooks and non-fiction. A poster promoted the 1987, and likely to be last-ever, Glastonbury CND Festival, with Elvis Costello, Van Morrison and the Communards headlining.

Jerry pressed buttons and listened, brow furrowed. I could just hear the *burr ... burr* of the ring.

'Hello, Clyde Submarine Base? Put me through to *HMS Repulse*, please ... yes, the control room ... and why not? Oh, I see. Sorry to have troubled you. Have a nice day now.'

He cancelled the call and replaced the handset. '*HMS Repulse* has left the base. Sailed on patrol.'

No Service

Immediately following the preceding events

'I'M OFF to see what Debbie's found out,' I said. 'Then I'll search our camper, see if Sarah took anything with her.'

'Hold on—' Jerry began, but I was out of the door, leaving it open, and running, head down against the driving rain.

Debbie had the green phone to her ear. She shook her head in a 'nothing doing' gesture. I pointed through the window at the VW. She nodded and raised a thumb.

Inside the camper van I began a search. I should have done this earlier, but I wasn't thinking straight.

The place was a shocking mess, with damp swimwear, towels and clothing scattered everywhere. There could have been a struggle here and you wouldn't know. Plus everything did stink of stale tobacco and marijuana.

Her Barbour jacket and red Kickers boots were missing. Was that a good sign? Mitch had said the spare helmet and leathers had gone. Sarah couldn't have taken the bike because I had it. So someone else must have removed the gear, to make it look as if she and I had gone joyriding together. Hence the lack of alarm when neither of us reappeared in the camp the previous evening.

The tiny sink and drainer overflowed with dirty mugs and plastic glasses. The sleeping bags were gritty with biscuit crumbs. The masthead of the latest issue of the camp's newsletter, *Faslane Focus*, peeped out from under Sarah's pillow.

I tossed aside the detritus of our motorhome life.

Had Sarah left of her own accord? If so she would have taken her toothbrush, makeup, purse, lighter and pills at the very least.

I flung open the flimsy melamine cupboard doors and opened the drawers, soon finding her toothbrush, makeup and pills. The foil strip of contraceptives showed she hadn't taken that day's dose.

I wondered if she'd walked or hitched into Garelochhead for cigarettes, but I found a whole packet of Benson & Hedges squirrelled away under a pair of knickers and, above the sink in the cupboard, her rolling tobacco and papers.

I descended through the sliding door, scooted round the bonnet in the rain and got in on the passenger side. The glovebox, fitted with a lock, was the nearest thing we had to a safe. I reached under the driver's seat for the keys, fumbled open the compartment and hinged it down.

Inside I found Sarah's pink felt jewellery bag containing beads, rings, ear studs and an antique silver bracelet, but not her jangly CND earrings. Underneath the drawstring bag nestled her Filofax, and behind that her purse and a spare box of her pills. I looked in the purse. It contained three pound coins, some ten p's for the phone and a five-pound note.

I put everything except the Filofax back and returned to the sleeping quarters.

The purple-and-pink organiser featured a pattern of interlocking embossed hearts. I'd teased her about it and she'd explained it was a Christmas present from her mum, but privately I thought it more likely a gift from a former lover.

I called it her 'Disorganiser' because of its random contents. These included till receipts, buttons, torn-off cinema tickets, a green one-pound note perhaps kept as a souvenir as they hadn't been legal tender for months, and classified ads for flat shares clipped from the *Evening Standard*.

She said it might be messy but it showed a lively mind and was far preferable to an anal obsession with neatness and order like certain people she could mention.

Inside the front cover she had stored her Press card, Barclaycard, British Library reader's ticket and driving licence among other ephemera of her modern life.

I turned to the Diary tab, focusing on the period since we'd met.

Work engagements, 'Mary & Paul, 'Cranks Ken+ Dad 1pm', 'Hair' ... nothing untoward, though I realised my pulse had picked up while I fingered through the weeks. If I was a bar of seaside rock the letters 'INSECURITY' would run all the way through me. I hadn't introduced Sarah to my parents yet, fearing that Mum would think her too clever for me and Dad would turn green with jealousy at my catch.

An engagement (assignation?) on Friday 9th September drew my eye. 'J 6pm.' Then another 'J' the following Wednesday, and on the one after that. Who was 'J'? She'd met him (or her?) ... I flipped the pages and counted up ... eight times since the beginning of August.

I turned to the address book tab. Several 'J's in the entries, scrawled in different pens plus a few in pencil. In fact, loads of 'J's—Jon, John, James, Julie. She had dozens of friends and, in the best Catholic tradition, even more relatives, including a prodigious quantity of siblings. She'd reeled off their names and ages to me. There were five. Had any of their names begun with a 'J'? Possibly. She'd also told me there had been a sixth, her eldest, Rory, who had been killed on military duty in Northern Ireland at the height of the Troubles.

I got out my own wallet and sneaked a look at the tiny print of Susie which I kept face down in the clear holder that also housed my Underground season ticket.

I'd told Sarah I was an only child.

Who was 'J'? I ran through our colleagues and the management team at *Today*. Several came to mind. A six o'clock meeting would be nothing unusual, though I did not remember her mentioning any of these appointments. Perhaps she had, when I wasn't listening.

No clue to her whereabouts inside the VW, anyway.

No note.

I glanced out of the window. Nobody around, and rain still falling.

No sense in having the thing and not using it.

I pulled out the Pocketphone. I would call Standen Motors again from here.

The phone was a real beauty, so light you could hold it to your ear for maybe ten minutes without your arm aching, and instead of buttons a flat control panel which responded to pressure.

A light labelled NSVC glowed. I guessed what it meant and sure enough, nothing happened when I keyed the numbers.

Jerry had got through, but I'd noticed he was on Vodafone. I wondered if my phone could roam between the two networks. A light labelled ROAM was out, so perhaps not. Unfamiliar with the niceties of mobiles, I needed the user guide, still in the box on Mitch's motorbike.

I pulled out notebook KS1. Radar said they'd written in their contact information. I found a Post-It note with a London telephone number and flipped through the blank pages right to the end looking for more.

Nothing.

No names, no address of the safe house.

Underneath the solitary phone number they'd written 'Memorise and Destroy' which seemed laughably melodramatic. Instead, after some trial and error, I programmed the number into my Pocketphone, and brought up my own number, beginning with 0401, and wrote that down.

I opened Sarah's stashed packet of B&H, apparently the last of our supply, and lit up. Should I remain at the peace camp, make more calls here or on the green phone, wait for developments? Or take the camper van and search for Sarah, stopping at all likely places: the newsagents, the corner shop, chemist, then hotels, B&Bs? If only I had a picture of her to show around!

I took out the Polaroids and shuffled through them. They must have used a waterproof housing for the camera. A crude solution, but it would have avoided the need to develop any films.

What the hell were these about?

I glanced outside. The rain had stopped and the sky brightened. I held the pictures up to the window to get more light on them. The bumps could be limpet mines. How had Jerry known that?

And how could I be sure the envelope had been left in the letter box on the gate, and that Jerry hadn't produced it himself and slipped it in with the post?

My headache had returned with vengeance. We had no aspirin.

I missed Sarah something rotten. I was scared for her, and guilty I hadn't protected her. So lovely, so precious, so vulnerable beneath that cheeky, assertive exterior.

I put the envelope in my anorak pocket and trudged over to the telephone caravan.

Inside I found Jerry standing and Debbie sitting, phone in hand, the Yellow Pages open in front of her.

'Anything?'

'I phoned all the newsagents in case she went to buy papers first thing. She would have bought them all, which anyone would have remembered. And she's not checked in to any of the hotels, and she's not in the Vale of Leven or the Glasgow Royal Infirmary. She's vanished. Ken, I phoned Boots and they have nothing under your name. I tried the other chemist too in case you forgot where you took them. Nada there either. Odd, isn't that, Jerry?'

Jerry said, 'Let's get everyone together again in the communal in ten minutes for a pow-wow. All right, Ken?' He shot me a meaningful look.

'Yeah. I'll fetch the Boots receipt. Debbie, you may think I'm half-witted, but I do know where I left my films. That's after I use the bog, I'm desperate for a crap.'

Debbie wrinkled her nose in disgust.

I crossed to the toilet caravan. The door stood open, indicating vacant. I glanced over my shoulder.

No one looking.

I shut the door from the outside, ducked behind the caravan and scrambled through the gap between the van and the brick wall along the boundary of the school grounds. Emerging, I came to the locked gate which led to the abandoned school, clambered over it and set off up the drive in search of a mobile signal.

Flight Mode

Moments later

I JOGGED up the incline round the hairpin bends. The Rocky Horror mansion came into view beyond the stone bridge. I paused for breath, turned to make sure I wasn't being pursued and took out the Pocketphone.

The No Service light was out.

I'd start with Sarah's parents—give Tracey on Reception my mobile number to call back on. I'd better ring my own folks too, but that could wait: one should call teachers at work only in an emergency, which this wasn't.

Quite.

Yet.

As my finger hovered over the keypad the phone rang.

I was so startled that I raised the Pocketphone to my ear, expecting to hear the caller's voice, before remembering I needed to accept the call. I pressed Send.

'It's me.'

I gripped the phone tightly, as if that would give me a physical connection to her. 'Thank Christ! How did you get this number? Everyone's pissing themselves with worry.'

'Listen, Ken. Are you alone?'

'Yes.' I spun around to confirm this. 'I'm up at the old school. Are you okay?'

'No.'

'Where are you?'

'I'm fine, but not at liberty. I'm being held captive.'

'Oh God, no. Shit. Are you all right? That happened to me too, but they weren't bad guys and they let me go. That's why I didn't show up. Who is holding you? When did this happen? Have they hurt you? Can you speak?'

'I am unharmed, being treated well, and nothing bad will happen to me, they say, provided you do everything I tell you without question.'

'Are these people with you now? Put them on. I demand to speak to them.'

'No, Ken, they won't speak to you. I need you to calm down and listen, do some things for me, to keep me safe. Ready?'

'Yes.'

'Call the Government and tell them *HMS Repulse* has been sabotaged with limpet mines.'

'I already know that. Photos arrived at the camp for me.'

'Listen. The mines will detonate if the sub surfaces. They must signal the sub not to surface but to keep a minimum depth of two hundred feet. Don't call the base, they can't contact the sub anyway, call the Ministry of Defence in London. Does anyone else know about the photos? You haven't shown them around, or called anyone?'

'No. But Jerry saw them. He delivered them to me.'

'Oh God, no. That's a disaster. Tell him to keep his mouth shut.'

She was speaking under duress, I judged, and reading lines from a script. I said, 'Will do. How can I get through to someone in authority who will believe me?'

'I'm coming to that. Take the photos and hand-deliver them to Margaret Thatcher. Do not call anyone else. Do not call the police or Clyde Submarine Base or involve the authorities in any way except the Government, or I will die. Also do not tell anyone I am being held hostage. Not even my family. Ken, love, promise me that.'

'I promise. How am I supposed to get near Margaret Thatcher? She's at the Tory conference in Brighton by now, with the biggest security operation in peacetime protecting her. They've got helicopters, the Royal Navy off the beach, snipers on all the buildings—'

'Ken, hush and listen, *please*. I am about to give you a codeword. That will get you through every government switchboard and open every door for you right up to No. 10, Downing Street. Ready?'

'Yes.'

'William Arthur Shaw. Repeat that back to me.'

'William Arthur Shaw. This is an IRA codeword?'

'No idea. They haven't said who they are. Please don't ask all these questions, just listen. You must remember the codeword, not write it down. As a mnemonic, the initials spell "was". Warn the Ministry of Defence. Get yourself down to Brighton. Give the photos to Thatcher. My captors will await confirmation, and they say they will kill me if they do not receive that confirmation by midnight.'

'Suppose I don't succeed? Something goes wrong? I need more time.'

'Not an option. Get this done, Ken. By yourself. I don't want to die. We have the best of our lives ahead of us. I'm so frightened … I miss you so much … I want to marry you … they've blindfolded me … but I'm trying to be strong for you … I've been visualising. That's a good idea, isn't it? Visualising me standing in my wedding dress at the door of the church, on Dad's arm, and you waiting at the altar, and I've been thinking about the music, and …' She trailed off, and I heard a sob, and another voice in the background, male, just audible, telling her to hurry.

'So you meant it? I mean, we—'

'Yes. They want me off the phone.' Then, louder, 'Ow! No, let me finish, you bastard! Let me say good—'

'Sarah! Wait! Don't go. How will they know I have delivered? Do I have to phone them or will you call again? Sarah? Speak to me, Sarah.'

But the line was dead.

Relief and fear fought within me for dominance. Sarah was alive and well, for now, but in desperate peril, as was *HMS Repulse*. I needed time to think this through, but I had no time.

I pocketed the phone, sprinted down the hill and raced to the communal caravan. Jerry opened the door. He must have been waiting for me. Joan sat on the horsehair-sprouting sofa, Colin, Spike and Mitch sat at the table reading the newspapers and Archie perched on a tiny plastic chair near the stove, colouring in his *Danger Mouse* book. Debbie must still be working the phone.

Jerry said, 'Been on a run, or just got the runs?'

Mitch added, 'Ye've hud time fur a full Turkish, ya funt.'

Chest heaving, I blurted out, 'Shut up, Mitch. Jerry, come outside. Just you. Everyone else stay where you are.'

They were all so surprised they complied, open-mouthed. I grabbed Jerry's arm and propelled him through the door out of earshot of the others.

'I've spoken to Sarah. She's fine, she's at home in Oxford. Took the train. She was homesick, too cold and wet here, and thought she was going down with a chest infection after her swim. I'm leaving now in the camper van to go south. Tell the others that much, but don't mention the photos to anyone, understand? Like you said, they got in touch, and I need you to do something.' I fixed him with what I hoped was a fierce stare.

'Sure, man. Anything. *Repulse* could blow any moment.'

'Keep everyone away from me for five minutes while I make a call. Then I'm leaving. Keep quiet about the photos. *Repulse* will be out of danger at least for the time being. Not a word to Debbie. And don't call the police, or the Clyde Submarine Base. Act as if you never saw the photos.'

'Wow. How did they contact you so fast? Did you get another note, or what? And when did you speak to Sarah? Debbie's been on the phone all the while. She's still in there, trying to trace your girl.'

The only way to explain was to show him the Pocketphone. I put my forefinger to my lips in a shushing gesture.

Jerry puffed out his cheeks. 'So Spike was right. You're no youngster on food stamps, are you? Who are you, Ken? And who is Sarah? Man, you've brought a whole shitload of trouble down on the peace camp. I'm disappointed in you. You want to make a call, use your own phone.'

'No service down here—never mind, I'll just leave and get out of your hair.'

'And you expect me not to share this with the others? That makes me complicit in your game. You *are* MI5, aren't you? Jesus, now they send kids in pairs posing as Romeo and bloody Juliet to spy on us.'

'Jerry, if word gets back to the police or military, *Repulse* is in grave danger. You saw the pictures. Just keep your mouth shut and everything will be all right. I must use the correct channels.'

Jerry sucked his teeth. 'I knew you two were up to something the minute you arrived. Should've told you to haul ass then.' He stamped his foot like an angry horse and turned around on the spot, kicking a stone in frustration which arced across the site and thumped into the office door. He said, 'You tell the others what you just told me. I'm not your bagman. Start with Debbie. You owe her that.'

'Y'know, I reckon you planted the photos, Jerry. You seem to know a lot about limpet mines suddenly. If we're frauds, so are you. I suggest you secure your shit, to use some American military vernacular.'

'You pompous little jerk-off! I'll secure your jaw.' He bunched his fist, but he wouldn't hit me, I was certain.

Instead, after a moment staring at me through narrowed eyes, Jerry turned and loped off towards the communal.

He knew more than he was letting on.

I considered telling Debbie that Sarah was fine, but that would raise more questions and lead to recriminations and abuse that I didn't have time for.

I scooted for our camper. With shaking, hasty hands I thrust aside the obstructions that had accumulated around the van—

Archie's red plastic pedal car, three bags of compost donated by a well-wisher, a milk crate half filled with empties. I opened both camp gates wide and jumped up into the driver's seat.

The faithful VW started first time.

I nosed forward. The other peace campers had descended from the communal and lined up like the Dirty Dozen. It was just as well they didn't have any shotguns. Debbie stared from the doorway of the telephone caravan, receiver in hand, bewilderment on her face. The others stood expressionless, all except little Archie, my last remaining friend in the place, who lifted his hand and waved. Ashamed of myself and our deception, I couldn't bring myself to wave back.

I spun the wheel, reversed out of the entrance, performed a three-point turn in the bus layby using lots of revs and set off southwards, my heart bounding in my chest like John Hurt's alien intent on escape.

The van rocked in the wind and veered to the right over the centre line. I'd left the roof up. I drew in to the verge, stopped and checked the phone.

No service.

Down here on the edge of the loch, the hills rising around me, I must be in a radio shadow. Reliable mobile telephony in rural areas like this clearly required a couple of years' more investment.

I hopped out to lower and latch the roof then set off again. Fourth gear, which had played up on the way north, now wouldn't engage at all, but I didn't have far to go. Just as well, with my speed restricted to 40mph in third.

I'd left the phone charger behind, and the Pocketphone was my only link to Sarah and the saboteurs. I'd better use public phones wherever possible, starting with the phone box down the road to call the Ministry of Defence.

William Arthur Shaw, William Arthur Shaw ...

As I drove, I rehearsed my lines out loud.

Double-Six

Tuesday 11th October 1988, 6.58pm, 24°C

DENNIS'S DRIVER, Stanley (never Stan) met me by the Arrivals barrier at Heathrow.

The chauffeur wrinkled his nose. 'Glad I wasn't sitting next to you on the flight, mate. You'd better have a wash and brush-up before you get in my nice clean Daimler. Here, I got the clobber from your flat.'

'Thanks, Stanley.' I grabbed the suit carrier and headed for the Gents. There I hung the bag inside the Disabled cubicle, stripped to the waist and did the best I could to make myself presentable, using wadded paper towels as a flannel.

I struggled into my shirt and suit, laced on the brogues, crammed my filthy, stinking camping gear into the suit carrier, put on the tie and ran my fingers through hair which resembled Rasta dreadlocks.

I wasn't a pretty sight even after this.

Stanley led me across the road to the short stay car park. Dennis sat in the back of his Double-Six, talking on the car phone.

I got in next to him and Stanley set off. The car was all chrome and walnut, a tad old-fashioned. The fold-down seatback tables were a smart touch. I guessed the mighty V12 engine had been the chief attraction.

'Yes, sir ... just so ... thank God I didn't print any of their stuff this morning ... yes, if I get an audience with the PM I'll tell her.' Dennis cancelled his call and turned to me. 'How do, Ken lad?'

'Bearing up. It's Sarah that matters.' Stanley halted at the car park barrier, inserted his token and we were on our way into the tunnel.

'Show me the pictures.'

'Hell. They're in my anorak. In the boot.'

Dennis leaned forward. 'Stanley, pull up and get out Ken's anorak. Right here.'

Stanley braked and stopped in the middle of the tunnel, producing immediate angry blasts from the drivers behind. He retrieved my anorak and passed it through the window. I handed the photos to Dennis and said, 'How many people know about this? The captors threatened to kill Sarah if word gets out.'

'Cool it, Ken. Just me and the proprietor. He's calling Charles Powell in Downing Street, who is Maggie's gatekeeper and will get straight through to her.'

'What about secretaries, telephonists?'

'They're all loyal dragons. And what else could I do? Even with your codeword—no, *especially* with your codeword, you'd not get within a mile of Thatcher. We had to involve a few people at top level. You say this Jerry character gave you the pictures?'

'They came in an envelope which Jerry claimed he found among the day's post. I told you last week I thought Jerry had rumbled us. Now I wonder if he is an FBI agent, a mole, even party to the conspiracy.'

'Voice those concerns when we get to Brighton. Now, what exactly was the message you relayed to the MOD?'

We emerged from the tunnel. I gestured at Stanley in front of me and raised my eyebrows. Dennis said, 'Stanley is the most trustworthy employee in News International. He hears all, says nowt. In't that a fact, Stanley?'

'Sorry sir, I wasn't listening. Please say all that again.'

Dennis chuckled. With patrician good looks and no hint of grey in his curly hair, the Yorkshireman seemed much younger than his years. In fact he was the same age as my dad.

I dug out my notebook. '"This is William Arthur Shaw. Polaris submarine *HMS Repulse* has six limpet mines attached to the hull. These will explode if the submarine surfaces. Radio the captain to maintain a minimum depth of two hundred feet." I repeated all this to the switchboard girl who replied, "Message received," and rang off. It has to be the IRA, timed to coincide with the Tory conference. Maximum bang for their buck in every way.'

Dennis said, 'Her triumphal return to Brighton shattered. Dozens of British sailors killed and a hundred million pounds worth of nuclear deterrent at the bottom of the Atlantic. No collateral damage. No civilian deaths. Devilish. Brilliant.' He reached into his seatback pocket, took out that day's *Daily Telegraph* and held up the front page. 'Did you see this?'

I shook my head.

They'd splashed the headline across three columns: '"We will not be cowed by thugs."' Tories see return to Brighton as victory over the IRA.'

Dennis read aloud, '"Mrs Thatcher last night demonstrated the Conservative Party's determination not to be 'cowed and bullied' by IRA terrorism when she made a defiant eve-of-conference return to Brighton's Grand Hotel ..." heck, will the Provos love that. Talk about a hostage to fortune.' He put down the paper. 'Still, blowing up a nuclear submarine sounds too sophisticated for the IRA.'

'I don't agree. The IRA are explosives experts. They could have sourced limpet mines from Libya, Russia or France. Remember the *Rainbow Warrior* that Mitterrand had sunk by his agents in New Zealand? They used limpet mines. *Repulse* was so poorly guarded, all the IRA had to do was swim up and attach them.'

'So you think these photos are genuine?' The editor held one of the underwater shots up to the interior light.

'Hard to fake a Polaroid. Probably why they chose them. Also, immediate results without processing. Dennis, I have to ask, did you have any idea something this big was going down when you sent Sarah and me to Faslane?'

'My source used the words "spectacular demonstration". I suppose blowing up a nuclear sub is just that. I didn't realise I would put you and Sarah in harm's way. I thought it would be just that, a demo. Otherwise I would have sent Ronnie Butterfield.' Ronnie was the grizzled, flak-jacketed, ex-Parachute Regiment Northern Ireland correspondent.

The editor produced a packet of Marlboro Lights and offered me one, which I seized with alacrity, though they had no flavour and I had chain-smoked on the BA Shuttle all the way down from Glasgow. I only had two B&H left, in fact.

Dennis leaned forward and pushed in the lighter. When it popped, he lit mine then his. He continued, 'In my defence, the pair of you were supposed to report on the story, not *be* the story.' He tapped the rolled-up copy of *Today* I had bought at Menzies in Departures and which lay on my lap. 'I couldn't print your stuff, for your sake as much as mine. Even if I didn't use your names in the by-line, I would have got grief for printing copy obtained illegally. I made it crystal clear not to break the law, you knobhead.' He dragged on his cigarette and glanced sideways at me. His face creased into a grin. 'Well done though. You both showed spirit and guts.'

'I can't forgive myself for letting Sarah take part.'

'You're not her keeper. Her piece was better than yours, by the way.'

'I know. She read it to me. She touched on all the issues like the environmental impact of Trident. So I'm disappointed you printed nothing either of us filed. Or any of my photos. How did they come out?'

'Don't sweat it. You've had plenty printed. As for the photos, see for yourself.' He took a fat envelope from his briefcase.

The first photo was the colour self-portrait I'd taken on arrival the previous Wednesday. Less than a week ago, but it seemed like months. We looked so happy together, me with my nerdy clip-on shades and she with the punky Chernobyl hairdo and enamel

CND earrings. In danger of welling up, I flipped through the stack of prints.

'You're a talented photographer, Ken.'

'Thanks.' I handed the photos back. 'Can't see with the courtesy light. I'll check them later.'

'Please run me through the kidnappings again. You made little sense when you phoned from the terminal.'

'Two guys nabbed me by impersonating road cops. They drugged me and held me overnight and claimed they were Special Branch and wanted to recruit me. They gave me this mobile.'

'Neat.'

'Did you bring the charger like I asked? It's almost out of juice and Sarah might call at any time.'

Stanley, hearing apparently restored, reached to his left and passed a polythene bag between the seats. Inside I found both 12 volt and mains chargers. I plugged the phone into the cigar socket. 'Thanks, Stanley.'

Dennis said, 'You reckon your two goons also lifted Sarah?'

'Has to be them. How else did they get the number of this baby?'

'What is its number? We'll need that.'

I recalled it from the memory. 'They also gave me a number which I thought was their Special Branch office. Here.' I brought up that number and showed Dennis. He noted that down too.

'What accents did they have? Ulster?'

'No. I couldn't place them. Not English, at least not actual England. West Country? I'm not good with accents.'

'You remember enough for the Yard to do Photofits of these guys?'

'Yes, but no police, or the gang will kill Sarah. These—' I held up the Polaroids—'pass from my hands into Thatcher's.'

'Won't happen, Ken. You phoned the Ministry of Defence with a bomb warning authenticated by an IRA codeword. You won't get an invitation to the Grand for a cup of tea with the PM.'

'What happens when we reach Brighton, then?'

He pointed upwards. 'Awaiting guidance from on high.'

'They'll know. They know everything. They'll kill Sarah. I must deliver the pics. Dennis, I love her. She means everything to me. They made her phone me. She was so brave.'

'A clever way to combine a bomb warning with proof of life,' Dennis mused. 'I wonder if they'll make her conduct the ransom negotiations …'

'You think that's likely? A ransom demand? I guessed they'd told us about the mines so they could claim credit when the sub disappears. If it's a ransom Sarah will have to negotiate for her own life and the sub crew's. If I lose her, my life will be over too. Boss, we got engaged yesterday. We're to be married.'

Dennis dropped his voice. 'Congratulations, especially as she's too good for you.'

'Yes, she is.' I turned to face the window and blinked away a tear.

Dennis put his hand on my arm. 'I'm joking, you silly sod. She's perfect for you. You're a sweet, lovely couple and she'll be a wife in a million. Hold on to that thought. Now listen. I dropped everything the moment you called. I came straight here, telling no one, to take you to Brighton in utmost secrecy. Though you're a smelly young wazzock who can't follow orders and deserves the sack.'

I turned to look at him and managed a smile. 'Yeah. I appreciate it. Thanks.'

'They'll have that phone off you. It could be bugged, did you think of that?'

'Christ. No. Shit. Could it be transmitting now? That would be a disaster.'

'I doubt it. You'd need a scanning receiver within a few hundred yards.'

'I must keep the phone on me all the time and in a signal service area for when they call. They'll come through at midnight to check I handed over the photos. This is how they will communicate with us, and it's our lifeline to Sarah.'

'Understood.'

'Dennis, whatever happens to *Repulse*, won't the IRA kill Sarah? She'll know too much ... codewords, descriptions of her kidnappers, what happened during the negotiations ...'

The editor twisted in his seat to face me. 'I think you have to prepare yourself for the worst. I've been trying to buck you up, with my usual lack of tact, but I won't pretend her situation is anything but perilous. Your immediate task is to play for time. We'll ask for an experienced police negotiator to coach you—'

'No! Any police involvement, they'll find out. I will not agree to that. But perhaps the call can be traced when they come through. I don't know how that works with a mobile, do you?'

'No. But where we're heading, there is plenty of expertise— bomb disposal, communications, intelligence services. All on site already. Thatcher only need click her fingers. Now I recommend you sit back and take a rest. It may be a long night.'

He folded up his *Telegraph,* stuffed it in the seat pocket and turned away, staring out of his window as the daylight faded. I leaned back on the squidgy leather upholstery and closed my eyes.

We'd kept up a steady 70mph in the fast lane since we joined the M25. I gave mental thanks for this motorway marvel that had ended the frustration of navigating around London. I had to give Thatcher credit for that, and for the Channel Tunnel too. And she'd shown guts after the IRA bombing in the same Brighton hotel four years ago. Whatever I thought of her politics, I admired her strength of character. Those personal qualities could be vital to me in the hours ahead. Margaret Thatcher wouldn't delay or dither, and she wouldn't be cowed. But could even she stand defiant and countenance the loss of a Polaris submarine? Surely not. But ... but ... if she held out against the IRA demands, that would be the death of Sarah ... or was she condemned to die anyway?

The questions buzzed around in my head like angry Scottish midges.

Yes, Minister

Tuesday 11th October 1988, 8.45pm, 21°C

THE RING OF Dennis's car phone woke me up. I'd been out for almost an hour. I felt worse, if anything: groggy, bleary-eyed, dry-mouthed. I saw a sign for Roedean School on the right, and the lights of a pier about a mile ahead. We'd entered the town from the east on the coast road.

'Understood,' Dennis murmured into his phone, then to me, 'Glad you got some shut-eye. We're about to meet George Younger.'

'The secretary of state for defence?'

'Yes. I know him. He's quiet, courteous and doesn't suffer fools.'

Stanley indicated and turned left for Brighton Marina. I said, 'In here?'

'It's outside the vehicle cordon and the proprietor has loaned his office for our use. I briefed Younger while you were snoring away, so he has the gist of the problem.'

Its V12 purring in contentment after its high-speed run, the Daimler entered the marina, a vulgar monument to Loadsamoney Britain. The developer, boxer-turned-property-tycoon George Walker, hadn't stinted. I rubbed the sleep from my eyes as I took in rows of swanky pastiche Georgian apartments overlooking the boats, a phony village square, a Gateway supermarket and a mock-Elizabethan tavern. Hoardings on scaffolding promised more consumer delights to come, including a multi-storey car park. We cruised past the construction works to the marina office. Stanley pulled up in a space marked Directors Only, next to another limo which had to be Younger's.

A beefy detective complete with earpiece and bulging dark suit stood with two armed, uniformed police officers, one with a powerful torch, the other with a beagle on a lead. Stanley opened the door for Dennis, who got out and exchanged a few words with this welcoming committee. Then the cop with the flashlight rapped on the rear window and beckoned me out.

'Good evening, sir.' He glanced at a photo of me on his clipboard. 'Please put the contents of your pockets down there—' he pointed at a metal box on the ground, '—also your watch, belt, wallet, coins, everything.' This I did, parting reluctantly with my phone and watch.

The cop pulled on a pair of blue latex gloves. He patted, or rather prodded, me down, getting very personal, even running his hand down my trousers and around my genitals. Meanwhile the beagle gave me a good sniff-over.

'Thank you, sir. I'll return your possessions once they've been checked.' He gave Dennis a more cursory search. The suited detective then ushered the pair of us into the office building and up open-tread wooden stairs to a door marked Managing Director.

Another identically dressed protection officer stood by the door, who said, 'The minister and his private secretary are ready for you.'

A poster print of George Walker in the ring, gloves up in the ready position, dominated one wall. Four people occupied the office. Three sat at the conference table. George Younger, in full evening dress; next to him, a pinstripe-suited man who must be the private secretary; and on Younger's other side a middle-aged woman with cropped dark hair, wearing a white blouse, cardigan and brooch.

Beside Walker's desk, by the picture windows, stood a squaddie about my age, in Royal Engineers uniform, with pens in his shirt breast pocket. He was screwing the base back on a telephone. He said, 'The room is clear, Minister,' picked up a bag of gear with leads dangling and exited.

George Younger rose, and I now saw he wore full Highland evening kit including a kilt and sporran. He was taller than he looked on television. 'Dennis!' he greeted my editor. 'And you must be Kenneth Sinclair.'

'Yes, sir.'

'Sit, sit. Introductions. Sheila Middleton from MI5, James Wheddon who is sitting in as my PPS while Brian Hawtin runs things in London.'

The table was laid with notebooks, pencils, tumblers and a water jug.

At a knock on the door, Younger called out, 'Come!'

A woman entered bearing a silver tray of coffee. Younger's first detective followed with a clear plastic box containing my possessions, which he placed in front of me, saying, 'We've sent the phone, watch and lighter for examination. We'll get them back to you as soon as possible.'

Younger eyed the pocket detritus in the box, which I'd transferred from anorak to suit, and included the envelope of Polaroids, the crushed packet of Benson & Hedges (two left), my pens, wallet and notebook, camper van keys complete with Grateful Dead dancing bears key fob and the end of the roll of Polo mints.

Everyone kept a straight face.

I was itching for a smoke but had looked in vain for ashtrays and didn't dare ask. I prayed someone else would lead the way and light up.

Sheila Middleton rose to pour the coffees, but Younger raised a hand. 'No, No. We mustn't let you mother us just because you are the only woman.' He poured from the insulated jug himself, splashing coffee in the saucers, but I understood how he had earned his sobriquet 'Gentleman George'.

'To business,' Younger said. 'Be warned. Not a word of this must ever get into the Press. Should a hostile nation or terrorist group learn that our nuclear deterrent has been compromised, they will never fear us again.

'The Official Secrets Act applies to all. Contrary to popular myth, you don't need to have read and signed the Act. No one should take heart from *Spycatcher* and think they can get rich and famous by publishing state secrets. Is that understood?'

People nodded or looked grave. Younger extended his hand and brought it down hard on the table with a slap. 'I said, is that understood?'

'Yes, Minister,' we chorused, all sitting up straighter. Younger's urbane demeanour had slipped, and when he put on his reading glasses, I thought his hands trembled a little. He composed himself, smiled all round and addressed Dennis.

'Thank you for not splashing the Faslane incursion over your front page like the *Express* did. The PM was not impressed. I feel that Nick Lloyd's chances of a gong on retirement have reduced to zero.'

My editor, who had told me he couldn't print my 'stuff' both for my sake and Sarah's, now said, 'I felt the Tom King story was stronger and more positive. I was pleased that neither Paxman nor Humphrys challenged you on-air about the intrusion either, sir.'

Younger looked embarrassed at this craven brown-nosing, as well he might. He said, 'The BBC are playing goody-goodies with us. They don't fancy the same fate as awaits the IBA,[16] and the new director general doesn't fancy the same fate as his predecessor.[17] They even greyed-out the story from the front page of the *Express* when Paxman and Marcus Fox reviewed the day's papers. With the notable exception of said *Express,* we stamped on the story.' He turned to me. 'Sometimes, even in a liberal democracy, the freedom of the Press must be tempered by national security considerations. The photos, please, Ken.'

---

[16] The Independent Broadcasting Authority, representing commercial television and radio stations, which Thatcher closed down following the broadcast of *Death on the Rock*, a Thames TV documentary about the killing by the SAS of three unarmed members of the IRA on Gibraltar.

[17] Alasdair Milne, who so infuriated Margaret Thatcher that she engineered his dismissal in 1987.

Middleton said, 'Hold them by the edges, gentlemen. I'll take the envelope.'

They passed the Polaroids around as directed. Younger turned to his secretary. 'How near is Sethia?'

'His helicopter landed at Waterhall as we left the Grand. He should be here any minute.'

Younger said, 'Then let's leave these for our naval expert's attention. Narendra Sethia is a distinguished retired submarine officer who happily was near at hand this afternoon and able to fly here immediately. Sheila, your witness.' He held out his hand, palm upwards, to indicate me.

Middleton said, 'Kenneth, did you get the number plate of the men who abducted you?'

'Ken is fine. The dark blue Cortina? Yes.' I flipped through my notebook and read it out.

'Good. Can you describe the woman in the safe house, as they called it?'

'She was the owner of the cottage. She brought me tea and toast. Old, about sixty or sixty-five. Permed, dyed white hair. Strong Scottish accent, almost a caricature. Think Janet in *Doctor Finlay's Casebook*.'

'Height?'

'Tiny. About five foot. Why does she matter?'

'They took you to what they claimed was a safe house, yet they let you look around in daylight then ride back to the peace camp. They didn't care that you'd be able to identify the place. That gives us concern for whoever's cottage it was. Not the small Scottish lady's, for sure.'

'Oh my God. She was one of them. And now they have Sarah.'

'Yes.'

'They're nothing to do with Special Branch or the security services, are they?'

Middleton said, 'No. The telephone number they gave you was a vacant office above a curry house in Kilburn High Road. And the call to your mobile came from an identical model of phone. The serial numbers of the two phones are consecutive, which proves that the men who kidnapped you also hold Sarah.

'We'll ask you to provide likenesses of all three kidnappers and a full debrief.'

I said, 'No police. If you involve the police, the hostage takers will kill Sarah.'

'Understood. We have a portable system which we'll bring to you. Operated by a civilian.'

'My kidnappers worked out I am a journalist. Easy enough. But how did they know about the body in the water at Faslane—the frogman? Or that I'd been on the raid, but not boarded *Repulse*?'

Middleton said, 'Good questions, but not ones we can deal with at this meeting. We wish to concentrate on identifying and finding these individuals and rescuing Sarah. Will you show us the area where you judge the hideout might have been?' She produced an AA road atlas.

I had crossed no water on my way back from Radar and Trapper, and the distance by Mitch's odometer was twenty-two miles. I'd joined the A811 west of Stirling, from the north. When I set off, led by the Cortina, I hadn't known in which direction I was heading. I'd been too woozy, too concerned about staying upright and controlling the Bonnie. Still, the information I had gleaned gave me a small zone.

I took a Brighton Marina pencil and drew a circle about five miles' diameter around the village of Thornhill.

'Excellent. A remote area. We can check every residence tomorrow morning. Well observed, Ken.'

'That's one reason he got the trainee post,' Dennis said, a trifle smugly.

Middleton continued, 'Ken, at the peace camp, an American calling himself Jerry gave you these photos, correct?'

'Not quite. He claimed to have found them in the camp's letter box on the gate. He and I opened the envelope together.'

'Did he say anything about the limpet mines?'

'He seemed to know what they were at once.'

'Did he mention timers, depth or distance fuses, anything at all like that?'

'No. I suggest you bring him in and have him questioned.'

Middleton said, 'We are doing just that. May I have Ken's photos please, Dennis?'

Dennis slid the thick packet over the table.

I said, 'The codeword was genuine?'

Middleton said, 'Sorry, I can't comment on that. And please don't say the words, Ken. Not even in here. Have you spoken to your parents or anyone besides Dennis about your kidnapping? What about the other peace campers?'

'No. Sarah said they would kill her if I told the police or anyone except the MOD. Now more and more people are getting involved—everyone here, and others who have answered phones, and this Sethia when he arrives. I'm sure I've seen his name somewhere. Who is he exactly?'

'As the minister said, a retired officer with appropriate expertise.'

'Hold on – is he the same chap who won the libel action a year or so ago against the *Mail on Sunday*? Something to do with a logbook? That was a naval officer with an Indian-sounding name.'

'I can't tell you anything except that Sethia is completely trustworthy, discreet and here to help us. And you.'

'Also, how can I be certain word won't get back to the IRA that I've disobeyed their instructions? They have moles too.'

'Don't assume it is the IRA. Did any of the other peace campers arouse your suspicions?'

'No.'

Middleton said, 'We need your fingerprints, Ken, and Sarah's, and if possible, Jerry's. Your camper van would be a good place to start.'

'Why do you need mine and Sarah's?'

'To eliminate them. Other fingerprints must belong to Jerry or persons unknown who handled the Polaroids or entered the camper. There may also be forensic evidence—fabric samples, explosives residue. And I'm sure you've read about the new DNA techniques which can identify individuals from a few drops of blood or sweat, even a single hair.'

'Yes.' I passed her the keys. 'Glasgow Airport long stay. Row H8.'

'Now please tell us about the phone call from Sarah.'

'I'd walked up the hill behind the camp as there was no signal at the bottom. She said she was unharmed and being treated well. She told me to calm down and listen, then said these exact words, "Call the Government and tell them *HMS Repulse* has been sabotaged with limpet mines." I said I had received the photos. She said the mines will detonate—'

A knock on the door was followed by the entry of a man with a jet-black full beard and moustache maybe ten years older than me. He carried a small black briefcase. Though dressed in mufti—jeans, T-shirt and jacket—he exuded confidence and a quiet superiority.

Younger said, 'This is Commander Narendra Sethia. Seth, it's a relief to see you. Good flight?'

'Yes, thank you, Minister.' Sethia sat.

Younger said, 'Sheila Middleton you know, James Wheddon my acting PPS, Dennis Hackett, editor of *Today*, and Ken Sinclair, reporter from the same newspaper. Coffee? James, you're nearest.'

Sheila Middleton you know. Narendra Sethia was another spook!

Sethia said, 'Press? What the hell are they doing here?'

'Dennis has full clearance. Our unfortunate Ken finds himself at the sharp and painful end of this business. He was working undercover at the Faslane peace camp with his colleague Sarah, who has been kidnapped. Ken is our sole link with the saboteurs.'

Younger's secretary pushed the Polaroids across to Sethia, who looked unconvinced. 'Hold them by the edges, Commander.'

Sethia lined up the photos. He took a magnifying glass from his briefcase and bent over the grainy images.

I sat back and looked around. The architect had designed the office to provide his client with a grandstand view of his empire. Windows on two sides overlooked the nautical action.

The wind had increased, and the clinking of masts and rigging floated up from the berthed yachts below us.

While the commander pored over the photos, I finished my coffee, now cold, and wondered what Younger had meant by saying Dennis had 'full clearance'.

The wall clock showed 9.20pm.

Dennis clearly knew much more about the unfolding drama than he had admitted. Was he an informer too? If you believed the newsroom gossip, Margaret Thatcher had the media in a stranglehold, with much of the Press reduced to an instrument of government propaganda. But I'd understood *Today* to be an independently minded, courageous, campaigning newspaper, despite its recent takeover by Rupert Murdoch. They hadn't moved us into Fortress Wapping along with the *Sun*, *The Times* and the *News of the World*.

The clock had crept on to 9.25pm before Sethia laid down his magnifying glass. 'What do we know about these devices?'

Younger said, 'Ken was just coming to that when you arrived. Ken, please continue with what Sarah told you about the mines.'

I consulted my notebook, taking my time like the commander. 'She said, "Call the Government and tell them *HMS Repulse* has been sabotaged with limpet mines which will detonate if the sub surfaces. They must signal the sub to keep a minimum depth of two hundred feet." She told me not to call anyone except the MOD — not the police — or she would die. So I really, really need this information to stay in this room. Then she asked who else knew about the photos. I said Jerry did, and she replied, quote, "That's a disaster, tell him to keep his mouth shut."'

Younger's man, head down, scribbled on his pad.

'Sarah told me to hand-deliver the photos to Margaret Thatcher, and to involve no one else or she would die. She gave me the codeword. Then I heard a male voice in the background, a kidnapper, telling her to get off the line. Then she... she ...'

I trailed off. My eyes filled with tears. I glanced around the table at anxious faces. I breathed in and out twice and fought to carry on, voice breaking. 'She said she didn't want to die ... she wanted to marry me ... and see me waiting at the altar while she stood at the church door on the arm of her dad ... You must find these bastards and rescue her.'

No one spoke for maybe ten seconds. Younger broke the silence, his voice low. 'Thank you, Ken.' He turned to Sethia. 'Commander, your verdict?'

'The pictures show six limpet mines attached to HMS *Repulse*, located to cause maximum damage.' He pointed at the photos. 'This mine is by the main engine condenser cooling intakes. This one is on the port side next to the missile compartment, and here is another to starboard in the same location. These two aft are near the screw, and the last is right by the torpedo tube bow caps.' He looked up. 'Any of these could blow a hole in the hull and sink *Repulse* with the loss of all hands.'

Younger said, 'What would be the range of consequences? Could there be a nuclear explosion?'

'A thermonuclear explosion? Very unlikely. A conventional explosion expelling radioactive material, more possible.'

'Reactor meltdown?'

'Again unlikely. The reactor would scram—shut down—probably on loss of electrical power. When USS *Thresher* was lost in 1963, the sub's hull collapsed and disintegrated, but the reactor remained shut down with no radiation from it detected. Most likely is that the limpet mine would set off a secondary explosion in the solid fuel of the missiles' rocket motors, causing complete loss of the boat and crew in seconds.'

His words hung in the air as we digested this horrific scenario.

Sethia continued, 'When did Northwood signal *Repulse* to alert them to the threat?'

Younger said, 'Within an hour of Ken calling the MOD. Forgive me, Ken and Dennis, if I don't reveal the orders that accompanied the sabotage warning.'

Dennis and I nodded.

Younger continued, 'What I can tell you both is that communication with a Polaris submarine on patrol is one-way. We can talk to them, but they can't reply. To do so would reveal their location, and the deterrent would be no more.'

'Not even in an emergency like this?' I asked.

'No. The at-sea deterrent must be continuous, and has been since June 1968. Should a crew member have an accident or fall ill, the sub won't call for help. Should he die, or even if there are multiple casualties, say from a fire, they'd keep the bodies in the freezer until the scheduled end of the patrol.'

'Can't another submarine take over—relieve the duty boat?' I asked.

Younger said, 'We don't—can't—discuss operational matters. Even the crews are not party to the deployment schedule and patrol areas. Seth, any questions for Ken?'

'No, but I have a question for Mrs Middleton. How can we be sure that Ken and Sarah are innocent parties? All this could be a hoax, a media prank, a piece of youthful mischief, or, worse, this young man and his partner are perpetrators in some plot to discredit the nuclear deterrent—embarrass the Government during the Conservative conference. Are you sure they are not themselves CND activists? Even if they started out kosher, they could have gone native after a week with the peace campers. Been indoctrinated. Done a Patty Hearst.'

Middleton took off her glasses and laid them on the table. 'Commander Sethia, we rule nothing out. However, I can assure everyone in this room and you in particular, Ken, that neither Sarah nor you are suspects and we have no reason to link you with this plot.'

She smiled at me, which I found deeply troubling.

I said, 'I'm shocked you would even consider us to be involved.'

'The two of you took part in an illegal break-in to the Clyde Submarine Base. I'd be negligent not to check you both out. But you were not arrested for what you did at Faslane, serious and stupid though it was. It's small beer compared to the threat to the nuclear deterrent and the lives of *Repulse's* crew.'

'And Sarah's life.' I glanced up at the wall clock, then addressed Younger. 'Minister, I have to hand those photos to Margaret Thatcher by midnight. Time is pressing.'

'Ken, no one, not even the Queen, can get into the Grand Hotel or any part of the Island Site without vetting, security clearance and a pass. The Polaroids go from here for fingerprint and other forensic tests. We'll make copies, which I'll hand to the Prime Minister tonight, well before the deadline.'

'The hostage takers were most specific. It must be me. Can you not make an exception in an emergency?' I half-rose from my seat.

Middleton said, 'Ken, calm down and use your head. Remember what happened in this very town at this very event four years ago. We are working on your clearance as we speak. The police will issue you a conference Press pass and you'll be able to attend while we stand by for developments. Maybe as soon as tomorrow. All right?'

Dennis, who had been quiet for some time, spoke up. 'May I make a suggestion, Secretary of State? I have clearance and a conference pass. Let me take the photos to Margaret Thatcher. That should satisfy the kidnappers.'

'Good idea. Ken, can you live with that?'

'If I must. What are your plans for me in the meantime?'

'We'll base you on *HMS Nurton*. That's the vessel patrolling off the beach. Commander Sethia will stay with you. They're working on your mobile phone to establish its frequencies so the radio operator on the ship can record both sides of any calls to it. We've alerted Cellnet so we can trace the calls.'

'One problem with that,' I said. 'Reception on these new miniature mobile phones is not great. I doubt the signal would penetrate a ship's steel hull.'

Younger chuckled. 'Then it's lucky for us that *Nurton* is made of wood.'

'Wood?'

Sethia said, 'Minesweepers must be non-magnetic. *Nurton* is constructed from an aluminium frame covered in mahogany. So reception will be fine even below decks. Better than ashore in a building.'

Younger said, 'Questions, anyone?'

I said, 'Does the Prime Minister know about the photos and the threat to *Repulse?*'

'Yes. As does No. 10, the proprietor of your newspaper and the switchboard operator at the MOD. No one else apart from the six of us in this room.'

Not quite correct: Stanley was in the loop.

Younger's secretary piped up, his first contribution to the discussion. 'Tracing mobile calls is not straightforward. The radio cells can be very large. A single transmitter on the British Telecom Tower serves all of Greater London. Likewise, there's only one for West Glasgow including Faslane and Drumchapel.'

Younger said, 'Let us hope they use regular telephones then. I have a question for Commander Sethia. How easy is it to fit a depth-actuated detonator to a limpet mine?'

The submariner said, 'It would be a simple modification.'

'I feared as much. We need to discuss the likely scenarios, of which there are two. First, the terrorists wish to blackmail us. If so, they will communicate their demands.

'This scenario suggests there is a way to defuse the mines once we comply or negotiate a settlement. Narendra, how could the terrorists do this, should they relent on their threat?'

The commander said, 'Good question, and one I can't answer. The idea of a mine is that once primed you cannot disable it. Tampering with it triggers a booby-trap switch. The device may also contain vibration and noise sensors to detect a drill or saw.'

Younger said, 'The even less welcome possibility is that they intend to blow up *Repulse* in any event. Then the advance warning would be to let them claim credit for the outrage. If the sub just blew up and sank on patrol, we would likely never discover why. We would not even know the submarine had sunk at all until it missed its end of patrol check-in.

'Let us pray that we are merely being blackmailed.

'Timings: the Prime Minister will look in at the Mayor's Reception around ten o'clock tonight. She will then go to her room to work on her speech for Friday. I am to meet her in the Napoleon Suite at eleven o'clock. I'll call ahead to advise that Dennis will accompany me.'

'Now I must return to my dinner with the National Union VIPs and hope my wife has saved me a doggy bag. Narendra and Ken, the marines are waiting at the dinghy dock to transfer you to *Nurton*. Once on board, stand by and await any communication on the phone. If it rings, we'll tape the call. Your brief, Ken, is to take any message, keep the call going as long as you can, but don't attempt to negotiate yourself. Understood?'

All at Sea

Tuesday 11th October 1988, around 10.30pm (watch confiscated)

OUTSIDE, STANLEY handed me my suit carrier. An armed police officer led Sethia and me through the rows of yachts which clinked, jostled and creaked at their moorings. We came to the dinghy jetty.

The wind had increased.

One commando stood on the dock holding the mooring rope of the rigid inflatable. A second sat inside at the wheel. Sethia descended with agility. I hesitated, uncertain how to emulate him. The rubber boat and the floating jetty were bobbing about so much it made me dizzy. I accepted a helping hand to avoid an otherwise-likely dunking.

As it was, I landed in a heap on the hard floor, legs in the air.

'Not used to boats?' Sethia asked and chuckled.

I scrambled up to perch on the side seat. 'No. I was brought up about as far from the sea as you can get in Britain.'

'Then I hope you won't suffer too much aboard *Nurton*. Very shallow draft. She'll roll like a pig in shit. I served on a 'Ton' as a midshipman. Most uncomfortable surface vessel in the whole damn Navy. You'd better put on a waterproof jacket now if you've got one in that carrier. And hold tight under way. This will be a bumpy ride.'

The helmsman throttled up. We burbled between the red and green lights which marked the marina entrance. Beyond the harbour walls the water became much rougher and the wind howled at gale force. The dinghy's engine roared as the helmsman applied full thrust. The RIB surged forward, nose up, and headed out to sea, rising over the swells and slapping down on the other side with tremendous bone-jarring crashes. Spray shot up and landed on us.

'Why are we going out so far?' I shouted.

'We have to get round the Palace Pier,' Sethia shouted back.

Give me four (or better, two) wheels and solid ground beneath me any day.

The pier came into view, lights ablaze. The funfair was lit up but not in motion, closed for the night. We thumped and crashed round the end of the pier. An ancient grey ship came into view with M1166 painted on its side which must be *HMS Nurton*.

The vessel was much smaller than I had imagined. It rolled and pitched at anchor like a toy plastic boat in a toddler's bath.

The commando at the helm threw the RIB's wheel clockwise. We banked and turned, throwing up yet more drenching spray. These Royal Marines were serious boy racers. I supposed it was what I'd do if I had a powerful boat to play with.

I battled to keep myself on the slippery seat and inside the wretched dinghy. The ride, unpleasant though it was, provided a few moments' forced respite from my chronic state of worry over Sarah.

We closed with *Nurton*. It would be a challenge to transfer from the bucking little boat to the sheer ladder which awaited us on the ship's side.

My anorak, not very waterproof at the best of times, had succumbed to the blizzards of spray. Cold seawater seeped into my suit and shirt. I shivered, partly because of the water and wind chill but more at the prospect of what might transpire this night.

The commando in the front got hold of the ladder and tied the dinghy to it. Sethia encouraged me on to the bottom rung and I climbed. He followed. I shinned up to the deck without mishap, where a seaman steadied me as I found my footing.

They sent down a net on a rope and hauled up our bags.

Sethia strode to a metal door and opened it. 'The Jimmy awaits us.' We descended an internal ladder to the inside accommodation. Even this wasn't simple with the rolling motion of the ship.

We clattered down a short corridor. I bounced off the walls at each lurch. The ship stank of diesel oil and the air was hot and humid. Sethia knocked on a door labelled Wardroom and we entered.

Inside waited a guy in a blue woolly pullover with epaulettes. He saluted Sethia and said, 'Welcome aboard, Commander. And you, Mr Sinclair. Peter Forbes, executive officer or XO for short.'

To my joy I saw my mobile phone, watch and lighter on the dining table. I grabbed and strapped on the TS-150. Spotting an ashtray, I asked, 'Is it allowed to smoke?'

Forbes chuckled. 'Sure. Might calm your nerves after your voyage.'

'And my stomach.' My insides were already protesting at the violent motion and the pervasive stench of fuel oil. My hands shook as I lit up my last-but-one B&H and inhaled.

Sethia looked on as Forbes said, 'The comms officer has rigged up a scanning receiver and tape recorder in the control room, tuned to the frequency of your mobile phone. He'll use headphones to keep the conversation confidential. No one else, including me and the Captain, will know what's on the tape, which will go straight ashore to the secretary of state.

'The two of you have exclusive use of the wardroom for tonight. Help yourself from the bar. Sam, our steward, has made up bunks for you in one of the cabins. Cookie has pot mess and tea always on the go. Heads and showers are on the deck below, right forrard. Questions, gentlemen?'

'Heads?' I queried.

'Bog. khazi. Crapper. And "right forrard" means downstairs at the pointy end, that's the one bouncing up and down like a lift on cocaine.

'I understand there's a visitor on his way to see you with some equipment, Ken. We're very limited for AC power points and the supply is rather rough and ready. I hope it will suffice. Anything else you need, press the call button for Sam.'

I examined my phone. The battery showed fully charged and as promised the signal seemed fine. I placed it back on the wardroom table as Forbes left us alone together.

Sethia said, 'I don't know about you, but I'm ready for a stiff drink.' He rose and inspected the glass-fronted bar cupboard. 'Brandy?'

'Yes please.' The temperature according to Casio was 29°C. Time 10.36pm. I shrugged off my wet anorak and hung it on the chair back, picked up my ciggy from the ashtray and dragged the smoke deep into my lungs.

Sethia handed me a crystal tumbler containing a generous measure and placed the broad-based decanter on the table between us. The spirit burned my throat in the most delightful way, warming me through to my stomach. Sethia topped me up at once.

'Now what?' I said.

'We wait.'

'They sent you to mind me.'

'Support you, Ken. Aren't you grateful for the company?'

'Very much.' I drank again, resisting the urge to drain the glass in one. This could be a long night and I needed my wits in order.

I glanced up at a framed colour portrait of the Queen in her coronation robes. 'Does every naval ship have her picture?'

Sethia followed my gaze. 'It's a good plan to remember who the owner is. On *Repulse* they've gone one better. They have the entire Royal Family—Queen Mum, Charles, Diana, the whole gruesome gang. Only it's the *Spitting Image* version of them. Some wag on the Port crew put it up after Her Maj came aboard.' He paused. 'This is off the record, right? I don't want to read our chat in the pages of your wretched rag.'

'You won't. Scout's honour.'

'Never?'

'Not without your prior say-so. I believe you've had a small run-in with the Press yourself not too long ago. Which you won handsomely.'

'Indeed.'

'They printed that you'd stolen the logbook of *Conqueror*, the sub that sank the *Belgrano*.'

'They did.'

'And now you work for MI5?'

Sethia tapped his nose but didn't answer. *HMS Nurton* bucked and tossed. The bar bottles clinked one way then the other. I sensed the blood drain from my face. Perhaps the brandy hadn't been such a bright idea. I said, 'I miss Sarah so much. We've known each other for only two months and already I can't imagine life without her. But that is what will happen. They'll kill her, won't they?'

'Let's hope not. The IRA have focused on military and police targets for years now. The last time they kidnapped a civilian was that Dutch businessman in the Seventies. Herrema? He escaped unhurt. To abduct and harm a young woman wouldn't play well with their American supporters.'

'*HMS Repulse*, however, is a great choice. The ultimate military target.'

'Indeed. I have friends aboard. Mostly crew, a couple of officers.'

We sat in silence for a few moments. I said, 'We can't even be sure they are IRA.' Sethia lifted the decanter and raised his eyebrows. I shook my head. 'Why didn't the other crew spot the limpet mines? Don't you send a diver down to check over the hull before sailing?'

'Yes, that's standard procedure. Perhaps there was an urgent need to deploy *Repulse* and corners were cut.'

'As long as *Repulse* remains submerged, she should be safe,' I said.

'For now. While we await another communication from the saboteurs.'

'Is there a way to get the crew out underwater without surfacing?'

'Yes, there are two escape hatches, one in the engine room and one in the torpedo compartment. You don a special suit and bob up to the surface. But we know from the photo of the nameplate that the saboteurs got on to the casing. They could easily have booby-trapped the hatch mechanisms. Anyway, you can't just abandon a nuclear missile submarine on the high seas.'

'Could the Navy order another sub like *Trafalgar* to rendezvous with *Repulse*, then send divers out to swim across and check the situation?'

'That's the stuff of Hollywood, I'm afraid. For divers to swim from one submarine to another in open sea would be a challenge at the best of times and next to impossible below 200 feet where there is little visibility. At those depths, saturation diving techniques would be required as with North Sea pipelaying.

'That requires long decompression stops. Also, RN ships and SSBNs on patrol never communicate. But these are desperate circumstances, and I imagine the Navy will rule nothing out.'

I warmed to my theme. 'Then once the divers have checked the escape hatches and disarmed any explosive charges, the crew can shut down the reactor and evacuate to a nearby surface ship.'

'Having removed or destroyed the nuclear codes, the boat's logs and everything else sensitive?'

'I guess.'

'And deactivated her sixteen missiles?'

'Yes, that would be a good idea ...'

'And set the demolition charges to sink her?'

'Demolition charges?'

'Every SSBN carries them. There are eighteen, with thirty-minute timers. Better to destroy the boat than let the enemy salvage her.

He continued, his handsome face grave. 'Scuttling his command would spell the end of the captain's career, even if it wasn't his fault. *Particularly* if it wasn't his fault. Bottom line is, I'm not sure HQ would take the risk of trying to evacuate in the way you suggest, failing, and the submarine sinking in one piece.'

'You mean they could order the captain to sacrifice himself and his crew by exploding the sub with all hands aboard?'

My pulse picked up as I considered the horror of what I had said. Sethia replied, 'Yes, as a last resort. The ultimate nightmare. Worse than a live launch command.' He raised the brandy again and this time I nodded. He half-filled both tumblers.

'All just to make sure the Soviets don't get their hands on it?'

'Yes.'

'Would he obey?'

'I don't know Geoff, the current captain. I wouldn't if I were in command. But the system has safeguards to make sure orders are obeyed. The dual interlock on the Polaris missiles isn't just to prevent a lone mad crewman or a terrorist firing a missile. It's also to ensure no single person can *stop* a launch. This is symbolised by the baseball bat which hangs on a hook in the weapons department. The XO would be ready to use it on the captain and then carry out the order to scuttle the boat, if the captain demurred.'

Sethia, undisturbed by *Nurton*'s motion, rose and paced around the wardroom.

My stomach gurgled. I gave up resisting and reached for my last cigarette, wondering when this photo ID expert would arrive. I didn't want any distraction when Sarah called, as I prayed she would, at the stroke of midnight.

Sethia peered out of the small porthole. 'Everyone's still up and about in the Grand Hotel. And the Zap Club on the beach is buzzing. That's one hell of a dive. Pity we can't scoot across for some action. Pick up a couple of girls. On second thoughts, perhaps not the girls, as we're both answered for.'

'Commander …'

'Call me Seth.'

'Seth … any suggestions how I should deal with this phone call from the kidnappers?'

'Tell the truth, but not necessarily the whole truth. If Sarah asks where you are, tell her. If she asks if you are alone, say yes apart from me, and explain who I am, keeping it vague. If she asks whether you handed the photos to Thatcher, say no, the best you could manage was your boss Dennis.

'You must assume her captors will listen in to your side of the conversation. I imagine they will use one of these same phones again, connected to a loudspeaker.'

'Yes, there's a car bracket accessory. I didn't realise you can eavesdrop on mobile conversations by radio.'

'Not secure at all. An ordinary police scanner will do it.. That will have to change. Some digital encoded system, if mobiles are to take off as a serious business tool.'

'I'm worried for Sarah's state of mind. She got tearful on the first call. She's a strong character, but she didn't seem to cope.'

'Try to prevent her from breaking down by remaining calm yourself. Listen to the message she relays, and any demands. Ask her to repeat everything. Question her about details. Keep the conversation going as long as you can.'

'So MI5 can trace the call?'

'Yes. They will also want to listen for clues to the kidnappers' whereabouts, better still to capture their voices. Background noises such as aircraft and road traffic could be vital to help pinpoint their location. The gang may be on the move—even phone in themselves, from a public phone box. That would be easy to trace, and although they would soon be gone, they may leave forensic evidence or be noticed by witnesses. Luck may be on our side. In fact, there's not much else going for us.'

'Suppose it's all a hoax?'

'Then nothing bad will happen, except to Maggie when the news gets out. Everyone's working on the assumption that the limpet mines are viable. So prolong the call. Finish with something short and positive like, "I love you. Stay strong. We will get through this together." Is that helpful?'

'Yes.' I stubbed out my final cigarette in the ashtray and drained the brandy glass, my hand shaking. 'How could the limpet mines be deactivated?'

'Maybe an acoustic signal. A sonar device. Sound travels well under water.'

'How would *Repulse* send such a signal?'

'I don't know. One possibility: there is a traitor in the crew ready to do it. But that seems unlikely, as he would be on a potential suicide mission. The IRA don't go in for that. Patrick likes to save his own skin. Now, have you eaten today?'

'One piece of toast and Marmite. One curly sandwich at Glasgow Airport.'

'Fancy a plate of *Nurton*'s finest cuisine?'

'No thanks. I don't feel too good, Seth.'

'A little scran will help. I'll rustle you up a portion.' He got to his feet and left the wardroom, sure-footed as a mountain goat.

I poured another slug of the brandy and drank it down in one, hoping it would settle my insides. I'd no idea you could get seasick so close to land. I stood up and staggered to the porthole. The shore lights shot up and down like yo-yos. *Nurton* heaved and pitched more than ever, in an unpleasant and unpredictable motion. One lurch to the left, one to the right, that would repeat a few times, then just as you were getting used to it, a big bastard roll from a different direction threatened to knock you off your feet and sweep everything off the table.

Time? 11.24pm. The digits swam in front of my watering eyes.

On this very night four years ago, in 1984, Patrick Magee's bomb exploded in the Grand Hotel two hours after midnight, killing five and injuring dozens more, including Norman Tebbitt's wife who was paralysed for life. The conference started as scheduled at 9.30am the next morning, Thatcher shaken but defiant.

How clever of the terrorists to attack this time on a different front.

My throat burned with acid reflux as the fiery spirit sloshed around my system and threatened to climb back up my oesophagus. My headache had returned. I needed a lie-down.

I retrieved my wallet from the anorak. It was damp from the drenching we'd endured in the rubber dinghy. I dried it off with the tea towel from the bar and opened it to check the photo of Susie.

The wardroom door opened and Sethia entered, holding two plates in one hand waiter-style. He placed them on the table with cutlery. 'I should have asked Sam to serve us, but we submariners don't stand on protocol.' He grinned.

The stew, like everything aboard this vessel, smelled of diesel oil. I took an experimental mouthful, then another. Seth tucked in with enthusiasm. He nodded at the photo in my open wallet. 'Pretty girl.'

'My sister Susie.'

'You're close, obviously. Where is she now?'

'She's dead.'

'Oh Lord. I'm sorry.'

'I carry her with me everywhere. I took this photo. I keep it to remind me never to allow another woman to suffer through my inaction or negligence.'

Sethia cleared his plate and put down his knife and fork. 'That's heavy stuff, Ken. Have you shared this with many people?'

I shook my head.

'With Sarah?'

'No. I will need to, if I ever see her again. I can't let her die, Narendra. Two on my conscience.'

'Do you want to tell me about it? Sounds like Susie has a bearing on the situation you find yourself in. And your state of mind.'

I looked up at him, then down at the two-by-two-inch colour print in the plastic display pouch. It showed Susie in one final, funny, pouting pose. Her golden ringlets, spookily like Sarah's punk hairdo, framed her chubby three-year-old face. She stood in her yellow-spotted swimsuit bottoms, she held Croco by the tail and she wore the red inflatable armbands which I would discover floating on the surface of the pool two minutes and forty seconds after I released the shutter and committed her image to celluloid.

I said, 'Not now,' slid the wallet into my suit pocket and toyed with my food. I was in danger of throwing up unless this bloody ship stopped thrashing around—swinging, tipping and bucking like a mean-tempered aquatic bronco.

My discomfort in every respect was obvious to Narendra, who said, 'More motion at slack water. Should be more comfortable when the tide sets from the other direction. I'm one of those annoying seafarers who has never suffered a day's seasickness in his life. Do you want to get your head down, Ken? I'll listen for the phone and bring it to you if it rings.'

I must have looked green. Time? 11.43pm. I felt dreadful. But was it worth lying down for a quarter of an hour? Suppose Sarah called before midnight?

No wonder the photo ID operator hadn't shown up. Impossible to board the minesweeper in these conditions.

'I think that might be a good idea.' I pushed back my chair to stand. *Nurton* wallowed and rolled. The chair tipped over with a crash. The bottles in the bar clanked one way and then the other, protected with little railings around the shelves.

I picked up my anorak from the floor and allowed Seth to put his arm around my shoulder, guiding me to the door like an old age pensioner. He helped me along the foul, hot corridor and into the officers' quarters, a small dormitory with two three-tier bunk beds. Even in here the stench was nauseous. The heat and humidity filled my throat and lungs.

They'd prepared a bottom bunk for me with a neatly folded work uniform and a towel laid out on the pillow. I pushed these aside and collapsed on to the mattress.

I was going to be sick. It was a matter of when, not if.

I lay there gripping the edges of the mattress like an unwilling passenger on a flying carpet. If anything, my innards were more fragile prone than upright. The wind had whipped the shallow seas off the beach into a frenzy. The lightweight wooden construction of the *Nurton* didn't help, nor the fact I was on the waterline down here. My pulse pounded in my ears, audible to me over the creaks and groans of the old tub. A landlubber lying down below, below, below …

I checked my watch. 12.10am. Another day. No call. Was my darling girl alive or dead?

Bitter saliva filled my mouth. My stomach announced the imminent expulsion of its contents with a gurgle like a drain probed by a plunger and ready to blow.

I rolled off the mattress to the brown lino floor, struggled to my feet, held on to the bunk uprights and made it to the corridor. The 'heads' were downstairs and to the front. I found the steep metal steps and descended. On the deck below I turned right. The floor rose and fell in a sickening fairground motion. Shower and toilet stalls lay ahead and unoccupied, thank God. I made it just in time, sank to my knees and vomited a stream of acrid, almost black liquid enriched with colourful chunks of the pusser's stew into the stainless-steel toilet. More heaving ensued at the sight and smell of this. The ship's motion was incredible: worse than an aircraft in heavy turbulence. Anchored to the seabed, *Nurton* snatched at her chain like a guard dog eager to attack.

The contents of the toilet bowl slopped around, some shooting back into my face. I grabbed the sides of the seat to steady myself.

Another wave of nausea convulsed my innards. This time I brought up less, but the cramping pain was worse. Agony. I understood now why people with seasickness said they wanted to die.

A distant warble became louder, a sound I'd only heard once before. A hand fell on my shoulder.

Into my ear Sethia said, 'Take the call, Ken.'

I shuffled round on my knees, pressed the Send button and croaked, 'Sarah, love, I did it, I did it. Mrs Thatcher has the photos. Tell them to let you go. I love you.'

'Very touching, but this is not Sarah.' A male voice, softly spoken but well amplified by the handset with no interference or distortion. 'You say you handed the photos to Thatcher?'

'They wouldn't let me into the Grand … hold on …' I turned back to the toilet bowl as my guts cramped with a fresh wave of pain. 'Sorry ... I gave the pictures to George Younger, secretary of state for def—'

'We know the bastard. Where are you now, Sinclair?'

I couldn't decide if it was Radar or Trapper on the line. One of the two. 'On board the minesweeper guarding the beach. No police, I swear. Put Sarah on, please.'

'She's not here. She is fine. She is well and bearing up bravely. Her fate is in your hands, Sinclair. Yours and the Prime Minister's.'

I grabbed the toilet bowl and hoisted myself up, twisting to sit with a thump on the seat. Sethia faced me, his expression combining concern and amusement. I suppose he'd endured more dramatic events than this, hundreds of feet below the Arctic icecap. He raised a thumb in encouragement.

I said into the mouthpiece, 'I'm listening,'

'Tell the devil bitch that unless she wants a hundred and forty-five lives on her conscience, the loss of her precious Polaris submarine, the end of her nuclear deterrent because *Repulse* is the only submarine currently fit for service, and the fall of her Government, she would be advised to do as we say.'

'Go on.'

'All Republican political prisoners in custody in Northern Ireland and the mainland, whether convicted or on remand, are to be released with full pardons. No exceptions, no negotiations, no delays. Once this is announced, we will provide instructions to neutralise the timed explosives attached to *HMS Repulse* and we will release our hostage. But the submarine must still not surface or rise to less than two hundred feet below sea level as the depth fuses will remain operative and detonate.

'To ensure that any undertaking provided by the British government is genuine and serious, there is a further condition and a deadline.'

'Which is?'

'Margaret Thatcher must announce the prisoner release in her speech to the Tory Party Conference on Friday.

'Should she fail to make this public undertaking, or prevaricate or procrastinate, we will kill Sarah Standen and allow the timers on the limpet mines to count down and destroy *Repulse*.

'Those timers are set to detonate at four-thirty pm BST[18] this Friday 14th October 1988.'

Narendra, watching me, had no idea what I was hearing. I tried to paint a reassuring expression on my face.

'Can I just run through the conditions once more? There's a lot to take in.'

'Play back the recording you're making, later.'

'I—I mean, what makes you think—'

'You're wasting time, Sinclair. The clock is ticking.'

'Give me proof that Sarah is alive, unharmed and being treated well.'

'You are in no position to demand anything. However, we are not monsters and we regret the Tory government has forced us to put Miss Standen in this position. You will have your proof of life later today.'

'Thank you.'

I waited for a response, but the caller had hung up.

Sethia raised his eyebrows in query. 'What?'

'Thatcher to release and pardon all Republican prisoners and announce this in her keynote speech on Friday. Or they will sink *Repulse*.'

'Clever. And as everyone suspected, the Provos are behind this.'

---

[18] British Summer Time: UK daylight savings time, one hour ahead of Greenwich Mean Time (GMT).

Full English

Wednesday 12th October 1988, 8.20am, 27°C

I DON'T RECALL how I got back to my bunk. I imagine Narendra Sethia put me to bed like a child, because when he woke me at 8.20am I was tucked up under the covers, wearing the cotton uniform shirt and trousers.

'Tea?' He held out a steaming tin mug. 'I guessed three sugars might help.'

'You guessed right. Hey—the boat has stopped rolling!'

'Ship, not boat. Though for maximum landlubber confusion, a submarine is always a boat and never a ship. Yes, the wind has dropped, the pressure is rising, the sun is threatening to shine. And we're on the move, as you can hear from the engine noise. Sadly, I can't report that all is right with the outside world.'

I sat up. 'What's happened? Another call? News?'

'No, nothing like that. Just general mayhem and consternation ashore. I congratulate you on how you handled the situation.' He grinned. 'Man, you were a funny sight, trying to hold it all in. Literally. Lucky it wasn't a Dan Dare videophone.'

'Commander, thank you. They chose well, sending you to mind me.' I managed a smile.

'Your suit took a direct hit from some accurate projectile vomiting.'

'Whoops. I've never felt more ill in my life.'

'A little too much brandy, and the pusser's stew—'

'Don't, please! My stomach is still sore. Though I do believe I could now keep down something solid.' I sipped the hot, sweet tea.

'Sam the steward has just sent a rating ashore with the Bootnecks,[19] to drop your suit off at the express dry cleaners. You'll have it back this afternoon, de-chundered and pressed. The rating also persuaded Boots the Chemist to let him in early to do some shopping for you.' The commander held up the familiar blue carrier bag. I peered inside. Disposable razors, toothbrush and toothpaste, shampoo sachets, soap and a roll-on deodorant. 'And the gutter press, otherwise known as the daily papers, young sir.' From an orange WH Smith bag Narendra produced copies of *Today*, the *Guardian* and *The Times*. 'And a full English, or your choice from the galley, awaits your convenience once you've abluted.'

What a difference a good night's sleep and a steady floor make! I finished my tea, got up, descended to the 'heads' and shaved, took a hot shower, the first for over a week, washed and dried my hair and climbed back up feeling almost human.

Seth and I ate alone in the wardroom watching BBC *Breakfast Time* on the colour set bolted to the sideboard. Jeremy Paxman had set up shop in the lobby of the Grand Hotel. *HMS Nurton* was visible through the bay window behind him, moving across the screen from left to right and then back again. We were steaming up and down between the two piers. I guessed that in the control room above us the crew were scanning their radars and sonars for seaborne, underwater and aerial threats. A futile effort, for sure. The IRA had bigger plans this day than the mere murder of the Prime Minister and her cabinet.

I'd surprised myself in the galley by accepting Cookie's full English offering, with white toast on the side and a jumbo mug of strong coffee. It's amazing how quickly seasickness clears up once the cause disappears.

We tucked in, watching Paxman review the daily newspapers, foppish in a slimline suit with a sky-blue silk handkerchief peeking

---

[19] Armed Forces nickname for the Royal Marines.

from his breast pocket. Tory colours: perhaps not the wisest choice for a BBC correspondent.

Behind Paxman, outside and beyond the concrete blocks which cordoned off the Grand, a gaggle of people came into view on the promenade, carrying placards on long poles.

'Demonstrators,' I said to Narendra.

'They won't last long. See that police van on the central reservation?'

I counted nine protesters. They clambered over the railings, faced the hotel and raised their banners. Young men and women, from the way they moved, though detail was poor on the fuzzy TV picture.

Their slogans, however, daubed in giant capitals, were easy enough to read.

'PUNKZ FOR PEACE'
'PAY OUR NURSES'
'SCRAP SECTION 28!'
'CONDOMS FOR PRISONERS!'

Two protesters carried a rolled-up banner between them which they now unfurled, holding up an end each:

'NO TRIDENT! NO CRUISE!'

If only they knew of the nuclear drama playing out inside the Grand Hotel—and hundreds of feet below the waves somewhere in the North Atlantic.

On screen, eight yellow-jacketed policemen emerged from their van and moved in on the demonstrators.

Paxman, unaware of the action in the background behind him, put down his copy of *The Times* and spoke to camera. 'That's it for the papers, now over to your local studio for the news where you are. Live coverage of the Conservative Party Conference follows at 9.25am. Goodbye from me.'

The picture cut away to the BBC South news presenter.

Sethia said, 'Did you recognise any of your lot?'

'No. I reckon that was Brighton CND.'

'The hard core travel all over.'

This was true: Colin, Joan and Debbie had been to Rosyth, London, Holland, Aldermaston and Greenham Common, often getting arrested. The pages of *Faslane Focus* glorified their exploits.

I pushed my empty plate aside and belched. 'Pardon me.' I'd surprised my digestive system with the fry-up.

Seth laughed, invited me to go back for seconds, which I declined, and said in that case he'd update me and brief me on the day's plan.

The commander pressed something under the table.

Seconds later the door opened and Sam the steward entered to clear our plates.

I said, 'Thanks for the shopping and taking in my suit.'

'Our pleasure, sir!'

I itched for a cigarette. Narendra Sethia glanced at me. Reading my mind, he smiled, pulled a pack out of his pocket and offered me one. 'I'll join you,' he said. 'Bad habit I got into at boarding school.' He lit mine and then one for himself.

I looked around the homely wardroom. Portrait of the Queen, deferential uniformed waiter, well-stocked bar and comfy chairs … the Royal Navy worked on the same principles of class and tradition as a Victorian gentlemen's club. Even aboard this smelly old wooden tub.

I waited, notebook and pencil in hand. Narendra rose and turned off the TV. He fetched his attaché case, took out a sheet of paper and passed it across.

I stared at the typed transcript of my phone conversation with the bombers.

'I can't let you keep it,' he said. 'This is the most sensitive document in the western world. Write nothing on your pad, please.'

I scanned the text, fear returning with a rush as the words, half-remembered from last night, leapt off the page as from a horror novel, puncturing the cosy domesticity of the wardroom.

'*Tell the devil bitch …*' '*No exceptions, no negotiations, no delays …*' '*We will kill Sarah Standen …*'

I looked up at Sethia and puffed out my cheeks. 'What chance Thatcher will comply?'

'Do as they demand in full? Approximately zero point zero. But this is a negotiation. She can counter-offer, play for time, make a gesture like releasing some minor felons. I'm not a politician, and I'm not party to the discussions. I'm a glorified messenger boy and your personal valet-stroke-PA right now. Bear up. All is not yet lost, either here or on *Repulse,* wherever she may be.'

I hoped I didn't look unconvinced.

He continued, 'They request you stay here while this plays out. The weather forecast is much better, so I don't expect a repeat of last night. You'll find your sea legs anyway. Even Nelson suffered for the first three days of every voyage, so there's no shame. You can go up on deck, visit the bridge, meet the captain. Prince Charles commanded a 'Ton'. *Bronington.* They're all named after English villages ending in 'ton', and —'

'Seth.'

He stopped rabbiting, met my gaze. 'I know. You want news of Sarah. The proof of life. Nothing yet. The commo and his deputy are listening upstairs around the clock in two-hour shifts for calls to your phone. You mustn't make any calls out.'

'Why not? I need to speak to Dennis. He may have something.'

'No, Ken. Think about it. If we can tune in to the frequency of the phone, so can the bad guys. A scanner in a hotel room on the sea front would do it.'

'You think they're in Brighton?'

'We must assume it's possible. They know you're here. For the same reason, we can't let you ashore. If they spot you with a police escort they'll guess the word is out. Should the Press print a peep about Sarah or *Repulse,* the negotiations will be over, our national security is down the khazi and events will spiral out of control.'

I picked up the transcript. 'Are they correct that *Repulse* is the only submarine fit for service?'

Narendra pursed his lips, looked away: deciding what to say. He drummed his neatly manicured fingernails on the table. Turned back to face me. Breathed in.

'What the hell. You know so much already. Don't repeat or print this anywhere, right? Agreed? Cub's honour?'

'Agreed.'

'*Renown* is under complete refit at Rosyth. *Resolution* you must have seen for yourself, hoisted out in the Admiralty Dock awaiting a decision. After the problems with her reactor, widely reported earlier in the year, despite all best efforts—'

'You mean the hairline cracks in the trouser leg joints?'

'Yes. And then a different, more mundane but still serious problem afflicted *Revenge* on QRA[20]. Christ, I'll be back in court and thrown in jail for sure if this gets out. Let's hope Sheila Middleton hasn't bugged the room.' He dropped his voice. 'Seawater had leaked into *Revenge*'s condensers, causing a reactor scram. She limped back on Monday under diesel power, three weeks before the scheduled end of her patrol.' I leaned closer, straining to hear him over the engines. 'They didn't dare bring her straight back into Faslane because the game would be up: two subs out of action as a matter of general knowledge, *Repulse* tied up, unarmed and not ready to take over... if they'd docked *Revenge*, well ...'

'No sub at sea. The dopiest Russian can count to four.'

'Precisely. So they scrambled to arm and provision *Repulse* ... and just when Geoff was about to sail, you and your friends mounted your stunt.

'Meanwhile, standing offshore, *Revenge* was running low on diesel. Down to fumes in the reserve tank. The proud record of twenty year's continuous nuclear deterrent hung by a thread. They just got away with it: *Repulse* left yesterday at 1am and *Revenge* arrived three hours later.'

'How do you know all this? You're no longer a serving officer, are you?'

---

[20] Quick Ready Alert (active patrol)

Sethia shook his head slowly. 'Don't ask. But you're right, should *Repulse* be sunk, or even damaged, the UK's deterrent would fail, causing incalculable political and diplomatic damage. It makes me glad I'm not on active service any more. Those Tridents are needed now, not in five years. The Polaris fleet is shot. Good old boats, but long overdue for retirement, held together with rubber bands and bits of string.'

'Your secrets are safe with me. I will not betray your trust.'

'You're a journalist. You'll do anything for the story.'

'No I won't. Help me save Sarah, and I'll do all I can to save the sub and its crew including your mates. Do you have the slightest detail, rumour, titbit of gossip about her to help me? Where is she? I am so bloody helpless sitting here waiting for the phone to ring like a lovelorn teenager.'

Narendra sighed. 'All right. Do you remember in the marina office I asked Sheila Middleton if you and Sarah could have been indoctrinated … even be spies or hostiles?'

'I remember. It was a valid question.'

'Well, they're happy that you aren't. They're not so sure about Sarah.'

My mouth dropped open. I screwed up my face in disbelief. 'That's ridiculous. I can vouch that she is a *bona fide* junior reporter. Just out of university, liberal attitudes but no extreme views, more into feminism than anything, comes from a respectable middle-class English family that runs a garage in Oxfordshire. I've worked with her, driven from London to Scotland with her, slept with her, proposed to her and she accepted. She says what she means and means what she says. Twenty-one years old, for Christ's sake, Seth, same age as me. Tell me how she is anything other than a victim of terrorism.'

'Hey, don't shoot the messenger. Take some time to think it over, and don't blame MI5 for covering all angles. When Sheila Middleton comes aboard later, keep it quiet that I warned you. Let her tell you.'

I took off my glasses, laid them down and rubbed my eyes. The reviving effect of the shower and the cooked breakfast had worn off fast. 'So MI5 are on their way. What else is in store for me on this godforsaken prison ship?'

'Calm it, Ken. Remember how well you did last night. The photo ID person is due too. Possibly with Sheila Middleton. But my stint as your minder is over. The time has come to say our farewells, I'm afraid.'

I polished my specs on the sleeve of my blue shirt and put them back on. 'Don't go just yet, Seth.'

'I'd much rather not.'

I doodled on my pad. A little girl, curly blonde hair, swimsuit, armbands, inflatable crocodile. 'Can we meet up again—stay in touch? You've been great.'

'Yes, Ken.'

I shaded in Susie's swim bottoms. 'My parents never blamed me, you know.'

He glanced at my doodle. 'For your sister?'

'Yes. I was thirteen.'

'What happened?'

'I thought you had to be off. It can wait.'

'No, I don't think it can. Tell me.'

I Don't Like Mondays

Wednesday 12th October 1988, 9.17am, 26°C

'SUSIE HAD BEEN pestering Mum to go in the pool. Mum was making us lunch in the villa kitchen. To take on the beach. She told Susie to find me. My parents had given me a Sony Stowaway for my birthday, the first model of what became the Walkman, and I was … you don't have time for this self-pity. It's none of your concern—'

'You got a Sony Walkman for your birthday. Go on.'

'I was lying on the sofa in my trunks listening to "I Don't like Mondays". The Boomtown Rats. Susie appeared. I could see the pool behind her. She came into the room. Held up Croco. I slid off one headphone and said, "I'll swim with you in a moment, Susie-Woozy." I reached for my camera, said "Smile!" and took the photo. Then I said, "Don't go in without me. Stay on the side, right?" She said, "Okay!" I remember it so well. I did say, "Stay on the side, right?" She did reply, "Okay!" I put my headphones back on, lay down and listened to the end of the song. Just that song. I'd paused at the start of the second chorus and the track is four minutes and nineteen seconds. From where I pressed Play again, there were two minutes, twenty-eight seconds left to play. Then I stood up straight away, but I couldn't see her. I went out on the patio. Her … armbands and Croco were floating on the surface, and at the bottom of the pool was a flash of yellow. Hard to see because the pump was going and the water was all ripples. You can guess how it ends.'

'She drowned. In those two minutes and twenty-eight seconds. You blame yourself, though you did nothing wrong.'

'I heard no splash or cry because Bob Geldof was at full volume. Stupid, so stupid. Mum hadn't heard anything either because the kitchen was round the back away from the pool.' My eyes had filled with tears yet again.

'I am so sorry. Have you had any counselling or support for this?'

'No. I carry her picture everywhere. It was much worse for Mum. Imagine losing your daughter, especially a late miracle as she was. Mum was perimenopausal when she got pregnant with Susie. Nine years after me. I was fine, they let me go to the funeral. "I Don't Like Mondays". The lyrics … I can't even say them. Do you know the song? Couldn't have been a worse choice.'

'Ken, when this business is over, seek professional support. Mental health is important, for men as much as women. Even in the armed forces they take it seriously these days.'

'I don't have any mental health issues. I am perfectly sane.'

'You were traumatised as a teenager. The wound is deep in your psyche, and the grief surfaces in situations like this. I've see it in crewmates many times. Small things trigger them. Some days, down there at four hundred feet, an officer's job is more counsellor than commander.'

I wiped my eyes on my uniform shirt sleeve. 'Will you give me your private phone number? Please, Commander? To help me through this, to give advice, and if Sarah dies …'

'Yes, of course. Pass me your notebook.'

I flipped to a clean page and pushed it over. He clicked his ball pen. 'This is a mobile phone they've lent me. Remember, mobiles are not secure. Anyone can hack in or overhear, so keep it cryptic.' He passed me a business card, for Trade Wind Yacht Charters. 'And this is my home number in St Vincent where I live most of the time.'

'Thanks.' A pause. 'You must go now.'

He glanced at his wristwatch. A Rolex Submariner. I pulled the sleeve of my blue shirt down over my Casio, clunky and gimmicky by comparison, all square edges and digital numbers. Flashy instead of classy like his.

'Yes.' We both rose.

We shook hands.

For the first time in my life I wanted to hug another man. My emotions were as scrambled as Cookie's eggs, with wariness, loss and neediness fighting for dominance in my addled, aching brain.

I couldn't hug him, of course. I settled for a wry grin, stepped back a pace, stood to attention and saluted, calling on those Wednesday afternoons square-bashing in the school CCF.

'Very good, Sinclair. Carry on.'

Narendra Sethia collected his attaché case, turned and left. The door closed behind him, leaving me standing to attention in the middle of the wardroom. I took my newspapers and collapsed into an armchair.

Dog on a Chain

Wednesday 12th October 1988, 9.29am, 26°C

MY POCKETPHONE didn't ring for the next hour as I read the papers from cover to cover. *Today* led with '600 SICK ON PLAGUE CRUISE' and a picture of Princess Diana opening a bowls club in Luton. *The Times* preferred 'MAJOR FIGHTS FOR £3bn LIMIT ON OVERSPEND'.

I ventured outside to the main deck, phone in pocket. Peering aloft, I spotted Forbes on the bridge. He beckoned me up, introduced me to the communications officer and the coxswain on the helm. In normal circumstances I would have enjoyed looking at the instruments and the joystick steering system, and asking about the big Bofors gun on the foredeck and the radio scanner and the tape recorder in the control room waiting for my call, but my heart was in my boots.

Back downstairs I turned up the television. David Dimbleby struggled to make the Tories interesting. Flipping with idle fingers through the TV listings, the most interesting daytime programme was a film: *Every Day Except Christmas* (1957, b/w): twelve hours in the life of the old Covent Garden.

Before that excitement, Channel 4 had a half-hour programme on interviewing skills at 1pm. I made a half-hearted decision to watch and take notes.

My Pocketphone didn't ring.

Desperate by now for a smoke, I reached under the table and pressed the call button to summon Sam.

He must have been on his break, because nothing happened.

For most of the morning I worried about Sarah. I imagined her terror, the ever-present fear of the choking arm around the neck, the glint of the knife approaching to slide between her ribs. Perhaps they were beating her, kneecapping her, subjecting her to mock executions, interrogating her, torturing her … raping her.

Where was my promised proof of life?

Was she already dead?

I toured the upper deck again. The Sussex police helicopter clattered into view, approached us and hovered directly overhead, making a hell of a din for a moment before tilting its nose forward and heading back to shore.

It was the only aircraft permitted within the five mile diameter air exclusion zone.

Nurton continued her patrol. I leaned on the railings and watched the Grand Hotel go by, then when *Nurton* did a U-turn at the damaged and derelict West Pier, I crossed over and watched again as we passed it going the other way.

Up and down, up and down, like a dog on a chain. I wondered if the captain was even aboard. Maybe the prospect of motoring across the same half-mile of grey sea all day had driven him ashore screaming to the pub.

The Royal Marines from the SBS[21] zipped about in their twin RIBs like flies circling an old horse, performing the occasional 'wheelie' in the water with much revving and heeling, I guessed just to break the monotony. They faced two more days of aimless patrolling. Would Younger keep me here all that time as well?

Boredom and fear are strange bedfellows. These conflicting emotions resolved into a chronic tension, tightening the muscles of my neck and back until, like a ventriloquist's wooden dummy, I could scarcely turn my head or unclench my jaw.

I revisited the galley and took a plate of fish and chips to the wardroom, where I ate alone, while on the TV, across the water, Thatcher's ministers preached to the converted.

Time slowed to a crawl.

---

[21] Special Boat Service.

My Pocketphone didn't ring.

At 4.05pm the door opened and Sheila Middleton entered, wearing the same outfit as the previous evening, shoulders hunched, looking like death warmed up.

I sat at the table and massaged my wire-taut neck. Twitching from nicotine withdrawal, I prepared for the worst.

She flopped into the seat that Seth had occupied. 'You played it cool on the phone. Well done.'

'I was in the toilet, having just thrown up.'

'So I hear. You wouldn't guess, from the tape. Did Seth take care of you?'

'He was wonderful. What a great guy. Did you trace the call?'

'Calls. The first one to you from Sarah originated from the Glasgow mobile mast. The second call came from a public phone box on the Drumchapel Estate outside Glasgow. So, it's possible they are all in Drumchapel. We might get lucky with photofits up there. That time of night, someone using the phone box might have been noticed by a dog walker or a housewife looking out of her kitchen window. If we're even luckier they may have come by car. The Cortina would link them to your abduction. Bad news on that score, I'm afraid.'

'What?'

'We found the "safe house" as you were told it was. The owner was not a Mrs McCready or anyone answering that description. The owner was a widow in her eighties. We found her in the woodshed with her throat cut.'

'My God.'

'The vicious murder of an innocent civilian, just to use her house for a few hours. A clear signal these people mean what they say.'

'They must be IRA Provisionals.'

'Not that simple, I'm afraid.'

'But the codeword they gave me ... that was genuine IRA?'

'Sorry, can't elaborate, any more than I could last night.'

'Any clues from the cottage—fingerprints, traces, notes?'

'Everything wiped clean, but we'll get something. We need to find that Cortina.'

'God, how awful about the cottage owner. To think she was tending her neat little garden, pottering around her kitchen, not a care ... and then ...' I glanced down at my watch. 'I'm going mad here waiting, nothing to do. Like the man said, the clock is ticking. Where is the chap to do these photo IDs, Sheila?'

'It's not a chap, it's a she, and a very bright she. Principal developer of the system. Everyone was worried about getting her and her equipment aboard in one piece, and about the power supply. She didn't dare risk blowing the circuit board as it's the only portable unit in the country. So, Plan B: you'll come with me to the marina office. I expect you're ready for some shore leave.'

'No police?'

'No police.'

'What else have you learned since last night? Any leads?'

Middleton sighed. 'We sent a team to your camper van and dusted it. They had to break in as we couldn't get the keys to Scotland in time. They got good prints from the plastic tumblers in the sink. Sarah's and yours, for elimination. I'll take your prints at the marina to get a full set and be sure which is which. Though we're fairly certain, unless you both wear lipstick.

'The same team paid a dawn call to the Faslane Peace Camp this morning. We dressed the agents up as civilian police and gave them a search warrant to show. They claimed they were investigating the break-in on Sunday night. They searched the camp and surroundings, including the old school, and questioned all the campers. Nothing suspicious found. They dusted Jerry's caravan and got his prints. They didn't let on about the Polaris photos. Jerry was all indignant, said the base intruders had been to court, were complying with their bail conditions and the police had no right to harass them while they were on remand. He threatened legal action.

'Jerry's fingerprints and yours are on the Polaroids, and the envelope they came in. We faxed Jerry's prints to New York and asked them if he's known to them under another name. The photos also carry your editor Dennis's prints. No others. We're testing the photos for forensic evidence. Explosives residue has its own chemical signature. If we find any it may lead us to the perpetrators.'

'Any news from the peace campers about Sarah? From Debbie in particular?'

'No. They all seemed to believe your story that Sarah had gone home and you'd followed. Debbie phoned Sarah's parents yesterday afternoon and spoke to her father, who had not seen her. Debbie left the camp after she made this phone call and no one has seen her since. The others claimed not to know her intentions. However, she didn't go into Helensburgh police station to progress the missing persons alert. I guess she believed your story too. Her present whereabouts are a mystery.'

'Debbie is very fond of Sarah and doesn't trust me an inch. I suspect she is conducting her own search.'

'We sent a second pair of agents to Islip to question Sarah's parents. That team have just reported in—that's why I am so late here. The mother was away visiting a relative. The father confirmed that Sarah hadn't been home. He also confirmed the telephone conversation with Debbie.

'They hadn't been overly worried, guessing that you and she were together, on the road and out of communication. The arrival of our agents spooked Sarah's dad, I fear.'

They're not so sure about Sarah ...' Seth's words echoed in my mind. *'Don't let on I warned you. Let her tell you.'* I sensed my knee jiggling up and down beneath the table and stilled it.

Middleton had said she'd be negligent not to vet us both, so I asked her anyway. 'Did you run the security checks on me and Sarah?'

'In progress. It seems Sarah's father is her mother's second husband. Did you know that?'

'No, but that would explain why she is much younger than her siblings. Half-siblings, they must be.'

As Susie was much younger than me.

Sarah hadn't mentioned her mother had remarried. So what? I hadn't told her about Susie. I'd said I was an only child, a white lie I often used to avoid having to recite the Susie story and then listen to dutiful expressions of shock and sympathy.

I glanced at Middleton. Her eyes were ringed with black. She'd been up all night. Before I could frame another question, she said, 'We have no suspicions about you, Ken, or Sarah, or your respective families. It's routine elimination work. We won't send the team up to your parents. If you're connected with Sarah's disappearance, you're the best double agent I've ever met, and you should be in my business.'

Either she was lying, or Seth had been wrong, then. With Sarah captive and in mortal danger, it was all academic. Middleton continued, 'You'd better change out of that uniform. Your suit is back, and the steward has shined your shoes. Can you be ready in five minutes?'

In four minutes I returned, suited and booted. I placed the Pocketphone in my shirt pocket like the dude in the advert, but the antenna poked up under my chin, so I settled for the inside suit pocket.

'Let's go,' Middleton said.

Sighting

Wednesday 12th October 1988, 4.25pm, 21°C

DOCTORS ARE NOT always white men; nurses are not always busty blondes. And a photo ID expert, I discovered, besides being female, can also be even younger than me, black, tall and trendy in slacks teamed with a burgundy leather jacket heavy on the zips.

She told me her name was Ursel and her family came from the Caribbean island of Grenada.

She set up her equipment on George Walker's conference table: a complete computer and monitor in a small suitcase no bigger than a cabin bag. The case lid hinged down to become a keyboard. The PC didn't have a mouse, the cool Apple Mac pointing and selection device which our subs also had on their Hastech terminals, but it was still impressive, with 256 levels of greyscale graphics.

I took my seat. The office floor seemed to heave and roll, as if we were at sea. This effect worsened if I closed my eyes.

Ursel explained that the software presented selections of head shapes, ears, noses and other features and merged them into a natural-looking face. She was working on a more advanced system that displayed full faces from the outset, she said.

We spent an hour building photographic-quality images of Trapper, Radar and Mrs McCready. It felt good to be doing something positive. The composites did resemble the suspects, though they all looked more villainous on screen than they had in actual life.

Middleton entered. She peered at the three images on Ursel's monitor. 'We'll get these faxed up to Scotland along with your fingerprints, which I'll take now, Ken.'

Her equipment was old school: an ink pad and two police fingerprint cards printed in 1985. She rolled each of my fingers from side to side and transferred the prints. 'That's it. I promise to keep you informed.'

Yeah, right, I thought.

She left me at the dinghy dock. I dropped into the waiting boat without help and we motored out of the harbour. Before the commando on the helm could throttle up and make conversation impossible, I said, 'I'm desperate for ciggies. Can we make a pit stop on the way back?'

He exchanged a glance with the other marine, who nodded. 'Sure, mate. We'll drop you on the beach below the Grand.'

'Will I get my feet wet?'

'Yes, if you put them in the water.' His colleague laughed and he joined in.

I buttoned up my jacket to keep any spray off my Pocketphone. I longed for it to ring, to hear Sarah's voice, to know she was alive.

We rounded the Palace Pier and the Grand Hotel hove into view, the balconies festooned with Tory banners: 'LEADING BRITAIN INTO THE 1990s'. Beside the hotel squatted the Brighton Centre, a brutalist concrete sarcophagus which would have suited an ambitious Nazi seeking a venue for an inaugural rally.

The tide was about half-in. The helmsman nosed the RIB up to the beach, his engine growling as if angry to be idling.

'Be quick, mate. We're supposed to stay on the water patrolling. Visible deterrent.'

I disembarked over the front without mishap, sliding down the rubber tube on my bum to the shore. I leapt away as a little wave approached and my brogues stayed dry. I scrambled up the first ridge of the beach, the large stones making progress difficult.

A flat-capped dog-walker with two Jack Russells on leads stopped at a safe distance to gawp at the big guys with their big guns, and maybe to wonder about the short bespectacled fellow in the grey lounge suit, and why he had got out of their boat here.

I hurried up the beach, the stones crunching under my shiny polished shoes, and ascended the decorative Victorian stairway to the promenade. At the top I spotted a newsagents on the King's Road a block east of the conference centre. It was after 5.30pm but the lights were on. Possibly run by hard-working Indians, like many corner shops these days.

I crossed the road and trotted to the shop. The bell jangled as I pushed through the door. I bought four packs of Benson & Hedges, a new lighter and some Extra Strong Mints. This left me out of cash.

Outside on the pavement I lit up and inhaled, closing my eyes for a second. The ground tilted beneath my feet. I took a moment to enjoy my smoke and look around.

Down on the beach, the marines clocked me skulking, and beckoned with exaggerated arm gestures, like airport ground crew marshalling a plane to its stand.

Back to the minesweeper. A little more comfortable than the camper van. Provided the wind didn't get up again. And what other choice did I have?

On the promenade, two people walked hand-in-hand towards the Palace Pier.

They resembled … no, impossible.

One was taller than the other and carried a rolled-up beach windbreak. The shorter wore a long coat that brushed the ground.

I dashed across the carriageway, too close in front of a minibus which blared its horn and flashed its headlights. Ignoring the squeal of brakes and the driver's shout of 'Bloody idiot!' I hopped over the low hedge on to the promenade.

The two lovers had pulled ahead of me. I threw down my cigarette and ground it into the concrete, less than half smoked.

As I drew closer, I became more and more certain.

Yes, as I'd thought, they were both women.

And the two were Debbie and Sarah, Debbie on the left as I approached from behind. She carried not a windbreak but the long anti-Trident banner I'd seen on TV that morning.

I put on a little sprint to catch up with them, my pulse quickening.

Tall, broad-shouldered, her blonde hair, her gait. Definitely Debbie. And by her side my Sarah, in an Afghan coat and red beanie cap I didn't know she owned, perhaps had borrowed, but also wearing, I now saw, her long jangly CND earrings.

Debbie let go of Sarah's hand and put her arm around my girl. Pulled her close, leaned down and kissed her on the cheek.

They'd betrayed me.

I could think of nothing else to do other than arrive behind them, panting, and blurt out, 'What are you two doing here together? I think I deserve some answers.'

They turned.

My heart sank. Or perhaps my spirits rose. Hard to tell my emotions. Conflicted: I wanted Sarah back, but if she'd been in the arms of Debbie ...? Yes, even then. Whatever Sarah wanted for herself I wanted for her. If that didn't feature me except on the sidelines, tough. Just let her be safe and unharmed.

But Debbie's companion was not Sarah. Nothing like her. Not even Sarah in disguise, but a much older woman in her thirties, attractive enough in a Bohemian way. But not my girl.

It took Debbie a moment to recognise me in my suit and tie.

I stood just as baffled. From behind, the other woman had resembled Sarah. Same height, same hair. Face-on, another person entirely, wearing Sarah's earrings.

'Where's Sarah?' I demanded.

Debbie said, 'No idea. That's her business, and if she doesn't want to speak to you neither do I. What are you doing here in Brighton, man?'

'I could ask you the same. Who's this with you, Debbie?'

'This is Beverley, the third swimmer, and how dare you be so rude to her?'

I jabbed my forefinger at the older woman. 'Why are you wearing my fiancée's earrings?'

'I take it you are the much-discussed Ken?'

'Shut up if you can't answer a question in plain English. Where is Sarah, Debbie?'

'I repeat, I don't know. Who are you, Ken? Why should we answer your questions?'

Beverley said, 'He's a spy. Spike and Jerry had that right.'

'I'm not a spy, I am a journalist.'

Debbie said, 'Aha. The truth will out. Hence the inky fingers?'

'I work for the *Today* newspaper. I'm sorry we misled you. Did Jerry send you down here, Debbie? To find me?'

Debbie said, 'It's always about you, isn't it? A journalist. Where's your story, Scoop? Nothing in *Today* or any other paper I've read since Tuesday. Are you saying Sarah is a journalist too?'

'Yes. My colleague.'

'A little workplace romance, eh? Or were you faking it? I'd expected more from Sarah. What an actress. She completely took me in. Damn her, and damn you. I've nothing more to say to you.'

Beverley took Debbie's free hand and clasped it. One person at least was pleased Sarah had turned out to be a phony.

'Take off my girl's earrings,' I said to her. 'How did you steal them? From the camper van?'

Debbie said, 'Don't you accuse her. Sarah gave them to me. Said they were uncomfortable. They didn't suit me, so I passed them on to Bev.'

Beverley said, 'I don't want the wretched things now.' She took off first the right and then the left earring and threw them down on the promenade.

We were attracting attention. A young mum with a kid in a pushchair stopped a little way ahead, uncertain whether to proceed. Other promenaders skirted us at a safe distance, heads turned away.

'Debbie, Sarah is still missing. I'm here to look for her. She's in dreadful danger.'

Debbie rolled her eyes. 'Jerry said you told him you and Sarah had split up, she took the train back to London and you followed in the camper van with your tail between your legs. All that nonsense about her going missing was just to save your dignity.'

'No, Debbie, it wasn't like that.'

'Jerry assured me Sarah was all right, so Beverley and I drove down here in Mindy as we'd always planned, to give Thatcher some grief during her rally. The reason we are here is nothing to do with Jerry. And sod-all to do with you, you lying, specious jerk. Now step aside.'

I said, 'Debbie, I understand, and Beverley, I'm sorry I snapped at you. I'm just so worried about Sarah. She didn't take the train anywhere. It was Jerry who was lying, not me. Can we have a civilised talk somewhere, please? Over a cup of tea? I'll explain everything.'

Debbie said, 'So you haven't split up? And she is still missing? Why would Jerry lie to us about all that?' She looked over my shoulder at something behind me. 'Who is the guy with the gun? I assume he's come for you?'

I spun around. The larger of the two commandos approached, his right forefinger extended over the trigger guard of his rifle. 'Sir, you have to come with us,' he said, his eyes on the women. 'Ladies, please leave this area.'

'This is a public space. We're doing nothing wrong. We're peace protesters.' Debbie unfurled a little of her banner.

'I don't care if you're Cinderella's ugly sisters, get your tits and bums out of here before I radio the cops and have you arrested.'

Debbie, her face reddening, opened her mouth to argue, but Beverley took her arm. 'Come on, Debs. These men are not worth it. No man is worth it.'

Debbie allowed Beverley to lead her away towards the pier.

I called after her, 'Debbie, I must see you! Where are you staying?'

Debbie twisted her head, half-turned and called out, 'You don't deserve it, but I'll see you, for Sarah's sake, not yours. Come to the

Crown pub, Grafton Street, at seven this evening. Alone, and no more bullshit.'

'I'll be there!' I stooped to retrieve Sarah's earrings from the dirt.

'What was all that about? You tryin' to get me court-martialled or what? A packet of fags, you said. Two minutes. Get your butt back here.' When I didn't move the commando reached out, grabbed the sleeve of my suit and spun me around, his face right in mine. 'Play any more tricks like that and I'll deck you, Mr Whoever-you-bloody-are-VIP-kid-arse-wipe.' He shoved me so hard I had to run a few paces to keep my balance, my arms flailing.

He caught up with me and seized me by the arm again, frog-marching me at a brisk pace. I heard a small yap and glanced to my left. The flat-capped dog walker stood with his Jack Russells, enjoying the show.

As we passed him, the commando growled, 'Move along, sir. Nothing to see here.'

One of the little dogs snarled, barked and leapt towards my legs, jerking at his lead. The OAP hauled it back and tottered off, muttering to himself.

Don't Look Now

Thursday 13th October 1988, 12.36am, 28°C

I'D HEARD THEM put the anchor down from my bunk. Tethered to the seabed, the minesweeper resumed its wallowing and rolling. Not so sickening as the night before, but enough to keep me awake.

The alcohol I'd consumed wasn't helping.

My Pocketphone lay on the pillow by my head. On arrival back on *Nurton* I was horrified to discover the battery dead. Had I missed the proof of life call from Sarah, or more threats and demands from the kidnappers?

To my great frustration, I failed to make the seven o'clock rendezvous with Debbie, denied permission to go ashore again. My pleas to Forbes went unheeded. I called Middleton as soon as my phone came back to life, but she refused to help either. I was a prisoner on this hulk. That's what they'd wanted all along.

Disobeying orders for a second time, I got the number of The Crown from Cellnet directory enquiries and phoned the pub at the appointed hour. Debbie and Beverley weren't in the bar, and the landlord didn't recognise my description of them.

I had no idea where they were staying.

I guessed Debbie had changed her mind about speaking to me again.

Sam had rigged up an extension lead so I could plug in my charger and sleep with the phone. I felt under my pillow and clasped the CND earrings, a physical reminder of Sarah. I must keep such things safe: the photos of her, her assorted possessions in the camper van, her clothing, her notebooks. They would provide some solace if I never saw her again.

Don't go there, Ken, I scolded myself.

All is not lost ...

But I couldn't reassure myself and sleep. *Wouldn't* sleep, until I knew she was safe and well. That meant speaking with her one-to-one. Nothing else would do. For the precious seconds I spoke to her I'd be certain she was alive.

I won't sleep ... but I *must* sleep, to be alert for what the night, or the next day, might bring.

Conflicted, as ever. Traumatised, with a deep wound in my psyche. Condemned to fail every girl I loved.

I turned on my front and buried my face in the pillow.

After a minute I overheated. What was the temperature in this black hole of a cabin? Prodding the backlight on Casio, now never off my wrist, gave the answer: 28°C.

Tropical at 12.46am. The six morphed into a seven as I stared at the digits.

I turned on my back and pushed off the sheet. I'd earlier bundled the blanket to the lino floor.

I concentrated on breathing evenly and deeply. In, out. In, out.

As I lay there in my underpants dozing off, my treacherous mind decided to replay the scene.

That scene. From *Don't Look Now*. The one where Donald Sutherland follows the little red-caped girl, she turns and it's a witch with a knife.

Sarah had turned around on the promenade and she wasn't Sarah, she was a middle-aged woman. A trigger to the terrors buried in the shallow grave of my subconscious.

That, and the talk of mental illness.

I didn't need this, not now.

The movie had given me nightmares for years. I'd watched it on VHS at the age of fifteen, unaware of the drowned child opening. I'd seen it with Phoebe, my first girlfriend. She'd brought the cassette round to watch at our place. Dad was out at a PTA and Mum was marking GCSE exam scripts in the study. We obviously didn't inform Mum it was an X-rated film.

I hadn't told Phoebe about Susie, never did, and after the horrific opening scene I was too insecure to say I couldn't watch the film through, fearing her ridicule.

Stupid. She was a sensitive, lovely girl who would have understood.

The famous sex scene with Julie Christie offered some respite, amid fumbling and mutual arousal, which subsided as the film turned ever darker, scarier, and we sat side by side too frightened even to blink, until …

Don't go there. Don't look. Now or ever.

Keep focus. Control and discipline, they are your friends.

The way to cope.

Perhaps I should see a shrink, or 'trick cyclist' as my father referred to them.

'When this business is over,' Seth had suggested. I clung to his words, fought to calm my racing heartbeat, vigilant for the ring tone in my ear, every muscle taut as a wire.

No chance of dropping off.

I sighed, opened my eyes and stared at the underside of the bunk above me. The slats were barely visible. The glow of the shore lights through the porthole provided the only illumination.

I debated whether to return to the wardroom, have a smoke and put in some more work on the bottle of Scotch: three-quarters full when I took it from the cabinet, and much less than half full when I rolled into my bunk at midnight.

Not a great idea, to get drunk, but I'd needed to blank out that seafront episode.

Little by little I sank into a torrid state of semi-consciousness. *Nurton* had quietened too, the rolling and the clanking of the anchor chain replaced by a rocking motion like a baby's cradle, albeit of industrial issue.

To sleep, but I hoped not to dream …

Friends in High Places

Thursday 13th October 1988, 4.30am, 28°C

'KEN! KEN!' An urgent whisper in my ear, a firm nudge on the shoulder.

'What ... who ...?'

'Forbes here. She wants to see you. Now.'

Groggy, I mumbled, 'Is it morning? I was fast asleep. Tell Middleton to wait.'

Forbes hissed, 'It's 4.30am. Not Middleton. Thatcher. The Prime Minister wants to meet you ashore. Now. Get down to the heads and brush your teeth, you stink of whisky. Dress in the wardroom. Quick now, man. God knows what's happened but you're about to find out.'

At 4.45am, in suit and tie, sucking an Extra Strong Mint, I asked Forbes, 'How do I look?'

'You can't wear that foul anorak. Here, take my Burb. It's raining out there.'

He helped me into his nice warm Burberry. I buckled the belt and we hurried up to the main deck, its boards slippery from the light rain.

I stared over the railings across the dark water. *Nurton* was close in to the shore, so close it surprised me she hadn't gone aground. The lobby of The Grand blazed with light, but all the bedroom windows were dark, except three in a row on the first floor which I knew belonged to the Napoleon Suite.

Forbes held a long torch to illuminate the ladder down to the waiting RIB. At sea level I was pleased to find a different crew to the ones I'd fallen out with earlier. These two were much more civil. Same uniform, same guns, same wary demeanour, though.

The tide was high, making my scramble up the stony beach much quicker.

The fishermen's sheds and kiosks built into the arches under the promenade, so cheery by day, now seemed sinister. The Zap Club also lay in darkness.

I climbed the stairs. At the top a uniformed, armed policeman awaited. 'This way, sir. We'll use the Empress Suite side entrance.'

We crossed the road and entered the Grand. At the security checkpoint a Press pass awaited me, complete with my name and picture. I took off Forbes's mac and hung the pass round my neck.

I emptied my pockets as requested by the constable.

'What's this?'

'My mobile phone. It's vital I keep it with me.'

He furrowed his brow. 'Expecting a call at five in the morning, are we, sir?'

'Yes. MI5 have already checked the phone.'

'MI5? Heh, heh!' The constable keyed his radio. 'Kenneth Sinclair has arrived. He has a mobile phone which he says he needs. Vital.'

A crackly reply: 'Confirmed that if it's an Excell Pocketphone he may bring it up.'

'Friends in high places. You won't need your cigarettes or lighter, though. Collect them when you leave.'

They body-searched me, swabbed my hands with cotton wool, tested this for explosives residue and put the phone through an X-ray machine.

A plain-clothes detective stepped forward. 'This way please, Mr Sinclair.'

The lift doors opened on the first floor. They'd stationed more detectives at each end of the corridor, by the stairwell and in the room opposite the Napoleon Suite. My escort knocked on the Prime Minister's door.

'Come.' Thatcher's voice.

I entered.

She wore a grey mid-length skirt, cream blouse and pale blue cardigan. Coiffed and made up, not in full warpaint, but a softer look. No hint of worry or fatigue. I wondered if she had just got up or had not yet been to bed.

It's true what they say about powerful people. An almost visible aura of authority and command surrounded Thatcher. Whatever you thought of her politics, in the flesh you could understand why Mitterrand, Reagan and Gorbachev held her in such awe.

She extended her hand. 'Kenneth. Thank you for coming at this early hour. I would like your advice on the challenging situation in which we find ourselves.'

I'd expected a secretary, and perhaps a Cabinet minister—Tom King, the Northern Ireland secretary, or George Younger—but I noticed only two chairs set at the small round table and realised this was a one-to-one.

'Let me hang up your mac. Can I offer you a drink? I am taking a fortifying whisky, but I can rustle up tea or coffee.'

'A whisky, thank you, Prime Minister. And may I wish you a happy birthday.' I should have declined the drink, but my hands trembled, and I needed one. Besides, it would help build a rapport between us to share a dram.

Thatcher glanced at her birthday cards, on a walnut console table beside the door. 'Thank you. I fear, however, it may not be my happiest anniversary.'

While she bustled to the sideboard and poured from a crystal decanter I glanced around. It appeared they'd rebuilt the suite as it was before the 1984 bomb which devastated the front of the hotel. The newspapers had printed the shocking pictures of the aftermath. In the refurbishment, only the furniture and décor had changed, and those not much.

A side door led to the bedroom, and I wondered if Denis was asleep in there, or if she'd roused and evicted him. Maybe he was smoking a cigarette and playing cards with the detectives across the corridor. That would be his style.

Two manila folders lay on the table, each containing around a dozen pages. They bore red 'TOP SECRET' stickers, and labels handwritten in marker pen: Kenneth William Sinclair, Sarah Anne Standen.

On the floor stood three red despatch boxes in a tidy stack, the top one open.

She'd been working on official papers when I arrived.

Thatcher handed me my glass. 'Shall we take in the view? They don't let me go to the window in daytime.'

She pulled the cord to draw back the chintzy floor-to-ceiling curtains from the French windows. We stood side by side. I saw *Nurton* still close in to the beach, or rather I saw her navigation lights and silhouette against the faintest fluorescence from the ocean.

Thatcher said, 'So reassuring, our wonderful Royal Navy. How vulnerable we were to an attack! A small boat and a rocket-propelled grenade fired straight into this suite. They could hardly have missed. This time, we have every contingency covered and an attack from seaward is no longer a threat. If only those responsible for the Clyde Submarine Base had shown similar imagination and foresight! *Extraordinary* lapses in security, to allow you and the protesters in from landward while the real terrorists swam up to the Polaris jetty.'

'Yes, they were lax.'

'Dennis Hackett showed me your photos from inside the base and your draft article. Both were excellent pieces of journalism, and I am heartily glad he decided not to print them. To think a gaggle of young people armed with nothing more than a pair of wire cutters could infiltrate an armed Polaris submarine! The most sensitive and powerful weapon in the United Kingdom!' She turned to face me, raised her glass. 'To you, Kenneth, and our wonderful free British Press. I wish you every success in your chosen career. And I toast your audacity. I need a little grit in my oyster.'

I mumbled something and raised my tumbler. Why this gushing paean of praise? Though welcome, it was surely insincere.

She said, 'Dennis tells me you lived undercover with the peace protesters. Kenneth, I do not believe any other country in the world would tolerate a permanent encampment of young people, who persist in breaking the law, on the doorstep of a nuclear weapons establishment. It is a tribute to the strength of our democracy and our tolerance of dissent.'

'What will happen to the three who got into *Repulse*?'

'Due process must prevail in the Scottish courts. I was interested, however, to read that the protesters cite technical irregularities with the bye-laws as their defence. The Ministry of Defence revised those bye-laws two years ago and I very much fear that Michael Heseltine may have been remiss in failing to authorise the changes himself, as the law required him to do. Should that be true, the defendants would have good grounds for having the case against them dismissed. Now shall we sit?'

She didn't quite wink at me, but the message came across loud and clear. Colin, Mitch, Spike and the girls would get off all charges, to avoid further embarrassing publicity.

At the round table, Thatcher said, 'May I see the Pocketphone?'

She examined it. 'A miracle of miniaturisation and visionary thinking by Nils Mårtensson. Mobile telephony will be a tremendous boon to our businessmen. I am proud of the role the Department of Trade and Industry played through a research grant.'

We each took a sip of Scotch.

'Kenneth, both you and your unfortunate colleague Miss Standen now have Secret Service files and will have for the rest of your lives. That is no reflection on your good names.'

'Thank you.'

'On confidentiality: we expect the judgement today from the Law Lords on the *Spycatcher* case. I fear it will go against us, driving a coach and horses through the current Official Secrets Act. Until we amend that Act, Secret Service officers, journalists like you and many others with classified information will feel emboldened to publish their own stories and memoirs, causing the greatest hazard to the security and defence of our nation.

'In your case, Kenneth, having read your file, the reference supplied by your employer Dennis Hackett and a glowing report from Commander Sethia, I am confident I can trust you, though you are young and ambitious. This is my proposition. I will be candid with you. You already know many classified secrets. I will tell you even more, provided you agree not to disclose the contents of this meeting or anything you learn from it to anyone, even Sarah.'

'Forever, Prime Minister?'

'No. That would be unfair on a working journalist. I give you permission to publish after my death, or in thirty years' time, whichever is the later, subject to your work first being vetted. Is that acceptable to you? If so, I require nothing more than your word and your handshake, whereas I will give you a handwritten note confirming what I have undertaken.'

She fixed me with the famous steely gaze under which so many had wilted and withered.

'I agree, Prime Minister. I will not let you down.'

'Good man.' We shook hands again, her grip dry, warm and firm. She continued, 'My thoughts are with you and Sarah as much as with the crew of *HMS Repulse*. You and I both know what it is like to lose someone close to you.'

My heart skipped a beat. 'Seth told you about Susie?'

'No, I learned it from MI5.' She opened my file and turned it towards me. Clipped to the inside cover was a photocopy of the *Nottingham Post* article, above the photo of the four of us I'd taken two days before Susie's death, using my tripod and shutter time delay.

'SUSIE MAJORCA POOL DEATH WAS ACCIDENT: CORONER'.

Thatcher took the photocopy and slipped it behind the other papers. She said, 'I have lost friends in tragic circumstances. Dear Airey Neave, my mentor. I miss him every day. Anthony Berry, in this very hotel four years ago. And many others.

'But I have never lost a loved one from my immediate family and can only imagine the heartbreak that must follow. Kenneth, the safety of your fiancée and colleague is paramount. Sarah is an innocent victim of this horrific, evil plot. I will do all in my power to deliver her back to you safe and sound. Which brings us to the matter in hand. The first of many problems we face over the next forty-eight hours is that we do not know our enemy.'

'The Provisional IRA, surely?'

'Not that simple, Kenneth.'

'But the codeword — that was genuine?'

'Yes. But there is a twofold problem with William Arthur Shaw. First, the IRA have never given a codeword to a journalist in person. They always telephone the police or a media organisation. Second, the codeword had already been used. This August, the IRA phoned a warning to the *Belfast Telegraph* of a bomb attack on the Royal Ulster Constabulary base in Ballygawley.

'But the warning was a diversion. There was no attack on the barracks. Instead the IRA detonated a roadside bomb outside the town, killing and maiming British soldiers on their way to their base in Omagh. We never made public that the codeword had been used. It appears probable, therefore, that the list of codewords fell into unauthorised hands, and the perpetrator used the wrong code.'

Reeling at the secrets Thatcher was revealing, I asked, 'Who has the list?'

'The police, Downing Street, the Ministry of Defence, the BBC, ITV, independent radio and selected newspapers including yours. It's a strange system that relies on careful communication and complete trust between sworn enemies. Delay, confusion or mistake can be fatal.

'We do not believe this was a mistake, and intelligence bears it out. The IRA are understood to be furious.

'Somebody stole the codeword list and is using it to frame the Provisionals.'

'A breakaway group? Unionists trying to discredit the IRA? Or it's a double bluff—it *is* the IRA, but they want deniability.'

Thatcher finished her Scotch and set down her glass. 'Kenneth, you are astute beyond your years.'

'How do you know the IRA are furious?'

She locked eyes with me. 'We speak to them. Not face to face, but through an intermediary, who reports that Martin McGuinness denies involvement and has even offered to help us find the perpetrators.'

This was extraordinary. Thatcher was giving me a news story that would make headlines around the world, should I walk out of here and dictate it to my news desk. Why entrust a callow cub reporter with such sensitive material? I said, 'Why would McGuinness not wish his prisoners released?'

'He and Gerry Adams don't want peace. Yet.'

'Yet?'

Thatcher sighed, the first time she had shown any sign of stress or fatigue. 'I had hoped that during my premiership I would bring peace to Northern Ireland. Peace must come. And come it will, through political engagement. Which means dealing with the IRA, via their proxy Sinn Féin.'

I said, 'If not the IRA, then who is responsible?'

'Whoever positioned the six limpet mines on *Repulse* did so with a skill beyond the IRA. I suspect Argentine involvement.'

'Revenge for the Falklands?'

She nodded. 'Disaffected former military personnel in that country have long vowed retribution for the sinking of the *Belgrano*. They could have made common cause with a splinter cell of Irish Republicans. The Argentines attempted to mine British naval ships in 1982, ships stationed in Gibraltar to support our Falklands task force. Spanish intelligence captured two Argentine commandos before they could carry out their plot. In their rental car local police found the limpet mines they intended to use. The type was as we see in the Polaroids. And we received this.' She bent down to the topmost despatch box and took out two sheets of paper. 'Received by fax at the Ministry of Defence yesterday afternoon.'

The heading read 'ENEMY WARSHIP HMS REPULSE' followed by 'John Edward Carew'.

'The next codeword?'

'Yes. He was an Irish sculptor of the nineteenth century.'

I scanned the first page.[22]

> We have seized the enemy warship known as H.M.S. Repulse and hold it hostage by six Limpet Mines in locations shown on Plan 'A'. Each Limpet Mine is equipped with two fuses: a Time Fuse set to 1630 hours BST on Friday, October 14th 1988 and a Depth Fuse set to 200 feet below sea level.
>
> The fore and aft escape hatches have also been booby-trapped.
>
> These devices can be deactivated only with a sonar transmitter set to frequencies which we will communicate to the British Government on compliance with our demands.

The document continued with advice to send *Repulse* to a deep-water location away from shipping lanes, shut down her reactor, disable her forty-eight nuclear warheads and inform other governments of the threat. Information about the mine disarming procedure followed, then more warnings about delays and prevarications that read as if a lawyer had drafted them.

---

[22] I received a copy of this document from the estate of George Younger in 2003.

Plan 'A' comprised a technical line drawing of each side of *Repulse* showing the locations of the mines, confirming what we already knew from the Polaroids.

I drew a deep breath and puffed out my cheeks. 'What do you intend to do, Prime Minister?'

'We have a choice of three unpalatable options.' She ticked them off on the fingers of her left hand. 'One: negotiate. Make concessions. Persuade the kidnappers to release Sarah and disarm the mines in return for progress on a peace process. Two: find them. Storm their hideout. Capture them alive, rescue Sarah, interrogate the kidnappers until they give up the disarming frequencies.'

'And the third option?'

'Concede their demands in full.'

I couldn't speak for maybe ten seconds. 'Give in? Release all the IRA prisoners? Including Patrick Magee who tried to kill you in this very suite?'

She averted her gaze. 'It may be the least worst option. Kenneth, at present, despite all efforts, we have not located the kidnappers.

'If we cannot make contact we cannot negotiate, if we cannot locate them we cannot storm their lair.

'In that case I must announce the unconditional releases and pardons.'

She turned to me, and to my alarm I noticed her eyes were moist with tears. 'It will spell the end of my premiership and political life, but so be it. I must serve God and country.'

She took a tissue from her sleeve and dabbed her eyes. She smiled at me and reached down for more papers. 'Kenneth, here is the redraft of my Friday keynote speech. A capitulation such as no British prime minister has ever made in war or peace. You may speed-read it.

'Any leak of the contents will spell certain death to Sarah and the crew of *HMS Repulse*. When you have finished I would like your opinion on which option to choose.'

She had written the draft in fountain pen on plain A4 paper, with confident strokes and few revisions.[23]

> NORTHERN IRELAND.
>
> When I came into office I quoted some words of St Francis of Assisi: 'Where there is discord, may we bring harmony. Where there is error, may we bring truth. Where there is doubt, may we bring faith. And where there is despair, may we bring hope.'
>
> 'Where there is despair ...' Madam President, can any part of our United Kingdom be in greater despair, or greater need of hope, than Northern Ireland? For almost twenty years now the people of this province, hard-working, devout people on both sides of the religious divide, have lived in fear. Fear that they, or their loved ones, may go to school or to work or to the shops and never return: killed by the bomb or the bullet.
>
> Madam President, we too know that fear. We have suffered the loss of dear friends and colleagues, seen battered bodies, hideously injured, some crippled for life, pulled from the debris of the bomber's handiwork, right here in Brighton. Like many others, some present today, we have been a victim of what we all euphemistically call 'The Troubles'.
>
> Madam President, Northern Ireland has been riven with conflict for too long.
>
> Enough is enough!

---

[23] This document was, to the best of my knowledge, never typed up, copied or shown to anyone except me. I received the original, sealed in an unopened envelope addressed to me, from the archivist at Churchill College, Cambridge in late 2015. For narrative purposes the text is abridged here.

So today I announce a fresh way forward. A bold way, not without risk, not without uncertainty, but sowing the seeds of a lasting peace and prosperity for all the people of the island of Ireland. For the problems of Northern Ireland are also the problems of the South, and no solution will endure unless it has the support of all the peoples of the entire island […]

The following peace initiative has been agreed by my Cabinet and has the strong backing of President Reagan.

All prisoners in custody, or charged, or under investigation in Northern Ireland or elsewhere for scheduled offences will be eligible for an unconditional accelerated programme of early release. This will apply, Madam President, not only to those affiliated to Republican groups such as the Provisional IRA, but also to Unionist and other groups. By 'accelerated' I mean months, not years.

All such releases will be subject to a declaration of ceasefire by the groups concerned […]

From this time (consult watch) on Friday, 14th October 1988, all men and women intent on further acts of political violence have a choice: abandon your plans, lay down your weapons and take part in the peace process, or face the full rigour of the judicial system, with no opportunity to enjoy the concessions I have outlined for existing prisoners.

Subject to the ceasefire holding, we will reduce the level of British Armed Forces deployed in Northern Ireland rapidly to a level appropriate to a normal peaceful society. We will reform the entire Police Service of the province to better serve all its peoples. We will resume multilateral talks aimed at introducing a new devolved Assembly with wide powers and solid safeguards for all communities. We will set up a Truth and Reconciliation Commission. We will remove high-security installations. We will cancel emergency powers. And we will introduce many other initiatives, set out in more detail in a Draft Memorandum of Peace to be published in days to come, which will also define the term 'scheduled offences'. [...]

I share the revulsion of setting free those who have used the bomb and the bullet. But those who have used such means are a minority, a small minority of the population. We should not allow them to stand in the way of peace, to control the agenda. The prize of peace is too great to give up. <u>And today it is within our grasp!</u> (Wait for any applause.)

Madam President, I ask all delegates here this afternoon, and all watching on television, listening on radio or reading this in their evening or daily newspaper, to reflect on the alternative to these proposals.

Endless violence.

There is no alternative to peace through a political process. We have started—no, re-started—that process here in Brighton today.

Peace <u>will</u> come to Northern Ireland.

EAST/WEST AND DEFENCE (Continue from earlier draft)

I put down the papers. 'Your cabinet and President Reagan have already given their blessing?'

'No, Kenneth. You are the first person apart from my husband Denis to read this. I plan to call an emergency Cabinet meeting here at the hotel at nine this morning and send the agreed draft to the Americans at midday.'

'Will you make the announcement about *HMS Repulse?* Warn other governments and so on?'

'No! We will make no such announcement. We must avoid a circus, such as surrounded the sinking of Soviet submarine K-219 two years ago. Do you know about that incident?'

'Yes, Prime Minister. Sarah and I spent a day in the British Museum reading every cutting for the past five years on nuclear submarines.'[24]

Thatcher rose from her seat. She crossed to the bay window and stared out to sea.

'They say the hour before dawn is the darkest. It seems so today.' She pulled the cord to close the curtains and returned to her seat. 'So, Kenneth. Your reaction to my peace proposal?'

'It is bold, it is ingenious. You are calling the Republicans' bluff by offering everything they have ever asked for, in return for a ceasefire. By extending the offer to the loyalists at the same time you avoid accusations of being partisan, or the suspicion that your hand has been forced. A disaster could become an opportunity.'

'Like the Falklands conflict? There are similarities.'

'That turned out to your advantage.'

'Yes, it did, and to the country's advantage too, but at the time it seemed my career was over. The shock of the invasion, the seemingly impossible task of restoring the islands to our sovereignty ... the loss of life, the sinking of the *Sheffield* ... then

---

[24] On 3rd October 1986 Russian *Navaga*-class ballistic nuclear submarine K-219 was disabled 680 miles northeast of Bermuda when seawater leaked into a missile tube, mixed with liquid rocket propellant and exploded. Several crew members died from radiation poisoning after shutting down the reactor manually from inside its shielded compartment. The remainder were rescued and the sub sank. By then ships of several nations were in attendance, purportedly to assist.

the bravery of the taskforce and our boys, the boost to the nation's morale and our great victory at the polls.

'Kenneth, can we create a lasting peace in Northern Ireland out of such a dastardly plot? The irony is that peace, whether it comes this year or in ten years' time, will flow from something like the proposal you have just read, which itself builds on Ted Heath's efforts in 1974.'

I said, 'By making this announcement, you gamble that the saboteurs will release the first frequency code so we can disable the time fuses on *Repulse.*'

'Yes. The process then becomes a negotiation, because *Repulse* can remain submerged for an extended period. As I am sure you know, Polaris patrols are limited only by the amount of food on board. The submarines have unlimited power, air and fresh water from the nuclear reactor.'

'What is the maximum endurance?'

'George Younger says that with strict rationing, *Repulse* could remain submerged and on active patrol with full deterrent capability for up to four months.'

I knew, but couldn't let on, that *Repulse had* to remain on patrol anyway, because none of the other three Polaris submarines was seaworthy.

I said, 'I think the peace option stands a better chance of success than storming the saboteurs' hideout, even if the security forces can find it, and even if you then take them alive. Why, short of torture, should they divulge the frequency?'

'I agree.' She closed the file in front of her, signifying the meeting was coming to an end. 'Thank you for your counsel.' She reached into her despatch box and came up with a No. 10 Downing Street 'Office of the Prime Minister' letterhead. She uncapped her fountain pen and said, 'This may help in writing your memoirs. Do not divulge its existence or contents. Remember, you must not publish until after my death, or thirty years have elapsed, whichever comes later. Either way you will still be in your prime.'

She wrote as follows:

TO WHOM IT MAY CONCERN

> Please assist Kenneth William Sinclair in any way you can with his researches into the 1988 Polaris Incursion and its aftermath. Kenneth has served the nation as an unpaid advisor. It is my hope and wish that he may tell his story free from obstruction, harassment or the fear of prosecution. I authorise and encourage you to share your recollections with Kenneth and to supply him with such material as you see fit, to enable him to provide an accurate account of the events of October 1988 and their repercussions.

She took back the letter and signed it with a flourish. She folded it, sealed it in a matching envelope and wrote my full name on the face. Across the flap she wrote, 'To be opened after my death but not before 1st November 2018 – Margaret Hilda Thatcher, Prime Minister of the United Kingdom, 13th October 1988.'

I tucked the envelope into my jacket and collected up my Pocketphone. We both rose to our feet.

'The letter will carry no legal weight in 2018, I am sure you realise. However, it may serve you as an introduction and a passport to some truths.'

'What more can I do here, Prime Minister? Do you want me to stay aboard *Nurton* until the end of the conference?'

'Kenneth, our belief is that you will receive no further calls on your Pocketphone and that future communications will be by fax. MI5 have all they want from you. The police will not charge you for any offences related to your incursion into Faslane earlier this week, nor for possession of the marijuana found in your camper van, though as a scientist and a mother I would counsel you to beware of mind-altering substances. You are therefore a free agent. I suggested to Dennis Hackett that he allow you to stay on here and attend the conference in your rightful role as a journalist. He agreed. We have found you a room at the Metropole, more comfortable than the minehunter, I hope.'

Thatcher opened the door. Two detectives stood ready to escort me out.

I turned to leave.

'Don't forget your mac, Kenneth!' She took down the Burberry and handed it to me.

The Call

Thursday 13th October 1988, 5.26am, 8°C

I COLLECTED MY smokes and lighter from the security point and exited the hotel.

I lit up underneath the leaded glass and wrought iron sign which simply stated 'GRAND' in confident capitals. My cigarette tip glowed in the darkness as I inhaled.

They'd radioed *Nurton* for the RIB and told me to wait at street level, staying within sight of the cop stationed outside the hotel main entrance.

No one else around, either on foot or on the road. The only sound was the low whisper of waves on the foreshore.

Darkest before dawn ...

Staring out over the water, I saw the RIB tied to the ship's ladder. Two shadowy figures descended from deck level.

Nurton had moved a few hundred metres offshore, I guessed because the tide was going out and there was less depth near the beach. This afforded me a few minutes' respite, for which I gave thanks.

I took off my pass and stowed it in my jacket pocket. I'd call Dennis later to get my instructions.

Thatcher had been generous to provide access for me. I would be in the hall for her keynote speech tomorrow afternoon, possibly at a turning point in history. I'd write my story in advance so I could file it within minutes.

My Pocketphone rang.

I dropped my ciggy, ground it out, removed the phone from my suit jacket and pressed the Send key all in one smooth movement.

'It's me.' A whisper, just audible above the waves.

'Sarah! Where are you? Have they freed you?'

'No. They're arguing about me outside. They left me alone with the phone. I've only got seconds.' She spoke fast, her voice soft and urgent, articulating every syllable.

'Where are you? How are you?'

'They moved me three times, some distance. I'm in an industrial area. A freight train line nearby. Planes overhead, low, on landing approach. Has to be Glasgow, Prestwick or Edinburgh, within five miles of the airport. Get them to trace this call. Any news on Thatcher? Will she meet their demands?'

'Yes, I believe she will.'

'They'll kill me anyway, Ken. The shorter one showed me the knife and how he would do it. I won't suffer, won't have time to feel any pain, he promised. But I don't want to die … get—'

The line went dead, and all my hopes died at the same instant.

Not because of Sarah's words, but because of what I'd picked up, faint in the background, a split second before the call ended.

She wouldn't be calling back.

I looked up. The marines had boarded the RIB. The whir of their starter motor cut through the predawn stillness, followed by the louder growl of the engine starting. I trotted up to the police officer on hotel sentry duty, my phone in hand yuppie-style.

'They're coming to collect me. I'll go down and wait at the bottom. I know the way.'

'Right you are, sir. Good night, or rather good morning.'

I turned and strode for the steps to the beach, dodging through the temporary concrete barriers. Not too fast, that would arouse his suspicion.

The RIB had set off. They turned on its coloured navigation lights and opened the throttle.

This would be touch and go.

I scampered down the steps. At the bottom, instead of heading to the spot on the beach where the dinghy would arrive, I lurked close to the arches and stepped crabwise in front of the fishermen's huts.

There wasn't much light down here, but I would be trapped by the powerful beams of the commando's torches if they shone them my way.

The RIB had arrived on the shore. One of the crew, torch in hand, was out of the boat and scanning the beach for me. Not finding me, he set off up towards the promenade.

I shimmied to my right. It wasn't far to the next street level access point, this one a ramp rather than steps.

The commando's beam probed ahead of him. Now it hovered over the stairway I had just descended, lighting up the ornate blue metalwork of the railings.

The moment I started up the ramp I would be visible. But maybe the railings with their large dolphin motifs would afford me a little cover if I crouched low.

My heart beat like a kettledrum.

The guy was shouting. 'Ken! Ken Sinclair!' The crackle of a handheld radio call reached my ears. Calling his mate. His boots crunched on the stones, approaching at a run now.

I reached the bottom of the ramp and saw the railings would only conceal me if I lay full length, face down.

Not an option. Better to keep moving and get lucky.

So I hoisted the mac like a showgirl performing the can-can and raced up the incline. My leather-soled brogues made a hell of a clattering racket. I slowed down, trod with more care, taking exaggerated paces like an Olympic walker, crouching low to present as little silhouette as possible.

I reached the promenade unchallenged.

I nipped behind the viewing shelter and peeped back towards the Grand. My pursuer had climbed the stairs which I had descended and was now crossing the King's Road in search of me at the hotel.

The police officer I'd tricked moved forward to meet him.

While they were both distracted I crossed the road myself, in full view and illuminated by the street lights if either man looked my way.

Neither did.

I darted past the first street on the other side, Cannon Place, which was filled with stacks of crash barriers stored ready for the morning's conference and too close to the Grand for comfort. I scuttled onwards and turned right at the next junction, crouching low until I was well out of sight from the main road.

Only then, as my pulse slowed and my breathing returned to normal, did I gather my thoughts and try to make sense of what I'd detected, faint but unmistakeable in the background of Sarah's call.

A blast on the airhorn of a large road vehicle, so prolonged that the Doppler effect caused the tone to drop in pitch as it passed by.

She hadn't wanted me to hear that and had cut the call.

She wasn't in Glasgow, or Prestwick, or Edinburgh, or any other Scottish city or any city at all.

She was in Faslane, at the peace camp or close nearby.

And she had lied to me.

Hitch

Thursday 13th October 1988, 5.40am, 8°C

I'D BEEN TO Brighton once before. I knew the railway station was in the centre of town and kept walking north.

A street sign told me I was in Queensbury Mews. Narrow and winding, the thoroughfare was probably once smart but now shabby and run-down, the houses divided into flats, the entrances spattered with bell pushes and name tags.

I followed my nose down a narrow alleyway by the Regency Tavern, through squares with imperial names—Russell, Clarence—turned right and emerged on to Queen's Road.

Early-morning traffic swished past in the gloom, headlights reflecting off the damp roadway. A cyclist pedalled past me, dressed in a suit and waterproof jacket. A commuter heading for the City.

Too early for a postman, but the whine and clink of a milk float caught my attention. I jogged up and accosted the milkman. 'Excuse me, I'm looking for the railway station?'

'Keep going this way, mate, you can't miss it, five minutes.'

I pulled Forbes's trench coat around me and hurried on. A sign ahead displayed the red-and-white double arrow British Rail logo. I'd drawn attention to myself for no reason.

I had to wait until 6am for the ticket office to open. I realised I was shaking. My watch showed 8°C, not cold, and it hadn't rained since I left the Grand, but I'd been up since 4.30am and the adrenaline kick from the phone call and evasive manoeuvres had worn off. I pushed into the waiting room, empty save for two old dears sitting side by side knitting who ignored me.

I needed another cigarette and got out the packet. Nineteen friendly soldiers left. When I put one between my lips and clicked my lighter, the larger of the old ladies coughed, wagged her finger and pointed at the No Smoking sign. I sighed and put the fag back. I'd warm myself up for a few minutes first and consider my options.

The door opened and in came the City gent who'd passed me earlier. He looked around as if expecting to see someone and went straight out again.

I patted my pockets. Apart from my phone, which from experience would hold its charge for about four hours (less if I made or received any more calls) I still had the letter from Thatcher, my wallet containing my Barclaycard (but no cash), my notebook, my new conference Press pass, a Brighton Marina biro, the jangly earrings and half a roll of Extra Strong Mints.

The credit card must be close to its £200 limit. The Glasgow to London British Airways ticket had cost me £75. I'd be in trouble if anyone telephoned Barclays for authorisation.

The comms officer on *Nurton* would have recorded my conversation with Sarah. How long until that tape reached MI5? Would they notice the HGV air horn in the background, so faint, masked by her voice whispering close to the handset? And how long to trace the call? They'd have to contact Cellnet and get the logs from their computer.

Not a quick process, surely?

Now I suspected where Sarah was being held, I had a duty to inform the authorities.

Common sense told me to walk back to the Grand, summon the RIB, brief Forbes and wait in the wardroom. The nice warm wardroom, just down the corridor from Cookie's galley, where bacon would be sizzling and coffee brewing at this very moment.

Instead I sat rooted to the bench. Why had I fled? My heart had overruled my head: insisted I hurry back to Scotland and find Sarah before Thatcher's SAS did. For with all their resources, within hours, by the end of the day latest, MI5 must reach the same conclusion as me: Sarah was in Faslane.

Why was she there? The most generous interpretation was that she'd told me the truth. Her kidnappers had moved her around, blindfolded, and she was back in Faslane, but did not know this. She'd cut the call because the thugs holding her had reappeared.

But although the railway line to Garelochhead ran within a few hundred metres of the peace camp, with thick woods in between I'd never heard a train on the tracks, let alone a freight train. And the airport lay at least twenty-five miles to the south east, so we never heard planes either. Why tell me those things?

Another possibility: her captors had forced her to make the call, to pretend she was alone for a moment, to deceive us and divert the search. They'd grabbed the phone and cut the connection when the lorry hooter sounded, aware like me what it suggested.

I opened my notebook and scribbled down the conversation in shorthand before I forgot it.

'They moved me three times ... I'm in an industrial area. Freight trains nearby. Planes low on landing approach ...' followed by, 'Get them to trace this call,' and 'Any news on Thatcher?'

Make her ask about Thatcher, that was plausible, but why get her to mention tracing the call?

The least appealing possibility was that Sarah had misled me on purpose. Maybe, fearing for my safety, she'd wanted to throw me off the scent. But in that case, why the blood-curdling comment about the knife? No need for that.

None of this made sense.

My head ached with the onset of a dehydration hangover. I took a mint from my pocket to allay the nicotine craving for another two minutes.

After one minute I crunched and swallowed the mint, exited the waiting room and lit up. I advanced on the Barclays cash point and inserted my Barclaycard. Drawing cash was safer than presenting the card at the ticket office and asking for a single fare to Garelochhead.

I requested £60.

'INSUFFICIENT BALANCE.'

Try again. I keyed in £40.

'INSUFFICIENT BALANCE.'

I tried a third time. With £20 I could get to London and into the office, where I would blag some expenses from the duty editor. Hopefully Dennis wasn't back yet.

'TRANSACTION DECLINED. CARD RETAINED. CONTACT CARD ISSUER.'

'Not working?'

I turned my head. It was the City gent yet again, wheeling his bike. I mumbled, 'Problem with my card,' and stepped away.

Destitute! What now? Call my parents? Call Seth on his mobile? Trudge back to the ship for a hearty breakfast, report my suspicions and attend the conference?

I walked out of the station intending to settle for the third option. My feet had other ideas, and propelled me down the underpass heading east.

I arrived at the junction with the main road and turned left. Traffic had built up and the sky was lightening in the east.

Light rain began to fall.

I loped along the pavement, hoping for a London-style double decker to appear which I could hop on and off without paying.

I'd seen one on the seafront, but they didn't seem to operate on this route.

I power-walked for half an hour, sticking my thumb out at every passing van or lorry. None stopped. This was poor hitchhiking territory, with local tradesman and builders in a hurry, few large vehicles and no suitable spots to wait.

At 7.30am, as dawn broke, I arrived at the roundabout leading to the dual carriageway and on towards the motorway.

I crossed the road and entered the filling station. In the loo I splashed some water on my face and dried my hair on the roller towel. Once again I looked like shit, but respectably-dressed shit at least. I hitched up Forbes's uniform Burberry and tightened the belt. This improved my appearance. I no longer resembled a kid who'd borrowed Dad's mac.

Back to my roadside vigil by the roundabout. The rain lashed down. I put up the collar, but water soon soaked my hair again and ran down my neck.

After thirty minutes, despite the warm raincoat, I shivered with cold. Water had penetrated my brogues to add to my misery. I was ready to give up and return to the seafront when an HGV drew up with an explosive exhalation of airbrakes.

'Hop up, mate.'

The beefy driver wore a Black Sabbath T-shirt, his name was Gavin and to my joy he was heading for Carlisle with a load of cheap clothing for market stalls. I shrugged off the soaking wet mac and hung it on the hook behind the passenger door.

He'd thought I was a car delivery driver, by my outfit, and asked me where my trade plates were. I played along and explained I was on my way to pick up an Austin Maestro MG in Glasgow for a customer in Edinburgh. Gavin's face creased with puzzlement at this unlikely itinerary. I babbled about the Maestro's fuel-injected two-litre engine, mused on why the customer hadn't waited six months by when he could have had the new Turbo model, said I preferred BMWs myself, switched tack to the upcoming Motor Show at the NEC and enthused about that like a contestant on Nicholas Parsons's *Just a Minute* until the driver's eyes glazed over and he reached for his CB microphone.

The cab was too noisy for conversation anyway, especially with his transistor radio strapped to the dashboard blaring Radio 1.

Gavin found someone to talk to about the traffic on the motorway and left me to my angst and my headache.

We rolled northwards at a steady 50mph. My head still hurt when we joined the M1.

At Toddington, Gavin indicated for the Granada services and pulled into the HGV park. I said I'd stay in the cab, but reasonably enough he insisted I accompany him. In the Burger King I watched him scarf down a trucker-sized egg and sausage muffin with tea while I breakfasted on Benson & Hedges and tap water. (I claimed I'd already eaten—I could hardly admit to being skint.)

We rose to leave and crossed to the Gents together. No one else inside. He took the urinal next to mine. I wish people wouldn't do that.

At the washbasins he stared at me in the mirror and said, 'You're no trade-plater, are you, pal? Glasgow to Edinburgh via Brighton, my arse. You're not even old enough to drive commercially. What are you—nineteen, twenty?'

Before I could reply he grabbed my arm, reached into my jacket side pocket and pulled out the Press pass by its chain-link lanyard. I reckon he'd spotted it while staring down at his cock in the urinals.

'A reporter, eh? What's your game, Mr Kenneth Sinclair? Doin' a piece on Tach fraud for the *Telegraph?* Cross-Channel smuggling? Or what? You picked the wrong guy, pal. Because I'm clean, me. Take your bleedin' story and shove it up your tight little bum. And tell your mates in the green Vauxhall to do likewise.'

'Green Vauxhall? What are you talking about?'

He gripped my arm harder. 'The car that's been trailing me since Crawley, overtook me to have a good gander then fell back. They filming me or what?'

'No. I mean, I know nothing about any car.'

'Well, here's something you will know all about.' Gavin let go of my sleeve, took a step backwards, squared up, swung his fist and unleashed a mighty haymaker into my midriff. No time to react or cry out. The pain was instant and agonising. I fell like a skittle to the piss-spattered tiles. Stars flashed before my eyes and my glasses fell off. Gavin threw down my pass, which skidded into a corner. I watched his boots march for the door as I gasped for breath and tried to speak, but no sound came out.

I struggled to my feet, still doubled up, retrieved my specs which were bent but not broken, scrambled into a stall and kicked the door shut.

And there I remained, head between my legs, for maybe ten minutes until the pain subsided to a bearable ache and my breathing returned to normal.

Back at the washbasin I dabbed my face and suit yet again with damp wadded paper towels. My stomach hurt like hell. Had he ruptured my spleen? I'd taken plenty of knocks on the rugby pitch but no one had ever hit me that hard. And my head still pulsed with pain.

Outside the rain had strengthened. No way could I resume hitching now I had lost my mac. Or rather Lieutenant Peter Forbes's mac.

I returned to the Burger King and sat at a table smoking. After ten minutes a server came across and told me to buy something or piss off.

I pissed off.

No symptoms of internal bleeding, which was something, and I could now stand almost upright.

The rain fell harder still, bouncing off the tarmac.

Tempting though it was to SOS Dennis for rescue, I resolved to try once more to hitch a ride. It should be easier from here, with every goods vehicle northbound and drivers refreshed and benevolent after their stop. My bedraggled appearance would soften their hearts.

I soon discovered how wrong you can be.

The very first lorry gave me a tremendous blast on his horn and accelerated past. The next few ignored me. Then the driver of a container truck leaned towards his open passenger window and shouted an unpleasant anatomical recommendation.

A less friendly bunch than I'd hoped for.

Next, a filthy white builder's van drove straight at me, mounting the pavement and chasing me on to the grass before he swerved back to the carriageway, giving me the middle finger as he departed.

The penny dropped. Gavin had been on Citizen's Band and warned every commercial driver within ten miles about me.

By now the rain had plastered my hair to my head, spattered my glasses and soaked through the shoulders of my suit jacket.

And I was losing the will to live.

I retreated to the porch of the Burger King, took out my phone, wiped it dry with my shirt front and keyed the number of the *Today* switchboard.

The same thing happened as at the school on Tuesday morning. As my finger hovered over the Send button, the phone rang with an incoming call.

'Middleton. We're in the car park, a lime-green Cavalier. In front of the Country Kitchen. Get yourself round here before you catch pneumonia.'

'You ... you've been following me?' I spun around, trying to spot their car. 'I'm not going back to Brighton. Leave me alone.'

'No, you're not going back to Brighton. Come down and we'll explain.'

I traipsed along the weedy pavement and turned at the sign saying 'CARS ONLY'.

I found the Cavalier, in a bilious colour that made my stomach churn anew.

Two people sat inside: Sheila Middleton in the back and the City gent from Brighton Station at the wheel, a pair of binoculars upright on the dashboard in front of him.

I got in beside Middleton. She said to the City gent: 'Start up. Get the heater going. He's like a drowned rat.'

'You followed me all this way? How? Why?'

The driver picked up a device from the passenger seat. Heavy-duty, military-styled. LED lights pulsed around a large central dial with a needle that oscillated like a piano metronome.

Middleton said, 'We installed a homing device in your phone the night you arrived. A wildlife tracker like twitchers use to keep tabs on birds. Endangered species. Such as you.' I met Middleton's gaze. Her face wore a sardonic grin. 'Sorry about that, but we didn't dare lose you. For your own safety.'

'So you want me to carry on to Scotland?'

'Yes. I wish you'd suggested that to me in Brighton instead of scarpering at dawn. Did you tell anyone your destination—the office, or your parents?'

'No.'

'Good. How about Thatcher? Did you tell her?'

'I promised the Prime Minister not to reveal anything we discussed.'

'Then you broke your promise soon enough. You told Sarah you thought Thatcher would meet the terrorists' demands.'

'She caught me unawares. How in God's name did they—she—know to call me at that instant? Just as I left the Grand?'

'We warned you the opposition would have eyes and ears in Brighton. A local sympathiser watched you, tipped them off. The dog walker.'

'The bloke in the flat cap with the two Jack Russells? He was ancient. And not on the promenade at five this morning.'

She said, 'My colleague Gerald here was smartly-dressed and on a bicycle. You didn't suspect him either. That dog walker was watching you all the time. At five this morning he staked you out from his rental above the fish and chip shop on the front. He listened in to police and naval radio traffic on his scanner, then stationed himself at his window and waited for you to emerge. A quick call to his cronies, and seconds later they make Sarah ring you. We've brought him in for questioning. No success yet. Where do you think they are holding her? Edinburgh, Prestwick or Glasgow? And how do you propose to search anywhere without transport?'

'I hadn't thought that far. I just wanted to get out of Brighton and up to Scotland. To be nearer her. I suppose I hoped she—they—would contact me again.'

'Give me a summary of your meeting with Margaret Thatcher, please, Ken.'

'No. I can't. Mustn't. Promised to keep it confidential.'

'Can you at least answer this: before Sarah called, did you have any plans to return to Scotland?'

'No. It was a spur of the moment decision.'

'That's better.' To Gerald, Middleton said, 'Fetch his stuff.'

City Gent got out, opened the boot and handed me my suit carrier and the Boots bag. 'More complimentary valet service. Your jeans, pullover, shirt, anorak, smalls. All washed, tumble-dried and ironed by Sam the steward. And your toiletries. Not forgetting the phone chargers you left behind on the ship.'

Middleton said, 'Are you aware how dangerous it will be to confront Sarah's kidnappers?'

'Yes.'

'We don't want two hostages to worry about.'

'So why are you happy for me to carry on alone?'

'I'm afraid you are the best chance we have. You are their chosen go-between. Tell them you are acting solo on your own initiative and they may believe you. We can help you, but you alone must make the contact.'

'How can you help?'

'We're tracing Sarah's call to you. I'll phone you with its area of origin later today. Different transmitters serve the three areas Sarah mentioned. We should be able to narrow the search down to one of those. Turn up there, put yourself around, they'll soon learn you're in town and pick you up. Play it canny and gain their confidence. Say you are an emissary from Thatcher. They'll trust you because they know you met her and spent an hour with her. Sarah gave that much away. They'll want to know whether the Prime Minister will comply with their demands. You are in pole position to broker a deal, or at least a delay, and get them to disclose the frequency to disarm the timer fuses.'

'You make it sound easy. But time is so short. What if I fail?'

'The last card we have to play is the SAS. But that could end in a bloodbath, everyone dead including you and Sarah, and no way to save *Repulse*.'

'What support will I have?'

Middleton opened her handbag. 'Here's a hundred pounds. Check in to the motel round the corner, have a rest, get dry and warm, charge up your phone. We'll deliver a car. Then proceed to Scotland. Call us day or night any time you need anything else.

'When you obtain the sonar frequency, call it straight in to Narendra Sethia on the mobile number he gave you.'

'Will do.'

'Ken ... good luck.'

I got out and headed for the motel. American-style, it was branded 'Travelodge', and basic though it would be, it appealed more than standing on the slip road in the driving rain with my thumb out.

Breakdown

Thursday 13th October 1988, 12.35pm, 21°C

A SHARP DOUBLE rap on the motel door woke me. I'd showered, changed, collapsed on the bed and gone out like a light.

Outside stood an Austin Maestro, sadly not the MG model with digital dashboard and voice synthesis but a humble 1.3 City. Adequate, though. And what did it matter, with Sarah's life at stake? I checked the car over, signed the documents, thanked the car hire guys, took the road atlas back to my room and sat at the little desk.

From Toddington to Faslane (for that was my destination, whatever Middleton's call trace revealed) I measured to be 400 miles. A lot of it on motorway. Say eight hours.

The time was 12.35pm. I could set out now and reach the camp by nine tonight. But what could I achieve arriving then apart from winding up whoever was in residence? Colin, Mitch, Spike—especially Mitch and Spike—would not be pleased to see me. They wouldn't let me stay over in a caravan.

No, it made more sense to arrive tomorrow morning. Thatcher's keynote speech, marking the end of the conference, would begin at 2.15pm. What she said would determine how events unfolded.

Suppose the gang had left and holed up elsewhere? My chances of finding them were slim to zero. Middleton had suggested I cruise around Prestwick, Glasgow and Edinburgh waiting for the bad guys to notice and nab me. A moment's thought revealed that plan as laughable.

I tapped my pencil on the wood-effect desktop. I could divert to Prestwick on the way up, but search large urban areas fifty miles apart? The idea was ludicrous, even if carried out by teams of special agents equipped with vehicles and radios. To rely on one person with no experience in surveillance, sleep-deprived, his head spinning with fatigue and anxiety, made no sense.

My gut told me the peace camp was the place to be. I'd corner Jerry there. I'd extract answers from him. A weedy guy, tall but effete, he wouldn't like a sharp poke in the ribs or his lapels grabbed. Thinking of Jerry, what had MI5 found out about him? Middleton had said her search team had found nothing incriminating at the camp. Why hadn't they taken Jerry in for a grilling even so?

The situation resembled a jigsaw of a thousand pieces, many missing, with no cover picture on the box.

Either the intelligence services knew more than they were admitting to me, or their puzzle pieces were as jumbled as mine.

Still, I had a sense of purpose now: a destination, a plan of sorts, clean dry clothing, money, transport and an Excell Pocketphone with some charge.

The folder on the desk listed all the other Travelodges. A Little Chef Lodge at Gretna Green appeared to be in the same chain, all part of the Forté empire.

Using the desk phone, I booked a room there for the night, packed up, checked out, hung my suit carrier behind the Maestro's driver's seat like a travelling representative and set off.

I lay the phone on the passenger seat, the charger plugged into the cigar lighter socket, which soon proved a nuisance as I had to keep unplugging it to use the lighter.

I resisted the urge to turn on the radio and distract myself, instead using the time alone to work through the various scenarios I might encounter in Scotland.

Six hours later, nearing Gretna, I'd experienced no epiphany, the phone hadn't rung, but my right leg twitched and spasmed. I'd made only two short pitstops since Toddington.

I was approaching the off-road layby where Sarah and I had stayed overnight on our journey north.

Here, shielded by trees from the A74, the only vehicle in our own free private camping site, we made up the VW's bed for the first time and relished the joys of being together, in employment, on an exciting mission and in love.

I pulled in to the layby. I collected up the assorted drink cartons, Mars Bar and sandwich wrappers accumulated during the journey, extracted the Maestro's overflowing ashtray and crossed to the concrete rubbish bin.

In the bottom lay the empty tin of Heinz beans with frankfurters we'd shared that night. Like my ashtray, the can contained many cigarette butts, but unlike my ashtray it also crawled with glossy maggots.

Sick at heart, I ran back to the car, sped away and arrived at Gretna Green Services ten minutes later, where I scoured the shop in vain for alcohol.

The Little Chef Lodge proved to be as well-equipped and functional as the Travelodge. Two suited guys in the lobby asked me what I was travelling in. I said an Austin Maestro and they both laughed. I guessed they drove Cavaliers.

The No Service light glowed on the Pocketphone, so I used the payphone. Middleton answered. 'Where are you?'

'Gretna Green. Why haven't you called? What news?'

'Nothing to report. Cellnet can't trace the call Sarah made to you for now. System down. Just carry on. I will call, the moment I hear. Good luck.'

I forgot to ask her about Jerry. I didn't trust the woman anyway.

The Little Chef curry proved a poor choice for supper, and I slept fitfully. I dreamt of Sarah, naked, walking zombie-like towards me through a forest, a gory knife protruding from her chest. She opened her mouth and frothy blood oozed out. Her mouth twisted into a mocking grin, but she didn't speak, only gurgled.

I jerked awake, heart racing. A rustling sound. From outside. Followed by a knock on the door.

I blurted out, 'Sarah, is that you?'

'Sorry mate, wrong room.'

A rep. Drunk.

I slumped back to the pillow.

Next morning, I was on the road at 10am, still dog-tired, and nauseous after a very full and greasy English—correction, Scottish—at the restaurant.

I didn't want to arrive late, but not too early either. Midday would be ideal.

As I drove, anxiety replaced the monotony of the previous day. I gripped the steering wheel and hunched over it, my nose almost on the windscreen, as if that would help me arrive sooner.

I tuned the radio to Jimmy Young. His inane patter didn't help. I wished I'd brought the tape compilation from the VW. A blast of cheery Rick Astley would provide a connection to Sarah, recall the carefree times of peace and love we'd enjoyed at Faslane.

My eyes flicked down to the digital clock.

10.30am. Six hours until the timer fuses on *HMS Repulse* detonated.

I switched to Radio 1, but they were playing the Boomtown Rats. Not *that* song, the one I never want to hear again, but 'Someone's Looking at You'. Still spooky. I turned it off and drove in silence.

As on the previous day, I made steady progress. No need for a stop. I skirted Glasgow and crossed the Clyde. On the other side of the river I sneaked a glance at the road atlas on the passenger seat. Around twenty-five miles to run.

Loch Lomond glinted through the trees.

Roundabout coming up. Left to Helensburgh. My stomach tightened with apprehension.

I identified the Citroën almost at once. They'd pulled the 2CV off the road by a field entrance. I'd never seen it before, but with CND symbols on the doors and flowers painted on the boot it could be none other. What had the girls called it? Mindy.

The huge bonnet, incorporating the air grille for the engine, stood open like the gaping maw of a basking crocodile.

Beverley sat behind the wheel, the sunroof rolled right back above her head. She twisted to look as I changed down and slowed.

No sign of Debbie. Perhaps they'd split up and gone separate ways from Brighton.

I pulled off the road, got out and smelled the burning at once.

She got out too. 'Ken! Are you following us or what, man? Why didn't you show at the bar in Brighton? Debbie was spitting blood. And why in the name of all that's holy are you back in Scotland? They'll tear you limb from limb at Faslane if you show up like that.'

'Like what?'

'All scrubbed and fluffy-haired in a brand-new motor, a rich kid in Daddy's car, a spy.'

'I couldn't make the meeting. I phoned the pub but missed you. You didn't say where you were staying. I'll explain everything, but not now. Time is short and Sarah is in danger. She's at the peace camp or close by.'

'Not as of yesterday she wasn't. We phoned Jerry.'

'I'll tell you about Jerry too. What's up with the 2CV? And where's Debbie?'

'We smelled burning. We opened the bonnet and smoke billowed out. I poured our water bottle over it and it seemed to work. Nobody stopped to help. I suggested we flag down a car, but Debbie said no, some cocky jerk would try and chat us up then abuse us when he realised we were lesbians. So she set off up the road to the roundabout. There's a cottage. She'll use their phone, call the camp and get Mitch to come out.'

'I know about motors too. Let me have a look.'

We peered into the engine compartment. These 2CVs were about as simple as a car could get. Air-cooled engine, front wheel drive, no frills, no electronics. I saw the problem at once. 'The heater tubes use cardboard as insulation. See? That dump hose has lost its Jubilee clip and fallen on the exhaust manifold. It's lucky you stopped and put out the fire or you could have lost the vehicle.'

I found a stick in the hedge and poked around the engine, brushing away the charred cardboard. 'No damage done. A hose clip and some cable ties will get you home. You'll need a new set of heater tubes for a permanent fix. I recommend solid rubber next time.'

'That's a relief. I thought Mindy was a goner.'

'Lucky I arrived. Hop in my car, we'll pick up Debbie and buy the bits in Helensburgh. Mitch can bring you back and fix Mindy. I'm afraid I won't have time.'

'I don't want to leave her.'

'Debbie?'

'No, you clot, Mindy. I'm in this field entrance and if the farmer arrives he'll shove the car out of the way with his tractor.'

'We'll push her clear. Leave a note.'

'No. I'll stay here and wait. We've got all our stuff in the boot. Banners, spray paints, cutters, climbing aids. If the cops spot the car, they'll stop and rummage around, plant evidence, revoke our bail. Will you pick up Debbie and go on with her? She can come back with Mitch. If Mitch isn't there, you must come back yourself. I can't imagine what you have to do at Faslane that's time-critical this afternoon.'

'You wouldn't believe me if I told you. Right-oh, I'll find Debbie. How long since she left?'

'Five minutes? She won't have reached the crossroads.' She looked up at me. 'Thanks for this, anyway.'

I soon reached Debbie, striding along the opposite carriageway to face the traffic, arms swinging, her big embroidered canvas bag over her shoulder.

No one behind me. I stopped in the road, engine running, opened the window and called out, 'Hi, Debbie.'

It took her a second to recognise me again. 'It's you. The bad penny. You *are* stalking us. Now what do you want?'

'Beverley said to pick you up and go on to Helensburgh. I can fix the car but need parts. Don't argue, hop in and I'll explain everything.'

Which to her credit she did.

'Chuck the road atlas in the back.' I put the Pocketphone on my lap.

'So. Explain everything.'

'Sarah has been kidnapped by Irish Republican terrorists, cold-blooded murderers. I suspect they're holding her in St Andrew's School. The old mansion. Last Sunday night, under cover of our stunt, their divers swam up to *HMS Repulse* and placed limpet mines on the hull. These will detonate at 4.30pm today unless I stop them. Jerry is an accomplice to this sabotage plot.'

Debbie turned her head to look at me. I met her gaze for two seconds. 'And are you still a journalist today, or have you adopted a different Walter Mitty identity?'

'Look in the glove box.'

She found my Press pass. She turned it over in her fingers. 'Right … your story is so far-fetched I am concerned it might be true.'

'Every word.'

She considered for a moment. 'So why are you driving alone back to Faslane hours before this deadline?'

'There is a way to disarm the mines, involving a code. I have the best chance of obtaining that code, because I was the chosen conduit for their demands.'

'Which are?'

'Usual Republican stuff … prisoner releases. They made me an unwitting go-between. I believe they'll want to hear what I say, thinking it must come from the Government. They gave me this phone. That's how I worked out where Sarah must be. The terrorists will accept I'm there to negotiate.'

'And are you?'

'No. I'm freelancing.'

'So what is the Government's plan?'

'No idea. Thatcher is likely to respond with deadly force if she discovers where the terrorists are. But despite top MI5 spooks on the case, they haven't worked out they're at Faslane. If it comes down to an armed raid, the marines or the SAS going in, Sarah will likely die in the crossfire, along with the gang, and *HMS Repulse* is doomed—which you might think an acceptable outcome.'

'Which bit of that might I find acceptable?'

'*Repulse* sunk.'

'Can the crew evacuate?'

'The escape towers are likely to be booby-trapped and depth fuses prevent them surfacing.'

'I'd be overjoyed to see a Polaris sub at the bottom of the ocean, but not with the crew aboard. I stand for peace, remember. If you're freelancing, what can you say or do?'

We arrived at the roundabout. Left to Helensburgh. 'I don't know, Debbie.'

'If they gave you that expensive mobile phone, and enlisted you as negotiator, why didn't they call you on it, to see what was happening?'

'They did, sort of. But that channel of communication seems to be closed now. Not sure why.'

'Are you being followed—tailed?'

'Don't know again. There's a radio tracker in the phone. MI5 can find me. But it only has a range of a mile or two, and I've seen no suspicious vehicles in my mirror all day. They think I'm heading to Glasgow, Prestwick or Edinburgh. So I hope I have several hours' head start. Enough to make this crazy journey pay off.'

'How can I help?'

I jerked my head to the left, trying to read her expression. 'You believe me and you'll help?'

'For Sarah's sake, and the crew's. Some of them are teenagers.'

'First, please tell me, Debbie, you and Sarah ... you seemed to have such rapport. Did you have a thing ...? I mean I saw you swimming, and she seemed to be naked in the water, and she is so lovely, I wouldn't blame—'

'Do I fancy Sarah? Yes. Did we have a fling? No. A few laughs, a few cuddles, girls' stuff. Women are not driven by sex, Ken, like you are. We make affectionate companions for each other. Men are natural competitors. Women are natural allies.' I sneaked another glance at her. Debbie's face displayed no artifice, no pretence. 'I'm not a threat to you, Ken, I never have been, and Sarah is into you in a big way. She defended you when I said you were a jerk. Which you can be. For example, when you harangued Bev and me on the seafront in Brighton, bullied me into meeting you and then never showed.'

'Circumstances beyond my control. I am sorry. I hadn't met Beverley before.'

'We're not an item either. Just good friends. We always go to the Tories' conference. Then on to Greenham Common to support the sisters. Back to Faslane today ready for the big demo tomorrow.'

'I did wonder about Beverley. She is rather old for you.'

'God, Ken, you are so middle-aged. You're twenty-one going on forty-five! Age is not the issue. I'm twenty-one, she's thirty-eight. Those are numbers. But I don't work by numbers. I'm not a computer or a robot. I am powered by love. I'm a gentle angry woman in a world of mad men. Gentle with the people I treasure. Angry with the men who want to blow up our world, bomb us back to the Stone Age, poison the air we breathe, the land and the oceans that sustain us. I'm angry with the politicians, mind, not the poor souls who work at the base or go down in the subs. Now what is your plan when we arrive in about ten minutes?'

'You said Sarah will never marry me. Did she tell you that?'

'She never mentioned marriage. I don't see her bowing down to the status quo of the patriarchy. Ken, put your neuroses to one side, man. We need a plan. The camp is packed full of folk preparing for tomorrow. Lots of little kids.'

'Get Jerry alone. Confront him. Say we know the kidnappers are up in the school. Smoke him out. He might arrange safe passage for me.'

'What makes you think Jerry is part of the conspiracy?'

'I have no proof. Are you aware the police raided the camp on Wednesday morning? After you left for Brighton?'

'Jerry mentioned it on the phone. Said they'd come on a fishing expedition.'

'Did you tell Colin, Mitch and everyone your plans?'

'Of course.'

'They pretended not to know, then.'

'Very sensible. We broke our bail conditions by going on the demo. Our local cops would have alerted the Brighton cops. Did they search the camp?'

'Yes, including the old school.'

'Yet you still believe the school is their hideout, and Jerry is their accomplice, though you have no evidence, and the rozzers couldn't find any either?'

'That's about the size of it, Debs. The clue was the vehicle hooter. The last call I received on this'—I lifted the Pocketphone—'was from Sarah. She was speaking under duress. In the background I heard a horn blaring. Like they do at five in the morning, to wake us up and wind us up.'

'You're clutching at straws, Ken. It could have been any vehicle anywhere.'

'I know.'

We entered Helensburgh.

I said, 'If Jerry is innocent, he won't mind coming with us up to the school. He knows about the mines attached to *Repulse*. Photos arrived in an envelope addressed to me and we opened it together. He tried to phone the base and warn them.'

'That rather torpedoes your theory, if you'll excuse the turn of phrase.'

'Yeah.' We drove into sudden sunlight. We cruised down the seafront, busy at lunchtime. Mothers pushed buggies containing well-wrapped toddlers along the pavement. A gaggle of school-children in uniform milled around on the promenade, three female teachers in a flap trying to keep them together.

I spotted the Palace Restaurant. How long since I'd bought the never-to-be-eaten fish and chips? Our engagement celebration meal. Less than three days ago. It seemed like months.

Debbie said, 'What parts do you need for Mindy?'

'A jumbo hose clip and some cable ties. Mitch will have them in his toolkit. Let's keep going.'

My heart rate picked up as we wound along the lochside road, past the point where Trapper and Radar abducted me.

Let her be here.

Let her survive.

Bait

Friday 14th October 1988, 1.10pm, 14°C, sunny intervals

WE ROUNDED the last bend and the peace camp appeared, wreathed in sunshine for once, its hoardings and caravans festive, the Welcome sign bright with fresh paint. For an instant my mind's eye conjured up an image of our faithful camper van backed up to the fence inside the gate. Just a gap there now, a vacant space where Sarah and I had worked, played, smoked and drank, laughed and made love, bickered and teased.

I parked alongside a beaten-up Minivan, its rear doors secured with rope. We entered the camp and I saw many new faces, although they all seemed to know Debbie and welcomed her with cheery greetings.

They'd roofed over the open space between the communal caravan and the office with blue tarpaulins, and set up trestle tables under this rudimentary shelter, at which women painted banners. At a further makeshift table formed from a cable reel a gaggle of pre-school children sat at work on smaller posters under the watchful eye of Joan.

Little Archie leapt down from his stool. 'Ken! You're in time for the big fence party!' He held up his poster which depicted a submarine in a dustbin with the words 'TRASH TRIDENT!' above in an adult hand.

'That's great painting, Archie. What's a fence party?'

'We march down and decorate the fence with lots and lots and lots of posters, and flowers, and love letters to the workers, and our special sign, and we sing songs, and plant bulbs, and you're allowed to paint your shadow on the pavement, the nice policeman came and said! And there will be zillions of us.'

Joan collected up Archie in her arms. 'Debbie! Welcome home. How was Brighton? And Greenham Common? Where's Beverley?' She glared at me as if she held me responsible for Bev's absence. 'And what's he doing back here with you?'

'We broke down. Ken picked me up. We need Mitch to fix Mindy. Is he around?'

'Happenin', Debs?' came the familiar cruel Glasgow brogue from behind me. 'And Ken the man. How's yer lassie, yer wee nyaff? Did ye get back together?'

I turned and said, 'Not yet, Mitch. Can you ride down to rescue Bev? You'll need a fifty-mil hose clip and some cable ties, even string would do, to get her home. Heater hose come off Mindy.'

'Nae problem. Whur's she broke doon?'

While Debbie briefed Mitch, I strode towards Jerry's caravan and flung open the door.

It was all cosy inside. Jerry stood fiddling with his handheld police scanner. He looked up in surprise and dismay. 'Ken! What are you doing here?'

I pulled the flimsy door shut behind me. 'I'm going up to the school, Jerry. Debbie knows everything.'

His face tilted down towards me, pale and pinched. 'Why would you do that? There's nothing to see up there. No one. The police searched all the buildings on Wednesday morning.'

His scanner burst to life. 'Patrol Two-Four to base. Radio check please. Over.'

He turned the device off. 'For tomorrow,' he explained. 'We'll know what the Plods are up to before they do. We're expecting Bruce Kent and five hundred for the march.'

The door opened and Debbie entered. Jerry's eyes flicked from me to her. 'Debs, tell Ken nothing's doing at the old school.'

Her eyes narrowed. 'In that case, there's no harm walking up to look, is there?'

He said, 'Don't. You're needed here. Colin and Spike will be back from Greencity Wholefoods with the lentils and rice any minute. Joan can't handle everything. We've got at least twenty to feed tonight. It's not fair of you to leave it all to her.'

I said, 'They're holding Sarah in the school, aren't they, Jerry?'

'Who are?' He blinked in feigned innocence.

'The people who planted the bombs on *HMS Repulse*. The people who passed the Polaroids to you. I should have realised, that morning you took me up the school. You pretended to search the house and sent me off to the dormitories. I thought at the time it was strange that you got inside so easily. The place is well boarded up. "I got in round the back." What bull crap. You'd set up a hideout for them.'

In the corner, Jerry's wood burner blazed as if just replenished with logs. Seeing my expression, he put down his precious scanner with trembling hands. I advanced on him and began with a sharp jab to the stomach, a baby brother of the one I'd received from Gavin. Jerry doubled up. I pushed him backwards, anger fuelling my strength. I shoved him up hard against his wood burner. The backs of his legs touched the glass doors. I grabbed his collar and bashed his head against the cast-iron flue pipe.

'Ow—shit, man! My chinos! My legs—you'll burn me!'

'That is the intention. They are up at the school, aren't they?'

Debbie stood to one side. She did not intervene.

'Let me go! Jesus, Mary and Joseph, Ken, are you mad? Debbie, tell him to stop! Get help! Call Mitch!'

I caught the first whiff of scorching fabric.

Singing started up outside. The banner mums, led by Joan's warbling soprano, and accompanied, I judged, by Archie and his little friends on percussion. Wooden spoons beaten on saucepan-lid cymbals and margarine-tub bongos.

'We all hate Maggie's big black submarines, scary submarines, horrid submarines, we all hate ...'

Debbie stood her ground and said, 'Mitch has left on his bike. No one outside can hear you.'

I held Jerry against the heat. He whimpered, 'It's for your own good, Ken! I'm just trying to protect you.'

'From what, Jerry?' I grabbed a handful of his hair and bashed his head on the stove pipe again, harder.

'Don't go there. You mustn't. You'll … they'll … they'll kill you.'

'I knew it.' I pulled him forward, shoved him on to his sofa and turned to Debbie, my breath whistling through my teeth. 'I'm going up the hill now.'

'We all hate Maggie's big black submarines, stinky submarines, pooey submarines …' The kids' turn, with their own gleeful chorus.

'I'll come with you,' Debbie said. 'Jerry, you are the scum of the earth. You snake. You spawn of the devil. You plausible, cowardly piece of shit. What have you done with Sarah?'

'Not me. Honest, I didn't know. They never told me their plan. Just a baby IED,[25] they said, on the night you all broke in. To disable the sub. Blow off the propeller, they hoped. Not to sink it. Not out at sea. Not to hurt anyone. Not to kidnap anyone. I swear, I knew nothing. You can't go up the hill. I mean it, they'll kill you. The deadline is four-thirty.'

Outside, the women and children carolled on unawares. 'Smelly submarines, yucky submarines …'

Jerry put his head in his hands. 'Call the Plods if you must. Call the commandos. But it won't help. Sarah will die if you do. No one can save her except Margaret Thatcher. I didn't want this to happen. You gotta believe me.'

'Let's go, Ken,' Debbie said.

'No, Debs. Stay here and mind this arsehole. See he doesn't tip off his mates using his Vodafone. They've got the twin of my Pocketphone up there, haven't they, Jerry?'

Jerry nodded, his face contorted with misery, whether real or confected I couldn't tell and didn't care. 'I won't warn them. I'm a peacemaker. I fight for justice. The law in defence of the common man. They fooled me. I'm a victim here, like you two.'

---

[25] Improvised Explosive Device.

Debbie said, 'I'll come with you, Ken, and stay out of sight. Give me your mobile. I'll hide in the trees, sound the alarm if there's trouble.'

'Right. Good idea.' I reached down to the floor and hoisted up Jerry's heavy Motorola rig. 'Even better, let's take his phone.'

'He can still call them from the camp telephone.'

Jerry struggled to his feet. 'I'll come with you. I know the way in. I have the key. I'll let you in. They won't suspect if I give the special knock.'

I looked from him to Debbie. She nodded. I said, 'All right. Not a word when we leave here. Look more cheerful as we go through the camp.'

I opened the door and stepped down. Jerry followed and Debbie brought up the rear as we hurried down the gravel path. At the gate I extracted the Pocketphone from the waistband of my jeans and handed it to Debbie. 'You key in the complete number then press Send,' I explained. From my notebook I tore out Sethia's cell number. 'They won't take you seriously at the Clyde Submarine Base. Call this guy Narendra Sethia if I'm not out in an hour. He's an ex-naval officer working for MI5.'

She nodded.

We squeezed between the Maestro and the minivan, both parked up close to the gate to avoid blocking the pull-in to the bus stop. I took up station on Jerry's left with Debbie on the right. I prepared to grab him, if he did a runner. And I'd give him the full Gavin if he shouted out to warn his cronies.

'How many of them?' I demanded.

'Don't know. They come from the other direction. Through the woods from Station Road. Two or three. Sometimes they leave her locked up.'

'Where are they holding her?'

Debbie said, 'Jerry, you go in with Ken and show him.'

'They have knives. They'll kill me. Do it yourself, man. They don't have a problem with you. You did what they told you. She's in the attic.'

'They locked my girl in the attic?' Rage built inside me. I willed myself not to give way to it, to stay in control.

The track curved to the left as we ascended, Jerry puffing a lot, me a little, Debbie the Olympic-class swimmer showing no sign of exertion. The mansion came into view, its boarded windows dead eyes.

'Which part of the house? The place is monstrous.'

'Keep going and I'll show you. Stay out of sight as long as possible. They don't always have a lookout, but today, they'll be edgy.'

We continued, keeping under cover of the saplings, and crossed the ornamental stone bridge. The river flowed underneath this down the hill to the culvert we'd used on the night of the raid.

Ahead lay open ground, a large area of tarmac in front of the mansion for car parking. On the right were playing fields. Two rugby goalposts protruded from waist-high grass and weeds. I hoped the troubled inmates of St Andrew's School had derived some pleasure from their sport. I doubted they'd enjoyed many happy days within the walls of the institution.

We halted, unable to proceed further without exposing ourselves to view.

'Wait there.' Jerry pointed out a large bushy fern beside the bridge. We ducked down behind it. From here we had a reasonable view of the front and east elevations of Shandon House. 'See that tower with the pyramid top? The one in the middle of the building?' I peered upwards at the grey ivy-clad walls. The architect had channelled his inner Brothers Grimm into multiple turrets with inverted ice-cream-cone roofs. I counted four from our vantage point alone, with enough slit windows for an entire family of Rapunzels.

I identified the tower he meant, surmounted by an orb and crucifix, the only square-sided one and the highest, rising priapically from the nether regions of the building, a giant erection in every sense.

Jerry said, 'We use a door on the north side. I'll give the knock, let you in, then run. I'm a dead man if they catch me.'

'Suppose they've left Sarah alone in the attic and there's no one else at home?'

'Then you make your way to that square tower. Up the main staircase, you can't miss it, keep going to the third floor. Take a right down the corridor signed "Sister and Sanatorium". Halfway down, stairs lead to the room just below the roof. That leftmost room with the dormer.' He pointed and glanced sidelong at me to see if I understood. 'Look, nearest the tiny tower with the slit window under the square parapet. To the left of the graffiti, see it now?'

I saw it. Beside the window, barely legible in faded red capitals and half-covered with ivy, someone had spray-painted, 'Up Yer Bum, Nuclear Scum'. It wasn't clear if that referred to the peace protesters or the submarine base in the loch below.

The parapet he'd pointed out featured battlements and squared-off crenellations, several of which sported CND logos. There must be access to this parapet from inside the building, as the platform was way beyond the reach of any ladder bar a firefighter's.

As if on cue from an unseen film director on the payroll of Hammer Productions, the sun ducked behind a large dark cloud. A keen breeze piped up, whirling the dead leaves on the car park into rustling eddies.

Jerry said, 'There's a door in the corner of that room leading to a spiral staircase which takes you up to the tower window. You'll find a ladder propped up on the landing. That gives access to a hatch in the ceiling. She's inside the pyramid roof. At the highest point of the house.'

'There's no window in the roof—so no light or air in the attic?'

'Plenty of air through the eaves and loose slates. There are lanterns and flashlights.'

'Jesus. Sarah's been imprisoned up there since Monday night?'

Jerry screwed up his weasely face in embarrassment. 'She's a strong girl. She'll be all right. I hope. This is not what I wanted.'

'Jerry, you bastard, you sat warming yourself in your caravan playing the innocent abroad, while my precious Sarah languished up there in the cold and dark?' I resisted the urge to punch him in the face.

Debbie did the job for me. She raised two clenched fists and boxed Jerry's ears. I'd never seen anyone do that before. The effect was most gratifying. With a yelp, Jerry fell forward from his crouching position, his beaky nose ending up in the clammy leaf mould. Debbie hauled him up by the collar.

'We need Jerry for a while, Debs. He deserves a good hiding but not now. Jerry, do we have to cross the car park? Wouldn't it be better to go around the rear of the buildings?'

'It's too overgrown that way and there are barbed wire coils which they planned to lay all round but never did. We'll be fine. Hug the building and we're out of sight from the upper floors. All the windows this side are boarded anyway.'

'You'll stay here, Debbie?'

'Yes. I'm ready.' She held up the phone.

'Here goes.' My pulse rate quickened.

I checked the time. 1.24pm.

Jerry and I stood and moved forward. I darted my eyes over the façade of the house, scanning for movement.

About halfway across, in the centre of the car park, Jerry said, 'You won't believe what it's like inside. Very dark, hard to get around. You'll need my flashlight. Furniture and trash and—'

At this point several things happened at once.

Moisture splattered my face and Jerry disappeared. Three gunshots cracked out, and something stung my cheek.

A group of crows, disturbed by the shots, clattered out of the oak tree on the playing field with caws of alarm.

I turned. The bullets had lifted Jerry and thrown him backwards. He lay on the weed-infested tarmac, arms outstretched, blood pooling from his head. Or to be precise, which I like to be, blood pooling from the mushy red, white and grey mess where his head had been.

I stared, trying to make sense of the scene. Two shots to the head in a tight group had left little by which to recognise Jerry. His face had exploded like a melon hit with a sledgehammer.

The third shot had entered his chest. Only a little blood stained his shirt. The expanding bullet had stopped his heart —no, destroyed it—in a millisecond. If I turned him over I knew all three exit wounds would be the size of tennis balls.

There was no need to check for a pulse. Anyway, you can't give CPR to someone missing both his nose and mouth.

My stomach heaved and churned. I averted my gaze, took and held a deep breath, and managed not to puke up.

Something ran down my cheek. I wiped it with the back of my hand. Blood, though whether mine, Jerry's or a combination I could not tell.

I'd seen the muzzle flashes in my peripheral vision: bright orange pulses from on high. The gunman had fired from the square crenellated parapet. I looked up and glimpsed a black balaclava-clad head duck behind a battlement.

I ran my hand over my cheek and winced at a stab of pain. Something sharp embedded there. I prised out a shard of glass. Closer examination showed it to be a sliver of Jerry's skull or jawbone.

The three shots had sounded in quick succession, delivered by a semi-automatic rifle, probably an AR-180 or an AK-47. Both weapons were popular with Republican paramilitaries. Twenty rounds in the magazine for the Armalite, thirty for the AK—more than enough to dispose of me too without reloading.

Most likely an Armalite with scope sights. Only a marksman of great skill could achieve that accuracy with a Kalashnikov.

But the gunman hadn't dropped me. I remained standing, unharmed except for the cheek, which bled profusely. My left hand was slippery with the stuff.

They didn't want me dead.

At least not yet.

Even so, I scuttled towards the cover of the house, moving closer to the gunman's position but presenting an ever-increasing downward angle of fire.

My advice to Debbie now seemed stupid. I hoped she wasn't attempting to call Seth but had instead dialled 999 for the police. From her hiding place she might not have seen Jerry's injuries, might decide to investigate. I prayed that instead she was running as fast as her long, muscular legs could carry her down the hill to get the children shut away and wait for help.

I reached Shandon House and stood with my back to the perforated metal sheeting which covered the front door, my bloody hand pressed to my cheek. I stole a quick glance upwards and to the left. I was out of the gunman's line of sight here, protected by the ice-cream cone tower above the portico which prevented him leaning over and shooting straight downwards through the top of my head.

Now what? Carry on, or do a runner?

I calculated they'd be more likely to shoot me if I ran away than if I advanced. They'd targeted Jerry, realising he'd betrayed them. If I ran, it could only be to raise the alarm.

Not what they wanted with Thatcher's speech about to start.

I checked my watch. The Iron Lady might be on her feet already.

I waited, trying to calm my breathing and dispel the image of Jerry, his head transformed by dumdum bullets into a grisly lump of raw meat.

Coward and rat though he was, he didn't deserve that fate.

Neither did Sarah or I.

The gang inside the mansion knew they were cornered. They wouldn't hesitate to dispose of her and me with equal callous cruelty unless they got … what? Even if Thatcher conceded all their demands, she wouldn't grant them safe passage from this place.

Except perhaps with us as hostages at gunpoint?

No. Not even then.

Neither of us would leave Shandon House alive.

I wished I'd kept my phone with me now. I was in a better position to brief the authorities.

The calls of the crows faded. Quiet returned, but not peace. I edged around the front of the house to the southwestern corner, keeping my back to the brickwork. I had to pass a large bay window. All boarded up at ground level, so no danger of being seen provided I hugged the wall. I glanced up. Two turrets clung to the corners of the bay at high level, resembling pepper pots, each with a long slit window. This place was more castle than mansion. Easy to defend. Hard to storm, even with crack troops.

I pressed on, fighting my way through brambles with thorny shoots that grabbed at my ankles as if animated by Disney. I half-expected them to whisper a warning: 'Don't go on! Don't go in!'

I rounded the northwestern corner. Ahead I should find the door Jerry had mentioned.

I realised the key was still in Jerry's pocket, along with his torch.

I'd have to return to the car park, cross the open expanse of tarmac and grope in the corpse's pockets. There would be more blood than before. My stomach heaved again at the prospect.

I pressed on in case they'd left the back door unlocked, as Jerry had said he found it when we came up earlier in search of Sarah.

Weeds and ivy enveloped the rear of the house, grown rampant in the two years since the school closed. I found a rusty hoe leaning in a recess and used that to hack a path through the nettles. The door, when I came upon it, was small, with 'Kitchen Deliveries' engraved into the stonework above the lintel.

The handle turned and the latch lifted. I pushed, and the door opened smoothly.

Although what I'd hoped for, this didn't seem right.

I edged in, holding my breath, fully expecting a welcoming committee armed with guns, knives or chloroform.

Nobody inside. No sound of voices, or footsteps.

Jerry's assassins didn't care if I showed up. Or they wanted me to show up, and were biding their time, waiting their moment to pounce.

I stood in a still room or boot room with a wooden draining board and an old-fashioned butler's sink.

I glanced down.

Recent footprints in the dirt on the tiled floor.

This was a trap, waiting to be sprung. I was the prey.

And Sarah was the bait.

Last Rites

Friday 14th October 1988, 1.38pm, 14°C

I TIPTOED across the room and opened the door in the opposite wall. I stood at the junction of two corridors.

I crept forward and peeped into the first room I came to. Daylight, filtered by grimy unboarded windows at high level, showed it to be tiled throughout in white, with soap dishes embedded in the walls every metre.

Above these dishes, metal conduits carried an electrical ring main all around. Once a communal shower room, converted to a laundry? The floor drains and mains outlets were suggestive of a Nazi torture chamber.

I advanced into the near-darkness, listening out every few paces and dabbing my bloody cheek with the cuff of my pullover.

I peered through the next doorway into a small room, again illuminated by a high window. The housekeeper's office, latterly the school secretary's lair. Filing cabinets, a desk and a phone remained *in situ*.

A bookshelf held a Bible and some religious trinkets: a garish ceramic Virgin Mary with baby Jesus in her lap, a white plastic angel holding a crucifix with 'Charity' painted on its surplice. Where were 'Faith' and 'Hope'? I found them on the floor together, next to a neatly-curled, desiccated dog turd.

Also on the floor lay scattered magazines. Porno mags. No — closer inspection revealed them to be catalogues, well-chewed by rodents, advertising sex aids. Explicit photographs showed the use of the products. 'Pleasure Prober', 'Honey Pot', 'Mr Pecker',

'School Canes All Lengths and Thicknesses.' Maybe the abandoned reading matter of the school janitor.

I carried on to the end of the corridor and passed under an ornamental arch. Enough light seeped around the boarded windows to reveal a grand hall some thirty metres long, stretching across the ground floor from side to side. Decorative plasterwork was much in evidence. Columns, pilasters, finials, the full Gothic Jacobethan monty. Carved stone owls stood sentry on ledges in nooks, moulded ropes twined around window frames.

At the far end, to my right, the floor-to-ceiling picture windows would have let in the evening sun had they not been boarded. At the other end, a wide and grand staircase rose to a half-landing with east-facing windows. From here, staircases on each side mounted to the upper floors.

I turned left, climbed the stairs, listening, running through Jerry's directions in my head. 'Keep going to the third floor' proved a challenge, as the stairs stopped at the second. I cast around and found the sign 'Sister and Sanatorium' on the wall above a fire hose reel. Perhaps Americans labelled their floors differently.

Up here, the rooms were plain and utilitarian, the ceilings lower. I guessed this was staff accommodation in the house's heyday, also accessible from a back staircase leading down to the kitchens. They hadn't bothered to board these windows.

I glanced through open doorways. Odd pieces of modern furniture remained. A red melamine table, wooden chairs stacked in twos seat to seat, a chest of drawers missing its drawers. In a toilet with a high Victorian chain flush, rolls of faded linoleum stood on end.

My trainers squeaked on boards once polished to a shine by the child inmates.

I came to a pinboard with notices still in place, curled and yellowing, some held by a single drawing pin.

<u>Sanatorium w/c Monday 2nd June 1986</u>
Machlachan, G.H.
Kelly, D.W.E.
Sweeney, P.
Visitors strictly by appointment with Sister.
<u>Not to change (no sports)</u>
Duffy, F.C.
Curran, J.P.
Boyle, D.D.

A colour photograph showed Sister Enid, one of the few women the boys would have come into contact with. She looked prim but friendly, wearing not a scary Sister of Mercy habit but modern blue tunic and white cap.

I passed on, glanced to my left through an uncovered window and realised I was in entirely the wrong part of the building. Below me lay the former stable block. The inner tower, rising from the stable yard, was free-standing: a separate structure, a folly, with its own heavy double entrance doors.

Why had Jerry sent me up here? Ten precious minutes wasted!

I'd answered my own question.

I turned on my heel to retrace my steps. I needed to get back to ground level, out of the door and further round the north side of the mansion to the stable yard, accessible through the wide archway I could now see.

What was that rustling?

Mice or birds, I judged.

But mice or birds don't whistle, at least not a louder and louder whistle with a rising tone, nor do they clink teaspoons in mugs.

I turned again and advanced on my original path, heart thumping.

Sarah emerged from the farthermost door off the corridor.

She said, 'I've made myself a last cup of tea. I can make you one too.'

I sprinted down to meet her. She wore her Kicker boots, grubby jeans and a thick blue cardigan much too big for her over a man's check shirt, untucked, the tails of which flapped around her thighs. She got her first good look at me as I neared.

'What bloody man is that?'[26]

'It's little me.'

'It's gone everywhere, my poor love. Did I nick you?'

'Has it stopped bleeding?'

She reached up and touched my cheek, tight with congealing blood. 'Not quite. Come into my parlour. I'll clean you up.'

She took my hand and led me into Sister Enid's anteroom.

Under a stainless-steel drainer and sink, an empty compartment would have housed a fridge or washing machine. On the drainer stood a plastic flagon of water with a dispenser tap, a Camping Gaz picnic stove with a single burner screwed straight on to the cylinder, the whistling kettle, two mugs, teabags, a carton of milk and a dirty packet of sugar with a spoon sticking out of it. A wooden chair, a window with grubby net curtains but no boarding and a large white metal wall cabinet with a red cross on it completed the inventory.

She said, 'They left the first aid kit. Isn't that lucky?' She opened the cabinet and took down a box of Elastoplast, gauze and a pair of scissors.

'You're free to roam around? Where are they?'

She gave me a bright smile. Her eyes told a different story. Red-rimmed, with dark bags underneath. She'd tied her hair back, her wonderful hair which always glowed with health, now lying flat and lifeless as if glued down to her scalp.

'Oh yes, this is my domain. Although I see myself as Miss Havisham rather than Lady Macbeth. Come here into the light.' She drew aside the grey net curtain, wadded the gauze and wetted it from the water flagon. I stepped up to her. She dabbed at my wound, her breath on my face an intimacy both familiar and troubling.

'Ouch!'

---

[26] *Macbeth* (1.2.1) King Duncan's exclamation when a wounded captain brings him news of Macbeth's bravery in battle.

'Sorry. A fragment of bone. Hold on.' She darted to the first aid box and returned with a pair of tweezers and plastic bottle. 'That's why it kept bleeding. Stand still.' With one hand to part the wound and tweezers in the other she probed for a minute then turned away. A small piece of Jerry pinged into the steel sink. 'All done. Don't move. A little sting now.' She took up the bottle and squeezed. I winced as the iodine flowed into the wound. She dabbed the skin around the area dry, cut a long strip of the Elastoplast and applied it. She stood back. 'Not pretty, but it will have to do.'

'Where are the kidnappers? The gunmen? Why are you so calm, my love? Come here.' I opened my arms.

'I must look a dreadful state. Probably a bit stinky too.'

'You look gorgeous.' I took her in my arms and after a moment's reluctance she yielded and embraced me, her hands patting my back, then encircling my waist. We kissed and for a second the world stopped turning and all was right, even if she'd run out of toothpaste or perhaps lost her toothbrush, very unlike her.

'Where are they?' I repeated. 'Have they hurt you? If you're free to move around, why can't we just get out of here? Are they up on the battlements still?'

She broke free, turned and faced the window, hoping I wouldn't notice the tears. She wiped a finger under each eye. 'I can go anywhere in the house and tower but I can't leave. Kinda "Hotel California".'

'Why not? Jerry said they left you alone for long periods.'

'I don't know why Jerry said that, and we can't ask him now. Ken, my love, there is no "they". "They" is just me.'

I screwed up my face at this conundrum. 'Just you?'

'Just little me. And now, little you.'

'Then who ... Jerry ... how ...'

'He was threatening everything.'

'What's "Everything"? Who killed Jerry, if it's only you here now?'

'You don't get it, do you? It's just me now, and it was just me then.'

'You mean, you …'

She gave a tiny nod. 'I think you'd better leave, Ken.'

'Leave? You mean leave you behind? When I've just rescued you? Why would I do that?'

'Are you saying you still love me, Ken? You'll stand by me?'

'I've missed you so much. I can't take this in. I'm not understanding the situation. But I'll always love you.'

She tilted her head to one side and raised her eyebrows. 'Do you still want to marry me?'

'I do. Though I never returned with the fish and chips. You have every right to retract. Did you mean it when I proposed and you replied, "Yes, of course?"'

'I mean what I say and say what I mean. You know that. It might prove difficult to arrange a wedding any time soon.'

'I can wait.'

'You see, I love you too. That is a complication. Of this situation.'

'Now you're talking in riddles.'

She turned for a second to wipe away more tears before they escaped down her cheeks. 'Let's get married. There's just time, before you leave.'

'Get married? Great! The sooner the better. We'll need a minister. And two witnesses. There's a submarine commander I met in Brighton. They're allowed to conduct a marriage, aren't they? I can phone him now. Oh no, I can't. I gave away my phone. But you've got yours, haven't you?'

'We'd need to go aboard his vessel. I don't believe they can marry people anywhere on a whim over the phone. Anyway, he's not here and we don't have time. Thatcher will be up on her hind legs braying at any moment.'

I glanced at my watch. 1.55pm. And 12°C, for the record. Or the register.

She said, 'To hell with the formalities. Let's marry each other. Right now. Right here. Please. Let's say our vows.'

'You mean like pretend?'

'I won't pretend if you don't. God will see and bless our union.'

My eyes were misting up too. 'I know! There are three angels downstairs. Faith, Hope and Charity. They're plastic, not in the best possible taste, but I dare say Faith would agree to be the minister and the other two the witnesses.'

She said, 'Go gather them up while I get ready for you.'

With a whoop I raced down the corridor, pattered down the stairs, swivelled around the pineapple finial on the newel post and skidded into the office with the porno catalogues and the mouse droppings. I scooped up the two fallen angels from the floor and Charity from the bookshelf and bounded upstairs.

On arriving in the sanatorium corridor, I heard her yell out, 'Not ready yet! I'll tell you when! Find some rings!' I scooted into the anteroom. I flung open the drawer next to the sink and found two hoses for connecting a washing machine. With the medical tweezers I picked out the rubber washers from the couplings. I tried one on my ring finger. Not ideal: too small and constricting. I rummaged, and at the very back of the drawer discovered a small cardboard box without a lid containing drawing pins, paper clips and two rusty brass split ring curtain hooks. This stroke of good luck seemed a most propitious omen.

Her voice echoed down the corridor. 'Ready when you are!'

I caught sight of my reflection in a plastic-framed mirror on the wall opposite. The patch of Elastoplast did nothing for me. Neither did my left hand caked with dried blood on the knuckles and under the fingernails. At the sink, I hurried to clean up using the gauze and hot water from the kettle.

'The bride's getting nervous she'll be jilted!'

'Coming!' I dried my hands on more gauze and stood to compose myself for what I hoped would be a dignified entry.

'Go into the sickbay and wait by the altar!'

They'd dismantled the metal-framed beds and piled them under the window, which had lost half its boarding. The room, a residual smell of Dettol lingering after two years, was otherwise empty apart from a pine chest of drawers on the far end wall. Sarah had pulled this out and spread a clean(ish) tea towel on top. I placed the rings and the three angels on the improvised altar, turned, stood and waited at attention.

Tease that she was, she kept me standing there for three minutes and thirty-five seconds. Had she jilted *me*—slipped away and down the stairs in her socks, Kickers under her arm?

She appeared in the doorway.

I gasped.

She wore the net curtain from the anteroom as a wedding veil and carried it off to perfection. As she entered, radiant and assured, my beautiful enigmatic bride glanced to left and right, acknowledging invisible friends and family in pews to each side with a nod or a smile. She stopped for a moment, looked back, checking her train or perhaps to encourage a little bridesmaid, then resumed her progress down the centre of the room.

'You'll have to imagine the bouquet,' she said. 'And the music. I wanted "Lagan Love" but I can only remember the first verse. I'll sing that.'

And she did, with a lilt in her voice that even I recognised as Irish.

> 'Where Lagan stream sings lullaby
> There blows a lily fair;
> The twilight gleam is in her eye
> The night is on her hair
> And like a love-sick Leanhaun-Shee
> Who has my heart in thrall
> Nor life I own nor liberty
> For love is lord of all.'

There wasn't a dry eye in the church. She arrived before me and stood expectantly, looking up from under fluttering eyelashes. I got the message, lifted her veil and said, 'Before we begin. The finishing touch.'

I produced the CND earrings from my pocket.

'Oh, great! I gave those to Debbie. Poor girl, I wanted her to have something to remember me by. Did she give them back to you?'

'Yes. You complained they pulled your earlobes down.'

'Well, they do. But a girl must suffer for her looks. Lovely to wear them one last time. Thank Debbie for me when you next see her.'

I handed the earrings over. 'Sorry, I lost the backs.'

'I'll take them off right after the ceremony.'

A thought struck me. 'Catholic or Protestant? We never discussed.'

'A bit of each would be fine. Whatever comes out. You start.'

I turned to the altar and picked up Faith. Holding her up beside my mouth, I did the amateur ventriloquist act with big grin and teeth just parted. 'In de gresence of God we are gathered here gogether teritness tharriage of Kennet and Sarah.'

She snorted with laughter. I replaced Faith. We joined hands and gazed into each other's eyes. She said, 'Seriously now.'

'I, Kenneth William, take you, Sarah Anne, to be my wife. To have and to hold from this day forward, for richer, for poorer, in sickness and in health, and I promise to love and cherish you all my life until death us do part.'

'You forgot "for better or for worse".'

'That too.'

'I, Sarah take you, Ken, to be my wedded husband. I promise to be true to you in good times and bad, in sickness and in health. I will love and honour you for all the days of my life.'

'Now the rings.' I placed hers on the outstretched finger. A little loose, but better than too tight. She admired it for a moment, then placed mine.

A perfect fit.

I picked up Faith and waggled her from side to side. 'You ay now giss de gride.' I threw the little figurine over my shoulder and we kissed.

She hadn't washed or showered for days, but I found that even more arousing. Her earthy, animal essence turned me on with a vengeance. We kissed long and with joy. I imagined the congregation watching with amusement and affection from their pews, getting restless, beginning to look at each other with eyebrows raised, glancing at their watches, fed up with the show and gasping for a glass of fizz.

They'd have to wait.

We came up for air and gazed at each other, her hazel eyes crossed to keep mine in focus. We began to explore each other's bodies, hands roaming under knitwear, our breathing now fast and shallow.

She whispered, 'I want you, Ken. You'll never abandon me, will you, whatever I've done?'

'No. I am yours forever. Like the vow says.'

We kissed again and when I next got the chance I said, 'While we're here, I'm wondering, just an idea, would you be happy to skip the reception and move straight on to the consummation?'

'I thought you'd never ask.' She glanced over her shoulder. 'Everyone's gone. Only the two of us left.' She reached down and her hand snaked into my waistband. 'Hmm. You seem to have already ticked the first box on the Pope's list with a fine *Erectio*. Let's see if you can complete his holy trinity of carnal delights.'

She unfastened my belt with practised fingers. She wasn't wearing a belt herself, so all I had to do was release the single popper and slide down her zip.

'The knickers are clean on today, in case you are wondering. Last pair.'

'Clean, grubby or none at all, I don't care, Mrs Sinclair!'

'Me neither. I'm ready for you, Mr Sinclair.'

'Yes, so you are.'

She bent to untie her laces, kicked off her boots and her jeans. I dropped my own jeans to my knees. I guided her backwards to the altar. With a flick of a hand I swept Hope and Charity to the floor. 'Sorry, girls! We need to clear the decks for action.'

The chest of drawers proved to be exactly the right height.

The Tower

Friday 14th October 1988, a few minutes later

I FETCHED the packet of cotton wool from the first aid cabinet. She used it, stuffed some more in her knickers then hopped around getting her jeans back on.

I'd banished the image of Jerry's mangled head from my mind, but reality now asserted itself. The surreal bubble of our reunion had burst. The hideous reality of what Sarah appeared to have done made me shiver.

The marriage had been make-believe but the murder of Jerry was real. Although right now, it felt the other way around.

She said, 'I wonder if I'm pregnant? I left my pills in the camper. What a happy thought to cling to.'

'Sarah, we need to cool it and think. Play for time. Do some serious talking. My hire car is down at the camp. We can be away in five minutes. There's enough fuel for Stranraer. How's your credit card? Mine's over the limit.'

She looked up from tying her boot laces. 'My darling Ken, I must return to the tower and wait for Thatcher's speech. Do you think there's a chance she'll release the prisoners?'

'It's possible. She had a draft finished when I saw her.'

'How was she?'

'Human. Vulnerable. It was her birthday. Sixty-three. She talked about a peace process. Come away with me. We'll work something out.'

She raised her voice. 'No, you idiot, they'll have the number plate of that car and circulate it to every port and airport. Drive yourself back to London on minor roads. I'll say you were never here. Get away from me. I'm an evil influence. *Qui Tangit Frangitur.* Should be my motto too.'

'I'll stay with you.'

'Why would you do that?'

'Because I love you. Because I need to understand what's happening. Because I meant the vows I made. Maybe more so than in a proper church. Above all because I have just found you and can't bear to lose you again. Whatever you've done we can deal with it, together.'

'Up to the tower we go then. But be aware ours could be the shortest marriage in history. Following the quickest-ever wedding ceremony.'

'How did you get drawn into this? Why? Were you ever kidnapped at all?'

'We'll talk upstairs. Do you have cigarettes?'

'Yes.' I produced my packet.

'Not here, we're late already. Up in the attic. We must move. Someone may have heard the shots and raised the alarm.'

'Debbie came with me as far as the bridge. She'll have seen Jerry go down, called the cops. Or the Plods.'

Sarah stood up, dressed, my bride transformed into a warrior ready for battle. 'Get your anorak on if you're coming.' She turned and headed for the door, then looked over her shoulder. She flashed me the old familiar seductive Sarah smile. 'To think I came down for a cup of tea! Which I never drank. Instead I'm married to a handsome and very randy young man! It's a fairy tale.'

'A very scary one. Let's hope there's a Happy Ever After.'

I followed her through the door, down to the ground floor and out of the rear entrance I'd used. She said, 'We left this one open. When the cops came on Wednesday they searched the house but not the tower. I doubt they even realised the tower existed.'

Sarah led me along a narrow path she'd hacked through the weeds and nettles. We passed under the archway into the stable yard. She produced a cast-iron key and unlocked the oak double doors.

She relocked the doors from the inside. Our footsteps clanged on the metal stairway as we ascended to the first floor of the folly, a single large square room, bare boards, empty and windowless. Upwards to the second floor. There seemed no practical use for the tower except as a lookout and to provide a central tall architectural feature for the rambling baronial hall.

The second-floor room came with a tall, narrow window in the centre of each wall. To the west I glimpsed high chimneys in two rows of four, like the funnels of a pair of steamships.

A heavy wooden ladder stood propped against the north wall providing access to a hatch. Sarah climbed up, pushed the cover aside, got a knee on the edge, hoisted herself into the loft and disappeared into the blackness.

I followed.

'Decision time,' she said, and touched my hand in the gloom. 'We need to pull up the ladder. Repel invaders. If you want to go, go now. Last chance. I'll come down and let you out, no problem. If you stay with me, you may die with me.'

Not sure how to respond, I bent down, grabbed the top of the ladder and heaved it into the loft. 'My God, that's heavy! You managed that by yourself?'

'Do I look weak and feeble?'

'No. Silly thing to say.'

'Shut the hatch and put the ladder across it, Ken. See the metal eyes bolted into the joists? Tie it to those with the blue ropes while I power up my rig.'

At first, by the light from the hatch, I could make out little inside the pyramid-shaped roof space. Sarah groped into the darkness. Her shadowy form hunched over something. I hoisted the ladder into position and lashed it.

No one would come up through the hatch in a hurry.

Or go down …

A small table light snapped on, illuminating a bizarre scene. In the centre of the boarded floor stood a camp bed, the sort you clip together. On that lay a sleeping bag. On that, the twin of my

Pocketphone. Beside the bed, a collapsible fisherman's chair. Scattered around the edges of the space, in the eaves, were cardboard boxes containing supplies of biscuits, cereal, bananas, confectionery, bottled water and cartons of milk.

On two upturned plastic beer crates she had rigged up a portable colour TV plugged into a mains inverter. That connected via thick jump leads to a pair of deep-cycle batteries of the kind used in boats and caravans. Also, I noted a scanning radio receiver like the one on *Nurton*; a chunky transistor radio with a long telescopic aerial; and another unit connected to a whip antenna.

A wooden crate looked very much as if it contained munitions. Were those dark pineapple shapes hand grenades?

A rooftop UHF TV aerial hung from the rafters, pointing southeast to Glasgow.

A bucket with a lid must serve as her toilet.

Sarah spread her arms. 'All home comforts.' She smiled, frighteningly normal.

Jerry must have helped her with all this stuff.

Was he the 'J' in Sarah's Filofax? Had she and Jerry met up in London in the weeks before we left, to arrange all these details?

I asked, 'What's the smaller radio?'

'This? VHF marine band. To speak to the submarine base.'

'You have weapons? Firearms?'

'Only the rifle.'

'Where is it?'

'I left it on the parapet. An Armalite with a scope.'

'I had no idea you could shoot. You never said.'

'To paraphrase Mandy Rice Davies, I wouldn't, would I?' She flashed a disarming grin. 'You were surprised enough when I showed up riding Mitch's bike.'

'What's in the box?'

'Stun grenades. Give me a ciggy, will you?'

I lit two and passed one to her. I suspected the grenades were the real thing, as the ones used by the marines in the loch had been.

She inhaled and said, 'I'm afraid I finished the Scotch. Still, it's better to be sober now. Take a pew on the fishing seat. I'll recline like Cleopatra on my couch.'

I sat. 'Let me get this crystal clear. It was you and you alone on the battlements in the balaclava who shot Jerry?'

'Correct.'

'Why did you kill Jerry?'

'When I saw him with you, I knew the bastard had betrayed us. He had the frequencies, you see. Now I must tune in to the Tories.' She bent over her electronics. 'Clear radio and TV reception up here. That's why we chose it. Also easy to defend. Command post and siege tower combined.'

I thought of Jerry. One moment at my side talking to me, the next a bloody carcass.

How could I get us both out of this?

I stared at Sarah hunched over the TV controls and tried to fight the tightness gripping my chest, to hold back the panic. 'Why did you make that call to me yesterday morning?'

'To throw you all off the scent. Which backfired. I guess you heard the HGV horn?'

'Yes.'

'But you didn't tell MI5 or anyone?'

'No.'

'That's good, if somewhat surprising.'

The television picture appeared, perfect as promised. An American soap. A woman with big blue eyes and precariously piled-up blonde hair was saying, 'It troubles you that I'm a woman of ability?'

A bushy-eyebrowed, moustachioed man in a garish Hawaiian shirt sipped his cocktail and answered, 'The best place for an able woman is in her home, having babies for an able man and taking care of all his needs.'

Sarah snorted with disgust and switched to BBC2. 'Good, they haven't started.' She sat on the camp bed.

I checked my watch by the backlight. 2.08pm, and colder up here, as you might expect, at 8°C. Why did I keep checking the temperature? A nervous tic, a momentary distraction from an unruly world, a way to know something for sure and derive comfort from that certainty, or just the nerdish equivalent of stroking a lucky rabbit's foot?

The TV showed a long shot from the back of the conference hall. The ministers and their wives sat in rows to either side of the vacant lectern like school teachers on Speech Day. I identified Geoffrey Howe, Willie Whitelaw, Norman Fowler and, with a start of recognition, George Younger.

To each side of the stage hung gigantic TV screens, the biggest I'd ever seen, inside eye-shaped art deco frames. There must have been a ton of scaffolding behind the scenes to hold up monitors that large. Centre stage, inside a flying saucer graphic, was the slogan 'LEADING BRITAIN INTO THE 1990s', signwritten in a retro 1930s sans-serif font.

A pair of Conservative torch logos completed the effect.

Pure Orwell.

Delegates occupied every seat. Union Jacks on sticks lay ready in the laps of women from the Shires, many in blue, and their husbands, many portly and in tweeds. In front of the stage a scruffy gaggle of photographers jostled for position as they awaited Thatcher's entrance. One of them tripped on a potted palm and knocked it over. A security guard waded in, perhaps concerned a brawl was brewing.

2.10pm. The temperature display morphed to 7°C as Casio adjusted to the conditions.

'I need you to explain, my darling,' I said, as gently as I could. 'How did you get involved in this plot and why are you here now?'

'The British government got me involved when they murdered my father and eldest brother in 1972, and another of my brothers in the Gareloch this week.'

'The diver caught in the propeller? That was your brother?'

'Yes. Liam was there to scout out the jetty, then lead Juan and Paulo to *Repulse* with the hardware.'

'Argentinians? Thatcher told me she suspected them of supplying the limpet mines.'

'She was well informed.'

'So you blame Thatcher for Liam's death?'

'I do. You know what it's like to lose an adored sibling. Imagine how much worse to lose your father and two brothers to State assassins.'

'You know about Susie? I never mentioned my sister to you.'

'Your mother told me.'

'Mum? But you haven't even met—'

'I was certain you lied to me about being an only child. I needed to understand why. I phoned your mum, told her who I was, that I was your girlfriend, and asked her straight out. She explained all about Susie, said you always kept her photo with you. I'd wondered why you kept sneaking glances at your wallet. It wasn't as if there was ever much money in it.' She smiled.

My brain reeled at this revelation. I'd challenge Mum. No point pursuing it now. 'Go on. The State murdered your family.'

'Da and Rory were going about their business when the British Army gunned them down in cold blood.'

'This was in Northern Ireland? They lived there—you all did?'

'Yes. It was 1972. Just after Bloody Sunday.'

My heart, already in my boots, sank yet further. 'Your family was—is—IRA?'

'Was.'

'How did you get hold of the Provisional IRA codewords?'

'I asked Pru at the right moment.'

'Prunella? The chief telephonist at the office? Pru the Prune?'

'Yes.'

'How did you achieve that? She's the fiercest old harridan in the building.'

'I got talking to her, befriended her. God knows she needed some companionship. Poor woman lives all alone in a tower block flat in Pimlico. When she invited me back there for a coffee after work one day, I made sure I had my vibrator in my handbag. I said I'd rather have wine than coffee, and within the hour I'd penetrated her defences, shall we say, and introduced her to a new world of fun and games. She said it was her first orgasm. So sad.'

'You seduced Pru the Prune and bedded her? And she gave you the list of codewords?'

'She didn't give me the list, but she told me the next two in line following a little probing. Shouted them out. Lucky the bedroom windows were closed. Oh look. Here comes Boadicea in full woad.'

Sarah turned towards the TV, picked up the remote control and increased the volume. The *Monty Python*-esque Hammond organ which provided musical punctuation to the Tories' proceedings struck up a cheesy rendition of 'Happy Birthday to You'. Everyone on stage stood and applauded. The delegates leapt to their feet, waved their banners and Union Jacks and cheered.

Thatcher entered, imperious in sapphire blue. She shook a few hands and took her place at the central lectern. There she exchanged greetings with Willie Whitelaw on her right and the stout chairwoman of the conference on her left. The latter occupied a bizarre carved wooden throne raised a foot or so above the stage.

Everyone sat. A smart young woman rushed up to Thatcher with a sheet of paper. The final version of the Prime Minister's Northern Ireland passage? I doubted she'd have included a surrender to the IRA on the autocue.

'Sarah love, it's been gnawing away at me, she denied it but I've got to ask you, especially if you did that to Pru the Prune … did you have an affair … have sex with Debbie too, in the peace camp?'

She said, 'I don't blame you for feeling insecure, but no. I'm not into women that much, though I did experiment a little at university. I'm into you, Kenneth Sinclair. I was prepared to fake it, but I never needed to. I fell in love with you that Friday night in the Chinatown noodle bar. I've treasured every minute we've spent together. You are a wonderful, gentle, caring, funny lover.

Yet I've treated you disgracefully. That's what has made all this so very complicated and distressing.'

On the TV, the applause died down and the rapturous delegates resumed their seats. The chairwoman piped up. 'Prime Minister, you have seen the warmth of your welcome here, more than any words of mine could adequately express. I am sure you will have seen that the conference is in very good heart. We have had a successful conference and we look forward to the final session which you are to address. I think the warmth of your welcome—'

Sarah said, 'Why don't you get off your throne, kneel down and lick her arse, you fat pompous cretin?' She jabbed the remote to cut the volume and turned to me. 'My Da and Rory went to check inventory at a warehouse near Crossmaglen. Someone had grassed them up. A British Army hit squad lay in wait. Illegal, undercover, not even in uniform. To this day we don't know which regiment. Six of the bastards shot two members of my family in cold blood. There were thirty-four bullets in Da and sixty-six in Rory. You saw Jerry. Imagine that times fifty. Wouldn't you want justice?'

On the TV, the conference president droned on. Thatcher, waiting patiently, took out a handkerchief and blew her nose. Had she been crying?

I said, 'Justice, yes. Revenge, no. At least not this way.'

'Remember Peter Carrington?' [27]

'The foreign secretary Maggie sacked for allowing Argentina to invade the Falklands?'

'Yes. Before that he was defence secretary under Edward Heath. In August 1971 he authorised the random detention of Republicans. Among hundreds of other innocent men they rounded up Da and Rory, who was only sixteen. The Army took them both to the *Maidstone,* moored in Belfast Harbour. The prison ship. Which ironically served as the depot ship for the submarine base here in the Sixties.'

---

[27] Peter Carington (sic), 6th Baron Carrington (1919-2018). For the arcane reason why his name is spelled in two different ways consult his Wikipedia entry.

'We climbed the Maidstone Gate on Monday morning.'

'From the hulk they helicoptered our men away at dead of night. Aboard the helicopter, the crew told the men the orders were to dump them at sea—'disappear' them. The chopper came to a hover, the crew opened the door and pushed them all out at gunpoint. Only they weren't at sea, they were three metres off the ground, hard concrete mind, at a secret base in Ballykelly. Inside the base they tortured our boys. Hooded them, deprived them of sleep, stood them up spreadeagled against a wall with their hands raised, all the time deafened by thunderous music. Wagner on a stadium sound system. When the boys collapsed they beat them with iron bars and stood them up again. This continued all night.'[28]

'That's dreadful. I'm so sorry. I wish you'd told me this earlier.'

'It got no mention in the Tory press. Things got worse and worse in the Six Counties, leading to Bloody Sunday. The British Army lost all control. Carrington ordered shoot-to-kill assassinations of Republican sympathisers suspected to be ringleaders. My Da and Rory were high on the list and targeted for execution. As simple as that.'

'And you were a young child.'

'I was five years old, Ken. I had to grow up fast. I loved Rory and Da. I walked behind the coffins with my bouquet holding Ma's hand.' She drew on her ciggy and closed her eyes. 'I can still see the guard of honour in my mind, so smart in their berets. One of them gave me his balaclava afterwards. I wore it earlier on the battlements.

'Imagine the pain for a bright, cheerful little girl who'd lost her father and favourite big brother. But my tears were of pride as well as sorrow. So glorious we were, Ken. So brave, so defiant. On a sunny June day. The tricolours fluttering … the gun salute, so loud and thrilling … Ma's tears of grief and rage, me with my posy and my favourite cuddly bunny. Collins, that was his name. Martin McGuinness was one of the bearers, along with my remaining

---

[28] In 1978 the British government admitted the helicopter incident and all these acts at the European Court of Human Rights.

brothers. That was before we split with the Provos. And then my memory goes fuzzy. Our life changed within the year. Ma met John Standen. He was British, but he understood. He persuaded Ma to bring what remained of her family to England with him, away from the Troubles. To protect me and the five boys as were—four now. He's a wonderful stepdad. He and Ma set up the garage. I went to school, and before long I'd lost my accent. Let's see how the Steel Bitch is doing.'

She pointed her remote and unmuted the sound. Flanked by her twin doppelgangers on the giant TVs, Thatcher was in full flow, bragging of her achievements.

> 'Now that we've halted and reversed the years of decline over which Labour presided, we are told that all we care about is "Loadsamoney". Because we give people the chance to better themselves, they accuse us of encouraging selfishness and greed. What nonsense. Does someone's natural desire to do well for himself, to build a better life for his family and provide opportunities for his children, does all this make him a materialist? Of course it doesn't.
>
> 'It makes him a decent human being, committed to his family and his community, and prepared to take responsibility on his own shoulders.
>
> 'The truth is that what we are actually encouraging is the best in human nature.'

With a feral cry of disgust Sarah beat her clenched fists on the metal frame of her camp bed and jabbed the Mute button. Her breath hissed between her teeth. She turned to me and forced a smile, perhaps aware she was on the verge of losing control. She said, 'That's better. You asked if my family and I are members of the IRA. No. We split from the Provisionals two years ago. We transferred our loyalties to Republican Sinn Féin. Gerry Adams and Martin McGuiness were gagging for peace. They see themselves as politicians on the world stage, strutting around claiming credit for an end to the Troubles, aiming one day to shake Thatcher's hand and have a cup of tea with the Queen at Buckingham Palace.'

'That will never happen.'

'So you say. I believe it could have, but it won't after today, if I stay strong.'

'What's wrong with an end to the Troubles and a peace process?'

'That is surrender—capitulation. Ireland would remain divided for another sixty years. Or a hundred. The Provos have a vested interest in partition. We believe in one united island of Ireland.'

'What is this Republican Sinn Féin?'

'Another breakaway. Led by Ruairí Ó Brádaigh. But he let us down too. They all let us down, disowned us. We formed our own cell, to keep the faith pure and to carry out this operation. A family business we are, in every sense.'

'If you split from the IRA, why do you want Thatcher to release IRA prisoners—start the very peace process you condemn?'

'To prevent it happening. Thatcher won't surrender. This way we neutralise both her and the Provos, I get to level the score for my dead menfolk, and there will never be a "peace process" as they call it. Jerry has the press release all ready.

'We frame the IRA for blowing up *Repulse.* How neat is that?'

'Jerry won't be filing any press releases.'

'Oh. So he won't. But Jerry was always expendable. Ma and the boys have a copy. They're away over the water. They'll fax it tomorrow, once *Repulse* is on the seabed.'

'Suppose Thatcher complies with your demands? She showed me her draft. It's a clever speech. She takes credit for starting a peace process by releasing all Republican and Protestant terrorists—'

Sarah stood up and screamed, 'We are not terrorists! We are soldiers defending our homeland. The British are the terrorists, the invaders, the torturers! No one in my family has done anything except defend our precious homeland against oppression! We regret every death!'

I said, 'Is our honeymoon over?'

She slumped down on the bed, ran her fingers through her hair and rubbed her eyes with her knuckles. 'No. We made our vows. I will keep mine. I know you will keep yours. Anyway, you're part of the family now. You're complicit.'

'I didn't expect this.'

'Come off it. You had a damned good idea what we were up to days ago. I gave you every opportunity to leave, Ken. You stayed. You don't have to support me, but you mustn't betray us, or you'll end up like Jerry.'

'I know you will never hurt me.'

'I won't, but I can't answer for the rest of the family. If we get out of this, some way, and you let us down, you are a dead man walking. Ma would see to that.'

My brain churned as I tried to find suitable words. 'She sounds a fearsome matriarch. I look forward to meeting her. I think.'

'You've met her already.'

'No, that day only your Dad came to lunch, if you remem —'

Sarah dropped her shoulders, pursed her lips, sucked in her cheeks, gathered her hair behind her head. She transformed before my eyes into an older, smaller woman. When she spoke, it was in a sing-song Scottish Highland accent. 'Ye'll be wantin' a piece of toast wi' Marmite, Ken my lad, I'm thinkin'.'

'That was your Ma? The sweet little lady at the safe house with the two goons who kidnapped me?'

'The two goons, as you call them, who treated you with such gentle care, are my eldest surviving brothers, Joe and Danny.'

'Joe … is he the "J" in your Filofax?'

'Yes.'

'Your mother is a superb actress.'

'Oscar material, like me. Any accent. And in case you were wondering, like me she doesn't shy from her responsibilities. She slit the throat of the cottage owner. Insisted, though it broke her heart to do it. She takes after her own father. You met him too.'

'The old guy with the Jack Russells.'

'Yes. Grandad has killed eight men. Taught Mum all the moves with knife and gun. She in turn taught me.'

Unable to respond to the unfolding catalogue of horrors, and to play for time, I said, 'Should we check in again with Thatcher?' I'd noticed enthusiastic applause from the delegates at Brighton, as if she'd reached the end of a section of her speech.

Sarah pressed the Mute button again.

> '—a marvellous record. And it doesn't stop at individuals. Many businesses are now giving a percentage of their profits to help the community in which they are situated. Is this materialism? Is this the selfish society? Are these the hallmarks of greed? The fact is that prosperity has created not the selfish society, but the *generous* society.'

Wild applause erupted from the floor, with dutiful clapping and nodding from the ministers and their wives on stage.

Sarah said, 'I'll keep her on low so we miss nothing.'

We watched together as the Prime Minister launched into a spirited defence of her handling of the economy. Thatcher looked uncomfortable. Was Northern Ireland next?

Sarah appeared a little calmer, so I said, 'Tell me about the limpet mines. I saw the fax you sent the MOD. Was all that correct? About the timer fuses, the depth fuses, the deadline?'

She looked up as if she'd forgotten I was there. 'Yes. The Argies enjoyed themselves coming up with the technical mods. The fax was all correct. You can tell me the exact time till the deadline, I'm sure.'

'I can. One hour, thirty-eight minutes until 4.30pm. You will reprieve *Repulse*, won't you, Sarah? Even if Thatcher doesn't come through with your demands? You've made your point. Scared them shitless. Why not call in the disarming frequency now? We'll split. Drive off into the sunset in my Maestro. The 1980s Bonnie and Clyde, that'll be us! We're about the same age as them, even better looking, and with bigger hair—'

'You're babbling, love. You've been talking to Jerry, haven't you? All shit, no balls, that man turned out to be.'

'He thought you'd planted a baby IED to damage *Repulse* in dock.'

'He said that? Thank God I dropped him.'

'Who else knows the frequency codes now he's dead?'

'Apart from our Argentinian friends, back in South America?' She batted her eyelashes and lisped in a baby voice, 'Only ickle me.'

'What are they? You can share them with me. I'm family. You said so.'

'If I tell you, do you promise not to overpower me and call the numbers in, using my sophisticated communication devices?' She waved a hand at her radios and held her Pocketphone up to her cheek.

I affected a carefree chuckle. 'Of course I won't. I don't want your mum coming after me with her carving knife!'

She leaned her head to one side. 'Hmm. Better not to give you the responsibility, I feel. Or the temptation. You've a soft heart, Ken. I love you for it, but you're transparent. I can't trust you right now. Sorry.' She turned back to the TV. 'Let's see how your other favourite woman is faring.'

> '—as clean as the Thames. We have led Europe in banning the dumping of harmful industrial waste in the North Sea. Given our record, we are well placed to take the lead in practical efforts to protect the wider world. We will work with them to end the destruction of the world's forests. We shall direct more of our overseas aid to help poor countries to protect their trees and plant new ones.'

Sarah sat up and said, 'She talks some sense at last.'

> '—join with others to seek further protection of the ozone layer—that global skin which protects life itself from ultraviolet radiation. We will work to cut down the use of fossil fuels, a cause of both acid rain and the greenhouse effect. And Madam President, that means a policy for safe, sensible and balanced use of nuclear power.'

Sarah said, 'I spoke too soon. I take back my last comment.'

Polite applause rippled around the conference hall. The ministers on stage feigned enthusiasm, except Cecil Parkinson, secretary of state for energy, who clapped with exaggerated arm movements like an overwound clockwork monkey. George Younger glanced down at his watch. I glanced at mine.

Northern Ireland next?

> 'It's we Conservatives who are not merely friends of the Earth—we are its guardians and trustees for generations to come. The core of Tory philosophy and the case for protecting the environment are the same. No generation has a freehold on this earth. All we have is a life tenancy—with a full repairing lease.'

Over the ensuing applause, Sarah said, echoing my thoughts, 'She must come to law and order soon. Ken my darling, I'm scared. What have I done?'

I got up from my chair and approached her, my head bowed to avoid banging the steep sloping roof. I held her by both arms. 'Save *HMS Repulse*. Use your VHF. Call the base with the timer deactivation instructions and then we can scarper. We'll ditch the car at Stranraer, go as foot passengers to Larne. Then fly on to South America.'

'Minus our passports, dodging the international manhunt with our pictures pinned up at every airport check-in?'

I fell silent. Thatcher was saying,

> 'Madam President, year in, year out, this Conservative government has taken action against crime—action on police numbers—on police powers—on firearms—on fraud—on prison building—on compensation for victims—on stiffer penalties.'

We were running out of time, and I had run out of ideas.

> '—Conservatives need no sermons from Socialists on the rule of law. We proposed tougher sentences for criminals who carry guns: they opposed them. We proposed that over-lenient sentences should be referred to the Appeal Court: Labour voted against. We condemned violence on the picket line: they equivocated. And, year after year, they will not support the Prevention of Terrorism Act—an act which is vital to the defeat of the IRA and which has saved so very many lives.'

Wild applause at that. The camera cut away to the audience, then to Willie Whitelaw who stared glumly ahead, then to the view from the back of the hall showing the bald bonces of the males of the Tory tribe.

It amazed me that they had allowed so many journalists and photographers to crowd right in front of the stage, within touching distance of Thatcher.

Tom King, the Northern Ireland minister, cast a nervous glance around the audience. He knew what was coming.

The applause subsided. Sarah said, 'Here we go.' She broke free of my grasp to get a better view of the TV.

> 'The terrorist threat to freedom is worldwide. It can never be met by appeasement. Give in to the terrorist and you breed more terrorism. At home

> and abroad our message is the same. We will not bargain, nor compromise, nor bend the knee to terrorists.'

Sarah growled, 'Bitch.'

> 'In our United Kingdom, the main terrorist threat has come from the IRA. Their minds twisted by hatred and fanaticism, they have tried to bomb and murder their way to their objective of tearing more than a million citizens out of the United Kingdom.'

Sarah rose from her seated position and stood, teeth bared. She shouted, 'They're *our* citizens. We want them back in *our* country, you arrogant, devilish, murdering witch!'

> 'The truth is that the whole IRA campaign is based on crushing democracy and smashing anyone who doesn't agree with them.'

Tom King raised his hand in a clenched-fist salute.

Sarah screamed, 'King, we missed you last year but we will get you next time. You bastards, all with bloody hands! You talk of democracy who stole our country!'

I said, 'Cool it, Sarah. You've lost. No surrender from Thatcher. Just defiance. Don't punish the innocent for the sins of the politicians.'

I noticed Thatcher's upper lip beading with sweat. What thoughts, what fears must be racing through her head? She paused, took a sip of water and continued.

> 'To all those who have suffered so much at their hands—to the Northern Ireland policemen and prison officers and their families, to the soldiers, the judges, the civil servants and their families—we offer our deepest admiration and thanks for defending democracy. And our thanks for facing

danger while keeping within the rule of law—unlike the terrorist who skulks in the shadows and shoots to kill.'

Sarah shouted, '*You* shot to kill! *Your* party shot my father and my brother! *Your* men killed another brother this week! Hear this: you have just sentenced your Polaris crew of men and boys to death. You had the chance. You had the time. You had the choice. I might have relented. I sent you my Ken here, my sweet dear man, my fiancé! You played with him. You sent him back to find me, to smoke me out. Too late! Failed! I am ahead of you. I win. Margaret Thatcher, I—have—had—enough—of—you!' Aside to me, in a normal voice, she said, 'Stand clear, Ken.'

With a swift movement she thrust her hand into her sleeping bag and withdrew it holding a pistol. I couldn't be sure of the make in the dim light. I heard the click as the safety came off.

Not a Glock, then. They don't have a safety.

She pushed the camp bed aside, grasped the gun in both hands, took up the Isosceles stance with elbows locked and feet shoulder-width apart and aimed at the portable TV.

'No!' I cried out.

Eyes wide, Sarah squeezed the trigger. A thunderous report echoed around the confined space. The TV tube imploded with a *whumph* followed by a tinkle of glass and the ping of the spent cartridge hitting the floor. The acrid smell of gunpowder reached my nostrils.

'Put down the gun.' I shouted. 'This is hopeless.' That got her attention. I stretched out my hand to take the gun from the woman I loved.

She half-turned, and for a moment I thought she would shoot me. She said, 'Don't come any closer, for your own safety, Ken.'

The smell of shorted electronics mixed with the hot gun smoke. Bizarrely, the TV audio continued to operate, Thatcher's hectoring tones now disembodied and distorted, the damaged loudspeaker cone transforming her voice into a Dalek's.

'—we will never give up the search for more effective ways of defeating the IRA. If the IRA think they can weary us or frighten us, they have made a terrible miscalculation.

'People sometimes say that it is wrong to use the word never in politics. I disagree; some things are of such fundamental importance that no other word is appropriate. So I say once again today that this Government will never surrender to the IRA.

'Never.'

Sarah levelled the gun a second time. With a cry of, 'They will all die!' she pumped the trigger and put three more shots into the television.

In the silence that followed I heard the faint clatter of a helicopter approaching from the west.

Meltdown

Friday 14th October 1988, 3.20pm, 7°C

I SAID, 'The marines are on their way.'

'More likely the SAS.'

The clattering of the rotors increased in volume. Minutes away. 'Now or never, Sarah. Tell me the code to save *Repulse*.'

'I agree with Thatcher on something. "Never" means never. I will no more surrender to her than she will to me.'

'She's got the bigger guns.'

'I only need one.'

'You won't hold out for long with a few grenades and a pistol.'

She lay on her camp bed, cradling the gun in her hands. I said, 'Put the safety on and give it to me.'

'No.'

We had to raise our voices to be heard over the thrashing helicopter blades.

This was madness.

I lunged to grab the weapon. Expecting my move, she raised a boot and gave me a firm shove backwards, connecting with my sore stomach. By the time I had recovered my balance, a matter of seconds, she was sitting up on the bed with the pistol at her own head. She said, 'Get out while you can, Ken love. I don't want you hurt. Untie the ladder, scram.'

I made a move to advance. She said, 'Another inch and I pull the trigger. You know I don't bluff.' Keeping her eyes on me, she reached over and turned on the marine VHF with her free hand. It lit up with the number 16 on the LCD display. 'Time to identify ourselves.' She unhooked the microphone and pulled it towards her. 'Clyde Submarine Base, Clyde Submarine Base, this is the Provisional IRA Active Service Unit in St Andrew's School. Over.'

We frame the IRA ... how neat is that?

Her words echoed in my head.

Response came at once. 'Station calling Clyde Submarine Base, say again.'

'Clyde Submarine Base, this is the IRA Active Service Unit occupying St Andrew's School, Shandon. Call off the helicopter. We have RPGs.[29] They're trained on the helicopter and we will fire unless it turns back. *Now.*'

'IRA unit, confirm how many you are and how many hostages.' A second voice, with rotor noise muffled in the background. The helicopter pilot or co-pilot.

'Five men, one woman, three hostages including a four-year-old child. Leave or face the consequences.'

'Stand by.'

The helicopter noise remained steady, then reduced.

She said, 'Good. They're retreating.'

'You'll get us both killed. What is the point, Sarah?'

'We'll stall them. Negotiate, once they withdraw.'

'They know the deadline as well as you do. Time is up.'

'What can they do? They daren't kill me.'

The *shhh* of the carrier wave sounded from the VHF radio as the pilot keyed his microphone. 'IRA unit, we saw two people only in the roof space of the central tower on our thermal imager. Confirm whereabouts of other personnel and hostages.'

Sarah wailed, a cry of frustration, anguish and defeat.

I said, 'Surrender. Say we'll go down to the ground floor with our hands up. I'll do it. Let me have the mic.' I inched towards her.

'No! She held the VHF mic in one hand and the gun, pointed at her head, in the other.

The pilot came on. 'IRA unit, leave the roof space and descend to ground level.'

---

[29] Rocket-Propelled Grenades

She pressed the Transmit button. 'No! *You* leave, or you will die in flames!'

The threat was hollow, and she knew it. With her eyes locked on mine, she turned off the VHF set. 'You go. I stay.'

'Put the gun down, come over here and let me give you a hug. We're gonna be just fine, you lovely wife.'

She dropped the gun on the camp bed. I exhaled with relief.

The helicopter noise increased as the pilot throttled up.

She had to shout now. 'Here they come. Cue the "Ride of the Valkyries". I'd hoped they wouldn't find me in time.'

'In time?'

'In time to torture me for the disarming frequency.' She glanced at her watch. 'They have thirty minutes in hand. Ken, I'm sorry. I don't dare risk being tortured.'

'Surrender. Turn the VHF back on and end this nightmare.'

'I love you, Ken.'

The distinctive *whump-whump* of the individual helicopter blades sounded dead overhead.

What followed seemed to happen in ultra slow motion, as if filmed at a thousand frames a second. She snatched up the gun and held it to her temple. She fumbled for a moment, struggling to keep it in position. I tugged the Maestro's keys from my pocket.

She wasn't used to shooting one-handed. I flung the keys straight at her. The silver Austin tag tumbled throughout its trajectory, glinting in the light from the table lamp. I don't know if she saw me throw it. Perhaps she mistook it for a moth, whirring out from its hiding place under a rafter. Anyway, she flinched as the key fob neared her, at the exact moment she squeezed the trigger.

The report boomed around the rafters as before. The spent cartridge spun away to the floor. Sarah slumped back. The gun fell from her hand to the bed. I clawed my way across to her on all fours. Had she missed? I knelt in front of her. Her eyes remained open. No entry wound on her right temple. No exit wound on the left side either, but that was no surprise, given the calibre of the weapon. Smaller bullets tend to enter the skull and ricochet around inside, causing worse damage than if they pass through and out the other side. Which can be survivable.

Then I noticed the blood, on the dark green canvas of the camp bed, behind her head. I leaned lower and closer.

The bullet had entered the back of her neck. She hadn't hit an artery or major vein, or the blood would be everywhere by now, but her spinal cord was damaged.

I didn't dare touch or move her.

Her eyes flickered.

She was alive!

And then her lips moved, too.

I said, 'Sarah, can you hear me?'

'Yes.' The smallest voice. Even with my ear right up to her mouth I could barely make out her words over the din of the hovering chopper. 'I missed. Silly me.'

'I'll call the helicopter on the VHF. They'll airlift you straight to hospital.'

'I can't feel my limbs, but I'm afraid I might live.'

'You'll be fine! There's not too much blood. You're conscious and you can talk. Hold on, my love.'

'They'll still torture me. Poke out my eyes. If I live, I'll rot in jail in a wheelchair forever.'

'No. They'll care for you.'

'I'll give you the frequencies. I'll save *Repulse*. If you promise one thing for me.'

'Anything.'

'Kill me, Ken. Shoot me as soon as I tell you. Two bullets to be certain. Be brave, my trusty spouse. 'Tis a glorious thing I do.'

I made a show of thinking about it for a second or so. 'I understand. I will do that for you.' I reached down and picked up the pistol. A Beretta M9 semi-automatic. 'What are the numbers, Sarah? Give me the code to disarm the time fuses first.'

'Point the gun at me and promise.'

'I promise.'

'Closer. Right up to my head or I won't tell you.'

The helicopter hovered, descending ever nearer. I did as she instructed, holding the warm gun against her temple.

She whispered, 'If you don't kill me I'll tell Ma to come for you. She'll show no mercy.'

'I'll do it. I swear on our wedding rings.'

'Rory. Rory, on the phone.'

Her eyes filmed over. She was losing consciousness. I said, 'Tell me the numbers, love. The cavalry is on the roof.' As I spoke, boots scrabbled and slates cracked just above our heads.

'Not ... good ... with numbers. Prefer words. It's Rory, on the phone.'

'Rory's dead, love. We can't get him on the phone. Stay with me, Sarah. Try to remember.'

'Rory is all you need. Goodbye, my darling. Kill me, Ken. I'm as good as dead anyway. A mercy killing. The most tender act of love. Two shots, remember.'

'I can't.'

'You can. You promised. Go on. Do it. Pull the trigger.'

'No.' I took the gun away from her temple and engaged the safety.

'You let your little sister down all those years ago. Don't let your wife down now.' Her eyes lost focus.

'My darling ... don't say that.'

'Do it for me. Shoot me, if you love me.'

'Sorry ... so sorry ...'

She blinked twice, then whispered, 'I still love you, you coward.'

More tramping and stamping up above. The rafters flexed. Then with a flash and a roar the roof exploded. The fabric of the tower shook. A jagged square hole opened up. I crouched and buried my head in my hands as daylight flooded in. Pieces of wood, shards of slate and fragments of roofing material cascaded on to us. The noise of the helicopter rose to an ear-splitting din and the downwash blew in debris, dust and smoke until the air was thick and choking. A tea-towel-sized piece of black felt dropped on

Sarah, covering her head. She couldn't move to brush it away. My ears rang from the explosion. My eyes filled with grit and dust and I coughed.

A frame charge, I just had time to work out, like the ones they used at the Iranian Embassy to blow in the windows and doors.

No sound from Sarah. I very much feared she had died.

Crashing and hammering started up above my head. More splintering of wood, larger pieces falling now as they used a sledgehammer to storm their way in.

The sunlight disappeared as a black shape filled the aperture in the roof. An SAS trooper dropped with a heavy thud to the attic floor. A terrifying vision, dressed all in black, his upper body encased in armour, his head covered by a flash hood, wearing a gas mask, only his eyes visible behind thick goggles, his Heckler and Koch fitted with a dazzling spotlight that played all around the attic space as he searched for more occupants.

'Sarah's hurt! Spinal injury! Get a paramedic! She needs urgent attention!' I shouted, pointing at where she lay covered in debris and dust.

The gas mask prevented him from speaking to me. He could communicate only with his team, using a radio built into his headgear. He did however give a 'thumbs up' sign. He pointed at the ladder. I got the message: a ground force was on its way to take us out of the building by the same route we had entered.

I untied the ladder, lifted one end and he took the other. To my surprise, he heaved the ladder up to the jagged hole in the roof. Before I could react, he grabbed me and produced a harness from his belt. By the time I realised what he was doing he had my arms inside the harness and the buckle snapped shut. He pointed at the ladder. I hesitated. He gave me a firm shove. I climbed the wooden rungs and scrambled out on to the steep sloping roof. There I found a second trooper crouched low on an undamaged section. They'd thrown a grappling line over the apex to provide a handhold and prevent them sliding off the slippery slates. Number Two pointed. I grabbed the safety line and sat on my bum, the downwash from the chopper's rotors blowing my hair into my eyes. Seconds later the first SAS man appeared beside me.

A thick fluffy rope snaked down from the helicopter, a Sea King, I fancied, though it was hard to be sure from underneath. A mighty aircraft, whatever it was. The second trooper caught the rope, which had steel rings spliced into it at intervals. He took thinner ropes from his pack, with snap carabiners at each end, and attached first me then himself to the fluffy rope. He grabbed me in a bear hug. The first trooper descended into the attic again to tend to Sarah.

Without warning the helicopter throttled up, the line came under tension and a second later I swung in the air above the pyramid roof of the tower in the embrace of my rescuer.

My stomach lurched as the vertical speed increased. We cleared the orb and cross on the rooftop. Soon the whole mansion came into view as we gained altitude, then we left it all behind.

The Sea King switched to forward motion, tilted downwards and thundered towards the Clyde Submarine Base.

I dangled on the rope, face to face with the gas-masked, armoured trooper, swaying from side to side as if on a hellish fairground ride. The helicopter adjusted its course and as we turned, I glimpsed a big red evening sun setting over the hills to the west of the Gareloch.

The sun warmed my cheek. I hoped that my beloved Sarah would survive to see another sunrise and feel its warmth again too.

Extraction

Friday 14th October 1988, a few minutes later

WE HOVERED above the centre spot of the football pitch. The helicopter lowered us to the grass, where my new bosom buddy released my buckles and shackle.

A small delegation awaited my arrival: an officer in naval uniform, a man in a suit and a Modplod. As we ducked clear of the helicopter's blades the naval officer shouted, 'Did you get the disarming frequencies, Ken?'

'They'll need a body board to bring her down. She shot herself, injured her neck and spine. Tell them to be careful. It won't be easy, lowering her through the hatch. She meant no harm. Make sure paramedics with spinal—'

'We're taking good care of Sarah, Ken. Leave her to us. Look at me. Did you get the codes? Let's go.' We set off at a jog. He pointed ahead. 'Out of that gate and across to the Commodore's office.'

I'd worked it out while dangling on my rope. I said, 'The first code at least, for the timed fuses, yes, I believe I have it. I'll need a phone.'

'You can make some calls later. What is the—'

'No. You don't understand. She gave me a word. I think—hope—the letters correspond to the numbers on a phone dial or keypad.'

'Go on.'

'First, promise you won't let them torture Sarah for the remaining codes.'

'We don't do that sort of thing in this country, Ken. I give you my solemn word we won't harm Sarah. They're working to save her life right now. What's the code, man?'

'A mnemonic. R-O-R-Y. Her dead brother. Find what numbers they represent.'

'Got it. Anything else?'

'Look after my girl. She got caught up in something bigger than she could cope with, that's all. Get her the best medical attention. She'll cooperate with you. As soon as we're through here, take me to her.'

'Of course. Here we are.'

A marine guarded the door to the admin block. He saluted and admitted us. We hurried up to the first floor and into the base commander's office. An orderly sat talking on a jumbo-sized telephone equipped with extra buttons and lights. I blinked to clear sawdust from my streaming eyes and examined another phone, not in use. I checked the letters RORY next to the numbers on the dial and called them out. 'Seven-six-seven-nine. Hertz, I imagine?'

The orderly wrote it down while the officer said, 'That's in the range for a sonar transmitter and makes sense. We have a secure line open to Fleet HQ in Northwood who will relay it to the surface task force shadowing *Repulse*.' He nodded to the orderly on the phone, who spoke close to the mouthpiece, articulating with exaggerated diction. 'The sonar frequency to transmit is seven dot six seven niner Kilohertz. I say again …'

The officer said, 'We won't hear from the danger zone for at least an hour. Ken, that was brave work and I apologise for the undignified extraction. Time, as you know, was against us. There's a team flying up from London to debrief you, but first I'm sure you'd like a break to freshen up.'

I said, 'Freshen up? I don't care what I look like. I want to go to Sarah. Now. You said I could. Where have they taken her?'

'I promise you'll see her. She's on her way to hospital. As soon as she arrives and they've stabilised her, I'll call you.'

The officer, who never gave me his name, handed me over to the Modplod, who escorted me to the officers' accommodation block. They called it the Wardroom like on a ship. A staffer led me to a perfectly pleasant ensuite room. Inside, yet again, I found a change of clothing, towels and wash kit laid out on the bed. The Royal Navy was punctilious with its housekeeping.

I asked if I was free to leave. The Plod said, 'Please stay in your room until the debrief team arrives. I'll be down the corridor if you need me. Dial 230. You won't get an outside line on the phone, I'm afraid. Take a shower, have a rest. Watch some telly.'

He couldn't have guessed how unwelcome his last suggestion was.

I ran a shower, as hot as I could stand, and washed the grime and dust of that hellish attic from my skin and out of my hair, along with the last of Jerry's and my own dried blood.

I dressed and collapsed on the bed.

The 4.30pm deadline came and went. I wondered if I'd interpreted Sarah's words correctly.

An hour later, with my head still in a whirl, the phone rang. I snatched up the receiver.

'Hi, it's Seth.'

'Seth! Thank God! What news?'

'The skimmer and the SSN[30] shadowing *Repulse* report no explosions or other problems. *Repulse* has continued on patrol, while they work out a way to deactivate the depth fuses. You saved the boat, Ken. We all thought you'd lead us to Sarah and hoped you'd talk her round. I never doubted you.'

'She shot herself and injured her neck. Paralysed, maybe for life. They haven't told me her condition, or even where they've taken her. Can you find out, Seth, and call me straight back?'

'I'll do my best.'

But his best wasn't good enough. He called again at 6pm to say he was sorry, but information was scanty, the various branches of the armed forces weren't communicating, phone lines were

---

[30] Surface ship and nuclear-powered attack submarine.

overloaded and he would continue to work on it. Waffle and bullshit: unworthy of him. I told him so and he didn't disagree.

I got no sense out of him or anyone else that day, or the next, when they released me without the promised debrief, took me to the airport and put me on the shuttle to London with a hundred pounds in cash 'to spend as I liked'—the total reward I received from my country.

I never saw Sarah again, alive or dead.

Transcript of Interview with Ken Sinclair

Tuesday 19th March 2019

Mark Hankin: 'So, obvious question, what happened to Sarah, Ken?'

Ken Sinclair: 'Ah, she ... well, oh, let me try and tell it in some sort of order. I learned nothing in Faslane. They just put me on the plane down to Heathrow and washed their hands of me. Back in London, my editor Dennis gave me a fortnight's compassionate leave. So I got on the phone the next day, but all the doors that had previously been open to me now slammed shut in my face. I couldn't get through to Sheila Middleton at MI5, or the Clyde Submarine Base, or the Ministry of Defence. Even my new best friend Margaret Thatcher "ghosted" me, as the youngsters say these days. My only ally was Narendra Sethia, now back home in St Vincent. If he wasn't in when I rang, his housekeeper would get him to phone me back, saving me a heavyweight fortune in 10p pieces. I begged him to tell me which hospital Sarah was in. He said he didn't know, and no one would tell him even if they knew, which he didn't think they did. I called Stoke Mandeville and every other spinal unit in the country. They either didn't have her or claimed not to. The former, I am now sure, but wasn't at the time. I rode out to Stoke Mandeville to check there. Admissions had no record. I ran into Jimmy Savile in a corridor, showed him Sarah's picture, asked him if he'd seen her. He said No too. He was nice as pie by the way. You would never have guessed. After

several more futile days I telephoned Debbie at the peace camp. I don't know why I hadn't thought of this earlier. Finally I got some answers. She said the Sea King returned to Shandon House about fifteen minutes after it left, landed there, or so she judged by the engine sounds, then took off almost immediately and headed due west out to sea, right over her head. Mark, I believe … sorry, give me a moment … this gets no better after thirty-one years, you know. I believe they tortured Sarah in that attic for the second code, executed her, zipped her and Jerry into body bags, wrapped them with chains and weights, flew the bodies out over deep water and dumped them. I contacted Sarah's father, stepfather actually in Oxford. Standen anyway. He claimed he had no idea where she was, or where the wretched mother, his wife who I knew as Mrs McCready, was, or the equally wretched son Liam. I'm not sure how much the stepdad knew about the plot. Maybe everything, maybe nothing. He certainly wasn't telling me. I called the police to report Sarah as a missing person. They referred the case within twenty-four hours to MI5 who buried it. Bottom line, Mark, Sarah disappeared off this earth. No funeral, no grave to visit and tend, no ashes, no inquest, no enquiry, no death certificate. Like she never existed. My God, they ruined my life too. I might as well have died with her. Wish I had. Not a day's peace have I had in the past thirty-one years. Thirty-one years, one month and four days, to be precise. I keep the record. Like a life sentence. Except it gets longer every day, not shorter. Not much to remember Sarah by except the photos and the recordings on my Dictaphone. No grave, oh Lord, poor girl, love of my life, wife for an hour, rotting at the bottom of the ocean, and I even lost the earrings. She … they… sorry—' [Unintelligible]
[Recording paused]
[Recording resumes]
MH: 'Are you sure you're all right to continue, Ken?'
KS: 'Yes. I want this on the record. Quote me on everything I say, won't you?'
MH: 'I'll transcribe the recording word for word.'

KS: 'Good. I got a call about a week later from Prunella Fisher, the switchboard operator at *Today*. She told me Dennis had sent round a memo saying that Sarah had resigned, journalism hadn't suited her, she had decided to enter the theatre and applied to RADA. I couldn't return to the paper after that. Couldn't live with the lies as well as the loss, see some other trainee sitting at Sarah's terminal. I told Pru what I thought had really happened. A week later, God forgive me, poor Pru was found dead in her flat. Painkiller overdose. If she left a suicide note, it never made it to the inquest. I suspect she did leave a note, confessing she'd disclosed the IRA codewords to Sarah. Another tragedy, another victim, another death on my, on my …'

MH: 'Ken, would you like to stop here?'

KS: 'No, no, I must push through this.'

MH: 'Shall we move on to the submarine then? How did they defuse the depth charges attached to *HMS Repulse*?'

KS: 'They didn't get the code off Sarah, that I learned from Seth. They devised a plan, but they had to find a sheltered harbour over two hundred feet deep where they could bring in surface support and send divers down. The place they normally use for stuff like this is Loch Ewe, but it wasn't deep enough. The only loch with deep water access all the way in was Loch Broom, so they ordered *Repulse* to make for there. They put her into a stationary hover sixty-five metres down and evacuated as many of the crew as they could through the escape hatches, which hadn't been tampered with. They had to leave almost fifty men aboard to shut down the reactor, navigate the boat and keep essential systems going under battery power only. Deep divers then fitted custom-made rubber bladders made by the Royal Engineers, over the limpet mines to seal watertight around them. With *Repulse* still at depth, they inflated these bladders to a pressure equivalent to two hundred and fifty feet of water depth. This fooled the hydrostatic fuses, so the sub could safely surface and proceed to Loch Ewe, where they docked her on the NATO Z-berth jetty and disembarked the rest of the crew. Next day the bomb disposal boys deactivated the limpet mines with tiny explosive charges which destroyed their electronics without setting off the big bangs. In the meantime *Revenge* had been repaired and had taken over the deterrent, so amazingly there was no break in nuclear cover. All the crews were sworn to secrecy, but they never breathe a word anyway, those guys, they're used to keeping their mouths shut, so no details of the incident ever got out. A few people in Loch Broom noticed the crew bobbing up in their yellow immersion suits, passing fishermen etcetera, can't hide anything from them, but they were told it was a routine training exercise.'

MH: 'Amazing. How did you accumulate the suitcase of records, Ken?'

KS: 'I thought I'd lost everything in the camper van at Glasgow Airport, but a few weeks later three large cardboard boxes arrived at my flat containing the whole lot—Sarah's notebooks, my Dictaphone and tapes, her Filofax, my camera, even our clothes and leftover food. That was Thatcher's doing, I'm certain. She wanted this story told, Mark. The fact they'd sent Sarah's belongings to me surely confirmed she was dead. Years later I received Thatcher's draft IRA concession speech in a brown envelope by courier, a year after her death, so that would be 2014. She'd bequeathed her archives to Churchill College, Cambridge, but it seems with instructions for that particular document to come to me. They didn't keep a copy of it at Churchill, and unsurprisingly you won't find it on the Thatcher Foundation website. More papers had arrived much earlier from George Younger's estate following his death in 2003. In December 2016 the Cabinet Office released documents about the original incursion to the National Archives at Kew. But nothing about the sabotage. They also redacted the map drawn up for Thatcher which showed how we reached *Repulse*.'

MH: 'Those details are corroborated in the camp newsletter. Do we have permission to reproduce that?'

KS: '*Faslane Focus*? No. It will be hard to establish the copyright owners. Only a few articles have by-lines. You'll have to do your best. Try the Mitchell Library in Glasgow. They've got a collection of stuff there. Ephemera. A special collection. The Spirit of Dissent, they call it. Or Revolt. Lots from the Peace Camp and CND. They're very helpful anyway. It's not publicly available, you'll need to arrange access by appointment.'

MH: 'I or my agent will handle that. Have you contacted the people in the manuscript who are still alive, like ▮▮▮▮, ▮▮▮▮ and ▮▮▮▮, to get their permissions to be featured?

KS: 'No. Sorry, Mark, again I'll have to leave that to you and your agent. Aside from ▮▮▮▮ none of them wanted anything to do with me after 1988. ▮▮▮▮ will be fine, though. Haven't spoken to her for many years, but she's still active in the anti-nuclear movement and you can find her on Facebook. Can't blame the others. I misled them, exploited them, lied to them. They thought I was a posh stuck-up git anyway. They were all acquitted, as Thatcher had hinted they would be. She sent an official to give evidence at their trial in September 1989. Ostensibly this guy was there as a prosecution witness, but in truth he was there to sabotage the case. *A propos* of nothing, he made a point of declaring in a loud firm voice that Michael Heseltine had never approved the changes to the local bye-laws under which the protesters were charged. The case was immediately dismissed and received almost no publicity, as Thatcher intended. Also, the disciplinary hearings against the Faslane Royal Marines and other officials whose failings allowed our incursion to happen were held in secret. Ten people were punished including the base commander who was sacked. Where was I? Narendra Sethia. Seth will be fine to appear as himself. He lives in the West Indies still, chartering boats. His card is in the suitcase. Please run the final manuscript by him for technical accuracy as well as his approval. He'll be expecting to hear from you. You'll have to take care with reproducing my photos. Copyright will now belong to News UK, as I took the pics in the course of my duties, at least the ones at the camp. And the company provided the camera, which I suppose therefore technically also still belongs to them. The selfie shots of me and

Sarah in the van and around the camp would be my copyright though, I should imagine.'

MH: 'They are lovely photos. You look so happy, innocent and—' [Knock on door]

KS: 'In love? That will be Milena. I'm afraid we'll have to stop there. Email me anything else and I'll look forward to your sample. How soon can you do that?'

MH: 'By this weekend.'

KS: 'Great. Bye for now, Mark, and thank you for coming all this way and taking this on. The USB drive is in the drawer. Yes, that one. Remember the suitcase. Ah, Milena, good timing, dear, we have finished, at least I am finished for today. Voice going. Brain going. Everything going except the hair, for some reason I've kept it all, not even grey, but we soldier—' [Recording ends]

Afterword by Mark Hankin

I emailed Ken Sinclair my rewrite of Chapter 4 ('Coitus Interruptus') in Kindle file format as he'd requested. On the Monday following our first meeting I returned to the hospice.

Sitting up in a high-backed chair by the window, looking much better than the previous week, Ken professed himself delighted with the results. We went through the text together, changing words and phrases in the dialogue, inserting little details here and there. Often he would refer me to an article, Dictaphone tape or some other piece of documentation from the suitcase, asking me to check to ensure complete accuracy.

Contrary to his (and my) fears, Ken did not die in the days or weeks following our first meeting. I believe he entered a period of remission, triggered perhaps by relief that his story was in safe hands, would be finished and almost certainly published. Sophie Silverman was already fielding offers and talking about an auction of the movie rights.

Conscious of the ticking clock, I put aside my other projects and worked exclusively on Ken's manuscript and records throughout April and May 2019. As both Ken and Sarah used Pitman shorthand, I had their respective reporters' notebooks transcribed by a journalist friend of mine. I listened to all the tapes and found it intensely poignant to hear Sarah's voice on some of them.

Altogether I paid Ken a further six visits over these two months, some of them several hours long. At the end of one session, misquoting Dickens, Ken said, 'You know, Mark, I realise now this was not just the worst of times for me. It was also the best of times. I was never more alive than during those few weeks in October

1988. My life since then has been half-lived in the shadow of those days.'

On Tuesday 4th June 2019 I was in the car on my way to Ken when I received a call from the hospice. Ken Sinclair had died at six o'clock that morning. The news came as a shock, as he'd seemed hale and chipper at our meeting the previous Friday. I was shaking so much I had to stop in a layby for ten minutes.

Perhaps it was for the best that Ken died before we reached the end of his narrative, and he never read my dramatisation of the final three chapters of the book. I believe it would have broken him to revisit the appalling and surreal scenes in Shandon House. We'd talked about what happened up there, and his own draft of the events was as usual full of facts, so I hope my version captures the spirit and essence of what passed between the doomed lovers in those last terrifying minutes.

Ken's funeral took place at Gedling Crematorium, a modern and rather beautiful facility in the countryside a few miles outside Nottingham. I joined around twenty mourners in a high-beamed chapel full of light and air. A long picture window on one side framed views of rolling countryside. I sat next to Narendra Sethia, who'd introduced himself to me in the waiting room. Imposing in stature, upright and dapper, comfortable in himself and looking younger than me, though he must have been around my age, he proved as charming in the flesh as he'd been on the phone and online. He'd offered me every assistance with my task. I looked forward to spending some time with him over a drink at the wake and telling him I'd soon have a complete draft ready for him to check[31].

The organ played softly as we awaited the entry of the family. I took a moment to reflect on Ken, his remarkable story and the high price he paid for his selfless contribution to the nation's security.

---

[31] It transpired that Narendra Sethia was almost the same age as me, and we had grown up living less than a mile from each other in the leafy Surrey town of Haslemere.

Towards the end of our encounters, Ken had told me something of his personal life since the Polaris affair. He left London and returned to the Midlands, where he worked on the *Nottingham Post* for several years before going freelance to write for magazines. He married (remarried as he put it) in the 1990s, but it didn't last—'she couldn't cope with the PTSD'—and there were no children. His father died in 2016 and soon after that his mother was diagnosed with dementia and moved into a care home.

In recent years his freelance assignments had dried up with the rise of the internet and the decline in print media. He'd blogged about motorbikes and guns before beginning work on his memoirs in late 2017.

It might have been better if Ken had died alongside his beloved Sarah in that attic.

'Here we go,' Seth whispered.

A small knot of Ken's relations entered, a nephew pushing Ken's mother in a wheelchair.

A sad little service ensued. A daughter of a cousin, aged about sixteen, stumbled through A.E. Housman's 'When I Was One-and-Twenty'. The minister, who had clearly never met Ken, delivered a plain vanilla eulogy. Worst of all, during the committal, everyone jumped out of their skin when Ken's mother wailed, 'I don't want to see Ken ever again! Where is Susie? Where's my darling little girl?'

No mention was made of 1988. I wondered how many of those present knew what had happened.

I suspected only Seth and I.

Notes and Acknowledgements

During the summer of 2019 I attempted to contact the Faslane peace campers resident in late 1988 to ask if they were happy to be portrayed as themselves in this book. I could not trace all of them, but of those I did, all but one were unwilling to appear in print, while two were extremely hostile to the story being told at all.

I understood their misgivings.

As a result, although events in the narrative such as the incursion into the Faslane base on the night of 9th/10th October 1988 did take place as described, the peace campers portrayed in these scenes are fictional characters, with any resemblance to their real counterparts purely coincidental.

The one peace protester of the time who expressed enthusiasm for my story was Jim ▓▓▓▓▓. Jim offered to show me around Faslane and answer any questions I might have. I drove to Scotland and spent Thursday 8th August 2019 with him. Softly-spoken, courteous and possessing an encyclopaedic knowledge of the area and the history of the submarine base, Jim provided invaluable assistance. In the afternoon we visited the peace camp. Accompanied by one of the residents, and closely monitored by MOD police both ashore and afloat in the loch, we retraced the route the protesters took towards the South Gate in the early hours of 10th October 1988. I nearly got arrested trying to take photographs of the defences.

We also paid a visit to spooky, abandoned Shandon House, bought by the Ministry of Defence in 1990 and left to decay ever since despite being a listed building.

During the incursion, Jim's role was to support 'Debbie' by waiting at the South Gate with a towel and dry clothes following her courageous swim in the icy waters of the Gareloch. I reallocated this job to Jerry in the narrative, mainly to keep the cast of characters to manageable proportions. I omitted or combined other characters elsewhere for the same reason. There is no suggestion that 'Jerry' is intended to portray Jim ▮▮▮▮▮, or that Jim played any part in the proceedings other than as above. Jim was not arrested or tried in connection with this raid. He asked me to redact his surname to avoid unwanted attention.

Narendra Sethia suggested we submit the full manuscript to the Ministry of Defence for clearance, which we did. Their somewhat snooty response—that everything in the book was either in the public domain or pure fiction, and therefore fine to publish—suited everyone nicely. I am also indebted to Narendra for fact-checking the manuscript.

Apart from well-known historical figures such as Margaret Thatcher and her ministers, any resemblance to other real people is coincidental. For the avoidance of doubt, as the lawyers say, the MI5 agent 'Sheila Middleton' does not represent Stella Rimington. In the last quarter of 1988 Dame Stella was director of counter-espionage at MI5 and would not have been working in the field. Other able women had by then also been promoted into senior roles within the service, of which 'Sheila' was an example.

Thanks to my wife Liz for taking on the unenviable task of first reader and critic of the manuscript.

Thanks to Kit Pike and Paul Stone for inspiration.

Thanks to the following who gave generously of their time, expertise and knowledge of the era: Commodore Eric Thompson MBE, former Polaris officer, later Commodore of Clyde Submarine Base; David Riddell, formerly responsible for MOD police security at Faslane; Alan Marett, who served on 'Ton' class minesweepers; Ian Johnson, former rating on nuclear submarines; Lucy Bennett, for transcription of Pitman shorthand; Jacqueline Smith and David Liston, who instructed me on Glasgow patois ('Weegie'); Paula

Larkin, curator of the *Spirit of Revolt* collection at the Mitchell Library in Glasgow; Mike Lee and Richard Paul-Jones, who advised me on Brighton in the 1980s, and Jonathan Hunt for reconstructing Sarah's CV on a vintage Apple ImageWriter II.

Any errors in the book are my sole responsibility.

Thanks to my agent Sophie Silverman for taking care of the big issues while making sure that the t's were crossed and the i's dotted, and to the team at Fast Editions for their diligence and high production values.

Replicas of Sarah's earrings handmade by JoannesJemsGifts. Newspaper cuttings and photographs reproduced under licence from the respective copyright holders. Cabinet papers reproduced under the Open Government Licence v3.0.

Mark Hankin
North Norfolk
England
May 2021

Appendix

▲ Shandon House, Faslane, photographed in August 2019. The listed building was acquired by the Ministry of Defence in 1990 and is now in an advanced state of dereliction

◀ Sarah Standen and Kenneth Sinclair on their first day at Faslane Peace Camp, Wednesday 5th October 1988

▲ Narendra Sethia, pictured when a Lieutenant in the Royal Navy, August 1980

CURRICULUM VITAE

KEY FACTS:

NAME: Kenneth William Sinclair

ADDRESS: 191B Dalling Road, Hammersmith, London W6 1BA

TELEPHONE: 01-654 4675

PLACE OF BIRTH: Mansfield, Notts

NATIONALITY: British subject

D. O. B: 19 January 1967

EDUCATION AND ACHIEVEMENTS:

1971 – 1978 Grosvenor School, West Bridgford, Notts

Prefect. Captain, Under 11 cricket team

1978 – 1985 Nottingham High School

GCE 'O' Levels attained at Grade C or higher: Mathematics, English Language, English Literature, Physics, Chemistry, Biology, French, Geography, History, Art, Metalwork

GCE 'A' Levels attained: English Literature (A), Mathematics (B), Economics (B)

Extra-curricular: represented school in Rugby 1st XV (fly half); and in Rifle Shooting (1984 Notts League Runners-Up)

Vice-President, Debating Society

Sixth Form Essay Prize (for 'Utopia is a Scary Place')

Secretary, Photographic Society

1985-1988 Robinson College, Cambridge

B.A. (Hons), Economics (2:1)

Photos Editor, 'Stop Press with Varsity' (independent student weekly paper)   /cont ...

Target shooting: member of Cambridge University Rifle Association team retaining Chancellors' Challenge Plate ('Varsity Match') 1987

ABOUT ME:

I am a well-rounded, capable individual with a solid track record of academic achievement and an impressive list of extra-curricular accomplishments. My passion is communication, both written and visual, through journalism and photo-journalism. I am also a keen sportsman. I have a Blue in Rifle Shooting and I enjoy keeping fit by playing rugby and squash.

With keen powers of observation and good interpersonal skills, I have 'set my sights' on a career in journalism, and believe I have the ambition, drive and ability to make a significant contribution.

CAREER:

8 August 1988 to present: Reporter, 'Today' newspaper, News International Group, Vauxhall Bridge Road, London SW1V 2TA Selected from over 200 candidates for one of two vacancies as Graduate Trainee Reporter on the pioneering full-colour tabloid newspaper founded by Eddie Shah.

Salary: £9,000 p.a.

Curriculum Vitae of

Sarah Anne Standen

Personal details

Date of birth: 3rd December 1966

Home address: Flat 2B, 57 Blackhill Road, London E10 7PL

Telephone: 01-323 4586

I am a confident, capable and independent person prepared to work hard to achieve my goals while maintaining a healthy balance between my career and personal life. I am reliable, resourceful and outgoing, a natural team player, and I relish the challenge of leadership.

My interests apart from literature include current affairs, politics, drama and swimming

Education

Rye St Antony School, Headington, Oxford 1970 - 1984

8 O-Level passes. A-Levels: English Literature (A), Geography (A), History (A)

Head Girl 1984

Exeter University, 1985 - 1988

B.A. Hons, English Literature (First Class)

Acting: Titania in A Midsummer Night's Dream, Lulu in The Birthday Party (Harold Pinter); various characters in Government Health Warning (Edinburgh Fringe comedy revue)

President, Students' Guild, 1987. Achievements: introduced lettings service with free legal support, Great Storm clean-up and associated wildlife welfare projects (owl/bird boxes)

Work Experience

Standen Motors, Islip, Oxford, 1984 - 1988
Part-time Receptionist and Administrator involved in all aspects of running a successful service business, deputising for Managing Director as required. Experience gained in operation of Intel 386 PC with VGA graphics running VisiCalc and WordPerfect 4.0

Appointments

Trainee Reporter, 'Today' newspaper, August 1988 -
Salary £9,500 pa

Jubilate Domina

(with apologies to Christopher Smart!)

For I will consider my Love Sarah.

For she is a good Catholic Girl except in certain important respects for which I give thanks and praise.

For at the first rays of the sun she pulls the duvet over her head and says go away.

For that she then peeps out and asks have I made her a cup of tea.

For she screams when I snatch the duvet off her especially in cold weather.

For having done what she has to do in the toilet she begins to consider herself.

For this she performs in ten degrees.

For first she looks upon her tongue in mirror.

For secondly she says Oh my God I will never drink again.

For thirdly she stretches upwards with her fingertips extended which is rather pretty.

For fourthly she bendeth over and toucheth her toes ditto.

For fifthly she washes herself or at least splashes some cold water about her face.

For sixthly she floppeth back into bed upon wash.

For seventhly she grabs her pillow from under my head with unseemly strength.

For eighthly she rubs herself against me.

For ninthly she twitches her nose and reaches down and says what's this I've found then.

For tenthly upon play she goes in quest of food to wit toast with jam for her and Marmite for me and the tea I failed to make earlier.

For she can swim for life.

For she can sleep for England.

▲ The article referred to by ex-Polaris rating 'Norman' at the camp fire meeting on Wednesday 5th October 1988

THE GUARDIAN
Monday February 15 1988

Near-meltdown on nuclear sub report denied

Peter Murtagh

THE electrical fault last month in a Polaris submarine based at Faslane, Scotland, was not dangerous and did not lead to a leak of radiation, the Ministry of Defence said at the weekend.

Nobody had been scrubbed down, said a spokesman. He described the fault as a "minor electrical malfunction" but refused to elaborate, or to confirm or deny details in the report.

HMS Resolution, Britain's first nuclear-powered ballistic missile submarine has a pressurised water-cooled reactor. It was built in 1967 and is equipped to carry 10 multiple nuclear warheads of 60 kilotons each.

The Observer newspaper had reported yesterday that the fault on January 26 was due to a failure in the reactor's primary cooling system because the power supply was cut off. The report said that a backup pump did not work and that an emergency power supply also failed to activate. Why the power failed was not known.

The newspaper quoted a former nuclear submarine officer as saying that the reactor could have been heading for a meltdown.

However, the ministry poured scorn on this assessment. Its spokesman said: "He does not know what he is talking about and was not on the sub at the time."

Mr Richard Webb, a former naval officer with the US Atomic Energy Commission, said that submarine personnel would have had to work very fast to avert a disaster.

He said that because of the build-up of heat in the reactor with the failure of the cooling system there could have been "some form of non-nuclear explosion but with enormous energy potential".

The ministry said that the Clyde public safety scheme — used to inform local people in the event of a nuclear emergency — had not been activated by the base commander.

Mr Dennis Canavan, the Labour MP for Falkirk west, accused the ministry of a cover-up. "The public are entitled to know exactly what dangers arise from the Government's nuclear defence policy," he said at the weekend.

▲ Rebuttal of the article opposite, published next day by the *Observer's* sister paper, the *Guardian*

  # Daily Express

TUESDAY OCTOBER 11 1988   ***   22p   TODAY'S TV: PAGE 22

WIN THIS SUPER NOVA —Page 26

TYSON v TYSON Ruthless Ruth calls the tune —Page 3

Defiant Maggie returns to Brighton but Biffen warns on Yuppie image

GRAND TO BE BACK!

By ROBERT GIBSON and BOB McGOWAN

MRS THATCHER and her entire Cabinet were back at the Grand in Brighton last night four years after the IRA tried to murder them in their beds.

The Prime Minister swept into the foyer of the restored hotel and reflected on the night she came so close to death.

"I stood here in the ruins that time. It is still very vivid," she said on her arrival for the Tory conference.

And as crowds cheered outside behind a security cordon and a police helicopter hovered above, she said: "It is good to be back. It is going to be a very moving week."

But her dreams of a trouble-free return to the South Coast did not last long.

Last night three of her former Ministers spoke out against her policies.

BULLIES

John Biffen urged the party to rid itself of the "yuppie" and "fat cat" image. He warned that the Tories should not vacate the middle ground, particularly as Neil Kinnock was steering Labour back towards the centre.

Leon Brittan said measures to control credit may have to be taken in the Spring.

And Michael Heseltine said the Chancellor should do more to curb the credit boom.

But last night the delegates' thoughts were inevitably on the bombing that killed five people in 1984.

Deputy chairman Peter Morrison summed up the mood: "The Conservatives, of all the parties, are not cowed by bullies, thugs and terrorists," he said.

Mrs Thatcher was asked about her memories of the outrage.

"One of my greatest recollections is

Page 2 Column 1

Mrs Thatcher in Brighton last night Picture: JOHN DOWNING

Piggott's 4 days of freedom

JAILED racing legend Lester Piggott went home to his Newmarket mansion last night.

Piggott, 52, sentenced to three years for tax evasion in a £2.8m fraud, left Highpoint Prison on a four-day break—a prelude to parole before the end of the month. He has served 11 months.

It is Piggott's fourth time outside—twice to visit his wife Susan.

The Repulse: Invaded by peace protesters

Security alert after raiders invade nuclear submarine's control room

By JAMES BUCHAN

A MAJOR security inquiry was underway last night after three peace protesters invaded the top secret control room of one of Britain's nuclear submarines.

The incident happened early yesterday at the Royal Navy base at Faslane in the Firth of Clyde, home to both nuclear and hunter killer submarines.

A full scale alert was launched when the men were found in the control room of Repulse, which carries 16 ballistic missiles.

A woman was picked up at a dry dock in the complex after swimming up the Gare Loch and another woman was found in a nearby fuel depot.

Surprised

The three men, who appeared in court yesterday afternoon, reached the submarine after cutting a hole in the perimeter fence of the base, said a Ministry of Defence spokesman in London.

Then they rushed past a sentry at the top of the gangway to Repulse and disappeared inside the vessel through a hatch on its deck.

"They were apprehended almost immediately, but had already managed to scrawl messages on the walls with felt tip pens," said the Defence spokesman.

Three men and two women appeared before Dumbarton Sheriff's Court.

One of the accused, Philip Jones, 25, said: "I am surprised we are charged only with boarding the submarine. We reached the control room."

Jones, Miles Vallance, 17, Ian Mills, 23, Pamela Banks, 18 and Barbara Francis, 44, all gave their addresses as The Peace Camp, Helensburgh, which lies just outside the perimeter fence.

The three men and Pamela Banks were accused of entering a restricted area and causing damage to the fence.

Barbara Francis was charged with being in the oil fuel depot at Garelochead, a mile away.

They were bailed to appear in court on October 28.

Last night local Labour MP John McPhil said: "Not only are we talking about individuals appearing to have breached the perimeter fence, but reaching the very core of the security operation at the nuclear heart of Repulse. It is an appalling admission."

▲ Margaret Thatcher's efforts to suppress news of the Faslane incursion were so successful that only one UK newspaper carried the story on its front page. There was no mention of the raid on UK radio or television

▲ November 1988 edition of the peace camp newsletter *Faslane Focus*, reporting on the incursion

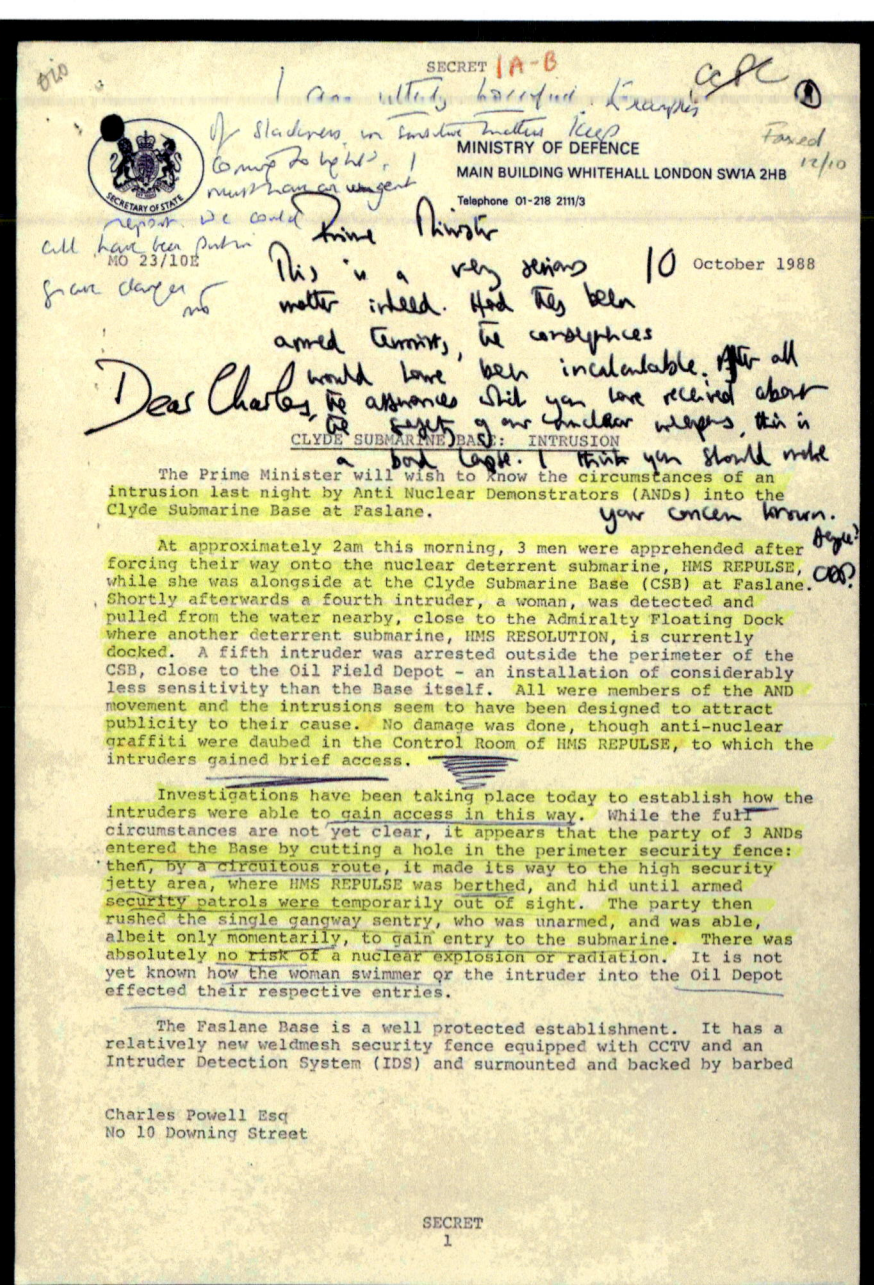

▲ Letter from Brian Hawtin, Ministry of Defence, to Charles Powell, private secretary to Margaret Thatcher, outlining the incursion into *HMS Repulse*

SECRET

coils. It is not, therefore, clear at this stage how the intruders succeeded in entering without the alarm being raised, though it has been established that the IDS was temporarily out of action during the weekend at the spot where the intruders are believed to have entered. Once in the Base, the intruders may have been helped by the presence on site of large quantities of contractor equipment (ladders, building materials), which could have provided both cover and assistance. Once they reached the jetty, they would appear to have concealed themselves and awaited a moment when all 4 armed patrolling sentries and the sentry on the submarine casing were out of sight in order to rush the gangway guard.

My Secretary of State takes a most serious view of this incident, particularly as HMS REPULSE was armed at the time of the intrusion. He has asked for a full inquiry to be conducted as a matter of urgency and a Board of Inquiry is now being convened by the Flag Officer Scotland and Northern Ireland for this purpose. The Secretary of State is aware of the Prime Minister's concerns on the subject of nuclear weapon security and will be taking a close personal interest in the outcome of the Inquiry in order to establish what remedial measures need to be taken to prevent a recurrence. He will report again at that stage.

Finally, the Prime Minister will wish to know that the Secretary of State is due to be interviewed by BBC Radio "Today" and BBC Breakfast Time television tomorrow morning and we can expect the intrusion to feature in both interviews.

Your sincerely,

Brian Hawtin

(B R HAWTIN)
Private Secretary

SECRET
2

SECRET

CLYDE SUBMARINE BASE - INTRUSION ON 9/10 OCTOBER 1988

INTRODUCTION

1 This report sets out the interim conclusions of the Board of Inquiry, which has been investigating the circumstances surrounding an intrusion by anti-nuclear demonstrators (AND) into the Clyde Submarine Base on the night of 9/10 October 1988.

2 The narrative of events contained in paragraphs 5 to 13 takes care to avoid anticipating the Board of Inquiry's final conclusions concerning individual culpability, except where the failure of individuals to observe standing orders has been clearly established.

3 The events of 9/10 October should be viewed in the context of the Clyde Submarine Base's concept of operations as set out in Standing Orders. The concept reads as follows: "The defence of the Base at Faslane is one of defence in depth, and frequent but irregular patrolling. This will include the surveillance and patrolling of the outer fence by static, walking and vehicle borne personnel. There will also be patrols and static guards operating within the Base itself. This policy allows for those with the detailed overall knowledge of the Base - the MDP and permanent Naval personnel - to operate in the areas they know best and personnel with little or no overall knowledge (newly arrived personnel) to man the observation posts."

4 Locations mentioned in the narrative below are shown in the map of Clyde Submarine Base at Annex A to this report.

NARRATIVE OF EVENTS

5 The first indication that intruders had gained access to the Base was the raising of the alarm by the Royal Marine sentry on the Green Area jetty at 0206 on Monday 10 October 1988. So far as it has been possible to establish, the sequence of events prior to this was as follows.

6 At 0133, 4 ANDs breached the perimeter security fence in Zone 11 (where the barbed coils on the outside base of the fence had been removed to allow work to be carried out) by cutting a portion of the weldmesh fence horizontally along part of its 3 metre length. Three of the ANDs then obtained entry by forcing the top and bottom sections of the severed weldmesh fence apart and slipping through, leaving the 2 sections of the fence to spring back together, making the cut invisible to close scrutiny. Their actions were not detected by the Perimeter Intruder Detection System (PIDS) because the alarm system appears to have been inhibited in the Police Control Room sometime between late Sunday afternoon and the

SECRET

▲ The Ministry of Defence interim report requested by Margaret Thatcher

SECRET

early hours of Monday morning. Responsibility for this action lies
has yet to be established. The CCTV at the perimeter fence
was operating on a normal scanning basis. Had the alarm
been activated, the cameras would automatically have
concentrated on the area of the breach.

7 Under normal circumstances the intruders would have been
delayed before proceeding further into the Base by three
large coils of barbed tape. These, however, had been removed
at the adjoining section (Zone 12) to enable engineering work
inside the perimeter to proceed. In addition, one of the MDP
patrols had recently been relieved for a refreshment break,
so that temporarily the adjacent patrol had a larger area to
cover. This could well have been noted by ANDs watching from
concealment.

8 The intruders then proceeded to the Maidstone Gate. There
was little opportunity for their detection en route as the
ground in this area, being of lesser security significance,
is lightly patrolled and affords both natural and building
cover. The intruders gained access to the Red Area (the
second most sensitive area) at the Maidstone Gate position.
This Area, which is under security surveillance by random
foot patrols, was congested by portacabins and construction
equipment owned by contractors engaged in site development.
The intruders were able to scale the gate by using a ladder
which they found. It is estimated that the intruders entered
the Red Area at about 0145 when 1 of the 2 foot patrols
permanently deployed in the Area was on a tea break without
relief. Because of pressure on MDP manpower this is usual
routine.

9 The intruders then moved through the Red Area past the
nuclear powered submarine, HMS TRAFALGAR, lying at No 3
Berth. It is reported that they contemplated attempting to
board TRAFALGAR but were dissuaded by a combination of the
Radiation Exclusion Zone signs which they saw there and the
presence of the watchkeeper on the conning tower. They were
not spotted by the watchkeeper in TRAFALGAR because of
contractors' impedimenta on the jetty. The intruders went on
undetected towards the locked gate at the northern access to
the Green Area. They penetrated the Green Area by climbing
the security gate using a number of large dustbins, which had
been lashed to the outside of the fence and which afforded
them a ready made ladder. Their intrusion unobserved into the
Green Area was further helped by some defective
floodlighting. Had there been 4 Royal Marine sentries on
patrol within the Green Area, as the orders stipulate,
instead of 3, as was the case on 9/10 October, it is possible
that a sentry would have been in position near the Access
Gate and would have observed the intruders as they scaled the
fence. The Royal Marine Detachment Commander had, however,
failed to ensure that the correct number of Royal Marine
guards were detailed as jetty sentries. The view of all the

SECRET

303

SECRET

other personnel on duty in the Green Area was obscured by the quantity of stores and equipment in the area. Additionally, 1 of the 2 MDP constables on foot patrol was not in position close to the Quartermaster's station at the jetty end of the gangway leading to HMS REPULSE because he too was on a refreshment break without relief.

10 The intruders were first sighted by the Quartermaster of REPULSE as they came into view around a container close to his security box. He initially thought that the 3 men were personnel from a Royal Maritime Auxiliary Service (RMAS) craft - which he assumed (incorrectly) to be moored further along the inboard side of the jetty - and, therefore, did not issue a challenge to them. Consequently, he was not alerted until the last moment when the intruders turned towards, and dashed down, the gangway. The gangway was protected by gates but these were broken and awaiting repair. As the intruders dashed down the gangway the Quartermaster shouted to the Royal Marine armed sentry on the jetty, who raised the alarm by radio but did not open fire because he did not consider the intruders to be hostile within the definition of his Rules of Engagement. When the intruders entered onto the gangway, the Royal Marine sentry was about 25 feet away and walking away from them. He therefore was too far away and had insufficient time to apply any restraint other than opening fire.

11 Contrary to Resolution Class Submarine Standing Orders, the Forward Main Access Hatch in REPULSE was open and unmanned as the casing sentry had gone aft to check the draught of the submarine. Arrangements, of which the Quartermaster was unaware, do exist for a Royal Marine sentry to replace the casing sentry when the latter is required to leave his position in order to undertake other duties. In the event the intruders were able to get down the access ladder and enter the Control Room where they were quickly arrested by duty personnel. Responsibility for applying the relevant orders relating to sentries and hatches rested with the Officer of the Day of HMS REPULSE.

12 After the alarm was raised by the Royal Marine sentry at 0206 a member of the public attempted to give a constable on duty at the South Gate of the Base some clothes for a swimmer whom he must have presumed had just been arrested. As a result of the subsequent search a female protester was discovered by a police boat sitting on the south west apron of the Admiralty Floating Dock. It would appear that she had swum the 150 meters from the loch bank to the floating dock in only a swimming costume and carrying an aerosol for slogan daubing in a plastic bag. It was apparent that she must have been out of the water for approximately an hour. The armed Royal Marine patrol on the Admiralty Floating Dock failed to spot the swimmer. This was almost certainly due to the poor lighting along the swimmer's approach route.

SECRET

SECRET

13 The Inquiry has reached the conclusion that the main aim of the intrusion was the daubing of slogans by the female AND swimmer on the Admiralty Floating Dock. The 3 men who succeeded in boarding HMS REPULSE - and on whom for obvious reasons attention has tended to focus - had intended to create a diversion by entering the Base elsewhere.

REMEDIAL MEASURES

14 Although the Board of Inquiry will need to complete its close and thorough examination of the evidence before final reccommendations are made, the above narrative indicates a number of measures which need to be implemented to improve security. The main ones are
  a) Further training and briefing of the MDP guard force to ensure greater familiarity with the operation, capabilities and limitations of the PIDS and its associated CCTV cameras;
  b) An MDP Inspector should be appointed to supervise the complete operation of the PIDS system;
  c) Additional patrols with dogs in any areas where the perimeter defences (whether PIDS or barbed coils) are temporarily out of action;
  d) Refreshment breaks for patrolling constables should be staggered in such a way as to ensure that maximum cover is maintained at all points and that there is no reduction of officers on patrol in the Green Area at any time;
  e) Strict compliance with standing orders, particularly with regard to submarine sentries and hatches;
  f) The provision of more secure gangway gates, allowing sentries to control access to berthed submarines more effectively;
  g) Immediate vicinity of submarine gangways to be kept clear of impedimenta;
  h) The 6 armed guards required to patrol the Green Area should always be present in the required numbers and should be better briefed and supervised in their duties;
  j) Windows of observation posts should be kept clear and spotlights kept free from defects;
  k) Barbed coils should be fitted to the top of the gates giving access to the Green Area;
  l) High intensity floodlighting should be installed at the southern end of the SSBN jetty to illuminate the foreshore and the external perimeter of the Admiralty Floating Dock;
  m) Joint Operating Instructions should be produced for MDP waterborne patrols and RM jetty sentries and for RM/RN/MDP patrols in the Green Area;
  n) The Red Area fence should be examined regularly for vulnerable points and kept free of impedimenta and well-lit.

15 When forwarding his interim report the Flag Officer separately instructed Commodore Clyde to implement as far as possible all its recommendations. Commodore Clyde has

SECRET

SECRET

reported to the Flag Officer that action is complete on 15 recommendations and is in hand on a further 6. The 2 actions remaining are outside Commodore Clyde's control and are being addressed separately.

SECRET

Printed in Great Britain
by Amazon